I0671204

Torn between two men, over 170 years in the past, I knew I couldn't have either of them, that doing so would upset the past as well as the future, but still…

Captain Charles Sanders rose above insanely gorgeous. He could turn the head of a mannequin. He was the classic image of a steroid muscle man on the front cover of a paperback romance, an easy six-feet-four—maybe five—inches tall. And the captain was much closer to my age than Carlos.

No wonder I, or rather, Carmena, was attracted to him. I wanted to gobble the officer up like milk chocolate, and in testimony, my mouth remained opened a bit too long. The captain's smile grew wider, and Carlos cleared his throat rather loudly.

I swallowed. "Captain. It's absolutely wonderful to see you." And it was.

Carlos, out of the captain's line of sight, rolled his eyes heavenward. I stumbled past the chairs behind my desk.

"Thank you, Carmena." His masculine voice wrapped invisible arms around me. "And may I say that it's always wonderful to see you?"

He glided across the room with the heat of a professional tango dancer. He took my hands and placed a long, slow kiss on the back of each one. Goosebumps rose on my arms, shivers did the whole up and down thing along my spine, and I wanted nothing more than to be alone with the man.

"I'm so glad you have recovered from that unfortunate circumstance." No matter what he said, his words oozed masculine sensuality.

"Carlos," I kept my toothy grin on the officer, "I've changed my mind about our last discussion. Perhaps you can attend to that other matter we were just dealing with."

"And what matter would that be, Carmena?" Carlos asked. He enunciated every syllable in the name and stood like a permanent fixture with his arms crossed.

I waved my hand. "Whatever. Just take care of it."

A psychic leaves her a present—but is it a blessing or a curse?

When Mandy Ruhe receives a sacred amulet from a mysterious woman she's never met, she is suddenly swept back in time to Texas 1845 and wakes up in the body of Carmena Luebber, owner of the Holiday Ranch. Unable to return to her own time, Mandy must assume Carmena's role. As she endeavors to discover why she was sent into the past, Mandy is caught up in the lives of the people who work for Carmena—their struggles and dreams—and ends up torn between two men in love with the woman she portrays. But Mandy is forced to admit that she can't have either one of them, no matter how much her heart wishes otherwise. Trapped in the past, she must complete an unknown task and find her way back to the present—before she messes up the future for everyone!

KUDOS for *Eve's Amulet*

In *Eve's Amulet ~ Book 1* by Carole Avila, Mandy Ruhe is given a necklace by a mysterious woman…Mandy doesn't believe in psychics, especially ones that try to tell the future, but she becomes suddenly unsure of herself when the woman's strange predictions begin to come true…Mandy is suddenly thrust back in time to 1845 Texas, Mandy spends the next several months trying to figure out why she has been sent to the past—and how to get back to the present…The plot is strong and has enough twists and turns to keep you riveted. *~ Taylor Jones, The Review Team of Taylor Jones & Regan Murphy*

The premise in *Eve's Amulet ~ Book 1* by Carole Avila is fascinating and something I'm sure most of us have fantasies about…Mandy, doesn't get to choose the time in the past that she is sent to, doesn't know why she is sent there, and has no idea how to get back to the present…Avila has a good handle on characterization…The plot is intriguing, the characters charming, and the writing very well done. *~ Regan Murphy, The Review Team of Taylor Jones & Regan Murphy*

ACKNOWLEDGMENTS

It often takes a community to create a written work. I appreciate everyone who has contributed to this story and to the Universe for giving me the words.

I am grateful to those who began Eve's Amulet's journey with me: Laurena Foegen, Patti Vickers, and my early editor, Maya Porter. To the Krav Maga trainer in Argentina who spent an hour with me on the phone; the people who machine-gunned my work at Gather.com where ego wasn't allowed; for the anonymous authors who provided valuable historical information at various websites; Paul Hischar for his enthusiasm and desire to see his students succeed in their own businesses; those who read early chapters and final drafts, sharing their very honest opinions at the Coffee House Writers Group and the Mt. San Antonio Community College Creative Writing Club (you guys are incredibly talented!) and the Mt. SAC Writer's Day Conference workshops; Bonnie Hearn Hill, for introducing me to Black Opal Books; Acquisitions Editor Lauri Wellington for helping when I needed it most; to the awesome copy and content editors Cora and Faith; Jack, for his help on the original cover; Sunny Frazier for all the invaluable information for writers; John Foegen for cheerleading and proofing--repeatedly; John & Ann Brantingham for their continued belief in me; Frank X. Haverkamp and his eagle eye; my loving Auntie Carmen Terrazas, for whom Carmena was named; Thanks to those who helped with the new revision—author Debby Wallace, Charles Sinclair Bartholomew, students in my creative writing classes at NWACC and the Writers Critique Group in Bella Vista. And to those dear friends who encouraged me, supporting my dream of writing and becoming a published author, especially Patty Vickers, Kristen Everts, Francesca Terzano, Therese Rumi, Janet Everts, Renee Barbee, Lauri Frew and especially Laura Moore.

I am filled with gratitude and thank you, thank you, thank you.

EVE'S AMULET

Book I
Revised Edition

Carole Avila

A Black Opal Books Publication

DEDICATION

This book is dedicated to the memory of
Laura A. Moore
The most amazing best friend ever
Who told me I was called to be a writer,

And to my beautiful and wondrous daughters—
Marisa, Jasmin, and Laurena,
Thank you for your unfailing inspiration, support, and love.

A Pink Hat

&

A Purple Hippo

CHAPTER 1

Texas, 1845:

D id you hear that?"

Carmena inclined her head toward the distorted glass panes over the steel-lined sink. She stared through a column of steam spiraling over a dainty porcelain cup, but the freshly brewed coffee never reached her lips.

Angela, the housekeeper of Holiday Ranch, and her nine-year-old daughter, Gracie, turned to the open window, and they all heard it again. Martino's warning, distant but clear enough.

"Sound the alarm!" Carmena shouted. She jumped to her feet, and her seat toppled over. "God willing, the men will hear it up in the canyon!" Chair legs screeched across the adobe tiles. Angela and Gracie hurried after Carmena to the enclosed rear porch. Carmena slipped on her muddy boots, and the frantic group bolted out the door. They looked up at Turtle Hill.

From the back patio, Martino, Angela's eleven-year-old son, was only a dark speck against the backdrop of the small mountain. The boy ran like a jackrabbit over scrub and rocks down to the ranch, yelling as loud as he could.

"Soldiers are coming! Soldiers!"

❧❦❧

Carmena sprinted toward the stables, issuing orders to Angela over her shoulder. "When you see any of the men, stop ringing the bell and head over to the barn. Get at least three milk cows up on the ridge!" In the same breath, she pointed at Gracie and yelled, "Get on upstairs to your hiding place!"

The wide-eyed girl pouted at the harsh reprimand and gripped her mother's skirt as Carmena dashed to the stables. Angela struck the rod inside the iron triangle, and the wild dinging alerted Jesse, one of the wranglers. She saw him hot-foot it from the farrier's shed, holding the top of his hat on his silvered head as he raced to the stables after Carmena. Just as Martino staggered to the base of the immense hill, Angela dropped the metal baton and spun around. Ignoring her daughter's tears, she stomped her foot and fisted one hand on her wide hip.

She pointed at the house and spoke in her heavy Spanish. "You heard Carmena. Go up to your room and hide!"

Angela's cotton skirt fanned in a circle as she hurried out the back gate. The housekeeper made her way to the barn and scuttled past the stables where Jesse was sliding a thick pad onto a nervous stallion.

℮ℑℰℑ

"Hold still now, Dandy," Jesse said to his horse as he hefted a worn leather saddle, carefully setting it on the pad. Veins bulged on the back of his hands as he gave a sharp tug and secured the leather straps around Dandy's belly. Normally standing stock still while being saddled, the horse stomped his hooves, and his ears flipped forward and back.

Jesse recognized the tension in Carmena's clenched jaw as she yanked lead ropes off the tack hooks outside of each stall. He helped her unlatch the doors and attach one rope after the other onto the halters of their best studs and broodmares, a few of which were in foal.

"Who's goin' up?" Jesse asked.

"You take this bunch. I'll get the other mares out of the paddocks. Maybe they'll follow Dusty up the hill." Carmena unlatched the bar on the last stall and hooked a lead rope onto Dusty's halter. "Damn it! I should've taken them up the hill like Carlos said!"

The wrangler kept silent and gathered the rest of the lead ropes as Carmena guided the horses out of their stalls. The animals fidgeted, and like Dandy, they nervously flicked their ears and pounded their hooves. Jesse's soft cooing gentled the horses a bit as he coaxed them to the center of the outbuilding. Once the muscular equines were gathered behind Jesse's mount, Carmena wasted no time in throwing a pad and saddle on Dusty.

"Where the hell is that boy?" she demanded.

A moment later, Martino stumbled into the stables. He hunched over and planted his hands on his knees, his chest heaving as sweat dripped off his grimy forehead.

Carmena pulled the knot out of her bandana and tied her long, unruly hair into a frizzy bundle. "Where are they? How many?"

Still out of breath, Martino drank in air between his words. "No more—" he gasped, "—than a dozen. They're comin' at a—slow gait. Still—a couple miles out." His slim body heaved up and down, fighting to regain his breath.

Jesse climbed onto his saddle and checked the horses behind him. In a level voice he said, "Lucky thing they ain't in the mood fer breedin'."

Carmena snapped at Jesse. "Do you have to be so damn calm all the time?"

He smiled and pressed his thighs into Dandy's sides, and the powerful stallion strode forward, leading a parade of horses out of the stables just as Gracie staggered inside. She cradled a baby goat in her arms, and its wooly nap bulged between her short fingers. Tears streamed over her pudgy cheeks.

Martino held a hand in front of his sister and gently pulled her out of harm's way as the procession of horses filed out of the barn. The weight of the goat threw Gracie off balance, and she tottered back a few steps over the hay-strewn floor. "Carmena, are they gonna take Hannah?"

"Dammit, Gracie!" Carmena scolded. "Put that kid down, and go on up to your room!" Then she turned her furious gaze to Martino. "Grab some of those ropes!"

A jerk of her chin indicated the lassos hanging on a large metal hook. Martino fetched them while Carmena placed a bridle over Dusty's head. In a single movement, she jumped up, swung a leg over her mount, and sat atop the mare. She hung the offered lassos around the saddle horn then glowered at the little girl still clutching the wooly baby goat.

"I won't tell you again to get on up to your room and hide, Gracie. Now! You need to follow orders so you don't get hurt!" She turned to the boy. "Martino, help your mother tie up some goats with the milk cows and get them up to the ridge. Then run over to the high meadow and tell the men what's happening. They probably didn't hear the alarm."

Carmena gripped her bridle with one hand, held the lassos in place with the other, and squeezed on the horse's flanks with her thighs. "C'mon, Dusty!" The beautiful tan mare galloped into the sunlight toward the paddocks.

Gracie stood her ground near the large wooden doors. The tiny goat uttered a "ma-a-a" in her arms.

Martino ushered her outside, speaking tenderly the way his father would when his sister didn't want to go to bed. "You heard Carmena. Go on up to your room."

"But what about Hannah?" Gracie rubbed her cheek against the animal's short bristles.

"The captain doesn't want a baby goat, so take Hannah up to your hiding place, but keep her quiet, and I'll tell Carmena I said you could bring her inside. Now get a move on."

"*Gracias*, Martino!" Gracie smiled and wobbled away, the pet goat snuggled in her arms. Martino walked backward, watching his sister until she disappeared through the side gate leading to the back patio off the kitchen.

Then he rushed to help his mother gather the cows and goats penned in the barn.

ℰↄℰↄ

"What was that?" Carlos, the ranch foreman, stared up toward the tree line.

Javier, Angela's husband and father to Martino and Gracie, tilted his head. "Sounds like a woodpecker."

"I thought it was the alarm," Carlos said.

Javier shook his head. "Nah. Believe me, I can hear the chow bell in my sleep. I didn't hear nothin'. Besides, them woodpeckers can imitate anything."

Both men faced the direction of the ranch in the valley below and listened. Steers grunted as they basked in the sun-warmed grass, ground squirrels twittered under the oaks, and scrub jays chirped from the high branches overhead.

Javier squinted at the cloudless sky. "Got a couple hours to go yet. I still say it woulda been easier to take the cattle and sheep to the east meadow down below instead of bringing 'em up here."

Carlos scanned the area. "I've been keeping a record each time the soldiers visit. It's been just over eleven weeks since they were here last. I don't want to take any chances."

"I bet that scalawag Franz is havin' a hog-killin' time helpin' hisself to more of our stock," Javier said. "But why thieve from us? There's lots a good ranches between here and San Antonio."

"We're about the only ones in Texas who breed thoroughbreds and saddlebreds."

"I bet the captain's out to sea when it comes to the lieutenant takin' our best horses and cattle or else I'd wager he'd clean Franz's plow for sure."

Carlos rubbed under the rim of his hat. "Even if they do come in the next few days, I'm pretty certain the cattle are safe up here."

"Only 'cause Franz is too dim-witted to send his soldiers to search up here for anythin'. Maybe you shoulda convinced Carmena to bring the horses up, too."

Carlos kneaded the tension out of his neck. "Let's give it another quarter hour before we see how Martino's doing with the sheep. Then we can all head down to the ranch for lunch."

❦❦❦

Gravel crunched under hooves as Lieutenant Franz and

ten of his men rode up the lengthy tree lined drive to Holiday Ranch. The lieutenant scoured the distant paddocks and corrals. It was a poor choice of pickings—a few old nags and too many yearlings, far too small for riding.

"Corporal Scott!"

The soldier, too young to grow a beard, rode to his commander's side. "Yes, sir?"

"Take half the men and see if there's anythin' more than buzzard bait in the stables and barn."

"Yes, sir!" Scott shouted in a deeper voice. He urged his horse forward. "Squad Two, move out and follow me!"

Four soldiers pulled out of line and followed the corporal away from the courtyard toward the outbuildings on the eastern side of the property. The rest of the men rode straight to the front of the villa where an enormous Mexican-tile fountain dominated the main entrance.

The men kept a few feet behind the lieutenant until he motioned for them to dismount at the hitching post near the adobe steps. Two sturdy pine doors with iron hardware barred the entrance. One door opened slowly, and the barrel of a long gun preceded Carmena.

Franz's soldiers raised their weapons and put her in their sights, but Carmena didn't back down. She leveled her rifle at the lieutenant's chest. It was futile to hold the man at gunpoint while the rest of his armed squadron had him covered, but she had to buy time for her ranch employees to hide their best income-producing animals.

"Miss Luebber. Well, ain't you the big sugar?" Franz tipped his hat. His gaze roamed down the line of her form-fitting gauchos, his eyes lingering on the bodice of her cotton blouse.

"What the hell do you want this time, Franz?"

"I was jest wonderin' where all yer purdy horses were at."

"I sold nearly all of our stock before you could get your stinkin' filthy hands on any more of them."

"Now, that ain't a polite way fer you to address a military officer, is it?" The lieutenant leaned against his saddle horn. "Why, accordin' to the Republic of Texas, I got me a perfect right to confiscate yer stock. President Jones knows it's better ta let some of his constituents lose a few horses and steers in exchange for military protection."

"I'm sure the president doesn't encourage the military to steal private property for personal gain."

The lieutenant pushed up the rim of his hat. More dirt clumped in the creases of his forehead than his neck. "Surely, Miss Luebber, you understand how we's protectin' the citizens of this great republic from sufferin' at the hands of them no count Comanche Indians to the west—" He pointed north. "— Cherokee to the east, and them Mexicans to the south, who still think Texas belongs ta them. Why, I'm doin' you a favor. The less you have, the less them Indians is likely ta steal from you. Y'all should be showin' me how much you appershiate what I'm tryin' ta do fer you."

The heavy weapon remained steady in her hold. "Spare me your bullshit, Franz. You're just a pathetic four-flusher interested in filling up your own purse."

Hardened eyes locked onto the woman. "Corporal Boyce, McFaddin. Please help Miss Luebber here with that terrible heavy gun."

Carmena confidently raised the rifle and pointed the single barrel between the lieutenant's eyes. "I'm warning you, Franz."

"Well, now, the way I see it, if you shoot me, my men will shoot you and take e'vra animal that's left on yer property. No doubt yer ranch hands will come an' rescue you but a course, they'll have ta be shot for innerferin' with the law."

"You're not the law. Not here or anywhere else!"

Franz slid off his horse and took a single step toward her. He peered into the barrel of Carmena's gun and stopped. "Cureton, Tankersley, Burnell! Take a look around. I recollect seein' a couple of youngins out back last time we visited. In fact, that little girl looked like she was just startin' ta ripen up."

The three soldiers shared confused glances.

"Move it!" the lieutenant shouted, and the soldiers scuttled toward the back of the house to search for the children.

Carmena clenched her jaw and curled her lip. "You're a disgusting pig!"

Franz noticed the infinitesimal droop in her shoulders. "Lower your weapon, Miss Luebber, and no one's gonna get hurt." He nodded to Boyce.

Boyce glanced at the Winchester, formidable in her hands. His steps were reluctant and heavy up the stairs. Carmena didn't flinch. Her well-aimed one-shot rifle focused on no one but Franz. The young soldier apprehensively pushed the steel barrel downward. Carmena never saw his apologetic eyes as her own were clouded with fury.

Boyce whispered to the enraged woman. "I'm sorry, ma'am. Jest doin' my job."

❦❦❦

Long before Boyce tugged the weapon from Carmena's grasp, Angela and Martino made it to the east side of the high meadow. They fumbled with ropes and set the small animals to graze with the sheep atop Turtle Hill. Then Angela sent her son across the ridge to find his father and Carlos with her desperate plea.

"Tell Carlos the captain is no here. Tell him it's the lieutenant!"

Halfway down the rugged terrain, Angela spotted Jesse following some soldiers into the barn. She forced herself to jostle to the bottom of the hill as a sharp pain speared her side. She leaned on a fence post and filled her lungs. The housekeeper heard a heated argument blare from the front of the house. Carmena's voice caught on the wind calling someone a disgusting pig. Though out of breath from her run up then down the hill, Angela sprinted across the yard. She reached the front of the house in time to see Carmena charge the lieutenant with a tightened fist shooting out like a locomotive toward his nose. Franz dodged the blow, and it grazed his jaw instead.

He raised his gun. "You stupid bitch! Yer gonna pay fer that!"

Carmena spun on her heel but didn't have time to distance herself from the officer's six-shooter. The solid steel barrel smashed against the back of her skull.

"No!" Angela screamed, her arms stretched forward.

Carmena tumbled, and her forehead smacked the edge of the fountain. Her body folded like a ribbon onto the gravel.

The lieutenant holstered his pistol and took in the disapproving frowns of his men. Boyce and McFaddin, enraged by the man's brutality, looked to one another for direction.

Franz rubbed his bruised jaw. "Serves her right fer attackin' a military officer."

Angela dropped beside Carmena and cradled her head on her apron. She barely heard Carmena say, "Get inside with Gracie. Don't let him touch her."

Blood oozed from the back of Carmena's scalp and dripped onto Angela's hand. "But, *mija*, you're bleeding!"

"Go," Carmena whispered just as she lost consciousness.

Angela's tears dripped onto Carmena's blouse. The housekeeper tenderly removed the young woman's head from her lap and with careful hands set the injured woman onto the ground, then scrambled to her feet.

"The captain will hear about this!"

Franz laughed. "Who'd ya think sent me?"

Angela cursed the man and ran through the open front door, pushing it nearly shut before she bounded up the stairs in search of her daughter.

Franz grabbed Carmena by the arm and hauled her limp body up the front steps, disregarding her head as it lobbed to the side.

"Stand guard!" he ordered his men.

Boyce pressed his lips together and grimaced at the rough hold the lieutenant had on the woman. McFaddin looked down and shuffled his feet.

Franz kicked the heavy door open. "Now I'm gonna show ya how ta treat yer superiors."

He dragged Carmena over the threshold and slammed the door behind him.

CHAPTER 2

California, 2017:

Outside the LAX baggage terminal, the first driver in a line of Yellow Cabs loaded my bags into the trunk with a practiced smile. He tore away from the curb and, at the risk of committing vehicular manslaughter, dodged through freeway traffic as if playing paintball, veering in and out of lanes to avoid a hit.

The stress of the drive reignited the pain at the back of my head and pounding above my brow, almost as annoying as the recurring western dream that plagued my sleep. Every night over the past few weeks, deep in the alpha state, I saw myself riding a big, dusty horse. Cowboys fought soldiers, but not a single Indian was in sight. A young soldier apologized, but I don't know what for.

At random intervals, a hot guy in a dark blue shirt had appeared like a gourmet truffle when I didn't even know I was craving one. His role was hard to figure out until he lifted me into his muscle-beach arms, his soft lips nuzzling my ear as he whispered enticing endearments. Tragedy struck in the buzz of the alarm. I stared up at the ceiling, my body warmed by the passionate, dreamy embrace, and my earlobe still tingled as if it really had been nibbled.

The taxi swerved into the next lane and jarred me from my thoughts. The driver rocketed into the diamond lane and zoomed past miles of concrete, the local preference over anything green. Once we were out of L.A., trees gradually became part of the landscape and breathing seemed easier.

An hour later, my cousin, Nicole, met me at the curb of her brick-fronted house in Montrose on the green foothills of the Angeles Crest Forest. She compressed my fragile nerves with a crushing bear hug.

"Mandy! It's so great to see you!"

While I paid the driver, she easily hefted my two largest bags from the trunk. Years of martial art classes paid off for her, demonstrated in her strength, as well as her quick and confident steps. Weighted down by an oversized purse and a small carry-on in each hand, I staggered away from the taxi and followed my cousin like a drunkard, each arm stretching to its fullest.

I grunted occasionally in response to Nicole's cheerful account of the weather as we crossed through a narrow walkway and up a flight of stairs attached to the side of the garage. Marco, Nicole's boyfriend, was a professional drummer and converted the garage below my new living quarters into a music studio. For that reason alone, my stay would be short.

Nicole led the way into the room and dropped my bags.

"Oh, my gosh! These hardwood floors are beautiful!" I spun in a slow circle. "And crown molding skirts the entire ceiling. I love it!"

My cousin smiled.

I examined the sheer maroon fabric panels covering three sets of French windows. Nicole opened the ones facing north to the Angeles Crest Forest, reminding me of the winter-bared woods I left behind in Arkansas. She opened another set of windows overlooking the brick driveway.

A round end table had been topped by an arrangement of photos of me and my cousin with a glass bowl I purchased for her from Eureka Springs, an amazing Victorian art community near my home. A series of colored reprints of Big Ben, Westminster Abbey, and London Bridge crowned the massive headboard. Other walls held a few professionally framed prints of Nicole in basic karate poses, along with two posters announcing martial art competitions.

My stoic aunt shaped Nicole into an obedient child, and

she grew into a compliant teen. While I secretly had a lion tattoo inked near my hip to rebel against my mother, Nicole remained a "good girl," accommodating the desires of others. Living with Marco in the fiery pit of sin, she finally managed to find a way to rebel against her ultra-conservative, judgmental mother.

Now if only Nicole could stand up to Marco.

Despite her physical strength, my cousin was an emotional weakling and placed the wants of her boyfriend over most of her own desires. She might as well forget about competing in martial arts. Marco wasn't keen on her leaving the house for any reason. He barely gave her permission to work part-time at a boutique in a nearby shopping district. If she hadn't already had black belts in Karate and Krav Maga when Marco first met her, I doubt he would have let her enroll in Tae Kwon Do classes.

Nicole helped me unpack the garment bags and a box of sentimental knickknacks I had shipped a few days prior. Everything else was left behind in Arkansas for packaging and delivery to a storage facility until I decided if I wanted to sell or rent my house.

Nicole zipped up and buttoned a pair of my jeans and draped them carefully over a wooden hanger. "Why did you say you moved to Arkansas in the first place?" she asked.

"You know. I got that weird inheritance."

"And you still haven't found out who it came from? I asked everyone in the family, and no one had any idea you even got an inheritance."

I shook my head. "I didn't find anything in my parents' papers, and I called the lawyer's office, but no one's ever heard of the attorney's name or the person who filed the will. They said at the courthouse in Texas that it might've been an old document, which is why it wasn't in their computers. And I'd have to pay some expensive processing fee if I wanted to find out who left me the money. I guess once I bought the house, it just didn't seem important."

"I wish you hadn't let Janet convince you to move back east," Nicole said of my best friend.

"Arkansas is beautiful country. And it's in the south central part of the country, not the east."

She shrugged. "It's east of the Rockies."

"It hasn't been so bad," I said.

"You mean it wasn't until Janet met that guy online and moved to Oregon a month after you got there."

"I admit, it was hard not knowing a single person, but it didn't really get bad until I got a speeding ticket a few months ago. I lost it in all my paperwork clutter, and it must have slipped through the cracks at the courthouse because it didn't turn into a warrant until recently."

"What? How fast were you going? Who gave you the ticket, and who cleared the warrant?" She interrogated me as if I'd confessed to armed robbery.

"Relax, Nicole," I held up my palms and let them slowly drop. "It wasn't a major event. I went to court a couple of days ago, and it was dismissed. And get this, the judge, who was very hot, flirted with me. Right there at the bench."

Nicole raised one eyebrow at me.

"Well, he didn't really say anything. It was more the way he looked at me. He even winked at me when I left the courtroom."

"Big deal." She waved off my remark. "A wink is like an empty promise. It's not a phone call or a date."

"But he did call me! Later that afternoon on his lunch break. He left a voicemail, asking me to take a ride on his property in his new Jeep and have a picnic by a creek and—" I sighed. "—he didn't know I'd be moving back to California in the next two days. I erased his message."

It seemed silly to postpone plans of moving because I had a small, yet indescribable connection to the man. I really wanted to go out with him. Any other time I would have jumped at the chance to date an attractive and available professional, especially one whi expressed an interest in me. But it didn't seem fair to make someone else responsible for my happiness. That was one of those things I had to find within, one of the reasons for returning to California after feeling so unaccomplished in Arkansas. And there was something else. Others had a sense of belonging, but I still needed to find my tribe, those who I could call family since Nicole was about my only blood relative after my parents died a few years back.

My reflection lasted no more than a few moments. "Thanks for doing this," I said to Nicole.

She smiled. "Not a problem. I'm really glad you came!" Nicole expressed more excitement in her voice than what I felt in my heart.

"I'm glad to be here. I guess it's time to concentrate on my future in California."

Nicole pressed out a crease in my jeans. "The job market's pretty bleak these days. The state is at maximum capacity in population and affordable housing. We've got one of the highest unemployment rates in the country."

So why did I bother returning? Just as the depressing thought started to have its way with me, Nicole said, "Wait ''til I tell you about Maizy!"

"The lady who used to live here?"

Nicole bobbed her head. Her eyes gleamed, and she described her former tenant, as if Maizy had been a Hollywood leading lady. "I wish you could've seen her, Mandy. It's like she didn't care what anyone thought about what she looked like or what she said." Nicole slipped a shirt on a hanger and buttoned it up to the neck. "She dressed in flowing skirts and billowy blouses and wore the most beautiful gemstone jewelry. She was amazing!" My cousin went quiet and scanned the room as though it was littered with listening devices. She whispered, "I think Maizy was a witch."

"You mean with a pointed black hat and bubbling caldron?" Skepticism saturated my words.

"Be serious," she scolded. "I mean the herbs and crystals and incense kind."

"A lot of people use those things, and it doesn't mean they're witches. Buddhists and Native Americans meditate all the time with that stuff."

"It wasn't just that," Nicole said. "One day when I was going to the gym, she stopped me in the driveway. She said, 'Marco doesn't want you to go to work, but he'll change his mind.' I had put in some applications at local shops, but I never told anyone that. Then the next day, Barbara called to say I got the job at Sweet Young Things, and Marco said it was okay!"

I plopped on the bed, tired of the moving process, and I refused to admit I was getting slightly spooked by the Maizy conversation.

"You probably forgot you told Maizy you wanted to work, and she convinced Marco to let you take on a part-time job."

"No! I never talked to her about it."

"Maybe Maizy could tell me if moving back to California was a good idea or not," I half joked. "Where is she now?"

"I don't know." Nicole slumped onto the bed. She stared out a window, focused on nothing. "She just said it was time to move on and left. You wouldn't believe what she told me. She said I'd get a raise in a week, and I did!" The framed prints of the martial arts events drew her attention and her voice softened. "She said I had great dreams that I was too cowardly to pursue."

My cousin looked as if she'd lost her black belt degrees, her expression almost as heartbreaking as my failure to find meaning in life, but the move back to California was my hope I could change that.

"I'm sure it was just a coincidence." I stood and nervously fussed with the window dressings. "Do you mind if I replace the curtains? These sheers are really cute, but someone could probably see in at night with the lights on."

Nicole ignored my paranoid remark. "Her predictions were more than coincidence, Mandy. And they weren't all good. She said Marco was going to get hurt when he fell off a horse."

"Stop right there." I held up my hands. "Now I know she's a fake. We all know Marco won't go near a horse, let alone ride one."

"Not everything she told me has had a chance to happen yet. She said we'd be getting a new blue car this month, but I can't see how when we're financially strapped after the remodel and paying off a few bills. But she did say we can control or change most everything that's going to happen to us by trusting the power of our own mind, and through prayer or meditation."

"In that case," I said, "anybody could tell you the future and never lose sleep over facing fraud charges. They'd simply argue that your prayers either were or weren't answered."

Nicole pulled back her head, a little attitude in her voice. "She told me you were coming, but you wouldn't be able to leave until you cleared up a warrant in Arkansas." When I laughed, she said, "I'm serious. She told me you got a speeding ticket from an officer with a funny name, and you were going thirteen miles over the speed limit. It would go into warrant, but the charges for failure to pay and to appear would be dropped by a man named Vincent."

I plunked down next to her on the bed, my mouth slacked open.

"What was the name of the officer who gave you the ticket, Mandy?"

"Dickie," I said. My jaw dropped a little lower. "I could never forget that name."

"And the judge who winked at you? What was his name?"

I swallowed back the lump in my throat. "Parker. The Honorable Vincent S. Parker."

"And?" she prompted. "What was the ticket for?"

I gaped at her. "For going thirteen miles over the speed limit. The judge dismissed the warrant." Now I understood Nicole's wild interest in my ticket. "You don't look as surprised as I am," I said.

"Because some of the things Maizy said already came true. I believe everything she told me."

A breeze lifted the curtains over the sink in the kitchenette, and a heavy shadow drifted across the room. Nicole glanced at it but gave more attention to the digital numbers on the microwave. She picked up my alarm clock and reset it to the correct time.

In less than a second, the gloomy mist faded. It was probably a cloud floating in front of the sun or the shadow of a bird gliding out of sight.

"Huh." I kept my eye on the open window. "I think the smog is getting thicker out here."

CHAPTER 3

Nicole sighed. "I'm bummed that Maizy left before you met her."

I shrugged and gazed around the beautiful room. "Her departure was my gain."

She touched my arm. "I saved the best for last. Maizy said to tell the next tenant, 'Good luck, and don't forget to wind it.'"

I blinked. "Why didn't you tell me sooner?"

"Because I figured you'd think it was a weird thing to say. What do you think she meant?"

"Heck if I know. I don't own a watch, and my alarm clock is digital." I jumped to my feet. "Oh! I have a music box!"

We stared at the wooden box on the dresser as if it were the only one left in the world. Nicole held her breath as I lifted the lid. "Time in a Bottle" tinkled out.

"It's already wound up. That's not it," she said, her lower lip protruding.

"Whatever she meant, we'll find out sooner or later." I waited a second and asked, "Um, did she, you know, tell you anything else? About me?"

Nicole crossed her arms and smirked.

"It's not like I believe in her silly predictions," I explained. "No harm in asking, right?"

Nicole slipped a scrap of paper out of her pocket and held it out to me. "Maizy said you'd ask and made me promise to wait until you did. She said not to give this to you until then."

"It's spooky enough that Maizy knew about my ticket and that I was going to court, but now this?"

"Here. Take it." She placed the yellowed and aged note in my palm. I unfolded it. The paper was more resilient than I'd expected from its fragile appearance. Altogether, it was no bigger than an index card.

"You're supposed to keep it with you until you don't need it anymore."

Words stuck in my throat.

Nicole pressed, "What does it say?"

"You haven't read it? I mean, after all, it's not even in an envelope."

"Maizy told me that respecting people's privacy is an obligation we all must practice."

"If she could dampen your curiosity, maybe she really is a witch."

Nicole playfully bumped my arm before resting her hands in her lap. "Just read it already."

In a split second, a wave of pressure crashed behind me, ending as quickly. I peeked over my shoulder. No one was there, yet I distinctly felt something press against my back.

My cousin didn't notice a thing, and my attention returned to the note. The first four lines of the poem were arranged in verse and written in beautifully scripted letters, resembling those on the Declaration of Independence. But the fifth and last line had been hastily scrawled across the bottom.

I read the first two sentences: "'Add the crone's advice at the end of this rhyme, then this note is passed on to the next in line.'"

"What does that mean?" Nicole asked.

"How should I know? Then it says 'Tis a gift you will find, but a curse it can be. If not used with wisdom, you'll dread eternity.' Huh. The meter's off in the last line. And there's still something missing, like a clue." I stared at the note and studied the penmanship. "It's strange that the first four lines are written in fancy calligraphy, but this last one is scribbled. You know, like a doctor wrote it."

"There's more?" Nicole brightened. "What does it say?"

"It says, 'He wears a pink hat and rides a purple hippo.'"

"What?"

"Here. Read it yourself. Not only does this last line make less sense than all the others, but it's written with a ballpoint pen."

Maizy's credibility had been crushed with ink.

I handed Nicole the paper, and she rolled her eyes. "I'm not going to let an inconvenient detail make me a skeptic," she said and continued examining the note.

Blood resumed its flow as soon as I stood up.

"It doesn't make any sense," Nicole said a few moments later. "I thought she gave you something important. Like the winning lottery numbers or your soul mate's address."

"Now, that would've made me a believer."

Nicole tossed the note, like a bad report card, onto the nightstand and half-heartedly invited me to her kitchen for lunch. She trudged out of the room, and her slow footsteps clunked elephant-like down the stairs, echoing her obvious disappointment.

After reading the note a second time, no hint of revelation came forth, so I slipped it into my back pocket just as the air shifted, as if someone walked into the room. Or out. I looked around, but no one was there.

I rushed out of the room and sprinted downstairs to join Nicole in the kitchen.

౿ఞ౿ఞ

Nicole was a vegan but, despite that, she whipped up some great dishes, probably the real reason Marco kept her under wraps. The only thing she did better was martial arts, yet her threat of a headlock did nothing to get me to talk about Maizy's poem again.

I returned to my room after lunch, grateful my cousin had turned down my offer to help wash the dishes. At first, I was going to add the poem to the top dresser drawer where only important things were stashed, like my phone charger and bamboo back scratcher. But instead, I read it once more, glad Nicole wasn't there to watch me take it seriously.

Ten minutes elapsed, and my frustration level grew higher. Although the entire matter freaked me out, the cryptic message intrigued me enough to keep it close. Back into my jeans pocket it went.

Measuring for new curtains to replace the sheers was a good diversion. I found my plastic storage container labeled "Misc. Tools" under the sink in the kitchenette. Halfway through aligning the fluorescent green measuring tape along the edge of a panel, a bright red hybrid pulled into the brick driveway below. My cousin ran to the car. Marco exited the passenger side like a jointless robot, his right arm in a sling and a nylon cast on his left leg.

Nicole cried out, "Babe! Are you all right?"

He smirked. "You mean aside from having a drumming arm out of commission and this huge obstruction velcroed over my leg?"

I hurried down the stairs and joined the group at the car.

"Marco, it's nice to see you." I gently hugged him. "But not like this."

Descended from a Zulu chief, Marco lost any trace of a fierce tribesman the moment he gave me his boyish smile. "Honestly, I'm okay. Mandy, this is my buddy, Theo."

I shook the driver's hand.

"My arm's broken but my leg is only sprained," Marco said to Nicole.

"Is that all?" She crossed her arms, put off by his nonchalance.

"Ask him how he did it," Theo urged. His white toothy grin contrasted his mocha complexion.

Marco frowned at his friend.

Nicole asked, "You weren't riding up at Wallace Ranch, were you?" She snuck a peek at me.

Wallace Ranch was a neat old place in Lake View Terrace where horses were rented out for trail riding.

"Think, Nicole. Why would I have been there?"

Theo snickered. "He would've been safer at the ranch."

Marco ignored him and started for the house. Theo and Nicole rushed to either side as he awkwardly managed the single crutch.

"Marco," Nicole threatened. "Tell me what happened!"

"I was at the gym and did a handstand."

"He tried to do a handstand," Theo cackled, but his laughter died quickly when Nicole stabbed him with knifepoint irises.

The injured man and concerned onlookers shuffled into the living room where Marco slumped into an overstuffed recliner. He dropped the aluminum crutch beside the chair in time for Nicole to catch it. Theo scurried to the refrigerator behind the bar adjacent to the living room.

"Decklan was showing off doing a handstand," Marco said. "And I dared him to try it with one hand."

Nicole set the crutch against the armchair. Theo raced back, vigorously shaking two small plastic cartons of dark green liquid and handed one to Marco.

"Then Mr. Big Shot here says—" Theo moved his head sideways with attitude. "Dog, anybody can stand on two hands, but let's see you do it on one."

"So I showed him how to do a handstand like a man," Marco said.

Theo roared. "Like a man with no arms! The guy falls on his skinny butt, and every single person in the gym cracked up. I almost wet my shorts!" He threw his head back as he laughed and missed Nicole frowning at him.

"I wouldn't have fallen if Decklan hadn't left a big ugly sweat stain on the leather," Marco explained. "I slipped on it and crashed like a freakin' drunk wino." Theo chortled again, and Marco rubbed his right arm. "The doctor says I can't play for at least six weeks. Damn!"

"Lucky thing the band isn't touring for a couple of months," Theo added.

Marco pursed his lips and dragged his fingers along the canvas sleeve. Nicole rubbed his shoulder, and he gave a poor attempt at a smile.

Though I kind of felt bad for the guy, Marco's predicament afforded me a longer stay without the noise.

I tried to lighten the mood. "Only in California would they use leather exercise mats."

Marco shook his head. "It wasn't a mat."

"Yeah," Theo added. "It was one of those gymnastic things with the two rings you do handstands on."

"A horse," Marco told him.

The hinges broke on my jaw, and Nicole's mouth dropped open, too.

Marco patted her hand. "Now, don't you go making a fuss over me just because I'm all laid up. Why don't you get your man something to eat?"

I yanked on my cousin's arm and dragged her open-mouthed toward the kitchen.

Marco grinned at Theo. "Sweet. I'm going to be a couch potato again."

"That's what you were while I was painting my patio furniture last week." Theo plopped onto the sofa and clicked on the TV while I continued to steer Nicole to the kitchen.

"I told you!" she whispered. "Maizy was right again!"

"Yeah, but that note she left makes absolutely no sense at all, so I'm still not convinced."

"Something probably has to happen first to understand what it means. Remember that line that said you'd find something?"

In the kitchen, I pulled the paper out of my pocket, and Nicole raised her eyebrows.

"What?" I dared, but she crossed her arms and kept quiet. I carefully unfolded the note. Nicole leaned over my shoulder.

"It says, ''Tis a gift you will find, but a curse it can be,'" I mused. "Who wants to find a gift that's a curse?"

Nicole clarified, "It says it can be a curse. It doesn't have to be one."

"Whatever."

I rubbed my forehead and sighed. The poem went back inside my pocket before I helped to prepare a meal for the new couch potato and his friend.

ഗ൦ഗ

Nicole let me borrow her car for a quick trip to the local linen shop where I purchased thick gold brocade curtains with tiny burgundy highlights to complement the comforter. The sheers slipped easily off the rods, and the new curtains fit as if they were tailor-made for the windows.

Scrunched like an accordion left to right, they looked great except when I peered at the last window frame on the left side of the bed. The window didn't shut all the way because the sash curved upward, leaving an eighth-inch gap in the middle. It was hard to believe Marco had overlooked such a major flaw. To top off my confusion, Nicole had opened each window in front of me without any hint of a problem.

I stashed the folded sheer curtains into a shopping bag and set them in the bathroom linen closet. Thinking of Marco's encased limbs convinced me to hold off on telling him about the sash, and I took a sustenance break. Nicole had stocked the petite refrigerator and cupboards with all kinds of healthy crap. I poured some granola and a cup of nonfat milk into a bowl.

What I'd give for a medium grilled steak and a Corona.

In the recliner, I aimed the remote at the flat screen, but it must have had a low battery. I pushed the power button over and over just to get the stupid thing to turn on, and then it wouldn't let me change the stations. Without getting up to manually change the TV, I was stuck with the *History Channel*. I munched on my granola while I watched a fascinating documentary on the life of Santa Anna, the Mexican dictator, emphasizing the crucial role his henchmen played and the demise of his political career.

After the program, and lacking any grace, I clambered out of the recliner and shut the TV off, mulling over how a carpenter might solve the sash problem. My fluorescent pink-handled flathead screwdriver was all I would need to detach the sill. Five minutes and a little elbow grease later, the entire slab of wood lifted neatly off the base of the window. I slipped my screwdriver into my back pocket and peered into the ledge.

What lay beneath the plank startled me more than my superior carpentry skills.

CHAPTER 4

An elegant silver chain with a hexagonal locket lay on the two-by-four hidden beneath the sill. I lifted the necklace, feeling a great rush of awe. The artifact—a gorgeous piece, heavy and maybe three inches in length—was as ornate as the pictures I'd seen of the Palace of Versailles. An ancient aura engulfed the charm, creating magic simply by its existence.

The silver chain looped through a bejeweled hook centered at the top of the amulet. Strands of intricately embossed silver curls of ivy snaked the silver treasure, and it was divided into six equal sections, with a silver cap on either end. After quickly testing a few sections, I realized each turned separately on an axle which must have run the length inside.

My shoulders flinched at an unexpected knock on the door.

"Who is it?" I said.

"It's me. Who else?"

It would be rude to deny Nicole a glimpse of the beautiful treasure. After all, I stumbled across it on her property.

"Door's open. C'mon in."

She immediately spied the plank of wood leaning against the disassembled windowsill. "What happened?" Then her eyes grew wide as she zoomed in on the necklace. It felt as if I'd been caught stealing.

"I found this while I was trying to fix the window."

She crossed the room in a few long strides and lifted the silver chain from my hand. "It's beautiful!"

"You didn't put it inside the frame?"

"No, of course not. I've never even seen it before."

I glanced down inside the wall. "There's not much dust on the wood where this was lying. It hasn't been here that long."

"Maybe this is the gift that was mentioned in the poem!"

I didn't want to get my hopes up. "Maybe one of the workmen lost it during the renovation."

"Since when are construction workers known to bring jewelry to a job site?" she asked. "And no one mentioned losing anything, much less an antique-looking pendant. Maybe Maizy left it behind!"

"Why would she leave something so valuable in a place where there was little chance of finding it?"

"What made you look inside the window in the first place?" Nicole asked.

I lifted the white enameled wood resting against the wall. "This sash was bowed, and I wanted to fix it."

"That's impossible. Everything in this room is in perfect condition."

"I'm telling you, the wood is curved, and the window didn't close all the way. Look at how this board bends." I slipped the wooden slat back into place and it conformed perfectly to the straight line of the frame. My knees went weak, and I croaked, "Oh, my."

Nicole flew to my side and held me upright. She latched an ankle onto a chair at the dining table and towed it toward us. I dropped onto the seat under the weight of disbelief.

"Really. It was warped."

She handed me the necklace. "Oh, I believe you. After everything else that's happened, I'd believe anything."

I stared at the window. Did I only imagine the buckled wood? Nicole was right when she said the room was in perfect condition. It seemed unlikely that Marco would miss a warped sash. But how could the exact same board that I removed because it was bent now be perfectly flat?

I rubbed the familiar ache that throbbed in my forehead as a dull pounding grew at the back of my skull.

As if jealous of my attention, the bulky piece of jewelry vibrated gently in my hand. It felt alive, and I almost dropped it, but at that point, my curiosity was stronger than my fear.

"What is it?" Nicole asked.

I snatched a floral-handled magnifying glass out of my toolbox and examined the sides of the hexagon-shaped charm. Brilliantly crafted, each of the six sides depicted a tiny scene from different eras of history.

Nicole's voice blurred into white noise as I stared at the object, this time without the magnifying glass. The minuscule images disappeared into the lacy curlicues enveloping the silver exterior.

Under the glass, pyramids and hieroglyphs of ancient Egypt took shape on one side of the amulet. Another side featured the Colosseum in its entirety and other Italian architecture. There was a representation of the old southwest with cowboys, grazing cattle, and a Spanish-style ranch. The scene felt vaguely familiar. South American ruins filled another of the six sides. I rolled the silver charm again and found a depiction of Westminster Abbey and Windsor Castle.

The last picture was the most captivating. The finely crafted silver created an entrancing outdoor landscape with undulating fields and a waterfall cascading through a canyon. Muscles in my neck tensed up when I noticed a rendering of a snake coiled on a branch in the center of an apple tree. There was no way to misinterpret the Garden of Eden.

An inexplicable feeling of dread loomed over me, and I sensed it was something harder to escape than my futile attempt at success in another state.

"Mandy!" Nicole's voice jarred me, engrossed as I was by the pendant. "What is it?"

I held the magnifying glass out to her, totally mute, and slouched, wide-eyed, back into the chair. For the next several minutes she ooh-ed and ah-ed as she examined the necklace.

Sufficiently filled with appreciation, she said, "This is it. This has to be the gift Maizy alluded to in the poem."

"What makes you think this necklace is connected to Maizy?"

Nicole dangled the charm from its chain and stood it upright in her palm. "I'm betting you can't find anything like this in Tiffany's. It's old. I'm not sure why the artist chose to illustrate these places, but they're all significant sites." At my blank expression, she explained further. "Each of these places is where a holy or mystical phenomenon occurred. The Egyptian pyramids, Incan ruins, and a famous English church."

"And the holiness of the Colosseum? How do you explain that?"

"The Vatican is located in Italy. And I don't have to recount the story of Eden."

"I don't recall a sacred incident taking place in the old west," I challenged. "How do you explain that?"

Nicole frowned at me. "Native American Indians. Their belief system is based on one of the oldest religions. Like the Druids, they connected to God through nature."

"But this is a picture of a ranch, not a teepee," I said.

"You just found it. You can't expect to understand everything about it."

We stared at the charm swinging innocently from its chain.

"How do you know all of this? About these sacred places, I mean."

She shrugged. "You know, online classes, history books, documentaries."

I was a top-rate slacker living in Arkansas while my cousin took advantage of her free time by educating herself and exercising her mind, learning of the world and the people in it. And nothing topped her devotion to martial arts, except a recent obsession with medieval England. The tournament posters she often stared at took on new meaning. They were all about unrealized dreams. Regret made a split-second appearance before it hid behind her usual cheery demeanor.

"There's one more thing that convinces me this is linked to Maizy's predictions and the note she left you."

I shook my head. "Please. Don't say anything more."

"I came up to tell you that Marco's mom called him just now. She and his dad came back from Vegas this morning. Iris won big. She hit a couple of huge jackpots, and one of them was a black, Maserati Granturismo coupe.

"Hah!" I sat forward and pointed an accusing finger at her, anxious to put the entire matter of fortune telling to rest. "Marco's mom is the one with a new car, not you or Marco, and it's black, not blue like Maizy predicted. It doesn't count!"

Nicole crossed her arms like an arrogant college professor about to point out the correct answer. "Iris told Marco that now that she has her fantasy car, she's giving us her BMW X-Three. She bought it for cash. Brand new. Two months ago. It's blue."

I slumped back into my chair. "Crap."

Nicole sat down, and her lovely green eyes appraised me. "What's wrong with having a little magic in your life?"

"Nothing." I gestured toward the necklace. "But this is... occult."

She smacked her forehead. "We're not talking human sacrifices and satanic rituals!"

"Earlier, you accused Maizy of being a witch," I reminded.

"I was a little more freaked out about it then."

I pointed to the necklace and sighed. "So what does this mean?"

"I don't know," she answered and set the charm on my palm. "Put it on. Wear it a while. See how it feels."

"I can't." I laid the necklace on the table as if it had cooties. "I'm simply not as curious as you, Nicole. Besides—" The truth whispered out of me. "It scares me."

"The first step in overcoming our fear is acknowledging it." She picked up the chain and draped it over my head.

"I told you that."

She nodded. "C'mon. I have to cook dinner for Marco before I go to work. And I'll make you something, too, if you keep me company."

We left my apartment and trekked downstairs to the kitchen. I tucked the necklace inside my shirt. It thumped my sternum every step of the way.

⌘⌘⌘

My cousin worked a four-hour shift that night while Marco and I sat in the living room eating dinner on the couch.

We watched a *National Geographic* special on mystical international locations, including Stonehenge and the Mayan temples. As if the program didn't spook me enough, Marco put on a taped episode of *Paranormal State.*

He handed me his plate. "How about second servings, Mandy?"

I probably should've been put off that he treated me like a servant just then, like he did Nicole, but I needed a break from the creepy programs. In the kitchen, I gladly spent five minutes dishing him another helping of a delicious vegan casserole and warming it up.

Watching all that stuff increased my uneasiness about the mysterious ornament hanging like a noose around my neck. Each time I fidgeted with the charm, it gently hummed against my skin, and the silver grew warm between my fingers. I slipped the jewelry back inside my shirt only to find myself twisting it again a few minutes later. Fascination and anxiety swirled in a nauseating mix, and I grew restless waiting for Nicole to return home.

Marco put on another unsettling program about modern-day ghost hunters, and that was all the heebie-jeebies my system could take.

"Would you like some tea or hot chocolate, Marco?"

"Man, what I'd do for a double-shot soy latte with extra foam right now," he said.

Generally too lazy to volunteer for any errands, I offered to drive to Starbucks, less than five minutes up Rosemont Avenue. Anything to get away from the TV programs adding to my sense of foreboding, but Marco thought twice about it.

"I'd better not," he said. "It might keep me up tonight. Thanks, anyway."

"Let me know if you change your mind."

A disturbing veil of doom followed me to the kitchen. I changed my mind about getting a drink, content to sit at the breakfast bar and toy with the necklace until my cousin finally strolled through the back door. I'd give her a minute to relax before I ranted about my fears.

Nicole glanced at the charm twirling between my fingers and said, "What's up?"

"Not much."

Marco ambled into the kitchen like Quasimodo, hunched over one crutch, his arm tucked into the sling, and a huge Cheshire Cat smile plastered on his face, just for Nicole.

"There's my woman!"

Nicole snuggled her way into his one-limbed squeeze. I would've gone upstairs to give them privacy, but I really needed to discuss my mounting feelings of unease with my cousin. I fidgeted with the sections of the necklace and waited while they completed their greetings.

"How are you, baby?" she asked.

"I'm fine. Your cousin is keeping me company."

Nicole's eyebrow rose up a bit. "I can't imagine she's said much tonight."

"Maybe that's why he values my company," I joked.

Some sections of the necklace were rotated out of place, and I set about twisting them to and fro to restore their original positions—a challenge without a magnifying glass.

"What's that thing you've been playing with all night, Mandy?"

Split second panic flashed in Nicole's eyes.

"The way you've been working that gizmo, you best hope it comes with some kind of warranty before it falls apart," he teased.

"Let's tell him," Nicole said.

"Tell me what?"

Nicole sparkled with excitement, unable to contain the secret of the charm and cryptic note.

Marco figured out what was coming. "Oh, no! I hope this isn't anything about that voo-doo nonsense and that Maizy lady."

While Nicole championed her former tenant, my eye caught movement at my feet. A fog seeped across the kitchen floor out of nowhere and surrounded me. Neither one of the two quarreling lovers seemed to notice. Panic strangled me like a boa constrictor as I started to shrink away from them. The overhead lights dimmed like a gas lamp, narrowing my field of vision. A steady pull on my body forced me to sink deeper into the miasma.

"Hey, what's going on?" I asked, but they continued their muted discussion.

Marco finally glanced at me, and his eyes went round. He mimed my name as though shouting it, but I heard nothing. Not reassuring.

Nicole wore the same mask of surprise. They stood at the brink of a tunnel as I floated backward, swallowed by the horizontal pit into a whirlpool of nothingness.

The last thing I remembered was the charm in my hands. Then the world turned black.

CHAPTER 5

Texas, 1845:

A colossal headache jackhammered at my skull. Pain ransacked every nerve ending, worse than the migraine I'd suffered before my court appearance. Motion sickness blossomed as my head swayed back and forth against my will. A struggle went into flitting open my lashes.

The fuzzy image of a moustached man came into view, and his tears dripped onto my face. Long brown hair dangled past his wide shoulders and stuck in the salty liquid on my cheeks. Decorative gold braiding sat on his wide shoulders and shiny gold buttons shimmered on the front of his dark blue jacket.

Yankee Jesus rocked me in his arms, and I wanted to throw up.

"Don't leave me," he whispered. His deep voice sounded like a lullaby, pulling some of my attention away from the pain and the need to vomit. "Carmena, come back to me."

It was the wrong name, but he said it like a soothing hot drink on a chilly day. I felt safe in his presence, inexplicably secure in an embrace so suffocating that it threatened to choke the air from my lungs.

My lashes fluttered all the way open. It felt like the man with the knockout looks wasn't holding me for the first time, but I couldn't recall seeing eyes bluer than the waters on a Caribbean postcard.

"Carmena!" His weak smile tried to nudge past his anguish. "Darling, stay with me!"

"Dude, why wouldn't I?" The small and scratchy voice didn't sound like my own, but apparently, he didn't care.

His long fingers swiped strands of tacky hair out of my face. "Forever more, I shall see to your every happiness, my love."

Deeply comforted, I gave him a trifling smile as I closed my eyes and lapsed into sleep.

℮∕ა℮∕ა

Something jabbed the backside of my body, like a hammock supported with rebar ropes. An ugly stink reminded me of the herbal poultices my great-grandma concocted for skinned knees. People whispered in a foreign language. A distant yell of "Hee-yah!" was followed by neighing, mooing, barking, bleating, and crowing.

I must have fallen and smacked my head. That would explain the confusing sounds and hallucinations. I probably had a concussion to boot.

Light penetrated my lids, forcing me to blink out the brightness. My head throbbed more than ever, and the room blurred, but I didn't miss the extreme close-up of a heavyset older woman smiling sweetly at me in a high-collared dress.

The cushy maternal image was, no doubt, a subconscious portrayal of my cousin.

There was no way for me to determine how much time had lapsed between seeing Yankee Jesus and Hispanic Nicole. I closed my eyes and felt a cool cloth press lightly on my forehead. Nicole chanted in Spanish, fluid rolls of the tongue like my private Pied Piper convincing me to follow her into wakefulness.

I opened my eyes and a tear flowed down her cheek.

"Your fever has broken, *muchacha. Gracias a Diós.* We thought we lost you."

Her floor length brown skirt rustled over layers of fabric with a hint of lace circling the bottom. Black leather lace-up boots peeked from beneath the brown cloth and the white utilitarian apron enhanced her wide waist.

"How could I let my imagination do this to you? I must be subconsciously jealous."

"I go see if the *caldo* is ready," she said, squinting her eyes.

Nicole's Mexican alter ego left the room. My aching brain vaguely recalled that *caldo* meant soup. My high school foreign language requirement finally paid off.

Too tired to question why she spoke another language, I let my sight wander to the golden tint enveloping the room. It was late afternoon. A breeze lifted the thin curtains.

I swear I had changed those.

I tried to make sense of the surroundings. My clever imagination had created the utmost authenticity in the 1800s décor. Although the vintage furniture looked too new, it contributed to the stylish Roy Rogers meets Zorro retro design.

Well-preserved glass hurricane oil lanterns topped superbly crafted pine end tables and another lantern hung from an iron hook next to the door. What felt like metal ropes on my back turned out to be leather straps tacked along all edges of the bed frame to brace the thick, down-feather mattress.

A light tap on the door announced a tall, dark-haired man who hesitated before entering. "*Buenas tardes*, Carmena." He said the name in a thick but decipherable Spanish accent. "Angela says your fever has broken."

I'd transformed Marco into a handsome Mexican ranchero, although I surprised myself by not conjuring up something truer to his roots, like a mighty African warlord. The Marcoman was quite attractive and muscular. Gray hair at his temples gave scarce hint of his age. His biker black leather vest and gold watch fob were fairly macho compared to the longsleeved, white shirt with a feminine round collar and a shoelace style tie, more like a ribbon knotted into a bow.

"How do you feel?"

"You mean aside from my head reeling worse than riding a rollercoaster in a backward loop after a pitcher of margaritas?" I mumbled. The Marco persona tilted his head and narrowed his gaze on me, and I felt the need to reassure him. "I'm cool."

He pushed himself off the doorjamb. "I'll get you a blanket." He started for an afghan thrown over a Victorian style chaise lounge in the corner.

"I mean, I'm much better."

"*Que bueno.*" He leaned back against the doorframe, relaxed, yet a tight jaw belied his tension.

"The captain took care of everything." A hint of a sneer distorted his features when he said the officer's rank.

The woman he'd called Angela bustled into the room carrying a serving tray. "Martino helped me get all the animals from the barn up the hill before the soldiers arrived. They were tied together like the paper chains the *niños* make for the Christmas tree!"

"Captain? Soldiers? Martino?" There was only one logical explanation for this bizarre hallucination. I was dreaming and couldn't wake myself up. I must have created a story based on my inner thoughts and feelings, changing people I knew into brilliant characters.

Hispanic Marco frowned and a small crease etched between his brows.

The woman set down a delicious-smelling bowl of chicken soup. "You eat and get well," she said. It sounded more like an order than reassurance. She helped me to sit nearly upright, fluffing the pillows behind me. The back of my head felt like a boxer used it for a punching a bag. My eyes clenched shut until the pain lessened and the rancid taste in my throat dissolved.

Angela patiently hand fed me with a polished, antique silver spoon. My starving body gladly accepted the savory concoction. It felt like I hadn't eaten for weeks. My taste buds endured torture waiting for each bite while she methodically dipped the spoon into the hot liquid, carefully scraping the bottom on the edge of the bowl.

My open mouth had only so much patience.

The woman jerked back as I grabbed the spoon and gulped down spoonfuls of the delicious broth. Golden liquid dribbled down my chin and I burped.

"Her appetite's back," the woman said.

"So are her manners," the man scoffed.

I patted my chest and burped again. "So what am I doing here?"

The woman gasped. "You don't remember?"

"No. The last I remember is seeing you and Marco disappearing right in front of me."

"Marco?" they asked one another.

"Carlos, she hit her head harder than we thought," the woman said. She pushed my chin to the left, inspected the side of my face, and looked back at the man. "It stopped bleeding, but I think you should get the doctor."

He uncrossed his arms. "It may not be safe to ride into town," he said and stood upright, ready to do her bidding, yet looked to me for permission.

"No need for a doctor," I told them.

The altered state was too realistic. What if I felt the breaking of skin if a doctor stabbed me with a needle? Worse yet, he might use leeches like they did in old western movies.

"You know, I really don't feel that bad. I'm just not remembering things too clearly." I looked from one to the other. "You'll have to fill in the blanks."

"The blanks?" the lady asked.

Even with accents, they obviously understood English, yet they questioned everything I said. I touched the knot on my temple, but the pain was worse at the back of my skull. I couldn't trust the experience to be real, although my senses said otherwise.

"Maybe I'll feel better once I soak in the Jacuzzi for a while."

Mouths remained open.

"The what?" the man asked.

"Let me draw a hot bath instead," the woman suggested.

This dream was getting out of hand. It was time to wake up and see Nicole and Marco in their regular bodies. These people, this room—while they were intriguing—I wanted to get back to life as I knew it. The images weren't terrible, but they didn't make sense, and nothing was in my control.

I lay back into the pillows, hoping more shuteye would end this imaginative yet brainless illusion, but a dreadful feeling cropped up, snapping my eyes open again.

What if I wasn't dreaming?

Nicole whispered something to Marco in Spanish. I heard *agua caliente*, which I knew to be hot water. I relaxed slightly. While the tub filled, I'd sleep, wake up, and things would be back to normal. Maybe that delicious *caldo* would turn out to be real.

The woman picked up the serving tray "Thank you," I said. "That was great. Maybe you can give me the recipe."

She giggled, a pleasing lilt similar to Nicole's laughter, but the Angela lady was more of a soprano. "The day you cook, we all die of the stomach poison. *Ay Diós!*" She walked out of the room, braying, her laughter fading with her footsteps.

I looked at the man she called Carlos and he lifted his shoulders, not defending my culinary skills. Then he rushed to the edge of the bed and knelt on his knee. He lowered his face close to mine. One large hand gently brushed my tangled hair from my forehead and the other tenderly stroked my cheek. His dark brown eyes welled, and he whispered, "I'm glad you pulled through, Carmena."

"Carmena?"

He smiled. "You'll feel better soon."

His firm lips were warm on my temple. He pressed another kiss onto my cheek. I turned my head and his lips grazed my ear. Desperation managed to climb its way into his irises, and I felt obligated to say something before he planted another kiss somewhere else on my face.

"Thank you, Mar—er—Carlos."

Tension eased from his features until no more than a few tiny wrinkles cornered his eyes, and only a single worry line furrowed his forehead.

"I'm sure I'll feel even better after I rest," I said.

"Of course," he growled. "Forgive me, Carmena, for thinking only of myself."

He stood and twisted a little knob on each of the lamps, and I relaxed as the room gradually darkened. His figure cut a large outline in the doorway. I didn't say anything, and he walked away.

It felt like a comic word bubble hovered over my head, except I had no words to fill it, nothing to describe the unbelievable characters, vivid surroundings, and my emotional and mental confusion. It was a welcome blessing when sleep came on to dull the colorful mirage.

As I succumbed to unconsciousness in the comfortable surroundings and headed back to the real world, my mind kept running over the same question.

Nicole was a vegan. Since when did she make chicken soup?

℘℘℘

Someone nudged my shoulder. Drowsy and unfocused, I rubbed at my lashes.

"How long have I been asleep?"

"Only an hour."

The reply was agreeable but highly disturbing with its Spanish accent. I bolted upright from the pillow. Pain, dizziness, and nausea engulfed me, and my "Aarrghh!" sounded more like a dog growling.

The woman jumped back, startled. "Don't worry," she spread out her fingers, patting the air. "The bath water is still hot." She went about relighting the hurricane lanterns one at a time.

I pushed the heels of my palms into my temples, and the counter-pressure alleviated some of the pain.

"What in the hell is going on here?" I demanded.

She clapped her hands. "You feel better! You take a bath, and I finish the dinner."

"Wait!" I cried. The woman watched me fumble out of bed. When my feet settled onto the cool wooden floor, I wobbled forward, tripping on a long garment entangled about my legs.

Even as a child, a floor-length cotton nightgown with ruffles on the cuffs or skirting the hem and a satin ribbon garroting my throat was never part of my wardrobe.

"¡*Cuidado!*" She ran forward to catch me.

My brain throbbed to some serious head-banging beat. "What the hell am I doing here? Where are my clothes?"

"Take your bath. We get you dressed later," the Angela woman said and peeled a piece of soiled gauze away from my skull. "You feel better when you wash the clouds out of your head."

She left me alone in the room, fully awake—only not. Barnyard noises continued to serenade from outside, and an evening breeze wafting through the open windows lifted strands of hair about my face. Slightly uneven ridges of plank flooring ran underfoot. The subtle touches felt real enough, proving my senses were intact.

My fingers fumbled with the ribbons and a myriad of buttons to relieve the chokehold at my throat. I felt a light vibration against my chest and looked down to see the silver amulet still hanging about my neck. I lifted it by the chain. It had to be connected to the distorted daydream.

Desperately wringing the sections of the charm this way and that did nothing to bring about the swarming mist that sucked me out of Nicole's kitchen and into this delusion. My sanity refused to let me believe this was anything more than a pleasant nightmare. Most likely, I dreamed too deeply to wake myself up.

That had to be it.

A door off the side of the bedroom led into a large bathroom, only there was no toilet or shower stall. The room was centered by a gargantuan claw-foot tub positioned at an angle. Other than a copper tube boring into the hardwood floor from the bottom of the tub, not a spigot or knob was in sight. A floor length mirror, in a frame of intricately tooled paisley swirls, stood like a piece of art in the corner. A large, brass urn sat in another corner, and only one purpose for it came to mind.

"Like that's gonna happen," I said to no one.

If this were a dream like I hoped, I wasn't sure I even needed to bathe, but standing around mulling over the situation didn't change a thing, and the hot bath lured me closer. The heavy nightgown dropped off my shoulders, and it seemed like fifty pounds of flannel clustered about my ankles. My body melted into the soothing hot water, and every muscle went limp under the liquid heat.

I swiped my hand across a tender, walnut-sized bump on the back of my head. My fingers came away not with gray brain matter, but dark brown slime and a terrible stink. It was the same smell I recognized when I first woke up, and it was a relief to shampoo it all away.

After I pulled the plug, the water level subsided, and an embarrassingly wide band of dirt clung to the inside edges of the white ceramic coating. Luck was on my side. No spray cleaner meant no clean up duty.

I shrugged, grateful. "Oh, well."

I towel dried my tangled hair with a rough piece of terry-cloth fabric, as though someone had forgotten the fabric softener, like it had been hung outside to dry. My reflection in the mirror eerily displayed a thinner body, flatter stomach, and thicker hair without split ends. Tone and definition highlighted the muscles in my arms and legs. My host body was definitely in better physical condition, but that wasn't the strange part.

I rubbed the tip of my fingers over my pelvic bone in about the same place my lion tattoo used to be.

Somewhere in the house, six deep gongs trembled in the air, announcing the hour and life outside the door. Worried the Angela woman or Carlos man would suddenly burst into the room, I hurried to the humongous wardrobe.

Among the vintage clothing were dark-brown gauchos, hanging next to an equally chic beige, cotton blouse sporting poufy, long sleeves. At least a dozen tiny cloth-covered buttons dotted each long cuff. A tan leather vest matched a pair of handmade designer boots. The satin corset on a sachet-scented hanger explained why my waist was so small. The bloomers were a bit much, but since I was dressing to the hilt, I thought, *What the heck,* and wore those, too.

The bedroom door opened to a wide hallway, and I stepped into an extraordinary historical other world. The plastered walls and adobe flooring covered in worn carpet runners were sufficient testimony to a human presence, although I saw no one. It was like walking through the pages of a coffee table picture book featuring Spanish architecture, the kind that commanded a few quiet moments of contemplating the past and who lived there.

The same dark beams as the ceilings in my bedroom stretched from one side of the building to the other. A few tables lined the long hallway topped with statuary, an occasional candleholder, and plants. Planter boxes hung outside small alcoves with arched windows. Every several feet, ornate metal hooks held more glass lanterns. I didn't see a light bulb anywhere.

No one was about, and I wasn't certain if I preferred being alone. Rather than search the upstairs rooms for the unique individuals who nursed me back to health, I followed my nose toward the stairwell and something smelling wonderfully edible.

The railings and banisters in the stairwell were detailed with loops and curls of wrought iron. Hundreds of crystal shards dangled on a chandelier suspended twenty-five feet above the first floor. Walls held original, desert-landscape paintings and portraits of unsmiling faces.

A huge grandfather clock greeted me at the bottom step of the curved, terra-cotta staircase. An expansive living area to the right brimmed with overstuffed velvet chairs, worn on the seats and armrests.

The mantle on the brick fireplace, a monstrous focal point, was taller than my shoulders. Layers of soot stained the hearth. The entire room was tastefully decorated for a mental prison.

A large tapestry of a coat of arms draped above the fireplace and depicted a knight's helmet, five tassels above it and a shield below it. Two triangular halves formed the shield, each centered with a fleur de lis, a diagonal dark strip, separating them. In the middle of the strip, a lion was poised, ready to strike.

It was the same lion that used to be tattooed on my hip.

CHAPTER 6

Most of the seats were occupied at a lengthy pine table centered in a huge formal dining room beyond the living area. There were three chairs on each side and armchairs at either end. As massive as it was, the table was almost dwarfed by the size of the room and the high ceilings.

A handsome young boy and cute little girl sat next to each other on the same side with the man named Carlos. Two other men were also seated, their backs to me. The man on the outside chair was lanky with silver-streaked hair. He tapped his fingers in succession on the tablecloth. The Mexican man in the middle chair had a slight roll of flesh hanging over the edges of his belt.

When Carlos and the children looked up, they collectively gasped. The men turned and were startled, too, as if I were naked. I looked behind me for gremlins then back to the expectant crowd.

Angela walked through the swinging door adjacent to the kitchen. She took one look at me and said, "¡Ay, Diós!" then set an urn of soup on the sideboard.

"What's wrong?"

The men smiled, even the young boy, but Angela and the little girl openly gaped.

"You never looked so…tempting," Carlos finally answered.

I didn't miss the other two men elbow each other.

"Next, we'll all have to dress in Sunday clothes for supper," Angela said.

The chubby Mexican guy chuckled. "Best bib and tucker I've seen, but it'll be hard to rope with wagon covers on your arms."

The old guy spoke up. "Don't listen ta their blather, ma'am. Ya look purdier than a mess a buzzards circlin' at sunset."

"Uhm—thanks," I told the elderly Anglo man.

Angela spooned *caldo* into our bowls, griping in Spanish. She finished serving and sat down beside the man with the love handles. He patted her, and they smiled at each other.

Two seats were available at either end of the table, but only one had a place setting. My chair evidently brooked the gap between Carlos and Angela.

"Aren't you going to sit down, Carmena?" the boy asked. The familiarity of the mismatched family heightened my sense of unease. I didn't know how I was supposed to respond—act like myself or the woman they called "Carmena?"

I nodded, too confused to answer aloud, and took the seat.

"It's Jesse's turn to say grace," the little girl said.

The lanky man, maybe sixty-five years old, turned out to be Jesse. His back curved forward in a calcium arch, yet I had the feeling he was resilient for his age. "Let us pray," he said. We bowed our heads. "And rejoice," he added, winking at me.

The rest looked up at him then at me, before returning to a reverent bow.

"Lard, we thank ya for allowin' Carmena ta remain with us, fer the abundance a food on this here table, an' fer the joy that y'all have brought each of us in so many ways at Holiday Ranch. May them no good soldiers who'er lower than a snake's belly in a wagon rut git what's comin' ta them. Amen."

"Amen," the rest of them repeated.

No one touched their spoons. All eyes locked on me.

"Right." I snapped a charming, hand-tatted napkin onto my lap and picked up a silver soupspoon at which point everyone eagerly delved into their *caldo*. Although I had a bowl earlier, it was as tasty and satisfying as the first. Someone had added a little spice to this batch that gave it some kick. Real comfort food, just what my nerves needed. But how could it be real?

I'd already sparked confusion and worry in Carlos and Angela, so instead of speaking during the meal, it seemed safer to remain silent. I eavesdropped on snippets of conversation while slurping the soup.

"Looks like the big goat broke her foot coming down the hill."

"Captain Sanders arrived lickety split."

"Franz's raid was shorely a bad time for a cow ta give birth, that's fer darn sure."

"I've got a five spot that says the ol' hen will lay an egg before that mean rooster crows."

"Nah, it's jest a sprain. I bandaged her all up. She'll be good as new in no time."

"We lost another chicken, Papa."

"That big heifer birthed herself while Franz tried to rob us blind."

"Them redback fivers are jest about worthless, and it's gonna get worse if we annex. I ain't takin' that bet."

"Javier," Angela said to the chubby fellow at her side then looked at the little girl, "Gracie, help me bring in the dinner."

They left the table and the swinging doors to the kitchen barely stopped flapping before they reentered the dining room. Javier held a cast iron pot with both hands, containing four delicious smelling baked chickens, small but probably lacking the modern-day hormones and water to fill them up. Angela trailed behind him with a ceramic bowl of pinto beans and jalapeños. Gracie held a platter of thick homemade flour tortillas.

If I didn't feel like I was in hell, I'd swear we were in heaven. Tortillas and beans weren't exactly on the Type-O diet, but as long as I had a flat stomach and small waist, I was going to take full advantage of the fantasy.

Angela set the beans on a trivet tray and rushed back into the kitchen, returning with a platter of corn on the cob.

"Carmena?" the boy asked. "Is it true the captain was here and knocked the lieutenant's galley west?"

"¡*Silencio, Martino!*" Javier admonished the boy.

"But, Papa, you said—"

Javier gave the boy the evil eye, and Martino dropped his head.

"It's fine, Javier." To the boy, I said, "It's true, sweetheart." I didn't miss the sideways glances that skimmed the table. Maybe it wasn't proper for an adult to address children with endearments in this other dimension. "I don't remember much right now about the captain being here and, uh, any galleys getting knocked any place." I took in the curiosity of the others and included them all in the discussion. "I guess I've forgotten a few things and hope that you'll all have patience with me while I recover."

"Oh, no!" and "Of course!" fluttered from one person to the next.

"Carmena?" Gracie asked. "Are you mad at me for letting Hannah in my room?"

"Of course not," I said. "You can let anyone you'd like in your room."

Gracie smiled, but for a few solid seconds, the rest stared at me like I was a carnival sideshow then quickly looked elsewhere. All except Carlos. Not once did he look at anyone else.

He touched my arm. "Jesse and Javier will ride into town tomorrow morning and will need you to give them money for supplies."

I folded my hands in my lap. "I thought it wasn't safe to ride into town."

Carlos and Angela exchanged glances.

"Good. Your memory is coming back." Carlos said. "We need the supplies. Besides, now I'm thinking the soldiers won't be returning any time soon. Not after the captain's involvement."

"That's fer darn sure," Jesse said, and Javier nodded.

Carlos tilted his head and squinted at me. "We'll talk later."

I didn't think any conversation could relieve me of my anxiety. My despair had nothing to do with soldiers. Instead, anxiety hit when Carlos asked me for money. I didn't even belong here, and I had already incurred new debt.

More cheerful conversation traveled around the table. We drank a fabulous roast-blend coffee and ate the best homemade flan to ever cross my taste buds.

By the end of the meal, the carved wooden buttons on my pants were ready to pop off. Satisfaction lasted until I gave thought to my predicament, and my nerves pressed the large meal into a brick inside my stomach.

The tailor-made clothes fit me perfectly, yet I had never tried them on. Everyone recognized me, but I didn't know a soul. And I had no idea how to return to my own reality.

Angela removed the dirty dishes from the table, and on autopilot I followed suit. She swatted at my hand. "Leave my job alone!"

My arm came out of harm's way. I had a lot to learn about my role in this mental time warp.

Javier and Jesse guffawed at Angela's reprimand. They pulled cigars from their pockets and strolled outside to the front porch as the children joined Angela in the kitchen for cleanup duty.

Carlos placed a hand on my lower back and gently supported my elbow. He escorted me through the living area. I assumed we were headed for the fancy parlor opposite the foyer and staircase. The room showed off tasteful tapestry-upholstered chairs and other dark Queen-Anne furniture. More etched-glass oil lamps created a very Victorian flavor.

Instead of entering the parlor, we turned left into a wide corridor of dark-wainscoted walls. Carlos continued to guide me as if I were an invalid. The long hallway displayed elaborate tables, an occasional chair, and huge potted houseplants, not to mention the artwork and sconces on the walls and standing candelabra. Nothing was overstated, yet each beautifully furnished section held its own as a showpiece.

Sturdy double doors led to a retreat that could have been part of a movie set. The dark-paneled library smelled of sweet, cherry tobacco and freshly oiled leather. Built-in bookshelves lined the octagon-shaped room. Leather-bound and cloth-covered manuscripts stamped in gold lettering filled the shelves to the fifteen-foot high ceilings. A tall brass, rolling ladder gleamed in a corner. A huge bay window draped in hunter-green velvet with golden tassels towered behind a colossal desk, large enough to seat six people were it a dining table.

The soft click of the closing door brought my attention back to Carlos, but my eyes never reached him. Instead, they froze on the life-sized portrait standing guard over the immense fireplace. The portrait of a woman defiantly stared back at me, a shadow over her smile—as if knowing one day this image would preserve the memory of her existence.

I had never in my life posed for a portrait, yet there I was painted on the canvas in a floor-length lavender gown and shiny brunette ringlets, thick brows, and rich brown eyes saturated with secrets. Long fingers extended from graceful hands, and I looked down to my own. The same limbs, but on her, they were exquisite.

Carlos's voice jarred me out of the mild trance. "You act as if you've never seen your mother's portrait."

I inhaled and managed to dampen the creepy sensation of a gradual invasive and alarming awareness.

The surroundings felt more…familiar.

It was hard to look away from my amazing likeness in the portrait, but I did and admired the desk covered with an array of crystal objects. An expertly cut inkwell, ashtray, and cigar box created an appealing arrangement in front of an elegant leather blotter. Every facet glittered jewel-like and created fragmented rainbows in delicate contrast to the solid brass fixtures.

Carlos selected a cigar to his liking and the lid of the crystal box rang brightly when he set it back in place. He neatly trimmed the cigar's end, and his cheeks caved in and out as he lit up. He motioned for me to take the extra-padded easy chair behind the desk, and the seat conformed to my body like a memory foam mattress.

He sat in one of two brass studded cordovan leather chairs opposite me and blew out a long stream of smoke that floated sensually over the desk.

His charming half-smile put me at ease. Instinctively, I liked Carlos and somehow knew he was an honest man of reputable counsel.

"Carmena, you have me worried."

He thought he was worried. Try living in phantasmagoria.

"What exactly worries you, Carlos?"

"I'm concerned that your current state of mind is… suffering. You seem to be having trouble adjusting after the incident with Franz."

"Really? Uh, how so?"

Carlos's eyes bore a hole into my feigned composure, a similar expression to the one staring at me from the image of Carmena's mother on the oiled canvas.

"You're not acting like yourself at all," he said. "In fact, I'm having a very hard time believing that you really are Carmena."

Carlos was an intelligent man, suspecting something amiss, yet he couldn't prove me an imposter any more than I could prove myself one.

"Why don't you tell me what you remember?" he asked.

"Why don't you tell me how I got these bumps on my head?"

"Always putting me in my place."

I didn't realize that was a pattern of mine, of Carmena's, at least not until that moment. I kept quiet.

Carlos sat back and relayed a violent story of soldiers raiding Carmena's ranch and a Lieutenant Franz trying to assault her. "By the time Javier and I rode down, you were on the living room floor, mostly undressed. Your head was bleeding."

"Son of a—" I jumped from the seat. My palms smacked the top of the desk, and I huffed like I'd spent too much time on a treadmill. Though not physically present during Carmena's vicious attack, the lumps on my head said otherwise. Somehow, I knew the fear and pain she had endured. "No wonder my head hurts so much!"

Carlos didn't budge at my outburst. "It's over. Take a slow, deep breath."

"You're right. This is just a dream."

His brows shot up, and I slunk back into the chair.
"Did Franz...you know..." I didn't want to ask. It might
have been Carmena who took the heat from the officer, but I
was in her body now.

Passion surged from Carlos like a rogue wave. "No. I
would've killed him if he had. I would've killed him regardless, except Franz was arrested after four of the soldiers
dragged Captain Sanders off of him."

"Man, the captain must be built like the Hulk!"

There was no reply to my comment, but Carlos narrowed
his eyes at me. I pressed my lips together and made a mental
note to curb my twenty-first century colloquialisms.

Carlos took a hit on his cigar and exhaled the aromatic
smoke. It spiraled into a curly tail up to the ceiling. A streak of
bitter sounding words in Spanish spewed from his mouth. As
soon as his speech slowed, he said, "Franz's face was barely
recognizable, and the captain's fists were covered in blood.
Angela found him cradling you—" He snorted. "—crying like
a baby. Angela checked your pulse, your breath. There was
none."

"I had a near death experience?" I asked in awe.

"A what?"

"Uh, I died but came back to life?"

I felt Carlos's suspicions pour over me. "I don't know exactly what happened, but you didn't die, and that's what matters."

"Why did Sanders beat the lieutenant so badly? I mean,
those things happened all the time back then—" Crap, if Carlos kept creasing his forehead like that, the lines would become permanent. "I mean, that happens quite a bit these days.
You know, men, soldiers, taking advantage of women."

"I don't know."

Carlos had just lied to me. I didn't know how I knew, but
I did. He didn't like something about the captain. "Last night, I
sent Javier into town to tell the captain that you were alive, and
I asked him to hold off on a visit until you were more well
rested. He sent you a note." Carlos jerked his chin. "It's there
in your desk drawer. As if soft solder will get him anywhere."

I tugged on the brass handle of the top center drawer and spied a folded, parchment note with an untouched wax seal securing it closed. *Carmena* was written with letters so artfully embellished, the name read like a poem. I didn't know what soft solder was, but I imagined it was something a girl could get used to.

Although interested in finding out more about the man who cried for me, truth be told, I was reluctant to know any more about the assault. I didn't think I wanted to discover anything else about this place or Carmena's life.

I pushed the drawer shut.

CHAPTER 7

Since my last nap, memories and snippets of images—not my own—popped in and out of my mind, but they were nothing I could grasp or make sense of. From the fragments of Carmena's memories, I knew that she highly regarded her foreman, but she had no romantic desires for him.

"Since when did you despise the captain so much?" Then I instantly realized the answer. Carlos loved me, or the woman I was supposed to be, and not like a sister. But it didn't feel like Carmena returned the same feelings for him.

I, on the other hand, thought Carlos was kind of hot for an older guy.

Captain Sanders had beaten up Lieutenant Franz because he'd fallen for me, or rather, Carmena, too. I barely knew what the captain looked like, but my senses reacted as if I did. A fascinating tightening in certain body parts convinced me Carmena was at least physically aroused by the officer, but it was hard to tell where her feelings ended and my own began.

At my breathy sigh, sparked by thoughts of the captain, Carlos's eyes sparked, and he leaned forward. His tranquil manner evaporated. The desk wasn't shelter enough to prevent his aura from heating my own. More than his mere protectiveness seared into me, but I felt compelled to remember the real Carmena's feelings about the man. I could sense the emotional battle raging inside her with two different kinds of love for two unique men, and with the responsibilities of her ranch warring against her enjoying anyone's affections.

For me, love won over work every time.

"You're blushing, Carmena."

That was easy to do when thinking about the two men, but Carlos probably would've been mortified to learn that thoughts of another man warmed Carmena's skin. And mine.

I had to change the subject. Fast.

I fidgeted with a corner of the blotter and stuttered, "Wha—what about the money for the trip into town that Javier and Jesse plan on making?"

Carlos appraised me as if deciphering abstract art. "Hmmm." He stubbed out the remaining cigar.

He pushed out of his chair and at one of the tall bookcases, he removed a thick manuscript, *Secrets of Irish Potato Farming*. The heavy book thudded on the blotter facing me, and Carlos lifted the linen cover. The pages, hollowed out, concealed multiple bundles of crisp bills bound with twine, enough money to buy a fast food franchise.

At my quick inhalation, he said, "So you've forgotten this as well. Do you remember your safe in the secret room off the bunkhouse?"

"Bunkhouse?"

"Apparently not. I think it best, Carmena, that you not mention this to anyone."

I lowered my voice. "Why not? Is someone here untrustworthy?"

"Of course not," he said. "But think of what would happen to the ranch morale if your mental capacity was called into question."

"You're right. I'll be more careful about what I say. Would you please give Jesse or Javier the money for the supplies?"

"I will."

Rather than reach across the desk for the money, he stalked around it like a panther and stood next to me. He drew dangerously close and pulled a few bills from one of the bundles. I pressed my back into the chair. Carlos smiled and leaned all the closer.

My heart did the whole miss-a-beat thing and guilt rose like an unwelcome zombie. If I ever returned home, would the real Carmena come back to a messed-up relationship with her most-trusted employee because of my lack of self-control? Could she even come back?

Anyway, time for a distraction.

As long as I had money, I might as well show Carmena's employees our, or her, thanks. Several bills slid easily from the smallest bundle. I handed them to Carlos, pushing them against his chest. He stepped back a bit.

"Angela deserves a little extra for protecting us and the remaining livestock. What do you think she'd like? Stationery? A bonnet?"

He laughed, and his thumb acted like a spout pouring invisible liquid down his throat.

"She's a drinker?"

"You know she likes to bend an elbow like the rest of us."

No, I didn't know. Carlos kept assuming I was Carmena. And everyone else did, too. "Well, then, get her whatever she needs to, uh, bend."

"Are you sure you're up to this right now?"

Carlos looked at me as if I were a math problem. We locked eyes. He made his move and leaned in. I extended my arm as far as it could reach, shoving several more bills at him. The cash flattened against his chest and put more space between us.

"I'm feeling fine. We should get something for Jesse and Javier, too."

Carlos sighed. "They'd choose cigars, but they'll refuse the gifts."

"It's not a gift. Remind them of how they earned it." He nodded. "I'd like to buy some shoes and clothing for Martino, Gracie, and Hannah. Speaking of which, why wasn't Hannah at dinner tonight?"

He squinted at me. "She eats in the barn."

"What?" The word went several notches higher than I intended. "Why doesn't she eat with us?"

"So, now you want to have a goat at the table?"

"Oh! Uh, I don't know what I was thinking!" I touched the knot over my brow as if that would compensate for my feeble reply and quickly moved on. "So, what about new things for Martino and Gracie?"

"You know that Javier and Angela have never allowed you to buy anything for the children except for Christmas and their birthdays."

"The children helped to keep the ranch and animals safe. Please tell Javier that he must buy new shoes, clothes, and some toys for the children."

"And now they're to get toys as well? You are unnaturally generous today, Carmena. You don't sound like yourself."

He paused for an explanation, and I gave one under pressure.

"Even the children kept us from getting ripped off."

"Ripped off?" he repeated, and his brows almost touched.

"Uh, they kept the soldiers from taking everything we had of value." I scrambled for another topic. "With Angela doing all of the cooking, housekeeping, and having two kids, why haven't we gotten a maid or another cook?"

"You keep forgetting how proud she is. She always refuses the extra help."

"How does she get all her work done?"

"The children, of course. Why do you act as if you don't remember anything?" Carlos snapped.

"The children shouldn't have to work so hard!" I snapped back.

"When did you change your mind about all the things the children can learn while working on the ranch? You called it a practical education."

"Things can change when you nearly lose your life."

Carlos crossed his arms. "You've been in that situation before, and it never affected you like this."

I shoved muscle into my voice. "Well, now it has!" My own arms crossed, but I hoped he wouldn't call my bluff. "I think when the men go into town, I'll have them make inquiries for a woman who can teach the children, as well as take on some of Angela's work. Come to think of it, Angela's clothing is as tattered as the children's. This is a cool, er, coolossus opportunity to buy her something new to wear. She'll need a new dress before we bring on any more help."

Carlos shook his head. "Every time you buy her one, she makes Javier return it."

"This time I'll tell her about it myself."

His lopsided grimace expressed no confidence in my power of persuasion.

"Don't worry. I know how to handle it. And you, Carlos? What do you want?"

He sighed, hefted the thick manuscript from my desk, and slid the literary decoy back onto the shelf. Then he stepped to the door, with the same gait as if he walked the plank, and looked back at me. "What I want, Carmena, is not for sale."

An ache rose in my chest, like a dull arrow from Cupid thudding against my heart. I knew, Carmena knew, he loved her. Yet, regardless of how attractive he was and how he made me feel, she saw him as an older brother or young uncle. Maybe even a father figure.

I had just enough air to choke out, "I wish I had it to give."

"As do I," he whispered, then he left the room.

That mournful quality in his half smile made me want to escape this place all the more. The door clicked shut, the tiny noise sounding like a volcanic eruption against the silence.

໒ঙ৩

It was bad enough incurring debt that wasn't my own, but now guilt had been added to the mix. A palpable sexual tension stood between Carlos and Carmena, or was it between him and me? I could barely tell the difference between Carmena's feelings and my own.

I remembered the letter Carlos had pointed out and opened the center desk drawer. Atop the crow-quill nibs, sticks of colored wax, and twiggy-looking pencils, I found the captain's note. My curiosity piqued. I used a gold letter opener from the drawer and slid it under the round seal.

Like Maizy's poem, the captain's letter was penned in a lovely script on elegant parchment.

My dearest Carmena,

> *Words cannot convey the relief I feel knowing that you are alive and faring well. Rest assured, Franz will never take liberty with you again, nor will he trespass upon your property. Carlos feels you should be allowed to regain your strength before I call, and rightly so. I know he holds your best interest at heart, almost as much as I do.*
>
> *My darling, I hope I have leave to call you such, as this recent tragedy has placed you in the forefront of my thoughts, more so than usual. I urge you to allow me to call on you when you are rested, as I feel there is an important matter we must discuss that may affect the rest of our lives.*
>
> *I am deeply and affectionately yours,*

Capt. Charles Patrick Sanders

My mind flooded with incomplete bits of emotion, gleaned from other letters Carmena had read and words of well-heeled passion about moonlit garden walks and not too lady-like thoughts. I rubbed the back of my hand, remembering the feel of warm lips against it.

Man, this had to stop before I forgot who I was.

No doubt about it, the captain had the hots for Carmena, and I'd bet a redback fiver that she might be in the process of feeling the same way about him. Powerful, genuine, glorious love. How unfair it would be to her, and the captain as well, to indulge myself in affections that weren't meant for me.

These caring people deserved more than what I had to offer. From Carmena's feelings I knew she loved them dearly and that they were all genuinely good at heart. It was far easier to be confused in California or pathetic in Arkansas, than to be accountable to them. Carlos, devoted and loyal, overlooked his comfort to see to mine. Everyone risked their lives keeping the soldiers from stealing my, or rather Carmena's, property.

I was caught in the sticky web of this other world, and the needs of these people felt all too real. They were depending on me to participate in their lives. No one had ever expected this much from me, and for some reason, I didn't want to let them down.

The rest of the day, I took refuge in Carmena's comfy master suite where the walls sheltered me from the non-reality outside. Curled up on a chaise lounge with a beautiful hand-made quilt, I waited as time passed slower than traffic on the 405 Freeway. The gauze curtains rose and fell like a ghost unable to detach itself from the rod. For several restless hours, I twisted the cogs of the silver amulet, but it yielded no results. With a magnifying glass, I found that the only picture that would perfectly line up, was that of the old Spanish style ranch.

Angela brought a tray of hot apple cobbler, oozing with gelatinous glaze, and coffee with a robust bouquet of Columbian beans. It smelled too good to pass up. The restaurant quality food didn't last long. I wolfed it down.

Normally, stress kept my appetite at bay. So what did it mean now that I ate like an abandoned pit bull?

Night was coming on, and I was confident a long sleep would free me of this place. I'd be rid of any responsibility for these dedicated people who obviously cared deeply for the real ranch owner.

But when I woke up the following morning, I was sorely disappointed.

ぐつやつ

Blazing white light forced its way under my lashes. One eye peeled open like a reluctant clamshell, the other stayed smushed against the pillow. A lavender sunrise peeked between the simple hemp curtains, and colorful Mexican tiles outlined the wood frame of the thick mission style windows. It took several blinks to adjust to the blinding glow of the lantern Angela held leveled at my face.

"Damn. I'm still here."

"Where else would you be?" the housekeeper asked.

A porcelain cup and saucer rattled on the nightstand, and coffee splashed over the rim. The steaming brown liquid may have been an incentive to raise the other lid, but ingesting another cup of coffee without heavy whipping cream and cinnamon stevia might prove a challenge. I didn't consider myself spoiled, just used to having things the way I liked them.

"I put medicine in your coffee for the pain in your head," Angela said.

"Thanks." The hot liquid was delicious even with the aftertaste of laudanum and without my usual added ingredients.

Angela hung the lantern on the hook next to the door and proceeded to light the other lamps in the room, altogether infusing the space with stadium lighting.

"You say good Texans never stay asleep after the sun gets up."

"It's not up yet," I mumbled and lay back down under the blankets.

Texas. That answered one question.

Instead of the annoying ruffled nightgown and its ribboned garrote, I'd slept in my camisole and bloomers. I thought it was a good idea until the comforter sailed off my body, and a whoosh of cold air pricked my skin.

"You always say the daylight only lasts for so long," my housekeeper sang without mercy and gathered the quilted cover in her arms. Disgruntled by her chipper demeanor, I tumbled out of bed and grabbed the coffee. Angela tossed the blanket on the bed and smirked.

Unwilling to urinate in a tiny brass urn, I trudged to the water closet down the hall. The wooden throne had no handle, and flushing required a bucket of water poured down a dark hole.

It was time to incorporate some twenty-first century improvements during my stay in Never, Never Land.

I'd ask Carlos if he could arrange for more modern plumbing and a host of other questions, like where exactly that secret room in the bunkhouse was located, what year it was, and when Carmena was born.

The amulet lay on a floral trivet tray, one of the few feminine luxuries in the room. If only I had never picked it up from its hiding place or pried the window open to begin with. Angry and frustrated, I ripped the necklace off the tray and wrenched the sections of the charm back and forth between my anxious fingers, but I was literally spinning my wheels. No dense fog appeared, not even a dark tunnel. Nothing to return me to my own place or time.

My physical senses—pinching my arm, biting my tongue, and accidentally hitting my head on the lantern by the door that added another bruise to my dinged-up skull—all told me that I was awake.

Of course, there were a few upsides to being caught in the waking nightmare, which included my enjoyment as a wealthy, single landowner. I had a team of loyal followers at my beck and call, a brutally handsome officer who actually wanted a commitment, and best of all, I didn't have to cook or clean. The feeling of being cherished replaced some of the sense of helplessness I should have felt at being displaced.

I dropped the chain around my neck. The amulet hummed, continuing to puzzle and frighten me, but even so, I had to keep it near as it was my only connection to my real existence.

CHAPTER 8

It would've been unfortunate to give anyone apoplexy by overdressing, yet I donned another brand new vintage ensemble, minus the corset. They were great for a night out on the town but not to spend the day in and doing anything routine, like breathing.

Instead of the gauchos, I wore a lovely ankle-length black, white, and blue striped skirt, spattered with mini bouquets of flowers. Gorgeous black leather boots had crisscrossed laces up to mid-calf with the era's famous sensible heel.

A mouthwatering aroma of breakfast foods hooked my nose and enticed me into following it downstairs to the dining room. No one sat at the table, but faint noises floated from the kitchen. I pushed open the swinging doors just in time to see Javier smacking Angela on the rear end.

Her eyes showed more white than Mt. Everest during a snowstorm. She immediately slapped her husband's hand away. "*De hay!*" she scolded with more embarrassment than conviction.

Javier grinned.

"What's for breakfast?" I asked.

Angela gave my latest outfit a head-to-toe assessment and pushed me back into the dining room.

"You don't belong in here." She shoved me toward my chair and said, "I feed you," then marched back into the kitchen.

In the short time I'd been here, I noticed her English, almost as flawless as Carlos's, diminished when she was flustered or caught in a perverted act, like being spanked.

Carlos entered the room while I waited for breakfast. "*Buenos días,* Carmena." He was definitely more upbeat since our last encounter.

"Good morning, Carlos. I need to speak with you privately later in the day, if you could spare an hour or so."

"You surprise me, Carmena. You never asked before, only ordered. And you never dressed like an elegant woman for ranch work." He bent over me and flicked a strand of hair behind my ear. "And you never smelled so grand."

I swatted his hand away. "And I'll bet I never had to beat you off with a stick."

Carlos chuckled and took his seat, not the least disconcerted by my reprimand. Gracie burst through the kitchen doors and Martino blocked them from swinging back inward as he helped Angela carry in plates of food.

"¡*Muchacha!*" Angela scolded. Gracie slowed her pace and looked over her shoulder at me. When I didn't respond, she looked farther back at her mother who said, "¡*Con cuidado!*" Carlos stared at me like I'd missed a herd of buffalo galloping by.

I guessed I was expected to scold the child.

"Yes, Gracie," I admonished without severity in my voice. I attempted to repeat what Angela said. "Cone-qwee-dah-doe."

Gracie giggled, and Angela said, "Don't speak to Gracie like that again," and went back into the kitchen.

"What did I say?" I asked Carlos as Javier and Jesse sauntered into the room.

"It's not what you said. It's how you said it," Javier explained.

"How did I say it?"

Javier smiled. "Like a gringo."

"I *am* a gringo."

Javier shrugged.

"Carmena was jest joshin'. Weren't ya, ma'am?" Jesse said. Before I had a chance to reply, he added, "And if ya don't mind me sayin' so, that's some getup. Y'all sure make a mash." He smiled politely and tipped the brim of his hat.

Angela brought in a platter of breakfast meats, and I glanced about at the others. I was the only one who didn't sport the same clothing. My crisp wardrobe was wrinkle-free and for the first time I wondered if my counterpart ever used it.

Like the day before, Gracie announced who was to lead the prayers and this morning her mother was the guest speaker.

Angela spoke in her heavy accent. "Let us pray." We bowed our heads. "Lord, we are grateful for all your goodness and for living on this ranch. Thank you, and Carmena, for to get the cigars for my husband and his best friend, Jesse. They are good men and deserve to have them." I heard the men shift in their chairs. "And the children will be glad to get new clothes, but they no need toys, and I no need a new dress."

Apparently, there were no secrets at Holiday Ranch. I looked up in time to catch Carlos's eye. He shook his head, and I kept quiet.

"Thank you for this food. Amen."

"Amen," we recited.

Between coffee refills, the men discussed the ride into town. I learned that the children fed many of the small animals, mucked stalls, and did some gardening. Inside, they set the table and helped Angela with laundry and washing dishes. We would've been in gross violation of modern-day child labor laws.

Angela told me after breakfast that the men were meeting Carlos in the library, which was perfect because I needed to chat with him before he checked on the cattle. Angela's prayer didn't hint that she knew of my plan to ask Javier and Jesse to do a preliminary search for another housekeeper. Maybe I could catch them before they started in on their conversation.

I walked the long corridor to the library. The muffled thunk of my leather heels didn't alert the husky voices squeezing through the tiny crack between the solid doors.

I heard Javier ask Carlos, "Do you think we're gonna hear from that mudsill? He shoulda contacted us by now."

"I'm not sure if Oswego is in on the coup against Herrera or not," Carlos said.

"It's dreadful dangerous work," Jesse said. "I'll be glad not ta see any of Oswego's men agin."

"Me, too," Carlos agreed. "But we still owe him half a shipment since that last disaster, and I'm pretty sure he's going to want it by hook or by crook, especially if there's a coup in the works."

"That damned curly wolf ain't worth another man dyin' for," Jesse said.

"Yeah. I'd hate to see any more men get shot," Javier muttered.

"I don't want to lose anyone else either, but we may if Oswego thinks we bilked him," Carlos said. "We'll have to plan this very carefully so nobody else dies."

During mealtimes no one had been melancholy enough to hint that anyone had been injured, let alone shot to death. Why would Carmena have involved the ranch in such a dangerous transaction? Or had the men acted independently? And what the hell was a curly wolf?

I backed away from the library and tiptoed farther down the hall toward the back of the house. Whatever the men discussed sounded risky, and I wanted no part of it. When the remote hadn't worked and I was stuck watching that History Channel documentary, the narrator mentioned the names Herrera and Oswego. They were important players associated with Santa Anna, the Mexican dictator. In the United States, that made them the bad guys.

For a second, I thought my cell phone vibrated, but it was the amulet, the buzzing stronger than ever. I gripped it through my blouse, my hand feeling a continuous thrum as heat gradually radiated through the cotton fabric. Before the metal could scald my chest, I yanked the silver chain over my cotton neckline.

The pendant swung like a hanging man, and the intricate curlicues lacing the sides glowed like white rivulets of light. I looked at the library doors, then back at the necklace, and somehow knew that the discussion between the men was relative to the strange reaction of the amulet.

I might've started to enjoy my other existence as a ranch owner, but what I overheard made me want to leave long before the rest of the mysterious shipment of goods was given to Oswego. I had to find a way back to my own time, before anyone else was killed.

Footsteps sounded inside the library, and I sped down the hall through two wide doors. I entered a cavernous room. I kept the handle pushed downward to keep the lock from clicking shut and quietly closed the door, slowly easing up on the handle. The normal cadences of the men's voices filled the hallway. The amulet stopped glowing, and I waited for it to cool before I stuffed it back inside my blouse.

I found myself in a lavish ballroom, void of furniture, surrounded by gold-leaf framed mirrors, twenty-foot-high painted ceilings, and a marble floor, shiny and clean. My steps sounded a dull echo as I crossed the expansive room to wide shuttered doors, much like the ones connecting the dining room to the kitchen. A short hallway housed sideboards and leaded glass front cabinetry that stored ridiculous amounts of stemware and china. More slatted doors on the other side of the small room led into the kitchen.

I decided to bury any memory of the private conversation between the men. It wasn't really my problem, especially since I planned on leaving soon, once I figured out a way to do that. For now, I'd share my plans of hiring a helper with Angela.

Trampling on Carlos's heart the day before in the library inspired me to kill two birds with one housekeeper. I'd scope out a new maid who'd also make a good match for Carlos. Maybe then he'd back off from Carmena.

I pulled out one of six padded barstools nestled under a huge pine chopping block and sat down with a view of Angela's bouncing backside as she scrubbed away at a pile of breakfast dishes.

Framed windows in the thickset adobe ran the length of the back wall and were topped with café style red-checked curtains. Wood counters and cupboards were everywhere, and shiny adobe squares covered the floor, the matte tiles disclosing the pattern of foot traffic. Cast iron pots hung from steel racks, and bowls of fruit and vegetables were centered on a huge oak island.

A red-painted metal hand pump sat next to a steel-lined sink. Shelves next to the stove were loaded with spices. A door to a small supply room was part way open, and I spied tall bags of dry goods and numerous shelves lined with food preserved in glass jars.

"I'd like to have a word with you, Angela."

The housekeeper glanced over her shoulder. She swiped her hands on her blue gingham apron and leaned against the wood counter. "*Sí*. What is it, Carmena?"

"It seems to me that you carry a lot of responsibility here."

"You don't like the way I do my job?" she asked as she pushed herself up from the counter.

"I adore the way you do your job," or at least I thought I did, "and that's exactly why I want to have another woman come in to alleviate your work load."

Her hand swatted the air. "I no need alleviating."

"Whomever we hire can live here and be a teacher for the children. Plus, she'll do all of your grunt work."

Curiosity struck. "What is this grunt work?"

"It means you can give the new lady the work you don't like." On inspiration, I quickly added, "And you'll be the boss of her."

I'd struck gold. Angela's eyes gleamed, and her chin rested in the V between her thumb and index finger. "I no like to pull feathers out of the chicken," she said.

"So, it's settled. I'll ask Javier to pick up a new dress for you." She started to protest, but I raised my hands and pushed back her objection. "After all, you must dress better than the people who work below you."

I wasn't the only one with an ego in new clothes. Angela gave her nose a tiny lift and said, "I'll wear the new dress."

"Great. I'll ask Javier and Jesse to make inquiries in town today for a maid who can also tutor the children. Then I'll interview a few women and find a match for, Car—uh, you."

Angela hummed a happy tune as she wiped down the butcher block. Her positive response gave me a sense of accomplishment, a feeling almost foreign to me.

In an effort to catch Javier and Jesse before they departed for town, I left the kitchen through the back door. For the first time since my doubtful arrival, I stepped outside of the house. The pre-dawn sky smacked me between the eyes. Spectacular streaks of fuchsia and cyan splashed in and out of eastern horizontal clouds.

It was the first time I'd ever seen an unpolluted sky.

A vegetable and herb garden thrived on a sizeable patch of land near the kitchen. Directly behind the house was what Carlos had called Turtle Hill, which was more like a small mountain. A cluster of rocks took the shape of a giant turtle in a crevice near the peak and readily explained its name.

Mexican pots and planter boxes skirted the patios and were filled with flowers and plants. A terra cotta fountain bubbled and small curved tiles in the ground created a channel that carried trickling run-off to the garden. A monstrous barbeque pit was centered in the main patio and wooden benches dotted the alcoves and gazebo.

Beyond the side gate, several structures sprinkled the ranch, which led me to another incredible discovery. The property was freaking ginormous. I saw the wranglers climb into a buckboard wagon near the barn and settle into their seats. Jesse was at the reins while Javier leaned against a plank backrest as if it was the seat of a Ferrari.

"Javier! Jesse!" I called out.

Jesse tugged on the reins, and the wagon rolled in my direction. The wooden vehicle met me halfway. The old fellow took off his hat and said, "Ma'am?"

"*¿Sí, señorita?*" Javier asked.

"Please, you guys. Call me Carmena." Jesse looked at me as if he'd been told to bow on one knee and address me as Your Highness.

"Y'all was sayin', ma'am?"

"Would one of you please make discreet inquiries in town as to who might be looking for work? I'm looking for a woman to help as a maid and tutor for the children."

Javier's eyes opened wider than Jesse's. Their chins dropped, and they looked at one another. "But I thought you were happy with my *Angelita!*" Javier said.

I smiled. "I am, and that's why I think it's important to hire another woman. Besides, more free time for her means more quality time with her husband."

The grin was slow in coming. "*Sí*. We can do this!" Javier and Jesse bobbed their heads.

"I'd like someone in their late twenties, early thirties." Just the right age for Carlos. "Not too young to be unskilled, but not too old to run out of gas."

Both men laughed and Jesse poked Javier with his elbow. "We wouldin' wanner ta have too much gas now, would we?"

I struggled against their taunting. "I mean energy, strength."

"Oh, yeah," Javier said. "Someone with plenty of gas!" The wagon creaked when they shouldered each other and whooped it up at my expense.

"Whatever," I said. "Javier, Angela will be in charge of the woman and needs a new dress appropriate for her station as, uh, the Household Supervisor in charge of the, um, domestic recruit. Remember, you're only looking for potential candidates for this position. Get their names and numbers, and Carlos and I will choose the person we're going to hire."

"Numbers?" Javier asked.

"You'll recollect, amigo, that Carmena ain't right in her upper story just yet." He twirled a finger at his temple. "Ain't that right, ma'am?"

"Absolutely, Jesse. Get names and a place where we can reach them. Thanks, guys."

I almost turned away from the wagon but had an afterthought. "And you boys get yourselves a couple of new shirts along with those cigars." They were about to protest, so I said,

"Your old shirts look a little shabby, and I want the ranch more well represented."

I'd realized Carlos didn't have me acknowledge Angela's thanks during prayer time because my workers were proud people. I was sure the men knew I was handing them a bunch of bull about the ranch being well represented, but it made it easier for them to accept the new shirts.

Javier kept his smile in place. "Can't look shabby married to the Household, whatever that was."

"Woo-wee! Betcha diddin know y'all was married ta such a high-falutin' woman!" Jesse smacked his friend on the shoulder before he smiled at me. "That's mighty nice a ya, ma'am. We could use some proper representin' on the ranch, 'specially bafore hirin' any new woman."

Javier laughed and tapped Jesse on the shoulder. "But my Angela may not wanna work with someone who has a lotta gas!"

The men hooted, and Jesse cracked the reins. "Hee-ha-ha-yah!" The team trotted toward the front of the property, their laughter dying down only with the distance.

Mission one was afoot—the search for an underling to help Angela with the potential of being an amorous match for Carlos.

CHAPTER 9

Mission two on the day's agenda involved questioning Carlos about the real Carmena. The thought of trekking across the vast landscape to the meadow where Carlos tended the cattle discouraged pursuing a question and answer session in that moment, so I decided to enjoy the fresh outdoors while exploring the other outbuildings.

Around the corner, following the same path as the wagon, an amazing view opened up of an expanse of green lawn between the road and the property, at least a football field long. The front of the property was protected by an enormous Spanish-styled fence paralleling the dirt road. Thick, white-plastered columns stood guard, topped with adobe tiles and fortressed with a six-foot row of black wrought-iron spears cemented inside a plaster base between each pillar.

Oak trees drew a line on either side of the lengthy trail that ran from the gates until it met the edge of a circular gravel driveway. A gigantic multi-level Telaveras fountain, the one I, or rather, Carmena, hit her forehead on, centered the turnabout in front of the Spanish style villa, the same one pictured on the amulet.

The home looked like a California mission in pristine condition. Towering arches fronted the mansion and red clay tiles scalloped the roof. Walls measured a foot thick and flower boxes adorned every deeply set window. Verandas offered the upstairs rooms a private retreat.

I spied Martino and Gracie carrying heavy buckets of grain to the stables, and I caught up to the children, snatching a pail from Gracie. "I can't believe you can carry two of these, Gracie. Do you want to leave your bucket here, and I'll come back for it?

She looked hopefully at Martino, but he shook his head. "Papa says carrying the heavy buckets will help my arms grow stronger," Gracie said.

"I think he meant longer. After today I might walk sideways for the rest of my life."

The children giggled, and their optimism gave me a lift. We cleaned out swivel trays mounted in the front corner of each stall and filled them with fresh grain. We sweated for three hours mucking stalls, and we returned to the silo to haul more grain for the horses in the corral.

Martino wiped sweat from his brow. "C'mon, Gracie. Now we feed the cows."

Gracie and I exchanged glances.

"I'd rather have diarrhea," I whined. The children burst into laughter.

We fed the cows and mucked more stalls. It was just after the noon hour when we finished the exhausting chores. After doing half a day's labor, I decided that we'd hire new ranch hands to relieve the children of the tiring work, as well as to help out with extra jobs, like hauling bath water.

A loud metal ringing perked up our ears.

"Chow time!" Martino announced. The children smiled, and I salivated on cue. Martino shoved the empty wheelbarrow into a corner as Gracie tore the rake from my hands and let it fall against a wall. In a heartbeat, the kids broke into a run.

"Come on!" Gracie yelled to me.

She raced her brother out of the barn. Although my morning of real work with the children was a lasting lesson in humility and appreciation, survival instinct took over, and I tore off after them. We raced to the well to wash up, and I elbowed them out of the way. No one was getting between me and my meal. Water splashed everywhere, and the kids laughed.

We shoved off from the well and I accidentally pushed Martino down in the process. "Sorry!" I called over my shoulder and kept running.

In the kitchen, my stomach protested when I remembered that we couldn't eat a morsel until the children set the table and prayers were said. Begrudgingly, while they laid out plates and utensils, I joined Angela in the kitchen to help her carry out the platters.

"Is Carlos going to eat? I really need to talk to him."

"He'll stay out in the meadow until dinner. He's afraid to leave the cattle alone," Angela said.

"Maybe I can pack a picnic lunch and take it up to him."

Angela smiled wide and toothy. "Only the two of you?"

"On second thought, I think I'll take the children, too," I added.

"*Ay-yai-yai*," she mumbled and pulled a picnic basket from a shelf. "That man has been nothing but kind to you."

I swiped a piece of fried chicken and the hot, seasoned meat tumbled across my tongue. "And I'm grateful to him, but that doesn't mean I have to show Carlos any more fondness than what's in my heart."

Angela scoffed. "I know you care much for him."

"I do," I admitted and grabbed a drumstick when she looked the other way. I spoke with my mouth crammed full of chicken. "I care for him as much as anyone else on the ranch. Don't worry, Angela. I'm sure that Carlos will find a woman who's right for him."

"A woman with manners!" Angela handed me a cloth napkin. "How can he meet anyone?" She spooned berry cobbler into a dish. "He's always working."

"Sometimes the perfect mate has a way of simply showing up on your doorstep," I said. Until I hired the right woman for Carlos, I wasn't going to disclose my brilliant matchmaking scheme to anyone.

The kitchen doors swung open and Martino and Gracie saw me with a piece of meat in either hand.

"Mama!" they yelled in unison.

"We're going to have lunch with Carlos." I stood between the kids and Angela as they each commandeered a piece of chicken. "How do I get up to where Carlos is?" I said to Angela as she continued packing.

She looked surprised. "You don't remember?"

"We know!" the kids sang out.

Angela fumbled for a quilt from a cabinet in the mudroom and piled it into my hands. Martino barely gave Gracie and me time to scuttle out the door after him. He carried the heavy basket but raced well ahead of us. We followed him westward up a gradual slope along the baseline of Turtle Hill.

Gracie held my hand and shepherded me along. We crossed at least three wooded ditches, but my body wasn't geared for scrambling out of them. "I should have worn my corset in case my sides burst open," I griped.

The jaunt took twenty minutes of tumbling down slopes and splashing through cold streams. The children laughed every time I squealed when a snake slithered into our path or hares sprinted for high ground.

Dirt smeared across any exposed patch of skin. My skirt had somehow ripped, a bird pooped on my blouse, and I smelled like a farm animal. But when we finally found Carlos, he showed no repugnance at my physical appearance. He must have been starving.

He snapped the quilt into the air, and it flitted to the ground like a parachute. Neither child had a sweet tooth for pie after the meal and ran down the knoll to play cowboys and Indians, using chicken bones for guns.

"Thanks for taking the time to have lunch with us."

"It's my pleasure, Carmena." A sensual vibration trilled in my ear when his mouth puckered, and he rolled the 'r' in the name.

I cleared my throat. "I need to ask you some questions. There's a lot I still don't remember, and I'm going crazy trying to figure things out on my own."

Carlos scrubbed his hands on a napkin and flicked a steel hinge on the stopper of a metal thermos. He took a swig of the tangy lemonade. "What do you need to know?"

"I know this is going to sound really crazy," I paused and ended up blurting out, "but what year is it and where are we?"

"Hah!" Carlos laughed. My face lacked any sign of humor, and the appropriate shock lifted his brows to his hairline.

"I didn't think it could be true!" He touched the side of my cheek. "I don't believe it!"

"You don't believe what?"

He sat in silent wonder.

"Honestly, Carlos, absolutely nothing you say will shock me any more than what I've already been through."

Rather than accuse me of lying or joking because I didn't know the date or our location, he said, "We're in the outskirts of what the locals call Fredericksburg, Texas and—" He kept his eyes glued on me.

"And?" I prompted.

Carlos opened his mouth a couple of times, about to speak, but each time he changed his mind and pressed his lips shut again.

"You look like a fish, Carlos. Tell me. It's okay," I reassured him. "Nothing can upset me."

"It's January eleventh, eighteen forty-five."

I'd lied. It was one thing to hope that the entire experience was a fantastic dream, but to have Carlos confirm my worst fear, that I was locked in the past, wasn't what I expected.

The earth spun too fast, the trees bent too far in the breeze, and I felt my lunch do a U-turn.

Then I collapsed.

ℰↃℰↃ

I heard Carlos say, "Breathe, Carmena. Take a deep breath."

It was fortunate that I was sitting on the blanket when reality knocked me unconscious. It proved a short fall. Carlos cradled me in his arms.

"Please tell me you threw up on your own shirt."

"I'm glad you didn't eat more cobbler," he said. "Are you all right?"

"What happened?" But I already knew.

From the documentary on Santa Anna I'd remembered that the "red fiver" Jesse was reluctant to bet against was also

known as a red back, the currency of the Texas Republic issued when President Lamar was in office. Texas would be
forced to annex to clean up their debt and I learned the annexation occurred during the mid-1840s, supporting what Carlos
just told me. But that would put me one-hundred and sixty-five
years before my time!

I wriggled out of Carlos's sinewy arms and sat up. Pungent aromas of sweet grass and pine tree sap and the distant
droning of a beehive were natural balms. My nausea almost
disappeared. Carlos handed me a cup of lemonade, and I took
a long swig as he wiped my lunch off his shirt with a bunch of
grass and leaves. He stuffed a napkin inside his shirt under the
stain and ignored the rest of the residue. He turned his attention back to me.

"Thanks," I said and used my sleeve for a napkin. "When
I asked what year it was, you said something couldn't be true.
What did you mean?"

"Just that I can't believe you've forgotten so much," he
said. "That's all."

In an instant, a wall closed between us. He poured himself
more lemonade and turned the rim of his cup like a large dial
but didn't drink.

It was just as well he went silent. My fragile belief system
couldn't take any more direct hits. The rest of our conversation
fixed on the ranch. A need rose within me to make changes. It
might have been a good way to keep distracted and maintain
my sanity before I was zapped back to my own time, and I sort
of liked the new feeling of being in charge and helping out.

"I want to order a larger stove for the kitchen with at least
four burners. We can give the old one to a needy family in the
area. I'd also like you to have plumbing installed in the
house."

"You've never been so generous, Carmena. Wanting to
give away a valuable stove, buying gifts for everyone, new
plumbing." He locked eyes with me. "It's not like you to spend
money as if it weren't yours."

"The convenience will be well worth the cost. I'm tired of
pouring water down the toilet. We already have irrigation for

the fountains. You can tap into those lines. We've got plenty of creeks to run the sewage off."

"Since when were you schooled on irrigation?"

I ignored his question. "How big is this property?

"You don't remember?"

"If I did, I wouldn't be asking." I sneered, but Carlos had a built-in buffer to Carmena's abrupt manner.

"Thirty-three hundred acres."

I swayed and coughed. "That's a lot of land." A slow sip of lemonade gave me time to regroup.

Carlos stood and offered his hand. "C'mon. Since you're so forgetful lately, I want to show you something." He shouted to the kids, "Stay put, you two. I'm going up the hill!" They waved and darted in and out of the saplings.

My legs turned to mush after Martino's steep shortcuts, and Carlos had to tow me to the crest of the knoll. Land sprawled in every direction. High desert scrub loomed north and east, and green hills rolled for miles to the west. Behind me from this vantage point, the ranch still remained as big as ever.

Verdant meadows covered the valley beyond. Mother Nature planted copses of trees along the glittering creeks that overflowed with runoff from the last rains. A decent-sized fresh water lake pooled smack in the middle of the landscape. Fenced ponds of black sludge were closed off to any straying cattle, and from Carmena's memory I recalled that was the primary reason we didn't have the cattle graze near the lake.

"Right now, we're on the top southeast end of Three-Hump Ridge. Most of this is yours," he pointed out.

In the very distant southwest, a tiny block dwelling sat at the base of a hill, at least a good fifteen miles from us. "What's that white building? Is it part of our property?"

"No," Carlos said. "That's on Sealsfield's land."

He tugged on my arm, but I resisted. "Is it a home? Who lives there?" So far, I had only met residents of the ranch.

"An old, crazy lady," he said. "Never go near there," he warned.

"Why not?"

"Just don't!"

It was the first time the man had raised his voice to me or told me what to do. My fists settled on my hips.

"Forgive me, Carmena," he grumbled. "Please, avoid going near there. The woman is unstable, and I am concerned for your safety in her presence."

"That's all you had to say." The awkward moment passed. "So who are the Sealsfield's?"

"Charles Sealsfield is an old German writer who came on the advice of the Adelsverein."

"The what?"

"The Adelsverein. It's an idealistic group that makes promises of Eden to other German immigrants, enticing them to buy Texan and other American land. Besides your father, Mr. Sealsfield was one of the lucky few to get a grant for this much property so far north that has water and good pastureland."

"So why don't you—er—we buy Sealsfield out?"

He tilted his head. I lost count of how many times he looked at me like that, as if I told him I wanted to marry Lieutenant Franz.

"You know that he won't sell to anyone," Carlos said. "I don't think he's even lived on his property for some time." His chin jerked up in the direction of the white cottage. "And Sealsfield lets that lunatic live there."

Carlos stood closer and his body heat zapped me like a solar flare. His large hand found a place on my back and I closed my eyes. The real Carmena didn't welcome the advances of her foreman, and I wondered how she could resist the allure of such a virile man. He turned my body to face his.

Carlos's voice dropped to a sensual purr, "Carmena."

I licked my lips, and he drew closer. Quiet settled as his dark irises fixed on my eyes and drained the air from my lungs.

"Carlos." I looked into his sultry orbs, the color of fertile soil, ripe and potent. "You smell awful." It wasn't exactly what I wanted to say, but I knew Carmena would be grateful.

He pinched his shirt collar and took a whiff. He chuckled and broke the trance as he took a step away from me, the remedy I needed to catch my breath.

"I'll escort you back to the ranch and change my shirt before riding back up to check the livestock."

I took a brief glimpse of the crazy lady's lodgings and felt the slight vibration of the amulet under my bodice.

Carlos took my hand for the downhill hike to our picnic site. There were more questions to ask, but for now I was content to pack up the basket and return to the house.

Carlos called to the kids. "*Vamanos, muchachos!*" They dropped their fake guns and started to run home. Carlos whistled to his stallion on the next grassy hill over. The horse raised his pointed ears. His black mane and coat shimmered under the sun as he galloped across the knoll.

"How did you teach him to do that?" I asked, amazed at the horse's obedience.

He gave me a sideways glance. "Your father taught me."

Pictures of Carlos popped into my mind—him as a teenager in the lower corral with a packet full of molasses treats. I nodded. "Oh, right."

"Since Hammerhead was a colt I've whistled before every feeding." Carlos pulled a sugar cube from his pocket. "But now, without a snack, he runs away from me."

The stallion, an easy seventeen hands high, charged across the grass. I ducked behind Carlos and he smiled at me over his shoulder, giving an appreciative downward glance at my hold on his arms.

The horse skidded to a stop, inches from us. Hammerhead sniffed at Carlos's shirt and whinnied, not liking the smell of my regurgitated lunch. Carlos nabbed the reins, gave Hammerhead the sugar, then sprang into the saddle. He took the picnic basket from me.

"Hop up."

"You've got to be kidding."

"Since when couldn't you climb into a saddle?"

I pursed my lips. He wouldn't believe me if I told him I'd never climbed on top of a horse by myself. I spied a fallen tree and clumsily crawled atop. "I'm not going to rip a good skirt," I explained.

Carlos gave my hem the once over. "It's already ripped. And stained."

I looked down at the soiled fabric, tattered around the hem. "Angela can fix it."

He huffed, then sidled the horse along the side of the tree. Skirt and petticoats flounced up as I swung my leg over the tremendous haunches. Carlos quickly turned his head in the other direction and inhaled sharply. I didn't blame him. It had been days since my legs were shaved. Women probably wore long garments in this era because disposable razors weren't invented yet.

The moment my bottom plopped on the back of Hammerhead's haunches, he sprinted into a breakneck run. I locked my arms about Carlos's waist to keep from slipping off. My palms warmed on his firm torso, and I impulsively held tighter.

The children laughed hysterically when Carlos galloped past them with me shrieking like a banshee. The kids would've seen a lot more than fabric if it weren't for my bloomers flying up my thighs. My breasts bounced hard against Carlos's back, and my rear slapped against the saddle blanket again and again as we galloped along the edge of Turtle Hill.

Carlos zigzagged past the outbuildings and charged into the darkened stables. Hammerhead skidded to an abrupt stop like a professional barrel racer alongside a loosely bundled hay bale, a sliver of light reflecting off his mane. My breathing matched the stallion's flanks as they heaved in and out against my legs. The pungent aroma of alfalfa filled my lungs on each inhale, and the only sound I heard was my own wildly pounding heart.

I was sure Carlos felt the swell of my heaving chest as I sucked in the musky oxygen. His knuckles turned white on the reins and the picnic basket, a death grip tighter than I had on his waist.

I would've flung myself off the stallion, but it wasn't that easy. If I swung my right leg over the rear, I'd land bottom up on the damp floor. If my left leg crossed over Hammerhead's backside, I might have landed on the bale, but there was the risk of falling off the small, nearly rectangular dried hay, which was at least two feet shorter and a foot narrower than the girth of the tree trunk.

"I'm stuck," I said and heard his heavy sigh. "It's not like I'm stuck on purpose!"

Carlos handed me the basket, whisked a leg forward over the stallion's head, and jumped onto the hay-strewn floor. He took the basket, set it down, then lifted his arms to me. I leaned forward and rested my hands on his shoulders. Gravity did the rest.

As I brought my leg over the horse, my breasts plunged into his face, and the cotton skirts scrunched up and smothered him. Without the fabric between us, it felt like I slid down the front of a flagpole. In the near dark and silence of the stables, we fixed our eyes on one another as my skirt slipped back down to my ankles.

Carlos's beefy arms made my hands anxious. My skin started to turn into liquid, and his body would soon absorb mine like a sponge. His large hands clamped onto either side of my hips and his fingers lightly kneaded my skin, molding me to his will.

I didn't move. I didn't speak, but I did manage to think. How many times did I have to remind myself that it would be careless to have an affair with the man, especially because he didn't exist in my time? Yet it didn't help that he was extremely fit and highly attractive. But Carmena didn't return his feelings, and that one guilty thought brought down the fragile house of cards.

My words were thick and hoarse. "Thank you for bringing me back."

I barely heard him reply. "You're welcome."

I leaned back and looked up.

"Carmena." He said the name like a magical incantation, but I wasn't granting any wishes that weren't mine to fulfill.

"No, Carlos."

"Why not?"

My mental faculties were already in question. Why not tell him I wasn't the real Carmena and didn't belong in this century?

"I don't think I can explain it," I said.

He released his hold with a jolt of hurt and stepped back. "You're different since you hit your head. I thought things were changing between us."

"I'm not sure what happened exactly, but you're right. I am different, but just because I can't return your feelings that doesn't mean you aren't important to me, Carlos." In my best damsel-in-distress tone, I said, "It would be horrible if I lost any of my friends here on the ranch but losing you would be devastating."

"I'll always be here for you, Carmena," he said, yet his passion was salted with anger.

Before either one of us uttered another word, we heard the team rolling over the gravel.

"Please tell Javier that I'll need his help bringing the cattle in," he said.

The formal request could have frosted glass. He climbed onto Hammerhead and galloped out of the stables, not bothering to change his shirt.

It may have been honorable not to hurt his feelings but depriving myself of smooching with Carlos didn't make me stop thinking about it. It took a few moments to get my breath on an even keel, straighten my clothes, and re-pin my hair before I scuttled outside.

Angela and the children crowded around the wagon. I joined them in a chorus line of wide-open mouths. We couldn't believe what the men brought home.

CHAPTER 10

Jesse jumped to the ground and removed a canvas blanket to uncover an assortment of objects in the wagon. The boxes, crates, and farm equipment were anticipated, as were several brown paper-wrapped gifts secured with twine, rewards for my employees. What caused our thunderstruck expressions was the unexpected visitor who sat next to Javier.

She was slender, maybe thirty. Not beautiful but naturally pretty—if she hadn't appeared gaunt with the ecru cotton dress draping off her shoulders. Prominent cheekbones jutted out of an oval face, and a dark lavender crescent under each eye pointed to a severe lack of sleep. Javier held the reins while Jesse took her hand and helped her out of the wagon. He made the introductions.

"Violet, I'd like y'all ta meet the mistress of Holiday Ranch, Carmena Luebber. Carmena—" Jesse proclaimed like a circus ringmaster. "—this here is Violet, our new domestic recruit!"

The woman gave my arm an enthusiastic seven-point-nine Richter scale handshake. "I'm so glad to meet you!"

I spoke through teeth glued shut and a false smile that fooled no one. "How do you do, Violet?"

"I'm fine now that I'm here. Jesse and Javier bragged up a storm all the way back from town, telling me how much they love working for you on Holiday Ranch."

"How nice of them." My brain went into gear. I extracted my arm before she shook it out of the socket and cocked my head to the side, the hollow smile still fixed in place. "Jesse, may I have a word with you?"

We speed-walked to the porch and stepped under the shade of a giant arch spanning the front entrance. "I asked you to make inquiries, not to bring a strange woman home with you," I quietly admonished.

"Now, ma'am, before y'all go an' git all riled up, lemme explain."

"It's too late. I am already riled up." My volume stayed down, despite my scorched temper. "There'd better be a damn good explanation for this," I hissed.

"Well, ma'am, like I was sayin'. Ol' Sal saw us in the gen'ral store. Y'all remember the gal with a boardin' house down the road a lick from the gen'ral store? She done said she couldin help overhearin' that we had us some work available."

Jesse was probably a used car salesman in a past life and gave me no time to comment.

"Ol' Sal's been pertectin' Miss Violet. Showed us her rifle. Wha, it's the biggest gun I ever done seen. So Javier an' me pulled the wagon round Ol' Sally's place an' met Miss Violet in the kitchen." He inhaled, but it was too short a breath for me to get a word in. "Why, she's sweeter than pie and a might intelligent. She'll have 'em kids learnin' letters and numbers faster than ol' Carlos ever did."

He refilled his lungs, and I took advantage of the split - second break.

"I am your employer, Jesse, and I would like to have interviewed her first." I glanced at the woman. The children plastered wide smiles on Violet, engaged in a happy conversation.

"The thing is—" Jesse leaned close and confided, "—Ol' Sal says Miss Violet's husband is fixin' on beatin' her within an inch a' her life and said he'd done kill any feller who steps in the way."

"Then why on earth did you take it upon yourselves to bring her here?" I screeched like I'd gone mad. The gathering at the wagon turned their ears toward my outburst.

Jesse leaned in even closer and spoke quietly. "'T'aint right an ol' woman should hafta defend a nice lady like Miss Violet. Wha, she done knows how ta cook, clean, an' muck a stall."

No doubt that was Jesse's number one reason why I should hire Violet.

"But, Jesse, I can't believe that you saw absolutely nothing wrong with your decision to bring Violet to the ranch without my say in the matter!"

We looked toward the handsome woman. Violet beamed at the children, absorbed by every word they were discussing. Angela's palms were pressed together as if her prayers for a maid and tutor were answered.

"You said so yourself. Her husband would kill anyone who stood in his way. What are we going to do when he finds out she's here?"

"Wha, he knows he'd be in mighty serious trouble if he sets one foot on yer land," Jesse said.

I pinched the skin together between my eyes to ward off a headache. "And why would such a violent man be afraid to set foot here?"

"Well, I reckon' Cap'in Sanders would pro'bly strap 'im upside down by his big toes if her husband came onta Holiday Ranch."

The patronizing tone remained in my voice. "And why would the captain do that?"

"Shucks, ma'am, y'all should know. Cap'in Sanders done tol' that yellow belly husband a hers if he ever set foot on yer land agin he'd throw him in the brig, strip his rank, an' take away all he owned."

"You're telling me that Violet's husband is—"

"Yes, ma'am. Lieutenant Franz."

Nothing fazed Jesse, not even the threat of uncertain death from one of the meanest men in uniform who killed, or tried to kill, Carmena. I gaped in the direction of the group. Angela and Gracie had escorted Violet inside, laughing all the way to the door, while Martino helped Javier unload the kitchen goods from the wagon onto a pushcart.

"We gotta get this other stuff unloaded into the storage shed!" Javier hollered.

"Carlos asked you to help round up the cattle!" I called back.

"Ah'll be there directly," Jesse called to Javier.

"Go, Jesse," I snapped. "We'll talk later. I need time to cool off."

"Yes, ma'am." Jesse appeared contrite. He walked backward and tried to reassure me. "She only needs room an' board. Says she don't want for nothin' else 'cept a restful night's sleep."

"I know exactly how she feels."

I stomped into the house in search of our new domestic recruit and punched one of the kitchen swinging doors from the empty dining room. It hit the wall, and I stepped out of the way before it ricocheted back. Everyone flinched. I stormed into the kitchen. Martino wisely kept focused on the small cart at the back door, setting bulging burlap sacks and small crates on the counters.

Violet had been bending over, picking a mess off the floor. She stood up and wiped her hands on her apron, unfazed by my hostile protest.

Angela recovered from my abrupt entrance and pulled out a chair for Gracie. "*Mija*, you sit while we put the food away." She handed her daughter an oatmeal cookie. Gracie smiled with a look of gratitude I'd never seen on a child's face outside of photos depicting starving children in third-world countries.

Angela gave the first directive to the new help.

"Violet, please help me stock these supplies inside the food cellar."

Gracie snacked while her mother and Violet carried boxes and jars inside the pantry.

Martino grabbed a cookie and made ready to leave. "I'm gonna help Jesse put the supplies in the barn cellar," he said to me.

That got my attention. "I didn't know we had a cellar in the barn."

He smiled devilishly. "The soldiers don't know either! That's where we store the—" He shoved the cookie into his mouth.

"Store the what?" I squinted at him.

Crumbs of oatmeal dropped onto Martino's shirt as he mumbled about helping Jesse deliver supplies around the ranch. He took off out the back door with the pushcart in tow.

Great. Even the kids were privy to things I didn't know. I sat on one of the stools at the massive butcher block and let my temper stew.

Angela came out of the cellar and poured me a cup of coffee. Violet snuck quick peeks at me while filling the larder and approached me as timidly as a stray dog. She wiped her hands on her new apron.

"Miss Luebber?"

"Please, call me Carmena," I snapped, not wanting to be polite to the woman.

"I know you're upset that Jesse and Javier brought me here."

"I can't deny the obvious."

She looked at the chair opposite me. "May I sit?"

I unintentionally waved as if granting royal permission.

Violet slid a chair out, sat down, and straightened her skirt. "I don't know exactly what happened the last time my—er—Georg came here with his men. Months ago, I had divorce papers drawn up with Beauford Jones, and since I had witnesses to testify to his abuse, I didn't even need Georg's signature. It's just that I was so fearful of him and couldn't tell him we were officially divorced."

"Please." I raised my hand. "You don't have to tell me this."

She nodded. "I know, but I'd like to, just the same. Georg mentioned that Captain Sanders would beat the…well, severely punish him if he ever set foot on your property, and I figured that I would also be safe here. But, more importantly, I saw that I wasn't the only one he bullied, and if other people were fighting him off, then I knew I could, too.

"We don't know that we're safe here," I said. Truthfully, my ego still smarted from Jesse and Javier making the decision to hire Violet without my consent. And I had no idea how Carlos was going to react to the news that her husband was the officer who tried to kill me.

"I know Georg," Violet said. "He's a boastful, arrogant man, but he's too much of a coward to go against someone in real authority, especially Captain Sanders. I thought you might understand why I need to be here. You have a reputation of being a fair and compassionate woman, and truth be told, I have no place else to go." Violet finalized her appeal, and tears filled her eyes. "Please. Let me stay."

At some point, Angela finished with the boxes and started peeling potatoes. She neglected the potato skin curling under her knife and transmitted a plea on Violet's behalf. For a moment, I glimpsed a familiar vulnerability deep in Angela's onyx irises before she returned to guiding the sharp knife under the brown peelings.

A heavy responsibility-laden sigh whooshed out of me, and maybe a little guilt was mixed in. "All right, Violet. You can stay."

She smiled and held my hand across the table. "Thank you, ma'am. You won't regret it."

"I expect you to tutor the children in math, reading, writing, and whatever else you're knowledgeable about for at least three hours during the day. You'll answer to Angela unless I, or Carlos, give you a direct order. You'll be paid with room and board and a very trifling allowance."

"Thank you," she said, her tears finally falling.

"There's another thing. People don't need to know what's happening under our roof. I expect complete loyalty and discretion from you, and in return, you'll be well treated."

"I understand," she said.

I gave her a paltry smile. "Welcome to Holiday Ranch."

She jumped off her chair and hugged me, weeping without shame. I shooed her away before I also cried like some stupid schoolgirl. Angela hugged Violet, and the two of them set about preparing dinner. They ignored me in favor of exchanging secret cooking shortcuts, and right then, Violet became a member of the piecemeal family.

Gracie returned moments later to collect dishes for table setting duty, one of the few chores she'd keep. I asked Gracie to place me at the opposite end of the table, next to Martino and Jesse. This would leave the space open at the other end where I usually sat between Carlos and Angela. Now it was Violet's seat, putting more distance between Carlos and me. Besides, the new seating arrangement would let me gauge Carlos's reaction to the new housekeeper from across the room.

A nap was exactly the thing I needed before dinner. Javier passed me in the living room as I headed upstairs, and he spoke just above a whisper.

"Carlos knows about our new helper. Jesse and I thought it best not ta mention her ex-husband's name."

"Good call. I didn't even think to ask what last name she goes by now."

"Her maiden name. Wright. Violet Wright," he said.

There had to be a sign in that. Jesse had found "Miss Wright" for Carlos.

☙❧☙

We all knew to keep mum about Violet's recent past, but there was no way to keep Carlos from ever finding out, and I hoped he'd be shot by Cupid before he did.

Aside from her apron, Violet was the only person not wearing new clothing to dinner. Jesse and Javier wore brand new shirts, Martino had new shoes and pants, and Gracie looked darling in a white pinafore and mary janes like I used to have in the first grade.

Angela brought out serving platters wearing her new dress, a plain, little-house-on-the-prairie, high-collared thing, but Javier stared at her as if she wore lingerie. For Angela, it represented her new status as lord, or lordess, of the house.

An amazing-smelling herb and nut-filled bread was neatly sliced on a platter that may have been deliberately set in front of Carlos. Violet walked out of the kitchen behind Angela, holding a large urn of French-onion soup. She placed the soup on the sideboard then sat down to pray with the rest of us.

Carlos glared at Violet when she took her place, but she tactfully ignored him. He then shot an eyeful of daggers my way at the farthest reach of the table.

"It's Carlos's turn to pray," Gracie announced.

We bowed our heads. "Dear Lord, we thank you for this food and for taking care of the members of our ranch family." He narrowed his gaze on Violet. "And we ask for patience, er, blessings on this meal and for blessings on all those who belong to this family. We are grateful, Lord, because those of us who received gifts today are members of this blessed family."

I cleared my throat, and Carlos scowled at me. "Amen," he said, and the rest of us echoed the response.

Angela let Violet serve. Grunt work.

The children described their new toys to Violet. The price of their gifts was worth the Fourth of July sparklers twinkling in their eyes. Gracie received a satin ribbon matching the one in her new doll's hair. Martino was given a slingshot with strict orders never to aim it at anyone.

We were a little apprehensive about asking Violet any personal questions that would somehow divulge her identity to Carlos. Thankfully, the cold disdain he bombarded her with in the short distance between them was a strong factor in preventing him from learning her former last name straight from the source.

Javier and Jesse lit up their cigars on the front porch after the meal was over, and Angela and Violet cleared the table. The kids ran upstairs to play with their new toys. I joined Carlos in the library to go over the daily recording of activity on the ranch, although my bones ached, and I wanted to conk out in bed for the night.

I trudged toward the desk and whined, "Do I have to be here for this?"

"Your father knew how important it was to keep the owner informed of the day's events, any change in assets and expenses—" He shut the doors behind him, and his smooth voice morphed into snarling. Hostility blasted out his eyes like a ten-alarm fire. "Or discuss changes in personnel. You could have at least informed me!"

I sat in my comfy chair, but Carlos stood. He crossed his arms and his nostrils flared.

"Informed you of what? That I hired a new employee?"

"That, too. But did you have to make your repulsion of me so noticeable by sitting at the other end of the table?"

"Oh! So that's why you're so upset?"

"I know what game you're up to, Carmena. I know you brought her here to steer my heart away from you, but it won't make any difference. My feelings are what they are."

I put on my best poker face. "If you think that Violet was intended as a romantic distraction, Carlos, you are mistaken. If that was my intent, I'm sure you would avoid her all the time. The truth is I had no idea Jesse and Javier would bring anyone home. And secondly, I wanted another woman to help Angela and to teach the children. Nothing more. You've made an assumption and a bad one at that."

Carlos walked to a window and rubbed his hand over the stubble on his chin. The dark night had blackened the glass, and he stared into his own reflection. "I see. I'm very sorry for making assumptions."

It was an insincere apology, but considering my deliberate deception, I accepted it.

"Do you mind telling me why you placed her next to me?" he asked.

"I had Violet sit next to Angela so she'd feel more at home with a table full of strangers. Like she was part of the... family."

It was an effective sting since he'd made a point to exclude Violet in his benediction. Carlos was the main reason I sat her next to him, but he didn't need to know all the details.

"I guess I behaved foolishly." His shoulders dropped, and this time I sensed embarrassment in his voice.

"It's okay. Let's forget this nonsense, shall we?"

He nodded.

"I need to ask another question. I don't know when I was born."

He whirled on me and lashed out. "For God's sake, Carmena. This has gone far enough!" Carlos took a good look at me and knew I wasn't faking. His eyes widened as the appropriate shock set in. "You don't know!"

"I can't be uninformed about one of the most basic facts in my life, now can I?"

"I want you to tell me exactly what you remember when we thought you died," he said.

I mulled it over. It seemed ludicrous to tell him what really happened, being sucked into a fog and landing in a time and place unfamiliar to me. On the other hand, I needed someone to confide in.

"Remember, you asked. Sit down," I instructed. "Just don't interrupt until I'm finished."

Carlos sat down, and I was certain he didn't know what to expect. The truth had been building like a pressure cooker, and I was relieved to tell my story. It gushed out rather easily.

"My name is Mandy Ruhe."

CHAPTER 11

I gave Carlos some historical updates during the narration. After all, California wouldn't become a state for five more years. He wore a mask of non-judgment during my story telling, but the more I described the phenomena leading up to the fateful day when I woke up in the captain's arms, the more his skin paled.

It took about three quarters of an hour to divulge my fantastic tale, finishing with how I fidgeted with the amulet each morning in hopes of getting back to my own time. The recital was bizarre to my own ears, and I didn't know if he thought I was crazy or if there was a smidgeon of belief on his part.

Silence bore down on the room until Carlos finally spoke. "Are you wearing this necklace now?"

I tugged on the chain and pulled it over my head. The amulet dangled over the desk.

"May I see it?" He held the offered amulet as if it was made of gold, and I handed him the magnifying glass. Carlos made the same sounds of appreciation as Nicole had when she first examined it.

"It looks exactly like Holiday Ranch! But none of these other pictures make any sense. They're like broken puzzles." He looked up at me. "You're truly not Carmena?"

"No," I answered. "Maybe a facet of her. I've been able to see more and more of her memories. Maybe this is a past life I lived as her."

Carlos frowned. "A past life?"

"Having lived before in another time, existing as another person."

He nodded. "Once, in town, I heard some Chinese men in the restaurant speak of such things."

"You believe me!" I accused Carlos. "Why don't I have to try to convince you to buy my story?"

"I don't know how this is possible," he said. "Yet, what you're saying is too incredible not to be true. Of course, it's hard to believe, but I can't help admitting that you've been unlike yourself, or Carmena, since Franz was here. Saying strange things, being kind to the children, buying gifts for everyone, and forgetting important details. That's not like the Carmena we know." He handed me the magnifying glass. "I can't help wonder where she's at. Do you know?" He sat forward and waited for word about the true object of his love.

"I'm sorry. I have no idea where, or when, she is. It's hard to be concerned about her situation when I'm sort of in the same boat."

"I imagine so." Disappointment seeped into his words.

"Will you teach me then? Tell me what Carmena was— uhm, is—like?"

"First," he stated, "you must promise me two things."

"That depends. What do you want?"

"I don't want you to tell anyone else about what has happened to you."

"C'mon, Carlos. You can't think I'd want to repeat this? I didn't even expect for you to believe me, let alone anyone else."

He exhaled in relief. "I also want you to tell me before you return to your own time."

"I don't know if I can return, let alone when, but I'll tell you if I find a way. In case I can't, I need to make the best of what I have here. I need to know about Carmena, her parents, and the history of the ranch."

Carlos set my amulet down and removed a key from his pocket. "Carmena keeps a copy of this key in her room," he said. He walked around the desk, knelt beside me, and unlocked the bottom drawer. He removed a heavy leather folder and two black ledgers then set them on the desk. He opened the folder. "These documents are all the births, baptisms, and any other important information for everyone on the ranch. Deeds and other legal papers are there, too." He placed them in front of me then dragged one of the bulky wing-backed chairs from the other side of the desk next to mine.

An unwelcome knock on the library door pulled me back from the edge of my seat.

"Come in," I said.

Angela stuck her head in. "I'm sorry to interrupt, Carmena, but Captain Sanders is here to see you."

I sighed and looked at Carlos, who was equally annoyed by the unexpected visit. I, because I hadn't primped and preened for the captain's visit, and Carlos, most likely because of the way he felt about the man.

"Please ask the captain to wait a moment."

Angela bowed and shut the door.

"Why on earth do you want to see him, especially now?" Carlos asked.

"He beat the crap out of Lieutenant Franz on Carmena's behalf. He saved my—her, somebody's—life. The least I can do is thank him."

Carlos didn't argue. Instead, he said, "May I remind you that his affections aren't meant for you, Mandy?"

"I don't even know the man! Don't worry. I'll keep the visit short on the pretense that I'm not myself."

Carlos smiled.

"I want you to escort the captain here from the parlor and stay with me, no matter how awkward. I can't have the man making any advances, or worse, during his visit."

"What could be worse?" he asked.

"Based on what he wrote in that letter, he may be thinking of proposing."

ᘓᘓᘓ

I stood behind my desk prepared to politely give the captain the boot. Carlos escorted him into the library. I recognized him instantly, and Cupid had at me with machine gun fire. It was Military Jesus, the man who rocked me in his arms and cried over me after the lieutenant's attack.

Captain Charles Sanders rose above insanely gorgeous. He could turn the head of a mannequin. He was the classic image of a steroid muscle man on the front cover of a paperback romance, an easy six-feet-four—maybe five—inches tall. And the captain was much closer to my age than Carlos.

No wonder I—or rather, Carmena—was attracted to him. I wanted to gobble the officer up like milk chocolate, and in testimony, my mouth remained opened a bit too long. The captain's smile grew wider, and Carlos cleared his throat rather loudly.

I swallowed. "Captain. It's absolutely wonderful to see you." And it was.

Carlos, out of the captain's line of sight, rolled his eyes heavenward. I stumbled past the chairs behind my desk.

"Thank you, Carmena." His masculine voice wrapped invisible arms around me. "And may I say that it's always wonderful to see you?"

He glided across the room with the heat of a professional tango dancer. He took my hands and placed a long, slow kiss on the back of each one. Goosebumps rose on my arms, shivers did the whole up and down thing along my spine, and I wanted nothing more than to be alone with the man.

"I'm so glad you have recovered from that unfortunate circumstance." No matter what he said, his words oozed masculine sensuality.

"Carlos," I kept my toothy grin on the officer, "I've changed my mind about our last discussion. Perhaps you can attend to that other matter we were just dealing with."

"And what matter would that be, Carmena?" Carlos asked. He enunciated every syllable in the name and stood like a permanent fixture with his arms crossed.

I waved my hand. "Whatever. Just take care of it."

The captain's blue eyes glittered more than the crown jewels under a spotlight, and his smile caressed me like a cashmere blanket.

"I don't understand, Carmena," Carlos said. "We were just discussing your poor condition after the lieutenant's attack."

"Is it true?" the captain asked, deep concern evident in his tone, and he held my hands tighter. "Are you unwell, Carmena?"

"Oh, no. I'm feeling much better now."

"Why don't we sit down?" Charles said. He took my arm, and I felt a girlish flutter in my solar plexus. We sat down on the leather settee, and Carlos seated himself on the matching chair directly across from us.

"How are you, Captain?"

"I'm very fine, especially now that I'm here, knowing you're well." His voice, smooth as French butter, made me want to melt into it.

We continued to hold hands, and my eyes held fast to his. "Carlos, is there something else you need?"

"Yes, actually. We need to finish the conversation we were having moments before the captain arrived in which you told me how fatigued you still felt since the attack."

Alarm washed across the handsome face. "Please, Carmena. You mustn't try to be brave for me." The captain unwittingly joined the enemy's side in the verbal tussle I was having with Carlos, and he abruptly stood. "Perhaps I can return another day."

I practically jumped on top of him and dragged him back down. "But I'm much better today!" I turned to Carlos and gave him a ferocious stink eye. "Aren't I looking much better, Carlos?"

"Well…" He rubbed his chin. "Now that you mention it, you do look a little pale."

The captain squeezed my hands, and I wished he would kiss them again. "I'm ashamed that I didn't consider your physical health more thoroughly before riding out." I made to protest, but he quickly added, "I'm also flattered that you don't want to send me off, Carmena, but we really do need to put your frail condition before all else." He glanced at Carlos. "I'm sure you'll be feeling better by next week."

"I'm sure I will be," I said, heartbroken that he readied to leave.

Warm lips brushed the back of my hands yet again, and the captain smiled. "Good evening, Carmena." He started for the library doors.

I trailed the captain like a love-struck teen, hoping he'd change his mind about staying. "It's much too late for anyone to be riding at this time of night."

"Surely you don't doubt the ability of a captain in the Texas Cavalry to take care of himself," Carlos said.

"I don't mean to insult you, Captain, but I fear for your safety," I lied. "There are so many highwaymen and all manner of vicious beasts out at night. We've plenty of guest rooms to see to your comfort."

"*¡Ay, Diós!*" Carlos muttered.

Charles took my hands in his. His smile couldn't get any wider, and my heart tried to jump out and rest in his dimples. "Don't worry about me, Carmena. Several of my men are waiting at the gate. Now, I insist that you get your rest, so that we may enjoy a proper visit upon my return."

"But I'm really feeling fine!"

"Thank you, Captain, for seeing to Carmena's needs before your own," Carlos said.

The Adonis made a gracious bow to Carlos. To me the captain said, "I will call on you next week when you're feeling much better, if I may?"

I pouted, despite the offer of another visit. "Of course."

He kissed my hands for the umpteenth time, and I wanted him to stay longer. Like a needy little puppy, I followed the captain to the door, but he said, "I will see myself out, Carmena. I'd prefer it if you sat down and rested."

"Of course. Anything you want, Captain." And I meant it.

He kept his smile in check, and Carlos huffed behind me.

The captain's long pointer finger stroked from my cheek to my chin, and he whispered, "Perhaps we'll have time later to share a few private moments together."

I sighed and brazenly admitted, "I'd really like that."

Carlos grunted. The captain grinned as he closed the library doors behind him.

I whirled around to face Carlos who openly smirked. I jabbed my fists on my hips and glared, but my dirty look had no impact.

Carlos took his seat at the desk and pointed to my own. "Now, let me think." He tapped the side of his cheek. "Where were we before you said how you wanted me to stay in the library with you during the captain's visit, no matter how awkward?"

"*Diós*," I griped and stomped across the room. I plopped down hard into my chair and crossed my arms.

Carlos laughed.

"Get on with it," I said. "What were you going to say?"

"I was about to tell you everything I know of the real Carmena Luebber."

ൟ

My composure returned once the captain left but his image embedded itself like a permanent photo in my mind as Carlos proceeded to tell me about Carmena. Finally, some things started to make sense in this other reality.

He showed me a few pictures of my twin self. It may have been the times, but Carmena wore a stern expression, as if smiling at the camera wasn't an option. She was the sole child of Heinrich and Carmen Luebber. There was one grainy picture of her mother in addition to the portrait over the fireplace. Later photos of Carmena's father showed a man strikingly similar to my own dad, Taber Ruhe.

"Why aren't these photographs framed and displayed?"

Carlos lifted a shoulder. "Carmena says some memories hurt more than others. Her father hung the portrait over the fireplace. That's the only reason it remains."

Carlos also said that Heinrich Luebber's best friend in Germany was a man named Alexander Eversmann, who introduced him to Gottfried Duden. Duden wrote many articles in German newspapers, encouraging an expansive migration to the United States, primarily Missouri. But it was tall tales of Texas from other German settlers that inspired Duden to write about it.

The land grant Luebber found was exactly like the fairytale descriptions. He was surprised years later to discover that very few acreages had an abundance of water sources and green landscapes equal to Holiday Ranch. He bought surrounding properties over the years and earned an esteemed reputation through his fair business dealings.

Those immigrants who made the difficult and costly transatlantic and transcontinental journey farther west to Texas blamed Gottfried Duden when they were met with the lack of hearty farmland. They didn't realize that they had purchased Texas property while in Germany that had been unseen by Duden.

The father of Lieutenant Franz was one of those landowner hopefuls, and he passed the bitter legacy and wasteland onto his son. The Franzs held Luebber partly responsible for their disappointing investments because of his close relationship with Duden and Eversmann, thinking Luebber had something to do with the unscrupulous businessmen who also believed that all of the land in Texas was equally valuable.

On February 12, 1817, four years after Carlos and his father, Juan Solis, joined the ranch family, Carmen Luebber died in childbirth. In honor of his dead wife, Luebber named his daughter after her mother but added an 'a' to the spelling.

Two years after Carmena was born, Carlos's father died of consumption.

As Carlos told me more about her, clear snippets of memories came alive, as if they were mine to begin with. When Carmena was barely eight years old and anxious to ride on her own, the girl managed to saddle her horse and sneak into town unescorted.

"Near sunset, she returned with a dirty and smelly hired hand," Carlos said.

"What! Who did she bring home?" I asked, wrinkling my nose.

"Jesse. He was a low-life alcoholic who needed more than a first aid kit to mend his broken life."

Jesse was given a bath, a new change of clothes, and was offered a cigar after dinner. He never touched a drop of liquor after that and became the hardest worker on the Luebber ranch.

When Carmena turned thirteen she rode alone to the northern most border of her father's land and met a group of Comanche women, children, and an injured chief. She convinced them to follow her to the ranch, and her father gave them a home until their chief was able to travel a few months later. That's when he had added on the secret room to the bunkhouse.

"The Indians moved on, but a family member comes back once every other year to trade, and lucky thing they do," Carlos said.

"Why is that?" I asked.

"When Carmena was seventeen, she and the señor returned from a visit with family friends. They had been staying at the Johnson Ranch, a sprawling property thirty miles east of Holiday Ranch." A layer of anguish covered every feature on Carlos's face. "The Luebber carriage had been attacked by renegade members of the Tonkawa tribe. Little Crow, the son of the injured Comanche chief, happened to be on his way to the ranch to make a trade and saw the attack in progress."

Carlos told how Little Crow and his three brothers fought off a dozen of their enemy but not before Heinrich Luebber had been killed. "Carmena held his body in the carriage and a pistol in her hand. Four of the Tonkawa had been shot to death. She listened to the señor divulge his last wishes. Keeping Holiday Ranch in the family was his top priority."

I felt a twang of remorse, recalling the loss of my own father who died in a violent car accident caused by a drunk driver. I knew exactly how Carmena felt, losing her father in her teens. But then she became an adult, and I fought to stay a child.

Carlos described a family of felons Carmena harbored during an unexpected windy spring storm on her nineteenth birthday, and a flashback snapped of horses traipsing over pieces of waterlogged decorations and flowers strewn about the ground.

Two strangers, a man and a very pregnant woman, sat together on one horse and Jesse held a shivering waif-like toddler in his saddle. After hearing their hard luck story, Jesse volunteered the ranch as a haven.

"Jesse's soft heart seemed to follow a pattern that always convinced him to overstep his boundaries and undermine my or Carmena's, authority in favor of doing a good deed, but it was she who convinced me to let the family stay," Carlos said. His complaint didn't sound like it held an ounce of animosity. "That was the night Carmena christened the property Holiday Ranch."

Carlos pulled a clipping from one of the side desk drawers. The headline read, *OUTLAW COUPLE WANTED FOR CONSPIRACY*. It was followed by a tagline. *Against the Republic of Texas and the United States*. It didn't include the publication name, but the date was June, 1832.

The article stated that south of the border, the Centralists wanted the couple, Alejandro and Maria Martinez for coup attempts against the ousted dictator, Antonio de Santa Anna. The opposing Federalists wanted them for inciting the population to adopt a democratic society. The cartoonish drawings didn't resemble Javier and Angela in the least.

I crumbled the newsprint into a little ball and placed it inside the ashtray, then lit a match to it.

Carlos shared every important event that occurred on the ranch and relayed every relevant detail of Carmena's family history. I picked up her memory as easily as Carlos readily accepted my absurd time-travel story, however true.

"You're holding something back from me, Carlos. I think you may know why I'm here. You accepted my being from the future way too easily."

"I assure you, Carmena—Mandy—I know nothing why you were brought here or where Carmena is." Carlos squirmed in his chair. "What year did you—When was it that you—"

"It was 2017." Thank God he was sitting down. Color drained from his face.

"No!" he whispered, and fear exploded in his eyes. Several moments passed before he spoke again. "Will the Republic be annexed? Will there be a war like Mexico promised?"

"I don't remember the exact day, but the Republic will be annexed in March, and will be admitted to the Union this December. That will result in an important war with Mexico next year."

Stunned by my lesson in future history, Carlos fell mute and the clock chimed seven times in the heavy silence as I watched him trudge to the windows with the knowledge of unborn history. His face reflected like a ghost against the pitch black of the glass.

At last, he said, "Will we be safe during the war?"

"Yes. The Mexican War will be fought mostly along the border or in Mexico. Everyone north of San Antonio will be very safe. Fredericksburg will be safe, which by the way, will be officially incorporated next year. Can you start converting any cash we have on hand into gold?"

Carlos gazed out the window. "Yes, but we should keep a very small supply of red backs until the annexation." He took a deep breath. "Now, if you don't mind, please tell me a little of two-thous—of the time from which you came."

CHAPTER 12

Carlos couldn't even say the year I came from, as if it was a curse capable of breaking open if spoken out loud. It took some thought to describe what the future looked like.

"We travel by car…um, steel wagons without horses. Most run on stuff called gasoline. We capture energy from the sun, wind, and water for power. We've created artificial light."

He scrunched his nose. "Artificial?"

"Light that doesn't use any kind of flame," I said. Carlos gasped, and I wondered if it was wise to continue.

"Go on, Mandy," Carlos encouraged from the window.

"We can travel in the sky around the world and have been to the moon and into outer space."

He swung around with a child's eyes of wonder. "How is that possible?"

"Someone invented airplanes, birdlike contraptions, and other vehicles that fly in the sky that go just about anywhere. It only takes a few hours to travel across the Atlantic."

"DaVinci was reputed to have drawn pictures of such things."

"What modern man has designed is much more sophisticated and more powerful. We use these in wartime to drop bombs on the enemy." I heard Carlos gasp again and lightened the topic. "We communicate by different means with people across the globe in less than a second with little objects called cell phones. Information is available in a split second with computers. We call all of these advancements 'technology.'"

He flushed. "*Diós!*"

"We had our first black president—"

Carlos nearly shouted, "What? It can't be!"

"Calm down." I flapped my hands in a poor attempt to settle him. "Hey! Since when are you a racist?"

"You don't understand. I don't care about the color." He walked back to his chair and sat down. "As long as they don't elect non-Christians into office."

I kept mum.

"I just don't know how a black man can qualify to be president," Carlos said.

"Educational opportunities have opened wide up in the future. The next president has been controversial to say the least." In no mood to debate religion and politics, I switched to economics. There's only a handful of super-wealthy people, and the disadvantaged ones try to get by. The world is full of random violence. We kill off animal species and whole tribes of people are lost in genocide."

"Genocide?"

"That's when you kill off an entire race of people."

His head bobbed up and down. "Indians. So, some things haven't changed all that much?"

"Huh," I mused. "I guess not."

He sighed. I waited, unsure if he wanted to hear more. Carlos fidgeted with one of the brass studs on the armrest.

"Are you...that is, in the future, are you spoken for?"

It was sweet, what he asked, and I sort of smiled. "No, Carlos. I can't even get a man in my life."

"You? Why not?"

"Too bossy, I guess."

"There is that," he said.

I stuck my tongue out at him, and he laughed.

"That's all I think I want to know right now. Thank you, Mandy." We sat quietly until Carlos held up the chain and asked, "What have you done with this device, your amulet, since you arrived?"

"I've been turning the sections constantly, like I did right before I disappeared. I'm not exactly sure what made it work."

"Perhaps we should put it from our minds and concentrate on getting you familiar with your new life." Carlos started to pocket the necklace, but I held out my open palm.

"It might be a poor act of faith on my part, but I can't let that jewelry out of my sight. It's the only physical connection to my life in the future."

He laid the amulet in my hand. "Such a treasure deserves great respect and care. There's no telling what would happen if you lost it."

"Don't you worry," I said and circled the chain over my head. "It can't get too much safer than hanging on my body."

Carlos took his leave, but I stopped him at the door. "Carlos. Please remember to address me as Carmena when we're with anyone else."

He bowed ever so slightly and said, "As you wish." His inflection hinted at resentment. He seemed angry. I didn't think I upset him by not handing over the amulet.

I think he was mad because I wasn't Carmena.

☙⧓❧

Twisting the amulet yielded nothing new, and I tucked the charm back into my shirt. It was late, and too tired to look at any more documents, I searched for Angela in the kitchen.

She walked out of the cellar, beaming. "Violet cleaned out the pantry. Everything is in excellent order!"

"Wonderful," I said, though I found it difficult to share her enthusiasm over the household task. "I need a bath drawn."

Violet sauntered in from the dining room with a dust rag in hand. Angela managed her new assistant like a pro.

"Please help Martino to draw water from the well, and then boil it for Carmena's bath," she told Violet.

"Yes, ma'am," Violet answered. "Would you like a cup of tea while you're waiting?" she asked me.

"Sure," I said.

Violet brewed a first-rate cup of black tea flavored with bergamot, which would later be called Earl Grey in England. before starting in on her task of schlepping water in from the

well with Martino. She poured the liquid into large copper vats
on the burners. The boy trudged out of the room with slumped
shoulders, and I thanked him for his efforts. I had already forgotten my intention to make life easier for the kids.

Violet pushed the caldrons around for maximum heat underneath.

"I'm planning to buy a new stove with more burners," I
told her.

She rubbernecked inside one of the cumbersome contain-
ers. "Now that would be a pleasurable sight." She added more
wood to the stove and poured tea for us after she sat down.

"And with new plumbing, we won't have to draw water
from the well for baths," I said.

"That just might be more welcome than a new stove."

"Do you like living in Texas, Violet? Even after all that
happened with your husband?"

She brightened. "I've never been happier. Your ranch is
the silver lining after Georg's abuse."

"Jesse did an advantageous thing when he brought you
here. Angela is more pleasant, Javier smiles more, and the
children are happier. And the rest of us eat more desserts than
ever."

Violet's laughter stilled as Carlos entered through the
back door after his nightly check around the property. Seeing
him reminded me that not every memory of the previous owner had been unearthed.

"Hey, Carlos, I haven't seen that room in the bunkhouse
yet."

Lightning bolts shot out of his eyes.

"Whatever," I mumbled.

"I know you think you can't trust me because I'm new
here, Carlos," Violet said. "One day I hope you can feel more
confident about my loyalty to the ranch."

He ignored her comment. "Martino said you were heating
water for Carmena's bath. Let me know when it's boiling, and
I'll help you take the water upstairs."

"I think I can handle it," she said.

"Fine," he replied. "I'll be up in my room when you change your mind."

As he stomped through the kitchen, she said, "I won't."

"Fine," he repeated with the same angry edge, the door swinging shut behind him.

"Did I miss something?" I asked, startled by Carlos's capacity to be rude and immature.

"He's been upset with me nearly all day."

"What did you do?"

"I was hauling water from the well for dinner because the kitchen pump wasn't working properly this afternoon. Carlos offered to haul the water for me, but I refused on account that it's important I stand on my own. I guess I insulted him by not letting him help. He stormed off earlier like he did just now."

"I imagine Carlos's outburst is nothing more than a trifle compared to your ex-husband's." She nodded. "Frankly, not only would I let Carlos carry the water, hell, I'd let him draw it from the well, too," I said.

She giggled. Her chipper demeanor and easy laugh put me at ease. Violet was the second person I'd met outside of those I lived with, and I wondered if they were all as nice.

"You must have met quite a few people in these parts, having lived on another farm and in town."

"Not really. Georg didn't like me to make friends," she answered. "Wait. I did meet the woman who lives on Sealsfield's land. But then, you must know all about her."

"Actually, we've never met."

"Her name is Sadie. Most people in these parts think she's a witch."

Great. The last time I had a discussion about witches, I ended up regretting it.

"I met Sadie only once, about a year ago, a day after a fearsome rain," Violet said. "I was riding into town when my buggy got stuck in some mud. I put grass and sand under the wheel to roll it out and was letting it dry up a bit. Sadie watched me from where she stood at the edge of a creek, collecting flowers and plants. Her dress was twisted up to her thighs, and she waded knee deep in ice-cold water as calm as could be.

"I asked if she needed a ride into town, but she shook her head and said, 'Come here. I want to show you something.' There's something about Sadie and how she makes you feel, like she's a queen to be obeyed. She showed me herbs to make poultices..." Violet's voice trailed off, and she stared off into la-la land for a moment.

"What is it?"

"Those poultices she taught me to make? They were for administering to minor cuts and bruises." She touched the skin under her eye.

"That's quite a story," I said, my thoughts churning like the boiling bath water. "I'll be up in my room." I left the kitchen with my tea.

If she was capable of divining a needed medicine for Violet, Sadie could have other special metaphysical abilities. Her knowledge might include something of the amulet, possibly knowing a way to get me back home.

A trip to the little white cottage moved to the top of my to-do list.

c∽ɔc∽ɔ

I'd have to figure out a way to get to Sadie's, since I had promised Carlos I wouldn't go near her. Someone else might know how to get to her home, but they might mention it to Carlos. And there was no telling to what lengths he would go to keep me away from her.

Violet interrupted my thoughts when she brought up the first two buckets of hot water. Martino kept a step behind with two more pails. His knuckles turned white and his muscles strained as he held tight to the handles.

There was no reason a boy that age should be hauling heavy buckets of water up the stairs, although asking the other men to help seemed unfair with the amount of work they did outside. And if Carlos's work kept him inside, he might be susceptible to a romantic intrigue with Violet. To free up Carlos's calendar, I needed to hire new field hands, and would do so under the pretense of them taking on the children's grueling workload.

The process of hiring would be turned over to Jesse. He obviously had a knack.

"Violet?"

"Yes, ma'am?"

I smiled. "You can call me Carmena."

"Yes, ma'am."

I shook my head. "Have you been talking to Jesse?"

"Ma'am?"

"Never mind," I sighed.

"I'll have Martino bring up more hot water, and then I'll bring in the rinse water."

"I think Martino needs to have his workload lightened. I'd prefer you to ask Carlos to bring up the water for our baths from here on out until I hire more hands."

Violet was about to protest but thought better of it. "Yes, ma'am," she mumbled.

"And please tell Angela that I'd like to know what I was wearing when I first, I mean, when I had been hurt. I need everything that was in my possession that day."

"Yes, ma'am," she said again and trudged out of the room. It wasn't a long wait before she returned with Carlos, each of them holding two buckets of hot water. Carlos appeared smug, no doubt pleased that Violet had to humble herself by asking for his help.

"Thank you, Carlos. I'll see you in the morning." He smiled at me but smirked at Violet, who remained unfazed. She knelt on the floor and slid a thin steamer trunk with brass corners and hinges from underneath my bed.

"Angela said the things you want are in this chest. She couldn't fix your blouse. She said you wore the things in this trunk under your dress and for some reason, Carlos told her not to—" Violet raised the lid and her eyes blew wide open. She continued slowly. "—not to mention it to anyone."

She removed my low-cut designer Brazilian jeans with the hot-pink handled screwdriver sticking out of a back pocket, and in her other hand she held my black leather Adidas running shoes with bright blue trim and Velcro closings. She held the clothing and shoes away from her body with outstretched arms as if she'd get an unmentionable disease if they got any closer.

Violet put a brake on any personal comment, but her eyes flitted from one foreign object to the other. She carefully set them atop my dresser before sliding the trunk back under the bed.

"Thank you, Violet. That will be all," I said like a royal.

She left the room, a puzzled expression still in place, and I snatched my jeans off the dresser the moment the door clicked shut.

The puzzling note from Maizy was still tucked securely in the back pocket of my pants. It was the first time I read the beautiful script in—was it three days or a week? I couldn't remember.

The cryptic poem and the scrawl at the bottom of the paper presented as much confusion as before. The note went into the top dresser drawer along with the untimely clothing.

I locked the bedroom door to escape into a brief watery retreat. For now, having a hot relaxing bath was what I needed to forget where I was, and remember who I was, or wasn't. At least now I had one thing that I didn't have before.

A hope of returning home.

ळ⁊ळ

After a sleepless night warring with my conscience, I lost and wrote the captain a brief note thanking him for his concern during his last visit and hinted strongly at another. I asked Jesse to deliver the message to him when he rode into town looking for some new ranch hands.

I helped the kids feed the animals in the barn again but had them skip mucking the stalls. It was grueling work for the kids, and I refused to let them do it. But I didn't do it either. Who wanted to muck stalls alone?

Jesse returned home from town in the afternoon and said, "I done delivered that note to the captain, but he wasn't about. His staff sergeant was at Sam Tucker's saloon. Said he'd get the message to the captain as soon as he found 'im."

"Did you put the word out for a couple of new men?"

"Sam Tucker said there's a couple a men bunkin' down at Ol' Sal's. They's been lookin' fer work, but Ol' Sal says they was helpin' with a cattle run for the Dobsons and ain't gonna be back 'til near the end of the week. She was talkin' to 'em jest the other night an' they done heard that no other place holds a candle to Holiday Ranch. I asked her to tell them fellers to head on up when they got back inta town."

"Good job, Jesse. Thanks."

He tilted the rim of his hat and left the kitchen with a cup of coffee in one hand and carrot cake in the other.

"Have you noticed everyone's getting a little bigger around the middle?" I asked Angela.

"Violet found a way to calm Carlos down. She says he has the sweet tooth."

"So, she exploits it, and we all suffer?"

"No one minds. Especially Carlos."

Ranching was hard work, and it wasn't necessary for the others to join a gym to keep the extra weight off. It didn't show on Carmena. Not yet anyways.

"Where is Carlos?" Anxious to visit Sadie, I thought to ask Carlos to take me on a short tour of the property, as opposed to raising his suspicion by asking him or anyone else how to get to her place.

"He's in the barn with Javier," Angela said.

"What's going on in the barn?"

"One of the heifers has a bump on her udder, and they're thinking of cutting it off."

"That's just great," I lied.

⌖⌖⌖

Familiar voices rounded the entrance to the barn, and I stopped in my tracks before someone took notice of my approach.

Javier's deep timbre was easy to recognize. "I think Oswego's forgotten all about it or else he woulda contacted us by now."

"Maybe them rumors 'bout Herrera's exile is true," Jesse said.

"If he's in that much trouble, maybe he doesn't have any money left to pay his men to pick up the rest of the shipment," Javier said.

There was an audible sigh.

"Considering what he paid us, Oswego won't forget about all those repeating rifles we still owe him," Carlos said.

The news left me breathless. I tiptoed away from the barn doors, too dizzy to run toward the house. I flattened my back against a nearby storage shed and splinters pricked through my dress, not at all uncomfortable compared to the thought of my men smuggling guns.

From the televised documentary, I remembered that Oswego was President Herrera's number one general and obeyed orders blindly. To what length would he go to get the remaining shipment of rifles?

The payroll ledger in the library revealed that Carmena's salary was fifty dollars a month, and she reinvested all of it back into the ranch. Gunrunning explained the ability to sustain the ranch when we could barely prosper with the limited breeding of livestock between military confiscations. But where did we get the money to purchase the guns?

The book full of crisp new bills in the library wasn't enough to continue maintaining the ranch in the long run. Carlos had mentioned a safe in the bunkhouse, yet that slush fund would run out sooner or later as well. He said we bartered for many things, but we still needed money to produce the things with which we bartered.

A fresh bucket of water sat next to the well, and I stumbled over to it. A splash of the cool liquid on my face revived me. The illegal line of work simply had to stop, as evidenced by the loss of life in the last raid, yet without the additional income I didn't know how we could legitimately generate the large sums of cash needed to effectively run the ranch. Also, there were too many things the ranch needed—basic conveniences like a new stove, indoor plumbing, and adequate clothing.

Perhaps I could call a meeting and ask for innovative ideas to contribute to the ranch's income. Maybe the guys could build furniture or the women make pies and cakes for the bakery in town. If we didn't use all our equipment, we might be able to sell some to local ranches. I needed to take stock of all the assets on the ranch.

Then it hit me. Take stock! Why not capitalize on my unique inside edge to create a portfolio that would help sustain the ranch by putting our assets in the stock exchange? I knew the names of large firms that made beaucoup bucks until the crash in 1929. We could make a fortune!

Sufficiently motivated, I ran back inside the house and holed up in the library to plan my next mission.

CHAPTER 13

It took a lot out of me to mastermind my idea. I needed a break after hours in the library and opted for a lone walk. I heard voices in the living room and headed for the ballroom instead, passing through the French doors to the back patios.

The west side of the house didn't provide as much shade, but I knew where I could find some. The late summer morning drew me to the front of the house and past the fountain. I meandered under the shadows of the generous oaks along the driveway. At the fence line, I looked back at the mansion and appreciated how long it took to walk the lengthy gravel drive.

The pounding of hooves turned my attention back to the road fronting the property. I was too far from the house to shout out a warning, and panic might have set in had it been more than two young soldiers nearing the front gates.

One rider stayed back, and the other boy cantered forward like a general in a military parade, both his back and mouth in straight lines. The familiar brand on the rump of his horse affirmed its origins, a stallion from Holiday Ranch. The boy pulled in his reins. It was the young corporal I had dreamed about, the one who apologized to me before Franz's attack.

I feigned confidence yet kept my distance as the soldier dismounted and walked toward the gate.

"Ma'am?" he bowed slightly.

"Corporal Boyce, is it?"

He stared straight ahead and pulled back his shoulders. "Yes, ma'am. My name is Boyce, however, due to conduct unbecomin' I was demoted in rank to private." He made eye contact and spoke in a less formal tone. "I'd like to apologize, Miss Luebber, for not using my brain and actin' like an…uhm, well, for not behavin' like a gentleman the last time I saw you."

The boy's face flushed, I guessed, not from the ride but from the apparent order to apologize.

"Thank you, Private Boyce. I appreciate your apology and trust that the next time any person is in trouble, especially a woman, she can count on your support?"

The young soldier snapped to attention. "Yes, ma'am!"

"I'm glad to hear it, but somehow I doubt you rode all this way to deliver an apology."

He stepped closer to the gate. "No, ma'am. Captain Sanders has asked that I also deliver a letter." He pulled a small envelope from his pocket and handed it to me through the wrought iron bars. Up close, I saw the sweat at the boy's brow and over his upper lip.

"Thank you, Private. Would you and your colleague like to come in for some refreshments before you take your leave?" You never knew when you'd need the help of some young soldiers.

The boy on the other horse looked hopeful, and Boyce's lip gave hint of a smile. "No, thank you, ma'am, but I do appreciate the offer, and I do appreciate you allowin' bygones to be bygones. If you don't mind, the captain has requested that I wait for your response and then immediately return to headquarters."

"Very well. Would you mind waiting here a few moments?"

"Not at all, ma'am."

I turned around and stepped back under the shade of the oaks.

Like the captain's previous note, my name was elegantly scribed on the parchment envelope, sealed with his majestic wax insignia. I unfolded the paper, and it became the letter.

My dearest Carmena,

It gave me immense pleasure to receive your most welcome correspondence. I would be honored if you allowed me to call on you within the coming week. At this point, my schedule does not permit me to offer an exact day and time for a visit as I have been charged with a special assignment, but I am in a grand state knowing that I may have liberty to do so.

Please inform the soldier accompanying this letter of your decision to receive me. I hope for an optimistic reply.

I am most affectionately yours, and yours alone,

Capt. Charles Patrick Sanders

Connected to Carmena, I couldn't tell if I experienced her feelings for the man or if I had developed my own. It took a few moments to rid myself of the silly grin brought on by the captain's note and his evocative closing.

When I could face the soldier with an uninterested reply, I said, "Private Boyce?"

The young man pressed against the gate. "Ma'am?"

"Please tell Captain Sanders that I am most agreeable to his suggestion."

"Yes, ma'am," he said and held his hand out for the letter. I pulled it back over my shoulder.

"I'll keep this. Thank you, Private."

"I'll relay your response immediately to the captain, ma'am. Good afternoon."

Boyce tipped his hat and ran to his horse. Then both soldiers took off at a gallop.

❧❧❧

Carlos gladly agreed to take me on a short tour of the ranch property, but only after he heard of the impending visit from Captain Sanders. I said I wanted to see what was behind Turtle Hill but gave no hint that I needed to learn the way to Sadie's cottage on my own.

Before breakfast Angela and Violet prepared our saddle-bags with lunch and filled our canteens. After I stuffed myself to the gills with a titanic breakfast, Carlos and I headed to the stables. My boot went into the stirrup, and I grunted audibly, trying to pull myself up onto my horse. Carlos pushed on my rump and my body heaved onto the saddle with the grace of a baby elephant. Dusty whinnied.

"It's Violet's fault. All those damn desserts." Miserable, I held the reins as Carlos strode around Hammerhead and lightly vaulted atop his horse.

"I suppose she shoved all those sugared cinnamon rolls down your throat?"

My nose shot upward, and I unintentionally snorted like Bertha, our largest sow.

Violet jogged into the stables. "Hold up!" She handed a bundle to Carlos. "I made some more of that pumpkin cake you enjoyed while you were measuring for the new stove in the kitchen."

She waited expectantly and looked as coy as Gracie, her hands behind her back, twisting from side to side.

"Thank you, Violet," Carlos said. "That's very kind of you."

"Think nothing of it." To me, she said, "You have a nice time on your ride, ma'am."

"Thank you, Violet. We'll be back in a few hours."

She lifted her skirts, and we watched her run out of the stables. My smile radiated victory in the matchmaking department. "You like Violet's pumpkin cake, huh?"

Carlos humphed at the sight of my triumphant grin.

The children ran beside our horses until Violet called them back to begin their lessons.

Our horses trotted toward the bottom of Turtle Hill, and I copied Carlos as he leaned slightly forward into the rising incline. We continued up the switchbacks, toward the turtle cut-out in the granite. To the east, stripes of magenta and yellow slashed the morning sky where the sun was gearing up to explode over the horizon. Thousands and thousands of tiny flowers colored the earth in pink, white, and purple.

We scaled the bumpy trail without conversation. I leaned well over forty-five degrees into Dusty's mane for the fifteen minutes it took to reach the top of Turtle Hill.

No wonder Franz wasn't willing to search up here for our livestock. The vertical stone walls behind the high meadow made the hill appear twice as tall and as difficult to climb from the bottom. Dusty and Hammerhead trotted across the dozen acres or so of dry grass then clopped into the entrance of the canyon.

The towering stone walls had been carved millions of years ago by glacial movement and precipitation. Noises echoed in every direction off the rock faces. Creatures darted around us, from horny toad lizards and occasional ground squirrels to buzzards clutching the sharp ledges above. The wind moaned, rushing river-like through the twisting stone trail. It would've been a spooky ride without Carlos's company.

I glanced at my broach, a watch, to time how long it took us to get through.

"How did you come to live at Holiday Ranch? Did Carmena's father hire you?" My words bounced back to me louder than expected.

"Not at first. When I was twelve, he found me and my father, Juan Solis, nearly dead on the property. Heavy rains flooded our small village, Palo Verde, and killed at least half of our family and friends. In the morning, most of the able villagers searched the debris for survivors, but a sudden mudslide buried every last one of them. My father and I were the only two able-bodied men remaining.

"After the slide, we left to scout for food and a new location for the village. We discovered higher ground, home to a small herd of buffalo and some wild horses. It was a good place that only took a day's travel through a wooded and rocky pass, and the children and older people could easily make the journey on foot. We were so excited to tell everyone that we found a new home for Palo Verde.

"We returned to the village only to find blackened circles where the rest of the huts used to stand. Everything—the trees, the gathering areas, and our homes were reduced to charred rubble. The blackened bodies of the remaining survivors, mostly women and children, were pierced with Comanche arrows. My father and I survived because we were gone."

Although it happened over three decades ago, Carlos described the events with fresh sorrow. I felt bad for having asked him to dredge up sad memories, but he continued the story.

"It started to rain again, and we had to leave the Lamorillos Valley. First, we rode to the new area we found, but the rains were heavy enough to flood it. We rode farther, for days, running out of food and losing our horses to animal attacks. Even though it was freezing, my father said we had to keep moving or else we'd die.

"We stumbled into this canyon and barely made it through to the other side before I collapsed in the high meadow. My father saw smoke rising from a chimney far below and started down the hill. A few men rushed from the barn and carried him into the bunkhouse. They barely heard him say 'my son' before passing out.

"Señor Luebber and one of his stable hands rode up Turtle Hill and found me. Your mother—Carmena's mother—nursed both of us back to health. The señor generously hired my father and let us sleep in the bunkhouse. It was like staying in a fancy hotel. My father said that we had to work hard for the señor because he saved our lives.

"Carmena's father always treated us like part of the family. The señor taught me impeccable English, and after my father died, he had me move into the main house. He started my training, preparing me to one day become the ranch foreman."

After telling of his childhood trauma, lightheartedness returned to his voice, and Carlos easily recounted other more upbeat stories from his youth. He'd nearly been bitten by a rattler when it crawled into his hat during his first overnight roundup, but it turned out to be dead, a practical joke the wranglers played as a form of initiation.

Another time, a bobcat spooked his horse and threw Carlos onto an apple cactus. When he was fifteen, no one was at the ranch except a wrangler with a broken arm. The wrangler had to talk Carlos through birthing a foal. Not one moment of Carlos's life was poorly spent. He had no regrets, other than unrequited love which he, thankfully, didn't mention.

Once we negotiated a small incline down and out of the canyon, the land opened to a lovely place teeming with the glow of spring. A relaxing lullaby of trickling water drained into a small creek at the base of the cliff. The horses had their fill of the spring water, and Dusty obediently pulled near the rock wall so I could have a drink. The cool liquid was naturally filtered, free of charge, and unflavored. Water never tasted so good.

Carlos squinted directly overhead then pointed to a gigantic shade tree far across the panoramic vista. "We'll stop there and have lunch before heading back. I think you'll appreciate the view of the valley when we get there."

We rode side by side over several grassy knolls, and my bottom started to rebel against the long ride. A little farther, I told myself, and I'd discover the way to Sadie's cottage. Maybe the old seer could offer a miraculous solution. The amulet vibrated on my chest, and I took it as a sign of being on the right path to getting back to my own time.

On the fifth or sixth verdant hillock, the giant oak tree stood out like a sentry commanding us to stop. It withstood time like my amulet, its branches reaching out in every direction.

"That's got to be the biggest oak I've ever seen."

"You don't recognize it?" He pulled on the reins, and Hammerhead immediately stopped. Carlos dismounted and helped me off Dusty, and the two horses grazed near some shrubs.

"I do know this place!" I looked up to the high limbs and at the lush surroundings. "There's a name for it."

"The Kissing Tree," Carlos said.

"So quaint. So 1800s. Did I name it that?"

"No," he said. "Javier kissed Angela here once, and it was a joke ever since. When he and Jesse pass by doing the quarterly fence repairs, Jesse gives the tree a wide berth. Says he's afraid Javier will go sweet on him."

"I can't even imagine Javier trying to put a lip lock on Jesse. Yee-uck!"

As promised, we sat on a ridge that provided a scenic vista of the rear portion of the Holiday Ranch property. And of course, there was Sadie's cottage, only a couple of miles out. Smoke drifted above the chimney.

"Isn't that the home you said belonged to that old lady?"

"Yes," Carlos replied, his voice sharp as cactus needles.

"Just asking. I need to get my bearings," I said as he laid out a quilt in the shade.

Luebber's Creek became a focal point on the east and yucca and agave dotted the range farther south. An underground stream fed the freshwater lake to the east, the same glistening lake I'd seen from afar when Carlos first pointed out where Sadie lived. The Sealsfield property was about two miles west. Maybe another twenty minutes, and I'd easily arrive at the cottage.

"It's beautiful!" When I turned to Carlos, he had already unpacked the food and spread it out on the blanket. "Why didn't you tell me you were setting up? I would've helped."

"I did." He smiled. "Twice."

"I'm sorry. I don't think I've ever seen so much earth in its natural state. It takes my breath away."

He stared at me. "I know how you feel. When I see something beautiful, I want to feast my eyes for as long as possible."

I shifted uncomfortably. "Let's eat."

The fresh roast beef sandwiches would've made Nicole become a meat eater. "So, we basically get back home from here the same way we came, right?"

He nodded as he chomped on his sandwich. "Right now, we're on Hahamonga Ridge. See those three humps?" He pointed to the tallest of the three points with craggy edges, a good distance away from us.

"Yeah."

"That's Three Hump Ridge. You head straight for the middle of those first two ridges to get home through Three Hump Canyon."

It was no more than a two-hour ride to Sadie's at a canter. My derriere could handle it.

We finished our sandwiches and chocolate cake. The one-hour stop turned into two as we discussed his goals, and it was no shock to find that every aspiration Carlos had was centered on the ranch. In the future, it might have been pitiful but in 1845, there was no better life than living comfortably at the place you called home with people you loved. Abundance had less to do with wealth than with a state of mind.

I shared stories of the future, focusing only on the positive—talking and moving pictures, The Beatles, man's first step on the moon, and Mother Teresa. I told him about medical advances and the capabilities of cell phones and computers and how we controlled our homes with them. I left him almost as breathless about the future as I was about all the open space.

Hypnotic buzzing from a nearby beehive soothed like a droning engine on a long car ride. My eyelids drooped, and I easily succumbed to a tranquil slumber. I woke with my body snuggled against Carlos, his back propped against the huge tree roots, his arms wrapped protectively around me.

I sat up, stretched my muscles, and yawned. "How long was I asleep?"

"About an hour."

"Did you sleep?"

"I was fantasizing," Carlos said. Sensuality oozed through his words.

I wished he'd stop doing that. It wouldn't do any good for either of us if I let temptation win me over. I pushed away from Carlos and straightened my clothes.

"Do we have an attorney in town?"

"Why?" he asked.

Saturating my voice in as much authority as possible, I answered, "Because."

He hesitated and narrowed his eyes. "Beauford Jones. You—Carmena—uses him for all our ranch business."

"I'd like to send someone into town soon to see when Jones is available. Whoever goes can also order the new stove."

"What do you want with Jones?"

"I may have gained back memories from Carmena, but I don't have her knowledge. Hey, since when do I have to ask your permission where ranch business is concerned?"

Carlos blushed, or maybe anger flushed the crimson into his cheeks. "Since you confessed you weren't Carmena."

I smirked. "And until you can prove otherwise, everyone on the ranch and in town will vouch for who I am."

"Fine. I'll arrange a meeting with Jones when we order the stove."

"Tomorrow," I said.

He stood abruptly and grabbed the plates and utensils off the blanket.

I packed up the food. "Look, Carlos. I see how frustrated you get when I ask so many questions. I want to spare you. Jones can give me basic but important information that you might take for granted that I already know."

He nodded without looking at me.

For now, Carlos didn't have to know about my intention to purchase stock.

I'd explain it. Eventually.

CHAPTER 14

Carlos rolled the blanket while I tucked the remaining food into the saddlebags. He took a swig of the lemonade. "It was nice to get some time off."

"You consider this time off?"

He nodded.

"Carlos, you need a vacation."

He swiped his hand in the air. "Why would I want to be any place else?" He tied the quilt to the back of his saddle. His head tilted slightly as he considered his words. "I'd rather discover the truth first hand than to live in regret for never having tried."

"That's pretty off the wall."

"Off the wall?" he questioned.

"Out of left field?"

Blank expression.

"A big change of subject?"

At that, he nodded agreement. "I believed it was the truth when you said you were from another time. You know more than Carmena. You say unfamiliar words and phrases that are...off the wall. And of course, there's the amulet. I never saw that amongst Carmena's things."

"Doesn't a girl generally keep those types of things in a drawer or jewelry box?"

"Carmena and I never had any secrets."

"I believe that. I see in her memories how honest you are with each other."

"Then let's be honest now, Mandy. You said you don't want to become involved because you don't share the same feelings for me as I do for you?"

"Yes."

"Are those Carmena's feelings or yours?"

I was shocked by his question, but it made sense. "Both of ours. I'm not totally certain what she feels, but for me, honestly, it's just lust. I know I'm eventually going to return home, and I don't want any hard feelings."

He touched my cheek, and his fingers splayed into my hair. He fisted a bundle of brunette curls in his hand. His words oozed out in a husky timbre. "What else matters when we both want each other?"

I shook my head. Carlos released my hair and threw his hands in the air.

"You'd go all soft on me," I said.

Now it was his turn to shake his head.

"Yes, Carlos. You'd read into it and hope for a commitment and try to convince me to stay, even if I found a way back. I just want to shag, but you want more."

"I'm shaggy, too!"

I laughed, but for Carlos, it wasn't a lighthearted moment.

His eyes smoldered. "Are you afraid to admit that we both have a mutual physical interest in each other?"

"No, I admit that."

"It seems as if we both want the same thing."

"Can you handle it, Carlos?" I dared him. "A one-shot deal?"

He nodded. "A one-shot deal. If those are our terms." He performed a head to toe inspection and gravitated closer. Electricity shot out of his body and parts of me quivered with the impact. He smiled like I had never seen him smile before, with a hunger that matched my own.

"Well?" Carlos asked.

"I'm debating on doing the right thing."

"How do you know what's the right thing to do?" he whispered into my ear.

"I suppose it just feels right," I whispered back.

"This is what feels right," he said and was on me like a wet suit.

He pushed my hair aside and kissed my neck, sending my mind reeling and vanquishing any feelings of apprehension. Carlos lifted me up and carried me to the top of a gargantuan tree root. We were face to face. Any doubts I had about being with him flew out the window as his firm chest pressed into mine, and I drew my hands up and down his muscled arms. His soft lips worked their way up my neck, to my ear and cheek, and toward my mouth. I closed my eyes and breathed him in, relishing his masculine aroma like a heady cologne.

One large hand tangled in my hair and the other groped for a place to settle. His lips honed in on mine. His tongue swam inside my mouth and evoked an immediate response.

We simultaneously pulled back, and I blurted out, "Ee-yew!"

Carlos was as confused as I was. "I feel like I just kissed...Dusty," he said.

"It could've been worse." I giggled and swiped my lips with my hankie.

"How?" he asked, as surprised as I was at the repulsive exchange.

"It could've felt like you kissed Dusty's rear end instead!" We both laughed. "What the hell happened?"

"We could try again," he said.

"Hell no! I'm no glutton for punishment."

"Thank goodness. I was only being polite."

We both wiped our mouths again, and I broke open the canteen of lemonade.

"Who would have guessed?" he said.

"Maybe, had it been in another lifetime." I handed him the canteen.

"I'm glad I'm alive now." He finished off the lemonade.

"But really, that was totally unexpected," I said, puzzled.

"It was like the magic just disappeared."

"Hmm, I think I know why. Carmena sees you as a broth-er, or uncle, or maybe as a father figure. Someone related."

"And I think the love I feel for you, for her, is like a little sister." He stroked my face with a finger. "A beautiful sister." He kissed my cheek.

"Let's not mention this to anyone."

"I wouldn't dream of it," he said.

I slugged him in the arm, and we saddled up.

Now that it was done, now that the attraction between us was reduced to a horse's ass, there was less exertion on my nerves during the ride home. As lovers, we crashed and burned, but as friends, our relationship soared to greater heights.

Without his romantic pursuit, Carlos and I could both move on. He was the biggest distraction next to Captain Sanders that kept me from wanting to return to my own time, and we surmounted the dilemma in the brief exchange.

Both horses breezed along the familiar trail toward Three Hump Canyon. They trotted through the rock walls without any direction from us. Carlos had mentioned the only danger riding through the pass was a landslide, but that there had never been a major one, so I felt unruffled at the thought of riding through on my own.

Before we started down the switchbacks of Turtle Hill, I put my hand on Carlos's arm. "You're a good friend, Carlos. Carmena's best friend." I had to lift completely off my saddle to reach him, and he let me kiss him on his jawline.

"As you are mine," he said.

He gently pressed his boots into Hammerhead's sides and Dusty trotted behind. We began the short leg back to the ranch, he with hope for a new future, and I with a renewed desire of returning home.

c∞o

By the time we made it to the ranch, the entire staff gathered to meet us, as if we'd been gone for days instead of hours. It was good to be back amidst the love embracing me, but my heart pinged as my mind momentarily recalled the details of my real home, not in California but in Arkansas, even though

I'd hadn't been there long. Even though I had no one there to greet me.

Maybe I'd get a dog. Or a horse.

Javier caught me when I hopped off Dusty and didn't let go until I was more balanced.

Jesse removed the saddlebags and gave us a quick accounting of the past few hours. "That heifer is doin' purdy good. Ain't a sign of a lump, but we done lost another a them chickens."

"Not even a feather to be had." Javier held onto Hammerhead's reins. "No sign of coyotes or any other tracks, either."

Carlos followed the men as they cooled the horses, and I lumbered up the stairs bull-legged to wash, looking forward to the outdoor dinner that Angela announced we were having.

The weather was perfect. Javier's mesquite barbequed ribs roasted over the large brick pit and a cool breeze spread the mouth-watering flavor all around the patio. Violet cooked the best-baked squash and fried potatoes, and of course, Angela's salsa, refried beans, and tortillas were the normal expected staples to complete the meal.

We dined around the pit, except for Carlos and Violet, who were engaged in a private conversation during most of the meal in the large gazebo with its own small fire burning between them. I happened to catch Angela gazing happily at them like a proud mother. Once I was over the allotted five-second jealousy streak for former lovers, I smiled as I witnessed my original plan in bloom.

After dinner, Carlos approached me in the kitchen. I took his plate and set it on the stack of dishes on the counter. "Let's skip inventory tonight," he suggested.

"No problem," I agreed.

Violet strolled into the kitchen and put on her apron. She pumped water into the metal sink.

Carlos stared at her then said to me, "I need to recheck the measurements for the stove."

"Of course, you do," I said, smothering a smile as I left him to his measuring.

For the first time in years, I went to bed and prayed. Anticipation of my visit with Sadie left my mind whirling and I asked that a stranger had the ability to provide the tiniest glimmer of insight, anything to help find a way to leave this place. I also prayed for the strength to leave despite my growing attachment to the people who lived on the ranch.

I tossed in bed most of the night and had to settle for only a few hours of sleep.

℘℘℘

A plate littered with crumbs sat on the counter behind Carlos. Violet's pumpkin cake and coffee was a great pre-breakfast snack for Angela and me, too. Carlos leaned against the counter, sated and in a good mood. Violet mixed pancake batter, and Angela kept an eye on a large skillet of bacon.

It was the perfect opportunity to suggest that Carlos take Violet into town. It was imperative I keep him away from the ranch, so I could visit Sadie. If Violet went with him, their errand might turn into a very leisurely trip, but Carlos surprised us all.

"No! It's out of the question!" He planted his hands firmly on the oak island. I was stunned by his insistence that Violet not accompany him, especially now that he had grown sweet on her.

"It only makes sense that the woman using the stove should be the one to order it," I said.

"Apparently you've forgotten about the threat of Lieutenant Franz."

The three of us women gasped in unison.

"You knew about Georg?" Violet asked. "How did you find out?"

His voice softened. "After the captain nearly killed him, he told me that Franz had never even beaten his wife, Violet, as badly."

Her chin dropped low.

"It's nothing to be ashamed of," I told her. "It wasn't your fault."

Angela put her arm around Violet. "You finally stood up to that...that *bendejo!*"

"The point is," Carlos said, "you've completely forgotten about the threat of the man. Jesse said Franz has been released while waiting a court-martial. Who knows where he's hiding out?"

"Are you afraid of him?" Angela challenged.

Carlos raised his voice, "Of course not! It's just that—" He looked at Violet. "I can't be taking care of business and acting like a guard dog at the same time."

"I assure you, Carlos, I won't get in the way if you want to get a shot at my ex-husband."

"No!" he said to Violet. "I won't permit you to go."

"Why not?" Angela asked. "Carmena can give her that little gun she keeps in her pocket when she leaves the ranch."

"And you heard her," I added. "Violet doesn't care if you take Franz out."

"Take him out where?" Violet asked.

"Uh, I mean, waste him." They still didn't get my meaning. "Kill the bastard."

The women nodded.

"It's settled," I said. "I'll give Violet my little gun, and the two of you can head into town after breakfast. Order the stove and let Beauford Jones know that I need to see him here at the ranch."

Carlos looked torn between spending some intimate time with Violet or seeing to her safety. He let us convince him that she'd be fine, especially with an early model Deringer in her pocket.

ℰↄℰↄ

Carlos waited for Violet out front by the tall fountain. I gave him my girl-sized single shot pistol and extra money for a new dress for Violet. He thanked me, but I didn't do it so she could pretty up for him. I needed him away from the ranch as long as possible.

The governess tumbled out the door fussing with her hair, and I saw a hint of color on her lips and cheeks. Carlos packed his handgun in his holster and settled a shotgun in the buckboard for solid insurance in case he ran into Franz or any of his followers.

Violet took his proffered hand, and he hoisted her up onto the seat. He placed my handgun in Violet's palm, and she slipped it into her pocket.

I ambled toward the doors and the crunch of gravel underfoot soothed me. I joined Angela on the front steps waving after the buckboard as it rolled through the shady drive. She leaned toward me.

"Does it bother you, Carmena? Carlos and Violet?"

"Not in the least. I was sort of hoping this would happen."

"I know you want him to have a companion, but what do you want?"

"It's going to take a lot more than a man to make me happy."

My remark distressed her. "How can you say that, *mijita*? You have the ranch and good people who care for you and each other. What more could you want than a good man?"

To take them all with me when I leave.

I voiced as much of the truth as possible. "I may need something that only time can give me."

She patted my shoulder and went inside, just in time for me to head out to Sadie's to find that missing something.

ℰↄℰↄ

I tucked Maizy's poem inside the deep pocket of my gauchos, and more than once, I felt for the amulet under my blouse.

Jesse helped me saddle Dusty. Once the tack was strapped on and tightened, I mounted up with the help of a small set of wooden stairs Jesse had built at Violet's request so the children could get up in a saddle for their formal riding lessons.

Dusty left the stables in a smooth trot, and I kept a loose hold on the reins, guiding her to the base of Turtle Hill. I leaned forward as she negotiated the rocky upward climb and my body lurched to and fro. It took nearly forty-five minutes to ride through the canyon at a slow clip with Carlos. I hoped to cut the time down by half with Dusty at a decent canter.

Around the first long bend, several large boulders cloistered to the left, rocks not piled there yesterday. If I mentioned the slide to Carlos, he'd want to know why I was riding alone in the canyon with conceivable dangers lurking at every turn. I'd ride more carefully through the stone corridor and let him discover the slide on his own.

The winds howled, and critters darted across the path. I would've been more freaked out if I hadn't heard the wind's eerie moaning on my previous ride. Buzzards sat on the cliff tops. "I'm still alive!" I called up to them. One flapped its wings before it settled down and sat patiently with the others while waiting for something to die.

Once out of the canyon, Dusty kept up a good pace across the grassy knolls, and I finally spotted the huge oak and the storybook house nestled beyond in a lightly forested area. Riding closer to the cottage, I spied flowers and an assortment of herbs growing in a fragrant garden. An arch intertwined with roses opened to a stone walkway leading up to the heavy front door. I saw a sliver of light through the pink shutters covering the windows, and smoke curled out the chimney.

I debated on where to dismount when an old woman opened the door. She was bent at the waist, with long flowing gray hair and a draping multi-colored skirt topped with a billowy purple blouse. A couple of colorful shawls swathed her shoulders and a scarf covered her head. She looked like a Hollywood gypsy, and leaned on a cane as gnarled as her hands, waving me in.

"Come," the old lady coaxed in a crackly whisper and shuffled back inside.

I tethered Dusty on the opposite side of the house. Carlos might go into cardiac arrest if he happened to see or hear about my horse in front of the one place he'd asked me never to go.

At the door, I heard the raspy voice call from inside, "Don't take all day about it!"

The door squeaked open to the pungent smell of a Hindu temple. Incense and candles burned everywhere. Garlands of herbs hung from the rafters, colorful crystals dotted shelves, and king-sized sparkling geodes stood majestically on the floor.

Sadie sat at a table, the top polished and warped as if the wooden slats were hundreds of years old. She pointed to the seat across from her. "Sit here, child." The timeworn chair creaked beneath me. She held out a knobby hand. "Let me see it."

"See what?" I asked.

"Come now. Let's not be coy." Not a muscle twitched in her outstretched hand, remarkable for her age. "Don't tell me you didn't bring it. You rode all this way and didn't bring it?"

"Exactly what was it you wanted me to bring?"

She peered across the table. Her eyes could bore through solid steel, and I faltered in my seat. "You're not a stupid woman but you have a hard time trusting. I have a feeling the hippo's going to be very good for you."

The last time the H-word was mentioned, I'd read it off the message from Maizy. I was struck mute and reached for the parchment paper in my vest pocket and placed it in Sadie's palm.

"That's better." She smiled, and her mood returned to that of a subdued little old lady.

I didn't think anything else she said could startle me until she held out her other hand.

"And now the amulet."

CHAPTER 15

Mesmerized by her uncanny knowledge, I pulled the chain from my blouse and lifted it over my head. I set the necklace into her open palm. The embossed curls on the charm gradually glowed brighter in a ghostly neon blue.

"Yes! Yes!" she sang happily, and after a few seconds the blue light dimmed out.

My throat finally opened. "Can you tell me what these things are for?"

"Why else would you be here?" She held up the charm. "This is Eve's Amulet. No one knows where it came from or how old it is. You've seen the pretty pictures?" Sadie stuck her hand in her pocket.

"Yes, but I needed a magnifying glass to—"

From a fold in her skirt, the woman pulled out a lens about four inches in diameter. It snapped into an iron frame that sat on top of the table and she placed the amulet beneath it. She whisked the silk scarf from her hair and twisted the long strands into a knob on top of her head. From another pocket she drew out two large tortoise shell combs and worked them back and forth into her scalp until they kept her hair confined in a knot of varying gray stripes. Already hunched, she had merely to lean forward a few inches before she looked down through the glass to the amulet.

"You've rearranged things. Scattered them out of order."

It felt like she'd accused me of a sin. "I've been trying to duplicate my actions when I first, uh, when I first, uhm…" I didn't know how to say it.

"When you first came here?" There was no shock or lunacy in those alert and insightful eyes, only the wisdom of a remarkably knowledgeable woman.

"Yes. I was fiddling with it before I zoned out."

"You went through the mist?"

I recalled the last image in my mind of Marco and Nicole, a dull cloud circling the edges of their bodies, frozen like statues, petrified at the site of me being vacuumed into a fog.

"Yes. I was surrounded by mist."

"Indecision. You didn't know what was in your heart. Do you know now?"

"Yes. I want to go home."

"No!" She slapped the table, and I jumped. "If that's all you wanted, you never would have gotten that inheritance or moved back to California!" Sadie smiled when I gaped. "Oh, yes. I know many things about you, Mandy. Ever wonder who left you that money?"

"It never occurred to me. I was told a distant relative had left it to me in his will."

"And you spent it all?"

I looked down at my hands and wrung them in my lap. "Most of it, yes."

"Foolish girl." She shook her head. "And now? Do you think you know how, and why, you should save a dollar?"

I nodded, dully reproached.

"So, tell me. What is the strongest desire of your heart? What do you yearn for with a thirst that no one else can quench?"

"I don't understand. What does that have to do with where I came from?"

"Everything!" she rasped as if she smoked one carton too many. "This amulet is for women who need to fulfill their secret passion, their most heartfelt wishes!" She touched the charm. "If you find out what it is you are seeking, that dream is fulfilled with this."

"How?"

"Who knows? But it does. Just like it worked for all the others who traveled through the fog and lived as their alter-ego."

"Their what?"

"Alter-ego. The one you need to learn from, like Carmena. The woman whose place you took. And not all travelers assume a new identity. Sometimes they just go as themselves."

"What happened to Carmena? Is she all right?"

Sadie waved her hands dismissively. "She's fine, she's fine. In another realm or maybe floating around in a dream state. Maybe in your body. Who knows? They're always perfectly safe, and when she comes back, you will return to your own life. It will be like neither one of you ever left."

At least that answered the question of Carmena's disappearance. Still, I had my doubts.

"How do you know this?"

"I know things," she whispered. "I am a guardian. Some of us protect the ancient secrets, and others make certain things go right. There are those of us who make certain the secrets are made known to those who need them. That's what I do. I take care of travelers."

"I don't understand, but I know that I shouldn't be here. In Texas, I mean."

"You think so?"

My nerves broke along the edges. It was frustrating not to get straight answers. Carlos came to mind. He'd cautioned me not to come.

"Bah. He knows. I told him," Sadie said, as though reading my thoughts.

"Carlos? He knows I'm here?" I jerked in my seat and waited for him to tear through the front door.

"He knows *why* you're here," she corrected. "Why do you think he's so mad at me? He told you never to come here, did he not?"

She threw curves at me left and right, and I felt I had no choice but to be completely honest. "Yes, but he never really told me why he didn't want me here."

"Men. They never change over the ages." She stood up and scuffled to the hearth. She took a ladle of wheat colored liquid from a bubbling caldron and poured it into an old ceramic mug. A little sloshed over the rim as she shuffled back to the table. "Drink this," she insisted, and set the cup before me.

"Is it a magic potion? Will it send me back?"

"Don't be silly. It's tea to calm your nerves."

I sniffed and, sure enough, I recognized the bouquet of chamomile and valerian. The beverage soothed me.

"That's better," she crooned. Sadie poured some of the steaming liquid into a white restaurant mug, and once she'd replaced the iron kettle over the fireplace, she sat back down.

"I told him he couldn't have Carmena."

"When did you tell him this?"

"A month before you arrived. He came to me to throw the cards."

"He came to see you? For a psychic reading? Carlos?" My voice rose an octave with each question.

Sadie squinted at me. "Did you lose your hearing when you came here?"

I shook my head. It was safer not to speak.

"I told him Carmena would leave, and a new woman would take her place from a different time."

"He knew I was coming?"

Tea dribbled out of my mouth. I dug frantically for the hankie in my sleeve and wiped my chin. At least I understood why Carlos so readily accepted my story. Sadie forewarned him that I was coming. He must have accused her of insanity to keep me from discovering the truth.

"Land sakes!" She rolled her eyes. "You sound like a broken record. Of course, he knew! Carlos thirsted for Carmena so badly, but it wasn't meant to be. I told him he was too old for her. Needed a woman to take care of him, not the other way around. Carmena isn't a nurturer."

"But will the real Carmena have a chance to learn how to be a nurturer? Where is she? What happened to her?" I couldn't help asking again.

She addressed me as if I were in kindergarten, speaking very slowly. "You're here—" She stabbed the table with her bony finger. "—and she's out there." Sadie looked upward, a brainless grin on her face, and flapped her hands like a bird before looking serious again.

"I'm trapped in Carmena's body, but why was I wearing my own clothes when I arrived? Shouldn't I have been in Carmena's clothes when I got here? I don't even have my lion tattoo anymore!"

Sadie shook her head and sighed. "I can't explain all the problems with time travel. Usually, everyone arrives in clothing of the era from the past, and it's not often a traveler occupies the body of another. But for whatever reason, you were meant to know what Carmena knows and to have your own possessions when you arrived. Perhaps they'll be needed later."

Sadie's voice morphed back into a strict school marm. "Carmena is not my responsibility. I have no idea what's going on with her. You're my traveler. Carmena belongs to someone else and you are each experiencing something different because you each have different lessons to learn to prepare you for something greater in the future." She held up her hands showing nothing to hide. "Don't ask me what or when. That is not mine to tell even if I knew. Just know that what goes on here with you has nothing to do with her. What I do know is that she will come back here when you leave. She'll know everything you've done when she returns, and you'll know everything about your own life if she was sent to yours and made any changes."

"Will I remember this place? The people?"

She shrugged, unconcerned.

"This is so incredible, knowing that I'm taking the place of a woman in the Old West to learn some kind of lesson. It's like destiny or something."

"Don't be so dramatic. Drink your tea." She didn't move or speak until I took a sip. Then she opened the parchment paper. "You see the first four lines?"

I didn't need to look at the note to know what she was referring to. "Yes. The poem."

"Those never change." She tapped the paper. "Never." She spoke the words out loud, not once glancing at the text. "'Add the crone's advice at the end of this rhyme.' That's me." She pointed at herself. "I'm the crone." Her head bobbed slightly, proudly confirming her part, and she continued reciting the poem. "'Then this note is passed on to the next in line.' I don't do that part. You do," she said. "''Tis a gift you will find but a curse it can be.' You get that now, don't you?"

"More than ever," I replied.

She continued. "'If not used with wisdom, you'll dread eternity.' The meter's off, but it still makes sense."

"I understand the wisdom part." I picked up the necklace. "It's not knowing how to use it that I'm dreading."

"Look," she said and took the amulet into her hands. Sadie held the charm by the cogs on either end. The veins on the back of her hands protruded as she pulled hard, and both end pieces slipped out to either side of the amulet on a thin metal wire. She twisted the end pieces like tiny hexagonal wheels, back and forth then pushed them back into place. "You forgot to wind it."

"But I didn't know how!"

"Well, now you do," she said matter-of-factly. "You take that back now. Go on, put it 'round your neck where it's safe."

I slipped the chain over my head.

"When you're ready to leave, you wind it up like I showed you. Then you line up the pictures."

"But I already tried that. They should have all been aligned when I put the picture of Holiday Ranch into place."

"You didn't wind it up like I showed you. Obstinate girl," she admonished. "And they only line up when you're ready to leave."

Finally, a way home. Tears declared mutiny, obscuring my vision.

Sadie saw the watery pools at the rim of my lower lashes. "Now, don't go and get all sappy on me. We aren't even finished."

"We're not?" I dried my eyes.

"Girl, have you gone daft on me? You have to add the crone's advice. Didn't you read this?" She handed Maizy's note back to me.

"I forgot."

"Don't you forget," she lectured with a crooked finger. "This is the part where you'll dread eternity if you don't write this down."

I patted my vest pockets. "Do you have a pen?"

Sadie scowled. "Not now!" She stabbed her finger onto the parchment and whispered, "You write this below the poem when you go back and not before. If you forget, you'll be sent somewhere else and never return home."

"But why?"

"I don't know. That's just the deal. If you mess it up for everyone to follow, then bam!" She slid her palms robustly against one another. "You get shipped off. That's how it works. I didn't make it up." Sadie hunched forward, and her eyes narrowed. "Remember. No matter what happens here, in this time, you must go back. The consequences will be worse than you could imagine if you don't return to your own time. And they won't just affect you, but many others in the past and future if you decide to stay. And for heaven sakes, don't lose the amulet. You'll never get back to your own time if you do."

"Do you know about my time?"

"You used to live in the perfect place until you went to live with that weak-kneed cousin of yours," she said.

"Nicole? She's great!"

"Bah! No backbone. Always letting that boyfriend tell her what to do. Women have had a hard time trusting their own thoughts. They forgot how to listen to the voice within. Too many distractions," she said. "Open your eyes to what's happening around you. People spend all day with TV, video games, internet, but not with other people." She leaned in my direction, and her eyes pierced my soul. "Technology is amazing but as it strengthens, the mind and spirit of humanity weakens. We forget how to be kind to one another."

She grabbed several dice from a bowl and tossed them onto the table. Instead of black dots on the uneven cubes, carved symbols resembling mathematical equations were etched on each side. Sadie spoke as her yellowed fingernail touched one die, then the next. "Live in the mountains. You must get land with its own water source and a greenhouse or two," she ordered. "Start planting fruit trees and vegetable gardens. Work through the floods and fires and earthquakes and hurricanes—they'll all continue until mother nature can help undo what man has done to her."

"Oh, man." I held my head and my temples, then took a swig of tea to calm my nerves. The drink was too thick and stuck like a lump in my throat. Sadie looked at me expectantly and created a pocket of silence for my benefit. Strangely, I wanted to placate her.

My voice finally returned to me. "I can't do all that by myself. I'm only one woman, uneducated and insignificant."

"You will always be an uneducated, insignificant woman until you uncover the truth about yourself. When you do, you will affect the world."

I was silent, blasted between the eyes by Sadie's comment and the power of my own potential.

"People must return to basics. Sew a dress. Build something. Learn how to heal yourselves naturally with what Mother Earth provides. And stop using plastic!" She sipped her tea, and her voice quieted. "Love what life has to offer. Show love to the planet." She sighed. "Just love. That's the secret to surviving. But who listens to an old lady with bent fingers, huh?"

She eyed me past her mug as she took a healthy swig. If it was for calming nerves, she needed to chug it down.

I wanted Sadie's approval but didn't think I'd get it. Still, I tried to tell her what I thought she wanted to hear. "I understand that no one wants to be accountable anymore. We don't have honor in the future. It's all about what our individual needs are and not the common good."

"Exactly!" She pounded the table with her bumpy fist, and I flinched. "Take that knowledge back with you, child. See how you can make a difference in the world, regardless of what era you're from. That's ultimately why you have come here."

"What do you mean?"

She sighed again. "That's enough for now." She pushed herself up from the table on arthritic hands and chanted under her breath, as if reciting an incantation. Sadie shuffled to cluttered shelves displaying dozens of bowls of different sizes and textures. When I thought she was going to choose one, she changed her mind and reached for another.

A bowl no bigger than half of a large orange caught her eye. Rather artistic, it seemed made of red leather and curlicues of black wire decorated the outside. She held it with two hands, as if made of glass, and set it on the table. She removed a piece of paper from the bowl without looking at its contents and handed it to me.

"Read it and commit it to memory," Sadie instructed.

In writing identical to the verse scripted at the bottom of Maizy's parchment paper, I read, "Kick up your heels and take charge!" It made as much sense as a guy with a pink hat and a purple hippo. That reminded me. "Why did you say that the hippo would be good for me?"

"Because it will be."

"But—"

"Carlos was right. You ask too many questions. You ask but don't seek. You speak but don't do. Stop wasting time, girl!" She held out her hand for the tiny scrap of paper, and I handed it over. "Now, what did it say?"

"'Kick up your heels and take charge!'" I recited.

"Good." She stood up, signaling the end of my visit. "Now next time, when you know in your heart that you should leave, don't forget to wind it!"

"I won't," I reassured her. "But how will I know it's time?"

Sadie patted my hand like a child who learned a valuable lesson. "You'll know."

I stood up, and she escorted me to the door. From that angle, I spied her coffee mug on the table. A multi-hued peace sign had been printed on the side with a cartoon image of a chubby hand holding up two fingers in a V.

I pointed at it. "Your cup—"

"Now, you be careful riding back. Watch out for that pile of rocks."

She spooked me good that time, and I forgot all about the mug.

"How did you know about the rocks?"

"Don't get all loopy on me and make a fuss that I'm knowing. I know. You know. All women got the know but most don't listen to it." She jabbed at my solar plexus with her pointy finger and spoke as sharply. "You feel it right there. That's why they call it gut instinct. The intuition, the inner voice. Call it what you want. You have to learn to listen and follow it."

Rubbing the tender spot on my chest, I asked, "But once I add the new line, who do I give the note to?"

"I told you." She kept moving toward the door. "Listen to that gut instinct of yours. It will tell you everything you need to know."

There were more questions I had yet to ask but she shoved me along, and her hand felt like a ball of wood as she pushed into my back.

"Should I set things right at the ranch before I leave?"

"That's what you're supposed to do! You won't be leaving until your work is done."

I tried to weasel another question in. "Why is my necklace called 'Eve's Amulet?'" I touched the lump under my blouse.

"Because that's what it's called. After all, it's all about her. About You. Me. It's about women who are going to save the world from itself. They never think they have it in them, but they do."

I was at the door's threshold and felt like a skydiver about to be kicked out of a plane. I held onto the doorframe and asked, "Why must I stay until my work is done?"

"For the love of God! Remember that verse you read?"

I recited, "Kick up your heels and take charge!"

"And keep an eye on those rocks," she reminded.

Her tiny front step barely left enough room for one person to stand. "Thank you, Sadie."

"What'd you call me?" she asked.

"Sadie. That's your name, right?"

She snorted and shut the door.

Flabbergasted, I stared at the wooden barrier. The woman had just kicked me out of her house.

CHAPTER 16

Dusty whinnied and pulled her reins loose as I scrambled onto the saddle from a tree stump. A gentle nudge sent her into an anxious gallop. Fresh air filled my lungs, and I chanted the puzzling "kick up your heels" line repeatedly, although I didn't have a single clue as to who would be the recipient of the poem or how to pass it along.

My tension seeped into the wind as Dusty tore across the rolling hills. My fear dissolved, and my skin tingled under the power that churned inside, filling me like a fleshy balloon that wanted to burst open. It was the first time I'd welcomed the future with open arms, even though I didn't know what to expect.

Dusty reached the cavernous walls of the canyon and I slowed her to a trot. Plenty of light poured in with the sun blazing directly overhead, close to noon. Hooves clip-clopped, the hollow sound as audible as the questions forming in my head that I should've asked Sadie while I had the chance.

Why did she lecture me on the condition of the world and on our pathetic collective state of mind in the future? Were the things she said about floods and government control stemming from her own issues of paranoia, or was there some kind of precognitive truth about it?

Sadie made it clear that I had to stay in this time until my work was finished. Did she mean making sure Violet and Carlos hooked up? Maybe she was referring to the successful creation of a stock portfolio for my employees. Perhaps I'd sneak in another visit before I left.

I had a lot to ponder and had almost forgotten Sadie's warning as my horse neared the pile of fallen stones. "Whoa," I called to Dusty, and she stopped directly in front of the rocks. They were spread wider and deeper than when I'd first rode past.

I heard a noise and spied dime-sized pebbles tumbling to the ground. Looking up, I saw them trickling down the canyon walls from the high cliff tops. A mournful wail, creepier than any of the noises I'd heard on the ride over, echoed between the stone walls, and I froze in the saddle.

Something was caught under the rocks.

More pebbles fell. I wanted to leave, but that gut feeling Sadie told me to listen to yelled at me, and I had to make an honest attempt to liberate the injured animal. It sounded again, a muffled growl. I sprang off Dusty and immediately kicked at rocks, latching onto the bigger ones and schlepping them away from the pile.

A pebble hit the top of my head. "Ouch!" More sprinkled down. I furiously dug my way into the pile and was unnerved when I touched a limb. A human hand. Large, hairy, warm, and securely attached to its owner. More pebbles rained down.

I ran back to my saddle and scooped the lariat from my pack, knotting it onto the man's wrist well enough to earn a scouting badge. He moaned again. Carmena's memories flooded into my mine and I knew exactly what to do and how to do it. I hurtled onto Dusty and wrapped the rope several times in a circle around the horn, then held on for dear life. My rear pressed into the saddle and Dusty, trained to obey the slightest body movements, slowly backed up as larger rocks crashed down.

"C'mon, Dusty!" I shouted and pressed my thighs harder into her flanks.

She stepped up the pace, and I prayed the man's shoulder remained attached. We extracted him from the granite prison just as a massive rock tumbled onto the spot where his head lay only seconds before. He groaned louder, but I continued to drag him past the bend, leaving a wide gap between us and the slide.

A thunderous roar assaulted my ears, and I jumped to the ground. I tore my vest off and tossed it on Dusty's head as small stones pelted my back. Then I dived on top of the man and shielded his body as the earth shook. A dirt cloud rounded the corner and the spray of dust forced me to shut my eyes. Dusty neighed, but soon silence settled along with the haze. A hard cough cleared the dust from my lungs.

Neither Carmena nor I was skilled enough in nursing as no hints of first aid came to the forefront of my thoughts. I at least ascertained that the man was alive by the slight movement of his chest. The moustached Mexican was dressed in grimy but well-sewn clothing, covered in fresh cuts, especially on his face and hands. Bruises colored his exposed skin, and dried blood clotted on his brow and stained one of his pant legs at the knee. Sticks poked out of his shirt pocket.

It was less than a quarter mile to the canyon opening. I decided to ride home to seek out help from my employees. "¡*Voy a consequir ayuda!*" I said. In case my Spanish was off and he understood English, I repeated, "I'll be back with help!" Hopefully the injured man was conscious enough to hear me.

I pulled my vest off Dusty and untied the lariat, shoving both into the saddlebag and sprung atop my horse. That was twice I'd mounted up like a pro without giving it any thought.

"Yaw!" I yelled, and Dusty took off like a rocket. We galloped at full speed. Maybe I could ride as well when I returned to my home in the future.

Long, heart-hammering minutes elapsed during my ride through and out of the canyon. From atop the monstrous hill, I saw Carlos steering the wagon from the main road up the gravel drive, Violet closer to his side than when they'd left. They couldn't hear me from the top of the hill and wouldn't have reason to look up when their eyes were most likely on each other. I rode down the switchbacks as fast as I dared, keeping my horse safe from any leg injuries. Just as Dusty touched the baseline of the hill, Carlos parked the wagon next to the gate nearest the kitchen.

"Carlos!" I shouted, nearly hyperventilating as Dusty galloped toward the buckboard. Carlos looked my way and his eyes flared open when he looked at my face contorted into a mask of panic.

"Carmena! What's wrong?" he shouted.

Violet threw her hands over her mouth. Carlos jumped out of the wagon and ran toward me. Dusty skidded to a stop inches in front of him.

"There's a man in the canyon!"

He shot off a barrage of questions. "Are you hurt? Is it a soldier? What were you doing riding in the canyon alone? Where the hell is Jesse? Javier?" His head jerked in every direction, frantically searching about for the ranch hands.

"Would you listen to me, dammit? There's an injured man in the canyon! He was caught in a rockslide."

"How bad is he hurt?"

"I can't tell, but he's still alive."

"I'll take the wagon up." He raised his hands to me, and I tumbled off the saddle and fell into his chest, nothing like the erotic episode during my first dismount off his horse in the stables.

"Find one of the men. I'll need help lifting the injured man," he said to me. "Tell Angela to get the bunkhouse ready. And have Martino cool Dusty off," he called to Violet as he sprang into the saddle. As she ran inside to relay the messages, he checked his pistol and rode away at a gallop.

I started for the back door off the kitchen, and Angela nearly collided with me. She pulled on my arm, and I followed her back across the patio.

"We'll boil water in the bunkhouse. First aid supplies are there, too, in the supply closet." She whipped out instructions in perfect English with her Spanish accent. "Violet, you stay with the children. When you see Jesse or Javier, tell one of them to watch for strangers, and send the other up to the canyon to help Carlos. Carmena, come with me."

I barely kept up with the woman, at least a dozen years my senior. In the bunkhouse, she leaned against the side of a large cabinet and shoved it to the left, uncovering a slightly discernible panel in the wall. She slid the board aside, and it opened to what had to be the secret room Carlos told me about. Once we were inside, she moved the dresser and panel back into place.

"Why will Carlos bring the man here and not to the main house?" I asked.

"You don't have all of your memory?"

I shook my head.

Angela prepared the bed as she answered. "We never know who we take in or why." She indicated the hearth with a tilt of her head. "Start a fire, then put water to boil." She covered the mattress with clean sheets and dragged a dark chest from underneath the bed. Precut strips of bed linen were rolled in various lengths for bandages. "He was in a landslide?"

"Yes." I wiped sweat from my forehead. "One of his legs was bleeding at the knee, and he had a nasty cut above his eye."

She removed the widest rolls from the box, as well as brown bottles filled with liquid and a brand -new bottle of fine whiskey. Laudanum and antiseptic.

We waited a while until we heard the creaky wagon stop outside the bunkhouse. Angela pulled back a door, camouflaged like the rest of the wall. Carlos and Jesse carried in the patient and plopped him on the bed. He had stringy long hair and a rough beard covered his jaw line. Angela barely glanced at the injured man, unaffected by the blood and grime covering his body.

"Jesse, please tell Javier I'd like him to keep watch while you see if there are any other unwelcome visitors about the property," Carlos said.

"Shore thing, Carlos." He hurried out the back door and pulled it shut behind him.

Angela tossed a clean rag at me. "Dip this in the hot water and wring it out." She knelt beside the bed, and I brought the cloth to her as Carlos rolled the man onto his back.

Angela looked like she'd been tazed at full power, instantly recognizing the man. She fell onto her bottom, her eyes plastered on his face as if he were a rattlesnake ready to strike.

"¡*Madre de Diós!*" she murmured.

"What is it?" Carlos asked. "Do you know him?" Angela's head bobbed. "Who is he?"

For a moment, I didn't think she would speak.

"Who is it?" Carlos persisted.

Angela swallowed hard, and her legs wobbled as Carlos helped her up. She pointed at the man. "It's him. It's Santa Anna."

"Santa Anna?" I asked. "The ousted Centralist Mexican dictator Santa Anna?"

"Yes. The same," Carlos snarled.

"Holy crap!" I said. "We have to get him out of here!"

"He's hurt bad. He needs a doctor!" Angela said.

"Do you realize what could happen if he's caught here?" Carlos asked. I suspected, but he spelled it out. "Not only is this man wanted dead by the Mexican government, but the United States hasn't forgotten that he declared war on Texas!" Distress looked foreign on Carlos's attractive face.

"I know that! I'm no stupid!" Angela yelled at him, her English deteriorating again. The injured man moaned. Worry filled her eyes. "He's very bad hurt."

"Harboring fugitives is one thing, but this—" Carlos motioned to the exiled politico. "—this is dangerous for us all!"

Angela's obvious torment told me that there was more at stake than she let on. "Why is it so important that we hide Santa Anna here?" I asked.

Tears spilled over and she wrapped her hands like a belt across her thick waist. Carlos grabbed a chair and placed it behind her. "*Sientate*," he ordered.

He reasoned with Angela while I dipped a rag into the hot water and wrung out the excess. Dry blood dotted the man's face, and he winced as I wiped his wounds.

"We must help him," Angela cried.

"Your days of political involvement are over," Carlos harshly reminded her. "You said so yourself."

"But this no is politics," she cried.

Carlos's words dripped sarcasm. "Oh, forgive me. The former president of Mexico was exiled to Cuba but is in Texas near the time of its annexation, the Mexicans want to reclaim the state and there is talk of a plot to overthrow Herrera. And you don't call that political?"

He stomped to the bed and tore a stick out of Santa Anna's pocket. He held it up as if he'd found a murder weapon. "And he stole our chickens!" Carlos threw the bone across the room. Angela cried softly and mumbled under her breath. "I can't hear you," he said. Disgust saturated his voice. "Speak up!"

It was a whisper but we both heard her, only Carlos refused to believe it. "What did you say?" he asked, astonished.

Angela screamed, and there was no denying what she swore at him. Carlos and I gaped at each other as the woman covered her shame-filled face with her hands.

Her back shook and, between heavy sobs she softly repeated, "He is my father!"

👁️‍🗨️

The injured man, a historical figure in my time, wheezed every so often between labored breaths in a painful sleep. Santa Anna may have been a greedy dictator, but he didn't mind a democratic society and approved of the numerous financial gains a democracy could offer—as long as he was in charge.

From public TV I also learned that he renounced the presidency from Mexico more times than he'd been exiled. In November of 1844, he attempted a coup against Paredes y Arrillaga, but it was a failed undertaking as Santa Anna's army deserted him. After that, he lost a great deal of credibility with citizens and politicos alike. His life was spared, but he was exiled to Cuba.

Carlos jarred me out of my recollections and dragged my attention into his bickering match with Angela. If he were a dog, his teeth would have been bared. "And have you forgotten who her father-in-law is, Carmena?"

"¡*Cabron*! Angela snarled. "We take action against the corrupt government when no one else bother. We no allow family to influence our duty to our people!"

"Who is Javier's father?" I asked anyone who'd answer.

The proud woman pointed her nose upward. "Joaquin Herrera."

"The current president of Mexico?" I asked, tottering in disbelief. From watching television, I'd learned that Jose Joaquin Herrera was an archenemy of Antonio de Santa Anna.

"The one and only," Carlos said. "Both Angela and Javier are bastard children of infamous politicos."

The amulet hummed and turned warm. "Does this have anything to do with the guns we were selling?"

Carlos filled me in. "Javier set it up. Herrera favored a dictatorship and when he learned his own son supported a democracy, he put a price on Javier's head. We needed money for the ranch to replace what the soldiers were taking of our stock, so Javier cut a deal with the Federalis who, at that time, also wanted Herrera out of office."

"This is very political," I said to Angela.

Santa Anna moaned, and Angela tended to his wounds.

Carlos lifted his chin toward the man. "Santa Anna has never been able to command the same respect of his people since he bought his own freedom when he signed the *Treaties of Velasco* that gave Texas to the United States. The latest Mexican party took him out of office before the treaty was even enacted." He wrinkled his nose at the dictator. "We should kill him now and be done with it."

I pulled Carlos to the door and whispered, "Don't forget, next year begins the Mexican-American war. It'll last for three years."

"What happened?" He shook his head and rephrased. "What will happen?"

"Herrera won't last long in office. He'll be exiled soon. His popularity will plummet when he decides not to try to win back Texas."

"What does that have to do with Santa Anna?"

"Santa Anna was, I mean, will be reinstated into office but then Paredes y Arrillaga will take over," I said. "He'll be responsible for starting the war, and Santa Anna will fight in it. The United States will win and not only claim ownership of

Texas, but Mexico will surrender a great deal of land, which will eventually become the southwest portion of the United States, all the way to the west coast."

Carlos's eyes shimmered. "And then the Republic will be free of the threat of Mexican control!"

"Eventually. Not long after the surrender, Santa Anna will resign and be forced out of the country again."

"If that's all true then it doesn't matter if Santa Anna survives or not."

"Except there's a minor flaw with that line of thinking." We watched as Angela checked her father for broken bones. I kept my voice down. "If Santa Anna doesn't go back, who's to say that his replacement doesn't win the war? I don't know what that will do to the rest of American history."

Carlos understood the implications of what I said. "I prefer living here than amidst the savagery of Mexico the way it is now."

"Mexico is barely stable in my time. It's been corrupted by drug cartels and a lack of control at every level of government and law enforcement."

Carlos rubbed his chin and walked over to the bed. He knelt down on one knee next to Angela. "You can tend to your father, but the moment he's able to ride, he'll be sent home."

"You can no make him go back, Carlos," she argued. "He's a wanted man! And he has the ribs broken."

Carlos turned my way and I shrugged. To Angela, he said, "I believe Santa Anna will leave on his own volition. Whether he decides to go back to Mexico or return to Cuba, we'll let him stay until he can ride, all right?"

She nodded.

Carlos lifted Santa Anna's back off the mattress and Angela removed his shirt. She wrapped long strips of fabric around his chest, repeating the process until the ribs were properly bandaged. Carlos removed the ex-dictator's pants and Angela gasped at the sight of what was left of her father's leg, lost in a battle seven years earlier. The stump was bloody and pulpy.

Carlos lifted the wood and cork prosthetic like a soiled diaper dangling by worn strips of leather. "I'll have Jesse clean this up. We can reattach it later."

The grimy fake leg joined the dirty pile of clothes on the floor, along with Santa Anna's six-shooter. Angela cleaned the gouge on his temple and several small wounds on his eyelids, then wrapped strips of fabric around his head and eyes to protect the cuts from infection. She fed her semi-conscious father some laudanum, and in no time the sounds of pain receded into quiet snoring.

"I go get my shawl. I'll be right back," Angela said and scurried out the door adjoining the bunkhouse.

I rubbed my arms and diverted my thoughts from the unlikely figure on the bed. "What happened in town today?"

Carlos kept an eye on Santa Anna. "Mr. Jones agreed to ride out the day after tomorrow, and I ordered the stove. You shouldn't have let Violet pick it out. She got the biggest and most expensive one." He shook his head. "It has six burners and two ovens. Mr. Fredericks said it was the kind they use in restaurants. I told her you'd probably want to cancel the order."

"A commercial stove. Good thinking!"

"¡Ay, Diós!" Carlos rolled his eyes. "I might add it's costing a fortune to ship. Almost twenty dollars, not to mention how much wood it's going to burn just to cook a meal. And it will take over six weeks to get here."

"It'll be worth every penny," I said.

"Speaking of every penny, there's something I want to show you." He double-checked that Santa Anna was strung out on laudanum before kicking aside a small carpet and lifting two false planks to reveal a safe in the floor. He twisted a large dial back and forth until the metal door popped open. "This is where you keep all your surplus savings." It was an impressive pile.

"I'll need most of it for my visit with Jones."

"This is all the money we have, and it has taken quite a long time to save it."

"Carlos, right now only two things matter to me. My amulet—you know how my life depends on it—and the lives of those who live on this ranch. So please, don't assume that I'll mismanage this money."

"Don't think I don't trust you. I simply question this particular decision, especially because you haven't even told me what it is."

We locked eyes and to his dismay, his concern went unheeded. I had him remove an obscene amount of currency, practically all of it, from the hiding place. He wrapped it in one of the bandages and handed me the makeshift package.

We replaced the floorboards. Carlos opened a small, hidden cupboard housing gears and pulleys. He held a knob on a metal wheel and cranked open two small, wooden framed glassless windows in the ceiling, a crude western version of a skylight for ventilation.

Angela returned and scarcely noticed our presence. She checked her father's breathing and felt his forehead with her palm before she settled into the chair next to the bed.

Then we left Angela to her notorious patient.

CHAPTER 17

Carlos slid the panel aside and fitted the cabinet neatly into place. No stranger could tell there was a door hidden behind the furniture leading to the secret room.

"We'll start taking shifts to watch for intruders but will have to hire more hands to pick up our chores for a time."

"We need more hands, regardless. There's plenty of room to board more men." We walked to the main house, and my mind filled with pictures of invasion by one of two governments from either side of the border.

"How will we replenish our assets if your plan fails?" Carlos asked.

"I don't believe that will be an issue. I won't go through with anything until I check out a few details with Jones."

The money fit neatly inside a large leather satchel, and we stashed it inside a hidden cupboard behind volumes of Shakespeare in the library. Carlos and I parted ways at the stairwell. I started for the kitchen, and he headed to his room.

"Carlos?"

He stopped at the landing.

"You and the men might start considering what you'd be doing with more time on your hands. If my idea works, you'll all become persons of leisure when I'm gone."

His expression held doubt and confusion. "What would the men and I do with so much time on our hands?"

"Why don't you start building your own homes? Here, at Holiday Ranch. There's plenty of land."

"Why would I want to live in another home?"

"Privacy?" I asked.

"You don't know everything I do," Carlos said.

I grinned. "No, but I've seen how many times you've measured for the new stove." He didn't reply. "Silence speaks louder than words, Romeo." That got a smile.

"Tomorrow we can send Jesse into town and see if those two fellows are back from Dobson's round up," Carlos said. "We can use them to free up our time for guard duty."

"Sounds good. If you need me, I'll be in the kitchen."

Discovering Santa Anna under a pile of rocks, compounded by my housekeeper and her husband's political connections, left me emotionally exhausted. A cup of Violet's tea would set things right, and then I'd eat a hearty snack.

Before I could take more than two steps, Carlos called from the stairs, "Carmena?"

I stopped mid-stride in the foyer. "What is it?"

He stepped into view. "What were you doing riding alone in the canyon?"

"Taking Dusty for a ride." So I left out some details. It wasn't like I was lying.

He stared at me a moment and said, "I see."

"Whatever." I resumed my walk to the kitchen.

Carlos called after me again. "What were you doing before you were in the canyon?"

I smiled at him, shook my head, and said, "*Ay, Diós.*"

೧୭೧୭

The next day was uneventful, considering that an exiled dictator was recovering on our property. Our patient slept well and remained in a laudanum-induced coma while his daughter kept vigil. Without Angela to relieve Violet of the extra work, everyone pitched in to help.

I delivered Angela's dinner to get a progress report and watched her polish off her food like a starving animal, inhaling without tasting. The only break she took was to use the outhouse when one of us brought her meals. The woman insisted on watching her father and since it was late when I offered to watch him, I was too tired to argue.

"How's he doing?"

"He's been asleep all day," she yawned.

"Let us know if you need anything," I said half-heartedly.

"I will," she assured me.

I left the bunkhouse and found Carlos taking a glass of milk and pumpkin cake up to his room.

"Carlos, I'll do guard duty after my visit with Beauford Jones tomorrow."

At the landing he nodded, his mouth full of dessert.

I spent a few hours in the library after the house lights went out with the accounting records at my desk and made note of every single asset on Holiday Ranch to prepare for the impending visit with my attorney. My fingers splayed over my chest. The amulet was there, quiet and waiting to be wound up.

Sleep took a while to come around and when it did, I slept long and hard. Child labor laws notwithstanding, I had another reason to hire more field hands. I was physically depleted by the extra chores I was unaccustomed to doing.

☙❧❦

Violet had a bath prepared when I woke up the next morning. I took one look at the steam rising up from the tub and said, "It's good to be a land owner."

This day had all the ingredients to be fabulous. The inner Mandy wanted to wield power like a man flexing muscles. I was starting to run an efficient ranch and had made some really good decisions. Despite the initial impression of my dainty skirt and blouse and turning heads at breakfast, I was ready to create a macho financial package with the attorney.

It was Martino's turn to pray, and he asked for blessings on the souls of the chickens that disappeared.

After the meal, I confidently retired to the library. Figures were rechecked that I planned to present to Jones, then I pulled the amulet out of hiding. I stroked the edges. The one thing Sadie said that made the biggest impression was to trust my gut instinct. It didn't feel like the right time to wind the jewelry. I quit fiddling with the charm and tucked it under my clothes.

While waiting for Jones to arrive, too much time on my hands played "what-if" scenarios in my head. What if my investment plan didn't pan out? What if something happened to Carlos—who would take over the ranch? What if I married the captain? What if I ignored Sadie's warning—would it be all that bad if I stayed?

Carlos walked into the library with Violet, and she announced the attorney's arrival. I asked her to show him to the parlor and offer him a buffet of finger sandwiches, desserts, and lemonade while I finished double-checking figures for our meeting. Carlos stood guard at the door.

"Carlos, would you please bring Jones in now?" I said about ten minutes later.

Carlos bowed slightly and returned with a short, rotund man who had remnants of chocolate cake on his tie and spots of lemonade on his vest. The garment rippled along the front closures, ready to launch buttons off at any moment.

"Mr. Jones, thank you for coming."

"Miss Luebber," the attorney said.

Violet brought in a silver service and poured out coffee. As Carlos halfway closed the door behind the housekeeper, I said, "Thank you, Carlos. That will be all."

Violet whipped her head around, looking just as confused as Carlos. He then slung jagged shards of betrayal at me with his icy stare, but I didn't back down. Had Carlos known what I was going to do in the meeting, he'd tell me I was crazy in front of my lawyer and have me institutionalized. I didn't repeat myself but remained standing and waited for him to leave the room.

"As you wish," he stated through tight lips and shut the door behind him and Violet.

Mr. Jones was as stunned as my manager. It was common knowledge that Carlos served as Carmena's right hand. Her right leg even. Without him, the ranch's most valuable asset, the connecting thread that held the property and its residents together, would crumble.

"What is it that I can do for you, Miss Luebber?"

"I'd like to make some investments. I'd also like to revise my will in case of any unforeseen accidents."

"That can be arranged. Investments, I mean. Not unforeseen accidents." He loosened his tie. "We'll need a witness for the will, of course."

"And there will be when we get to that. I've issued some drafts. I'll have Jesse accompany you back into town and make a deposit for me at the bank. Please disperse the drafts accordingly."

The little gnome of a man was polite and reserved. "Very well."

"The first draft is for twenty-five hundred."

He nearly choked. "Dollars?"

"Yes. I'd like you to invest it for me in steel through the New York Stock Exchange."

"Twenty-five hundred? In steel?"

"You're right," I replied. "Make it five thousand." He choked again. "Are you all right, Mr. Jones?" He waved me off. "The next draft is for twenty-five hundred, for something a bit riskier."

"Miss Luebber! Stocks are highly unstable, not to mention that many disreputable scallywags are engaged in the practice of swindling money from unsuspecting people."

"Do you want to vent any other objections before we proceed?"

"I most certainly do! It's unheard of for a single woman to be making such important decisions on her own, especially when it comes to investing in stock certificates. Why, you need to keep your money safe, in the bank, until you get married and then your husband can handle your financial affairs. Until then, at the very least, have Mr. Solis participate in these decisions."

"Despite your lack of confidence in me, Mr. Jones, I wish to make these investments," I said.

"You'd be a fool to waste so much money!" Various shades of cranberry dappled his pudgy cheeks.

"Mr. Jones, please remember that as my attorney, and with regards to stocks, I am not soliciting any advice, legal or otherwise. Do you understand?"

"Yes, I do." His flustered red cheeks and round head made him look like a tomato. He wiped his shiny pate with a handkerchief. "But I ask that you note my protest, especially to Mr. Solis."

"So noted. Now, what do you know of any advancements in technology?" I asked him.

"Tech what?" he asked.

"Hmm." I thought a moment. "Inventions. What's out there?"

"People are always trying to make money, claiming they made something or other to change the world. Why, just last week I received a letter from my brother, telling me about a man who says he is working on communicating by sound through telegraphs. A bunch of codswallop, if you ask me."

"Who is the inventor who's claiming that?"

Beauford contemplated the ceiling as if the name floated above us. "Let me think," he mused and tapped his temple. "I can't imagine anyone in their right mind wanting to invest—"

Dealing first hand with sexual inequality and the Neanderthal male beliefs of the time lit a fire under my frustration level. My voice may have risen a tad louder than I intended.

"For goodness sakes, man! What the hell is his name?"

There was an immediate knock on the door, and Carlos peeked in. "Do you need me, Carmena?"

In my most demure voice, I replied, "No, Carlos. We're fine."

I waited. He glared suspiciously at the attorney then closed the door.

I turned to Beauford. "His name?"

"I believe it was Morse."

"Samuel Morse?" I asked, amazed.

"Yes, I think so. I'm greatly relieved that you've heard of this lunatic. He is trying to take credit for inventing the telegraph, claiming he owns the patent. If you are even minutely associated with this modern-day brigand, Lord knows what people will think of you. Why, thinking he can make voices heard across telegraph wires. Imagine that nonsense!" Mr. Jones shook his head in disbelief.

My heart skipped a few beats. In high school, I learned that Morse invented the first successful electronic transmission of data that would blast the doors wide open to telephone communications, and Morse code would be used for international communication on the high seas until 1999. Holiday Ranch could make a fortune and I was going to use any means possible, especially my knowledge of the future, to make it happen.

"Contact Samuel Morse," I told Beauford. "And tell him we'll fund five-thousand dollars of the legal and research fees with a share in any patents."

"That's preposterous! Besides, you said twenty-five hundred a minute ago."

"Did I? I've only just changed my mind. Five thousand." I dipped my quill in the crystal inkbottle and prepared new drafts. "I've heard discussion of a firm that is in the process of forming next year called American Telegraph. They're on the verge of inventing those machines that make voices carry over the wire. The moment you hear it is available for public trading, we'll buy in with five thousand."

"Miss Luebber!" he objected.

"You're right. Ten thousand. I'm telling you, Beauford, telephones are going to be the wave of the future. You should invest in them yourself."

He glimpsed at the door and spoke in a harsh whisper, "This is ludicrous. I cannot advocate these, these…whimsical decisions of yours."

"I've already noted your protest, Mr. Jones."

He wiped his face with his already damp handkerchief.

"I'd also like ten thousand in gold shares."

"Gold is a fortune right now!" he bellowed. "Why, it's over twenty-one dollars an ounce!"

Carlos opened the door again. "Carmena?"

Jones faltered, unable to get out a sound.

"I believe Mr. Jones has recovered now, but I'm sure he wants you to acknowledge his protest. Thank you, Carlos."

Carlos directed a beady warning at each of us before he slowly shut the door.

I leaned toward my attorney. "Let's face it, Beauford. Texas is destined for annexation. You would do well to convert your own holdings."

His chin rose up a fraction. "At least we're in agreement on one thing."

I smiled and handed him another check. "And here is a draft for five thousand to be invested in Harrisburg Railroad."

More sweat rained from his brow. His handkerchief was drenched but he kept mopping his head. Visibly distressed, Beauford said, "You'd be wise to keep your money in the bank. Railroads are just a whimsy until they open up more wagon trails."

"Something tells me they'll be around for a very long time to come."

"A foolish waste of money," he argued.

"Just wait until they invent freeways."

"I beg your pardon?"

I ignored him and handed him a paper across the desk scribed by myself with a quill, passable for a first-time calligrapher. "Here is a prepared list of names. These people will inherit any asset in my name, including the stocks, in the event of my death or disappearance."

He took the paper.

"Listen carefully, Mr. Jones. There are specific instructions here regarding my will. The stocks will be owned as share-and-share alike with right of survivorship, under two conditions. Write this down," I ordered.

He scowled and pulled a notepad from his valise while I paced behind my desk.

"First, the stocks, regardless of their value, must be sold before September 1, 1929. Every single one of them, regardless of how well they may be doing."

He eyed me like I'd gone off the deep end. "I've never heard of such a thing. Besides, why would anyone care what's going to happen so far into the future?"

"I want to ensure that the ranch is still here for generations to come. Regardless if it's an emotional decision, see that this stipulation is included in the will. Perhaps we can include a threat which instructs that the assets be turned over to the state if my wishes can't be granted."

"I don't know if this can be done. It's not like you can dictate when stocks are sold, as if you owned some type of a business."

"Incorporation!" I startled him, and he flew back into his chair. "You're a genius, Beauford." He blushed. "Set it up. It's imperative that Holiday Ranch be kept in the foremost working condition, whether it serves as a breeding farm, cattle ranch, or any other business."

"Surely you're poking fun!"

I shook my head.

"You want to incorporate a ranch? That's utterly ridiculous! Besides, your land is riddled with sludge, and everyone knows the military has been confiscating your livestock. Do you have any bad debts you're not telling me about, Miss Luebber?"

"I'll pretend I didn't hear that remark, Mr. Jones. Now, the other stipulation is that as long as anyone is living on the ranch, they will receive the dividends, share-and-share-alike. At the very least, even if the stocks are worthless, whoever resides here will be able to produce a healthy income from whatever type of work or service is offered. And if we're a corporation, the stocks belong to the ranch and will convey with the ranch if someone tries to sell it. That should be a big enough threat to keep it in the family."

"You're not even married," he pointed out. "You have no family."

I paused for dramatic effect and spoke in a low, deliberate tone. "All the people on Holiday Ranch are my family, Mr. Jones. And I expect you, above all, to remember that."

He acquiesced a few seconds before he protested yet again. "But you just said there's a chance the stocks won't give you a profit. There may not be enough to run the ranch."

"Let's just say that I trust my gut instinct."

"Absolute madness," he mumbled as he scribbled out my instructions. "You said you wanted to keep your cash on-hand, close to home where it's safe. This is quite the gamble you're taking. Absolute madness!"

I stared Beauford down until he huffed, and his defiant chin remained in place.

"Lastly, I want to buy Charles Sealsfield's land."

Beauford Jones hit his limit. He jumped out of his chair and roared, "How am I to do that? People, wealthy people, have been trying to buy his acreage for years! German royalty offered to buy it, and the man outright refused! And now the man can't even be located!" The red-faced attorney whipped out his handkerchief, but it flopped over, limp and saturated with moisture.

I called through the walls, "I'm okay, Carlos! Mr. Jones, you are huffing and puffing like a wild boar! Will you please calm down?" I tugged on the hankie in my sleeve, half the size of his. For a second, he stared at the skimpy fabric but took it and proceeded to wipe his head. He handed it back to me, but I shooed it off. "Keep it."

I poured a generous amount of brandy at the serving tray and handed him the snifter. "Here. Bend an elbow." The round man slugged back the drink. "Better?"

"Yes. Thank you." He composed himself and asked, "What makes you think Sealsfield will sell you his land?"

"Every man has his price. Find his." I handed him a bank note. My steadfast resolve probably kept my attorney from further arguments against the purchase.

"I trust you will safeguard this blank draft, Beauford?"

He took the note and raised his nose, as if offended I had to ask. "Of course, Miss Luebber. You know I'll have to first locate the man before I can negotiate a deal," he quietly stated.

"I will pay for any legitimate expenses required for the search."

"Now, as for the fee for my services..." The arrogant Beauford Jones I saw in Carmena's memories came to life.

I handed him a final draft. "There's enough here to cover your time, as well as expenses for a trip to New York and back to purchase the stocks and file for incorporation."

He read the amount and kept his eyeballs in their sockets. He stuttered, "Uh, thank you, Miss Luebber. It has certainly been a most interesting visit." He gathered the checks and paperwork off my desk. "I'll prepare the first draft of the will and deliver it within a week."

"Two days, Beauford." The retainer I gave him warranted overnight delivery, but I took in account the long ride back into town and the lack of FedEx couriers.

"But it will take time to draft!" I gave him a twenty-first century gangsta stare. "Two days," he mumbled.

"See that the bank has my money insured before you leave town. Once all this business is completed, I want any extra cash in the bank to be converted to gold. How long does it normally take to process the stocks?"

"They're very efficient these days. Once I get the drafts to the Exchange, you will immediately begin to make, or lose profit," he said. "You should receive a written accounting of your investments in as little as ten weeks. The certificates will only take about four months to print."

"Purchase the stocks no later than the end of the week." I shouted at the doors. "Carlos!" He entered the room a fraction of a second later.

"Yes, Carmena?" His words were frosted over.

"I'd like Jesse to ride into town with Mr. Jones. See that he's armed."

"I'll inform him." He could've been waylaid by pirates, yet Carlos reacted as if I asked him daily to send an armed man into town with my lawyer.

"Please see Mr. Jones to the parlor."

"I sure hope you know what you're doing, Miss Luebber," Beauford said.

I smiled. "So do I, Mr. Jones. So do I."

CHAPTER 18

Beauford Jones waddled out the room. I knew it cost Carlos to keep quiet, but he held his tongue and followed Jones to the parlor.

I pulled the satchel out of the hidden cupboard and set it on an end table. From my chair, I savored a spectacular Remington view framed by the bay window.

Jesse hurried into the library. "Yull be needin' me ta run ya an errand, ma'am?"

My sights lingered on the scenery as I considered accent reduction for Jesse.

"Please escort Mr. Jones back to town. Take that satchel on the settee to the bank and make certain this money is deposited and insured. Please bring me a receipt."

"Yes, ma'am," he said and picked up the small valise on the way out of the room, shutting me inside with my thoughts as I peered out the window.

Contradictions filled the Texan topography. Green flourished where water flowed through refreshing creeks, but over the next ridge the land could be thirsty and hostile. The differences slugged a person right in the stomach, yet the choice was to accept it or move on.

Contrasts formed me, too. Some parts were rich and welcomed, and other aspects weren't so appealing. Sometimes it felt like parts of my soul had dried up. I spent a lot of time alone to avoid knowing what people thought of me, yet I was miserable as a hermit. Without self-acceptance, I couldn't expect anyone else to accept me either.

I wasted time not valuing who I was or appreciating what I was capable of doing. In short, I was stagnant in action and personal growth. It took me three steps back to see that I was too fearful to move one step forward.

This was the mist Sadie mentioned. She said it was indecision and accused me of not knowing what I wanted in my heart. Sadie was right, but now I knew what I wanted. Before experiencing life as a ranch owner, I wished for things that weren't meant to be, for things that didn't resonate with who I was. I did things that held no passion and shunned responsibility for insecurity.

Before my heart had pleaded "Take me," but now I wanted to be like Texas. I wanted to thunder proudly, "Take me as I am or leave me!" Sure, there was room for improvement, but I would determine what changes to make and make them on my own terms.

Hiring the services of Beauford Jones set things right at the ranch. The operations and finances would be turned over to those who embraced this place as home and took the land to heart. Now I had to set things right for myself. I had a taste of home on the tip of my tongue and relished the thought of my trip back. I wanted to bite into life and at last know its true flavor.

The past week felt like it had passed in the span of months. My gut instinct told me my time to leave the western frontier was drawing near. Once we sent Santa Anna on his way, I'd be ready to go home.

A knock on the open door shook me from my insightful revelations but not one thing had the capacity to diminish my newfound hunger to return to the future.

"Mandy? May I come in now?" Carlos asked. A bit of sarcasm singed his words.

I continued to face the provocative landscape. "Come in."

Carlos closed the door. "Are you going to tell me what's going on?"

"Yes. Please sit down."

He sat, but I remained spellbound by the natural view that inspired my newfound awareness, and my voice reflected its transformative peace. "I invested nearly all of our cash in stocks, gold, and developmental research. Oh, and land."

I turned in my chair and witnessed Carlos jumping from his seat as if he'd sat on a pinecone.

"You what?"

"I knew you'd disagree, and that's why I didn't want you attending our meeting. It's my hope to reap a profit on the ranch and not get on the bad side of the law to stay in the black."

"Then stop spending money like a woman. Buying dresses, a stove that burns more wood than a locomotive, not to mention plumbing!"

"I'm only having Beauford purchase stocks that I know did well from a historical perspective. Gold will never get lower than it is now. Trust me. At the turn of the century, land will be at a premium in Texas, especially when the need for oil arises."

"What the hell do we need oil for? We've fenced ponds of the damn sludge so the cattle won't fall in!"

I smiled. "Remember those cars I told you about? They need oil converted to gasoline to make them run."

He snorted. "And will there be enough of these cars to use all the oil?"

"Millions. More than there are horses."

His eyes filled with revelation. Carlos bobbed his head up and down, and he rubbed his chin. His voice returned to its normal sensual drawl. "Very clever, Mandy."

"There will also be an industrial revolution at the turn of the century. Oil will become a valuable commodity to make all the machinery run."

"But what about now?" he said. "The military takes whatever it can of our livestock from right under our noses."

"Through a meeting with Captain Sanders, I think I can arrange a deal with the cavalry. I'll permit them to take livestock, provided we can recoup our losses by not handing over large numbers of our income-producing animals, mainly the ones for breeding."

"In the meantime, how much longer will they steal from us?"

"Not long," I replied. "A resolution will be passed in a couple of weeks stating the intent to secede, and Texas will become a state by the end of the year. Then the cavalry will concentrate on border wars. For now, we have enough to purchase more cattle and horses. At the turn of the century, after cars are invented, horses will only be used for sport and recreation, but cattle will still produce an income."

"How much livestock were you thinking of buying? What breeds do you want to purchase?"

"Whatever you prefer," I told him.

"Whatever I prefer?"

"Yes. I plan on turning the entire operations of the ranch over to you when I leave."

"But where will that leave the ranch without you?"

"When I leave, I'm quite certain Carmena will come back. She'll have to learn how to nurture herself, to take it easy like the rest of you. If any of you want to work hard, that's your prerogative, but at least you'll have the option."

Carlos scrunched his nose. "I don't mind seeing Violet and Angela with less work, but men must have something honest to do."

"You can make money doing what you love. Build furniture, compose music, write books. You can give back to the community. Build a home for orphans or buy books for a town library. Whatever turns you on."

"Turns me on?"

"Whatever excites you. Do whatever your passion is to give your life meaning."

The insight at that moment had been unintentional, but it impacted me with a hard-hitting realization. My life didn't hold any meaning. I had no passion for anything. That was why I left Arkansas and moved in with my cousin.

"This might work." Carlos gave approval to my plans just as Angela knocked on the door and poked her head inside the room.

"Do you have a moment?" she asked.

"Yes," Carlos and I answered. Carlos deferred to me and stood. He held the door for Angela and left the room.

"What do you need, Angela?"

"Please come see to our guest. He tried to take the bandages off his head and eyes. He says he wants to leave, but he may be dreaming like you did after your accident."

"I'll see him for a moment, but then I have to relieve Javier for the next watch." I left the library and Angela followed. She fidgeted with the hem of her apron and pressed her lips together. It didn't take someone like Sadie to figure out what was going on.

"You don't want to see him alone. That's why you came to get me?"

"*Sí,*" she admitted. "We no part on good terms."

"What happened," I asked.

She shrugged. "Javier and I tried to have Santa Anna killed."

"What?"

"We try to end dictatorship in Mexico," she explained, as if murder was a no brainer solution. "A revolutionary was hired for to shoot him during the fight at San Juan de Ulua, but Santa Anna was hit in his foot with the cannon. His leg got the infection and had to be cut off. We no expect to see him again, especially in Texas."

We approached the bunkhouse and heard Gracie's voice echo from somewhere in the direction of the patio. "Mama? Mama?"

"I be back," Angela said and scurried off to find her daughter.

I opened the way to the secret room and was hit with a smell found in hospitals or around sick people. Santa Anna snored. A long strip of linen had been wrapped around his head and now littered the floor. I felt his forehead with the back of my hand. His skin was warmer than a normal temperature.

Santa Anna snapped to life and caught my wrist in an iron grip. "*¿Dónde 'stoy?*" He was feverish, beaded with sweat, his words slurring under the influence of laudanum.

"*Está en la casa Luebber.*"

"You speak Spanish very well," he said.

"*Gracias*. I'm surprised you speak English at all."

"Know thy enemy." He licked his chapped lips. "What day is this?"

"You would do well to let go of my arm." He glanced at his hand and released his hold. "The eighteenth of January," I answered.

"How far is it to Mexico?"

"A long way, even for a man without a fever, broken ribs, and a missing leg."

He pulled back the blanket and lifted his thigh, examining the bandaged stump attached to his cleaned artificial limb. "You've been taking care of me?"

"Not personally. My domestic supervisor has been looking after you. Are you hungry?"

"A bit."

I was about to offer Angela's famous *caldo* when I heard her speaking loudly from the next room.

"What is it that you want with Carmena, Captain Sanders?"

Santa Anna stared at me as I gawked toward the open door like a kid at a peep show. I threw a spare quilt over his personal belongings, then lifted the blankets off the man and bounced on top of him. I pushed him with my bottom closer to the wall.

Heavy blankets over layers of skirts worked up an instant sweat. Santa Anna's hands took full advantage of my predicament. The woolen blanket barely settled before Captain Sanders appeared in the doorway.

One look at me, and he rushed across the room. "Carmena, what's wrong?"

"Stay where you are!" I pleaded and slapped at my bedfellow's wandering hand. Angela scurried behind the captain and pulled on his arm.

"Don't get close," she said.

"Oh!" I moaned as my heel absorbed the hit against Santa Anna's wooden leg. "Angela, the doctor told you no visitors!"

"I'm sorry, Carmena. The captain insisted on seeing you."

"What's wrong?" He stepped forward, but Angela kept a steady grip on his arm.

"Uh, she minister to the Indian family last week. They, uh, all die of the pox. We don't know if Carmena has it."

For the way he looked, Angela might as well have told the captain he'd lost his commission and was being shipped to Turkey.

She wrung out the cloth floating in murky gray water used to wipe down Santa Anna's perspiration. The filmy fabric pressed across my forehead, and I gagged despite the cool relief.

A hand cupped my breast. I kept the blanket to my neck with my free hand and pretended to shiver as I dragged the unwanted arm off me.

The captain saw the spare quilt on the floor hiding Santa Anna's clothes and gun. "She needs to keep warm." He moved fast and stooped over to pick up the quilt.

"No!" Angela and I yelled in unison.

"More blankets make her too hot," Angela explained.

"Then let's take that one off," he said and approached the bed.

"No!" we yelled again.

"Then she be too cold," Angela said.

The captain rubbed his fingers together, like he had an itch to fix the problem. "Perhaps I should fetch a doctor."

"Uh, he came. Says for everyone to stay away." Angela lied like a third-rate lawyer.

"Isn't it too cold for Carmena in here?" he asked.

Angela kept up the fast thinking. "The doctor say she must be in the isolation."

"Captain," I said, "I am well cared for. It disturbs me greatly that you refuse to leave."

"I'm sorry, Carmena." Sincerity seeped through his words. "I only want to see you well."

"And I—" *Kack!* "—only want to see to your health." *Kack! Kack!* I coughed pathetically as I ripped Santa Anna's hand off my bottom. "I implore you to leave, Captain."

He pouted, a sensitive man with hurt feelings, and started to trudge out of the room. At the last second, I threw him a bone and called him by his first name as sensually as an invalid could. "Charles?"

He pirouetted on his heel. "Yes, Carmena?"

"Will you come back and see me when I'm feeling better?" The remark included a bonus of batted lashes.

He smiled. "Of course. Send word into town when you're feeling better, and I'll come as quickly as possible. I, uh—" He looked at Angela then at me. "I brought you a present."

He pulled a small box wrapped in Victorian paper from his pants pocket and set it on the dresser. Then he pulled a small envelope from his inside jacket pocket. Vacillating between handing it to Angela or leaving it with the gift, he leaned the card against the box.

"I didn't intend this as a get well gift, but it could be."

"Thank you, and for your visit, Charles."

The man didn't budge. Angela stood behind him, her eyes rolling heavenward.

"I'm afraid I need my rest now. Angela, please see the captain out." I planted my head on the pillow, trying not to choke on the smell of sweat from the man glued to my backside.

Discouraging roving hands, I coughed again, only much louder this time to cover up the muffled cry when I kicked the ex-president's good leg. I closed my eyes under the pretense of succumbing to sleep.

Sanders left the room, and I heard him tell Angela, "Now you heard. She wants me to come back the moment she's feeling better."

"*Sí, señor.* We send for you." Angela finally escorted him out, and the bunkhouse door slammed shut. I ripped the blanket off my perspiring body and tumbled off the bed. Santa Anna was also sweating but happily so.

"You animal!" I was too upset to sling any effective insults.

Santa Anna smiled like the devil. "You're welcome to stay."

"That wouldn't be appropriate nor desirable." I straightened my skirt and wiped my forehead with my sleeve.

"No one but your housekeeper would know."

Angela entered the room, and his features paled. Instant recognition collided as if a sledgehammer smashed full force against a brick wall.

"Like I said, that wouldn't be appropriate."

Santa Anna glared at Angela. "*¿Que haces aquí?*"

"I live here," she snapped.

"You traitor!" Santa Anna tried to get up, but pain forced his body back down.

"You will behave, or you will be put out, even if you no well."

The line sounded rehearsed, even with the bad grammar. Santa Anna looked my way. I crossed my arms and let him think Angela called the shots.

"So be it." He covered himself and kept surveillance on his daughter. "As long as you don't try to kill me in my sleep!"

She sneered and turned up her nose. "Mexico is free of your corruption. To kill you now serves no purpose."

"Angela, if you prefer, we can have someone else look after him," I said.

She lifted her chin. "I no afraid of him."

From the way she glowered at the man, I almost feared for his safety.

"I'll ask Violet to prepare him some *caldo*." To her father, I said, "Sir, as Angela has pointed out, our hospitality will be extended to you as long as you abide by our rules. You are not permitted to leave this room."

"Believe me, I have no intention of staying much longer," he wheezed.

"Angela and I will be back shortly with your lunch. Don't do anything stupid," I warned.

"You have more faith in my condition than I do." He closed his eyes, but I doubt he was anywhere near sleep.

I shoved the gift and card from Charles into my pockets before I slid the false door into place and left the bunkhouse.

಄಄಄

"There'd better be a damned good reason why your husband isn't on watch! The captain must have seen you enter the
bunkhouse and followed!"

I stormed into the kitchen and Angela trudged behind me,
shaken by the confrontation with her father, then my outburst.

"Where the hell is Javier?" I shouted.

"He—he—went to Three Hump Canyon with Carlos,"
Violet stammered. Her eyes bounced from me to Angela.

"He was supposed to be on a bloody watch until I relieved
him," I shouted. "Sanders nearly caught our guest enjoying the
accommodations here at Holiday Inn!" I shook my head. "I
mean Ranch."

Violet's eyes puddled. Angela draped her arm protectively
over her co-worker's shoulders.

"Angela will be taking food back to our guest, and I'm
going to the barn to take watch."

"Shall I fix you a lunch?" Violet asked, her head down-
cast.

"No. After lying in bed with that foul man, I've lost my
appetite."

She gulped air, and I shot a threatening glance at the
woman.

"Angela, I want you to eat something. You look worse
than your father."

Violet's eyes would have ripped open if they widened
much more. She tried to appease me with a freshly brewed cup
of hot coffee, and it worked. Rather than rush to the lookout
post to take watch, I let the liquid soothe me while she prepared lunch for our patient.

"Angela, eat here before going back to the bunkhouse."
She made to protest but I added, "He's not going anywhere for
the next fifteen minutes."

Grateful for a break, sustenance, and company, Angela
chomped the sandwich without the grace and good manners
she used at the dinner table.

"Why do you want to take care of him?" I blatantly asked. "The man has no morals or scruples and obviously doesn't care about you."

Angela pinched the sandwich crust in her fingers and kept silent.

"When was the last time you saw him?"

She bit into her sandwich like a savage beast. I thought she'd choke on her words more than her meal. Under the influence of raw emotions, she'd lost her grammar again. "I last saw him before Javier and I come here." Angela sipped her coffee and continued. "After the Junta convince Herrera to exile Santa Anna, I come home from a meeting, and my father jump out and he hold a knife to my throat like this." Her index finger rammed tight under her chin. "He say, 'The next time I see you in Mexico, I order you hanged for the treason.' He no kill me even though I betray him."

"So, you're taking care of your father for not killing you?"

"*Sí*. And then I owe him nothing."

CHAPTER 19

It was a short walk to the barn. I scaled a ladder to the top of the building. A small ledge and seat were built atop the structure for keeping watch. The little wooden bench lacked comfort, perhaps so that the person on duty wouldn't fall asleep. Hunger hit, and I regretted not having brought up some lunch.

From the perch, I visually feasted on wide-open views in three directions with Turtle Hill behind me. If a military search party descended upon the ranch looking for Mexican outlaws, or if the same outlaws wanted to perform a search and rescue for Santa Anna, I was sure they'd take the direct approach and ride straight through the front gates.

The thought of soldiers reminded me of Charles, and I pulled the card and gift he'd brought me out of my pocket.

My name was written in his graceful penmanship. The carefully scribed words spoke volumes on the rough parchment.

My dearest Carmena,

How glad I was to receive your note expressing your delight in my visit last week. It gave me great joy to lay my eyes upon your beautiful smile. I am most profoundly honored that you welcomed my company. Please accept this token of my esteem. I can't say why, but it strongly reminded me of you.

> *I am most deeply and affectionately yours,*
>
> ## Capt. Charles Patrick Sanders

The box in my pocket was a quaint floral tin knotted with a pink satin ribbon and a dried pink rose slipped inside the knot. The tin opened to cherubed paper that covered a hand-carved ivory box. Elephants had yet to become an endangered species.

I lifted the lid and found a lovely bracelet, gold by the look of it with colorful cloisonné figures dangling from tiny gold rings. Every other charm was a rose-colored bonnet swinging to and fro, and in between each, a cute lavender hippopotamus.

Pink hats and purple hippos. A serendipitous act of the universe.

༺༻

I did guard duty for the next six hours wondering if the captain's gift was a divine message of sorts, but I couldn't make sense of it, other than it was a heck of a coincidence to have a line on the poem describing the gift from the captain.

After my watch, I walked to the bunkhouse. If Santa Anna was awake, I wanted to ask him a few questions before I ate dinner.

Angela looked up at me from a rocking chair. She yawned and stretched her arms. Blankets rustled, and we looked at her father beaded with sweat. Angela laid an afghan aside and helped Santa Anna sit upright.

"Pour the medicine into the spoon," she pointed at the opium tincture on the table. I measured the liquid and spooned it into his mouth. Santa Anna choked but swallowed it all and sank down into the folds of the pillows and covers.

His eyes slit open, and Angela asked, "Are you hungry?"

He licked his mouth. "Perhaps later."

"What are you doing in Texas, especially this far north?" I asked him without ceremony.

A tiny smile lifted a corner of his mouth. "So charming and polite, you gringos."

"Answer the question," I demanded.

He looked at me with more than disdain. "If this were still Mexico, I'd have you shot."

"With an attitude like that, you might never leave this place alive. We might have to post a guard in the room."

"I found my way from Havana by boat to the Texas border," Santa Anna said. "I was sleeping. Too much tequila to ease the burden of this painful stump of a leg." He glowered at Angela. She shifted and looked at the floor. "Once we were on the main road, the *stupidos* hired to drive the wagon went north instead of south."

"That still doesn't explain how you managed to get this far north," I said.

A clever smile crossed his lips, one that a skilled poker player knew how to use. "We were ambushed by soldiers near San Antonio. I escaped but had no idea where I was. I thought I'd head for higher ground, walking for days until rocks rained on my head."

"He's lying," Angela said.

His eyes cut through her. "What do you know of me? You hate me! You tried to have me killed!"

Angela stood. "I want you removed from office because you no good a leader! And if I no do it, many others wanted you dead!"

"¡*Mientierosa*!" Santa Anna tried to sit up, but his efforts were futile. He gave into weakness and dropped back to his pillow. "This is the thanks I get for putting you in school when no one else wanted you?"

"If you no hurt people, you kill them. Better for me to be in the convent than with you."

Santa Anna morphed before our eyes, from a hysterical man, high on laudanum, to a deadly calm disposition. He spoke evenly, wickedly. "The nuns didn't want you. I had to pay them to keep you. Otherwise, you would've been on the street. Like your mother."

Angela inhaled a breath as sharp as his words. "¡*Mientieroso*! My mother—she die to give me life!"

"Your mother was the village whore who didn't want to be tied down to a child! She was a colonel's niece, and I had to take care of you or suffer demotion."

Angela was too stunned to reply and kept her hands over her mouth. It dawned on me that Santa Anna spoke English for my benefit, to witness the humiliation he poured on his daughter.

I stepped in between them and made a T with my hands. "Time out."

A lone tear dripped down Angela's face, and her shoulders drooped. Santa Anna's voice grew feeble as the laudanum took effect. He slurred his words, but he managed to eke out his insults.

"I let the nuns give you a name, gave them a pouch of gold, and saw you once a year as the colonel ordered." Smug satisfaction and drool puddled in the corner of his mouth. Unable to remain conscious, he lapsed into sleep and snored.

I handed Angela a fresh hankie, and she wiped at her tears. I didn't know what to do to comfort her, to dull the cutting edge of her father's revelation.

"You said he was good at hurting people. He's not picking on you, Angela. He's just…being himself." She gave me an anemic smile. "You ready to let me and Violet start taking shifts?"

She shook her head. "No. I finish my job. I no care he is my father." Her shaky grammar told me otherwise, but I let her do what she felt was necessary for her own emotional benefit. Fortunately, she had already eaten. No telling how long it would take for her appetite to return.

"I'm going to grab a bite to eat."

"*Gracias,* Carmena."

As I slid the panel into place, I glanced back and saw that Angela's saddened demeanor had transformed into a hard shell, and I doubted Santa Anna would ever be able to pene-

trate it again. I had yet to justify his own daughter's willing-
ness to assassinate him or anyone for political reasons, but I
could understand why people hated the man.

Angry and hungry, a nasty combination, I stormed toward
the house. My earlier raging about the captain's surprise visit
was no secret. The moment I entered the dining room, I was
furious all over again. No one had the nerve to speak, knowing
I was looking for a verbal brawl.

I decided to call a last minute dinner meeting for the
adults to discuss the matter of housing our unlikely guest. Jesse told Angela she had to attend, per my orders. Angela let
Gracie think she and her brother were rewarded with a rare
treat of eating in the tree house next to the barn. Martino
would signal us if he saw any sign of military personnel or
strangers with a simple but effective alarm. A stack of empty
tin cans would make a disturbing racket if they toppled to the
ground.

Angela said grace before the meal. "Dear Lord, we ask
you to bless this food and our family. Have mercy on those
sinners who no have an ounce of love in their cold hearts, and
even bless those who are angry at people who no deserve it."
She glanced at me. "And even bless those—" Angela was
about to add more but I cleared my throat too loudly, and she
said, "Amen."

"Amen," we repeated.

The women wore their beautiful new dresses, but my poor
attitude drew any notice away from them. I opened the discussion by retelling of the close call during Sander's visit.

"I take full responsibility," Carlos explained. "I told
Javier to come up to the canyon and forgot to ask him to wait
until you took over his watch. I thought you'd go straight to
the barn after I saw you in the library."

"It's my fault. Carlos didn't know I asked you to speak to
our guest," Angela said.

"Regardless of how many excuses we make for each other
that doesn't detract from the need to have a lookout at all
times. From here on out, one person will stay on watch until
our guest leaves. Martino will have the shortest shift from one

to four, until we get some hired hands to help out. I don't think Sanders will send anyone around at night, so we'll end the shifts at midnight and begin again at five."

Carlos eyed me. His half smile was the confirmation I needed to know that the soulful transformation I experienced in the library had taken effect. I had grown up.

"Are you gonna turn the guest over to the law?" Javier asked me.

"He'll decide where he'd like to go, and we'll make sure he has a ride to get there."

"The sooner we git him on the other side of the Rio Grandy, the better fer us," Jesse said.

"He's not fit for travel," Angela said.

"How long will it take before he's ready to ride?" Violet asked. We were surprised to hear her speak up, unaccustomed to her participation in a mealtime conversation.

She waited, and Angela lifted a shoulder with her answer. "He can leave in a day or so, but it will be painful."

"Jesse found two men in town who might be able to work here," Carlos said.

"They're mighty fine fellas," Jesse assured us. "Turns out my folks was kin to theirs and theys in need of a decent place to live an' work."

"Their names are Joseph Ziegfried and Roy Duncan," Carlos said.

"You're joking!" I laughed. "Ziegfried and Roy?" My tee-hee died down in light of the blank stares. I coughed. "Whatever. If we can trust them, why not bring them on earlier? Even if they saw you-know-who, they might not recognize him."

"Jesse, ride into town tomorrow and see if they're back from Dobson's round up," Carlos ordered.

"Set up a meeting here with Captain Sanders while you're at it," I said, and a table full of curious eyes looked my way.

"You should wait a bit longer before he finds out you don't have the pox," Angela said. "You were on your death bed, after all." She turned to the others to explain. "The captain lost his color and was going to cry like a baby when he saw

Carmena sweating in bed." Snickers skimmed the room, and
Carlos guffawed rather rudely.

"I'd be sweating, too, if I were stuck that close to the
man," Javier said.

Jesse slapped his knee and grinned. "That's too close fer
me to be with any man!"

"We'll need a bigger table," Violet said, returning to the
topic of extra hands at the ranch. The rest of us looked at her.

"You don't have to sit at the same table to be family,"
Javier reminded her.

Carlos smiled. "Holiday Ranch is growing all the time.
Soon we'll be making some substantial purchases of cattle and
horses, provided Carmena can negotiate a contract with the
military. That's why she needs to meet with Sanders."

The rest looked at me in awe, tackling a big monster like
the U.S. government.

He continued. "In addition to new field hands that come
on after Ziegfried and Duncan, we plan on hiring more wranglers and perhaps another maid. We'll have to draw a line between ranch hands and family and will discuss the changes in
our duties."

"For now, it's only two men," Violet said. "We can add
another leaf to the table. There's plenty of room."

"Why we need more people working here?" Angela asked
defensively.

"Yeah. What sort of work will that leave the rest of us?"
Javier inquired. Everyone cast their eyes on Carlos and me.

"Great," I said to Carlos. "I hired a crew with high work
ethics."

"When the new help arrives, each of you can determine
which jobs you're better suited to," Carlos explained. "We'll
discuss the upcoming changes in personnel after Beauford
Jones comes back from completing a business transaction for
Carmena."

I added, "The thing is, you'll all have more free time to
do the things you enjoy once these changes take place."

No one spoke up. No one seemed excited about the
thought of not working so hard.

"C'mon, Violet," Angela said. "Let's get the pies."

We started in on a second pot of coffee with dessert.

"Violet, if you had all the time and money in the world, what would you do?" I asked.

"I'd do some more oil painting."

Carlos put his hand over hers. "I didn't know you knew how to paint."

"Some," she said. Modesty tinted her words and pink blotched her cheeks.

The rest joined in and shared their if-I-could dreams. I didn't know Angela knew how to needlepoint or that Jesse carved wooden animals in his spare time. Javier wanted to build a fort for the kids. And Carlos? The way he was ogling the woman next to him, I'd bet he'd be sweet on spending more time with Violet.

I worked at my desk in the library after dinner to cover all the points possible in the proposed contract for the captain. I showed the written agreement with the military to Carlos when he came in for the nightly accounting.

He was astounded by my legalese and asked if I was an attorney in my past life.

ℰↄℰↄ

Everyone bedded down for the night, except Jesse, who took watch, and Angela, who resumed her care of Santa Anna. In my room, I pulled a nightgown over my head, weary from an exhausting day. The bed was like a magnet, but something was wrong.

I didn't feel the familiar weight of the amulet bump against my chest. My hand probed for the charm, but it wasn't there. A thorough and frantic pat down of every fold in my clothes didn't produce the necklace. Sadie warned me not to lose the only way back to my own time.

Prior to my meeting with Beauford Jones, I debated whether to wind it up or not, but I couldn't remember the last time I touched it after that. Although no one except Carlos and

Angela had ever seen the necklace, I was positive that if anyone on the ranch had spotted it, they would've said so.

With an oil lamp in hand, I spent a few quiet hours downstairs searching the library, scouring the kitchen, and combing
through the dining room without success. It was too dark to
hunt anywhere outside. There was no choice for me but to wait
for morning.

With the amulet lost, the way home was closed forever. I
thought that by creating financial independence for the ranch
and its inhabitants, I'd be buying my return to the future. Lately, every decision I made was in the best interest of the people
whom I'd grown incredibly attached to during my short stay. It
wouldn't be short if I didn't find the necklace, and Sadie
warned me of the consequences if I remained in the past.

I had to tell Carlos. Only he knew how significant the
amulet was to me.

I fell into a restless sleep and anticipated the joy in finding the necklace, but more so, the repercussions if I didn't.

CHAPTER 20

Javier was bent out of shape about having to conduct a day-long jewelry hunt when he preferred to do chores. Nonetheless, he spent hours searching each outbuilding on the property. Martino and Gracie went through the entire second story and most of the first with the women, but our time was wasted. Angela searched the bunkhouse, and Violet rummaged through the parlor and library without any luck.

Jesse came back from town and let me know that he bumped into Sanders, who asked how I was feeling. He told the captain I didn't have the pox, and on my behalf, Jesse extended an offer of lunch to the captain on Saturday, three days away. Charles readily accepted and that threw the house into an uproar.

The captain had no idea that our hospitality was part of a plan to ask him to serve as an intermediary between the U.S. Cavalry and Holiday Ranch. He also had no idea that we were nursing the exiled Mexican president back to health.

In town, Jesse caught up with Joe and Roy. They finished their cattle run early. Jesse had no trouble convincing them to start working immediately at the ranch, and again, on my behalf, he insisted we pay their room and board for the past month at Ol' Sally's.

The moment Joe and Roy arrived, they were introduced to everyone and given a quick tour of the property. Carlos made certain to tell them to keep mum about the injured Mexican we had been nursing. He gave them strict orders not to enter the small apartment off the bunkhouse but to report any suspicious activity.

The men found their new accommodations superior to the perfumed and lacy rooms provided by Ol' Sally. For their first job they joined in the search for my amulet, but even with the added help, my necklace was still missing by the time Angela rang the supper bell.

I cancelled the futile search.

Violet took it upon herself to add another leaf to the large dining table to accommodate the new field hands.

It was Gracie's turn to say the blessing. "Thank you, God, for our two new friends." Approving smiles were bestowed on the men and the young girl for her sweet benediction. "And please, God," she prayed, "help us find Carmena's jewelry because Papa says the men are wasting too much time on such nonsense."

"Ouch!" Carlos exclaimed and scolded Javier, "You kicked the wrong leg!"

"Shhh!" Violet admonished.

"Go ahead, Gracie," I said as I glared at her father. "You are allowed to say whatever you want during prayer time."

Gracie continued. "And if we can't find Carmena's necklace, please help her get more jewelry because Mama says Carmena will feel much better when she gets some."

Grunts and chuckles went around the table. "Whatever," I said. "Gracie, that's enough."

Carlos grinned. "You did give her permission—"

"Finish your blessing, Gracie," I said, cutting him off. "Now. Please!"

"Amen," she said.

"Amen," the rest of us joined in.

Before I could snap my napkin open, our nerves collectively lurched at the sound of clattering hooves. The men jumped from their seats.

"Stand guard with the women and children," I told Javier. "If you hear anything amiss, head for a safe-room." I pointed to the children. "Stay quiet."

Jesse, Joe, Roy, and I followed Carlos to the front door. Carlos opened the tiny window on the door and whispered, "I can only see one horse. No rider."

He latched the little window closed. From a hidden cupboard near the entryway, Carlos removed three rifles and handed them to the men. "Jesse and Roy, go 'round the back and keep us covered from the outside," he whispered.

They flew down the hall on light feet, through the ballroom, and exited the rear doors.

A knock sounded on the door. I peeked through the window on the door and only saw a hat. I shook my head at Carlos.

"Joe, stand behind the parlor door and come out if you hear a ruckus," he whispered. Joe nodded and took a rifle, quick to tiptoe into the parlor.

Carlos put a pistol in my palm and my arm dropped. I caught the barrel and held it upright with my left hand. I stood behind the door and signaled with a jerk of my chin for Carlos to open it.

Carlos slowly pulled the door open then exhaled. "Just a moment, Mr. Jones."

I blew out a stream of relief, glad to hand the heavy gun to Carlos. He set our weapons in the corner behind the door.

I pulled the door open and said, "Mr. Jones. Please come in."

"Good evening, Miss Luebber. Mr. Solis," the stocky man said, taking his hat off.

"We were just about to sit down to dinner, Mr. Jones. Would you care to join us?"

"No, thank you. I had a rather late lunch."

"Let's sit in the parlor, shall we?" I said, forgetting all about Joe's hiding place.

On cue, Joe nonchalantly stepped out of the parlor with the gun pointed at the ceiling, rubbing the barrel with his handkerchief. He handed the rifle to Carlos. "I got her all oiled an' cleaned up fer ya like ya asked."

"Thank you, Joe. Dinner is about to be served."

"I'll jest wash my hands an' sit down directly. Good evenin', Mr. Jones."

"Mr. Ziegfried, it's nice to see you. I hear you and Roy are now employed by Holiday Ranch."

"We are, and we're glad fer it." Joe smiled and tipped his hat before he walked to the dining room.

In the parlor, Carlos extended his arm toward the settee, rifle in hand. "Please have a seat, Mr. Jones." The attorney made himself comfortable, and Carlos left the room to put the guns away.

"I assume you've brought the revised will, Mr. Jones?" I said.

"The draft is finished, and I'm sure you'll approve. Here is your copy."

I didn't take it and asked, "Why a draft and not a completed document?"

Beauford smiled and handed it off to Carlos when he returned to the parlor. The attorney explained. "You'll be happy to know, Miss Luebber, that the reason I could not deliver a finished document in a timely manner is because of the guest I happened to be entertaining this week."

"Please don't think that having a guest is an acceptable excuse for any delay." My missing amulet sparked more responsibility for my ranch family, and if I was stuck here permanently, every decision would affect me as well.

"Carmena," Carlos said as if he were silently instructing me on etiquette. "Go on, Mr. Jones."

Beauford looked as if he was about to burst at the seams. "My guest this week has been a fellow attorney from New York, one Mr. Martin Sansburg. We discussed business relative to the meeting we conducted here last week."

"What did you find out?" Carlos asked.

"In a confidential conversation, Mr. Sansburg mentioned the name of a particular landowner who is no longer residing in this country but continues to own a very desirable piece of property."

"Sealsfield," Carlos said.

"Precisely. At one time, Mr. Sealsfield was residing in England, and Mr. Sansburg happened to be acquainted with his solicitor in London."

"Excellent," Carlos said.

"As it happens, the solicitor, Mr. Miles Thompson, is expected to be in New York on business in the next month or so. I dispatched a letter to the gentleman with word of your offer to Mr. Sealsfield for his land."

"But what if Thompson is no longer his attorney?" Carlos asked.

"On the off chance he is not, I told Mr. Sansburg I was at liberty to offer a small incentive to make a letter of introduction to the correct solicitor."

"I'm impressed, Beauford," I said.

"Well done," Carlos added.

He smiled. "Very well, then. That concludes my business here. Please look over the will, and let me know if you require any changes."

We all stood and headed for the front door.

"How long do you think we'll have to wait for a reply?" I asked.

"If I haven't received a reply in a reasonable time by post, say within a month or so, I will travel back east and attempt a personal search for Mr. Thompson at the address I've been supplied."

Carlos smiled. "Excellent. Please let Carmena or me know the moment you hear anything."

"I shall, Mr. Solis." Beauford put on his hat, and we said our final good-byes.

We headed back to the dining room, where everyone had been waiting for us to join them for the meal.

∂∞∂

Although I'd called off the search for my amulet, I spent hours the next morning going over every square inch of my room and the library. Angela found me on my hands and knees inspecting the floor beneath my desk. She said that Santa Anna was well enough to leave the ranch, and the ex-politico wanted to have a word with me.

Clean-shaven, Santa Anna was attractive, despite the bandaged ribs and weight loss due to his injuries. His daughter had washed and mended his old clothes, and he wore them like a designer suit. He stood when I entered the room, a gentleman, but he had the visage of a piranha.

From the threshold of the bunkhouse door, Angela addressed her estranged father. "A horse is ready for you. Food and water are in the saddle bags, enough for three-days." Her grammar was perfect.

"Thank you, Angela," Santa Anna said through tight lips.

"I'll be in the kitchen," she told me. She glanced at her father, then took her leave.

Sadie warned me to heed my gut instinct. Right then, my feminine intuition was screaming. The man had crushed a lot of people to get to the top, stole land when it suited him, and ordered men killed who disagreed with his politics. I wouldn't take what he had to say lightly.

"Miss Luebber, how nice that you came by," Santa Anna said without an ounce of sincerity.

"It will be a relief to get you off my property."

"Obviously, you are not one for formalities."

"No, I'm not one for bullshit."

Santa Anna bowed slightly. "There is something I need to discuss with you." He motioned to the chair. "Please, sit down," he said as if I were his guest.

I felt the chair was a psychological ploy to put me in a place of submission, lower than him. I was over a foot shorter than him as it was. "I'll stand, thank you."

"As you wish." He took the chair and crossed his legs like a person who had the upper hand. "If you remember, Carmena—" He called me by my new first name and the familiarity grated on my ears like a scratched chalkboard. "Several months ago, a business arrangement with the Mexican government was only partially completed."

I knew instantly what he referred to. The botched shipment of guns. "I don't know how you know that, but it didn't involve you, Antonio."

He didn't like being called by his first name either. Through a scorn-filled smile, he said, "Oh, but I plan on collecting for Herrera. Besides, my sources say he will soon be exiled." I knew it from the History Channel but how did he? My surprise pleased him. "The man no longer has the *cojones* to remain in office."

"And you think you do? Antonio, you were exiled. No one wants you back in power."

"Oh, I'll have to lick a few boot straps but that's a small price to pay to return to my country."

"Texas won her independence," I reminded him. "Why do you need more weapons?"

"That is none of your concern, but what you should know is that I expect the rest of the shipment."

"I owe you nothing."

He spoke with annoying casualty. "There's a storage facility, a deserted farm, twenty-two miles south of here above the Guadalupe Creek. You'll find quite a few guns and ammunition stored there."

Henry Castro's ranch. When Castro heard of a large land grant, he abandoned the small farm and migrated about 150 miles farther south. His dream was to create his own settlement of Castroville, east of San Antonio.

"How do you know it's being used as a storage facility?"

Santa Anna smiled and examined his fingernails. "Deliver my order three nights from now at the most eastern part of the Lomorillos Valley shortly after midnight. Wait along the tree line at the edge of the forest until my men arrive."

"So that's why you came this far north."

"If it wasn't for that damned landslide that spooked my men, we would've been finished with this days ago."

"Why don't you and your men raid the Castro Ranch yourselves?"

"I haven't enough men at my disposal."

"And you say they want you back when you can't even find anyone to follow you?"

He curled his lip like a growling dog.

"You have no hope of winning a war against The States or a coup against Herrera." That perked his ears right up. "I, too, am well informed. In fact, I can guarantee that even if you succeed, you won't be in office for more than two years." The History Channel said so.

"You would make a formidable adversary, Carmena." This time he said my name like it was dessert. "Come with me, and I will make you a lucky woman."

"Even if I didn't find you so repulsive, I doubt your wife would approve."

He glowered and stood. His steps were long and deliberate, the limp on his makeshift prosthetic barely visible. Had it not been for his height, we'd be nose to nose. I stood my ground, and thankfully my wide-legged gauchos and thick leather boots hid my shaking knees.

"I'm telling you, Antonio. There's no point in starting a war. The American troops outnumber and outclass your soldiers. And what the hell makes you think for one second I'd risk my men to get you the shipment in the first place?"

He smiled. If he had an ace up his sleeve, he'd pull it out now.

And he did.

From his pocket, he retrieved the silver chain attached to my amulet. The charm twirled and reflected the candlelight off every tiny curve. Santa Anna was older, but he was also faster. I tried to grab the necklace and his long arm held it out of reach. My hand snatched at empty space.

"Where the hell did you get that?" I demanded.

"Our encounter under the blankets was rewarding in so many ways." Santa Anna moistened his lips. Negotiating wasn't one of my strong suits, and I didn't know how to play this game, but I had to try.

"There's no monetary value to that trinket, Antonio, and this isn't a very polite way to thank me for my hospitality."

"This means more to you than life itself. Isn't that what you said? Perhaps it is as valuable as a shipment of guns and ammunition?"

Santa Anna dropped my necklace back into his pocket and leaned forward, his other hand resting on the hilt of his gun. "Only because I admire you, Carmena, do I promise to return it when you deliver the guns." He lifted a strand of my hair and smelled it. "I find it erotic to blackmail such an exquisite woman."

I shoved his hand away, and his temper blazed. He stomped to the door, and I looked about for an object to conk over his head.

"I will shoot anyone who tries to stop me," he said with his back to me. And I knew he would. A great number of his people capitulated to his intimidating threats because they knew he'd see them through.

The man strolled through the common room, and I followed him. Jesse stood outside the bunkhouse and held Dusty's reins. I wouldn't risk Jesse's life by asking him, unarmed, to stop Santa Anna. The ex-president mounted my horse.

"Two nights, Carmena." It tweaked my nerves every time he said my name.

He kicked Dusty into a gallop and wasted no time in getting off my property. I ran a short way after my horse and Jesse followed. In the nearly faded sunset a trio of shadows came out of nowhere and waited on their mounts for Santa Anna under the Holiday Ranch arch at the entrance of the gravel drive. They must have been scouting our property for days. A cloud of dust trailed after the ex-president and his cohorts.

"Why in the hell did you give him my horse?" I asked Jesse.

"Gee, ma'am, y'all know how that ol' girl is meaner than a snake when Carlos or you ain't ridin' her. She'll buck him off 'bout the two mile mark afore she comes back home."

That was true. Dusty had been well trained by my foreman.

"Where's Carlos?"

"Last I saw he was findin' another excuse ta visit the kitchen."

"Thank you, Jesse. Please see that Angela remembers to clean up the back room in the bunkhouse."

He knew I referred to the secret room that wasn't much of a secret now that Santa Anna and the captain had visited.

My thoughts whirled as I jogged to the kitchen to find Carlos. The amulet seemed a petty reason to put the lives of our ranch family at risk. But I'd still put them in jeopardy if I didn't heed Sadie's warning by upsetting the balance of both the past and future when I didn't return home.

It wasn't only my life and the lives of those I grew to care for on the ranch that I had to consider. Now complete strangers, people I would never meet, could be caught in a ripple effect of consequences if I didn't do the right thing.

Responsibility had some terrible downsides, and I had a feeling I was going to find out how terrible they could be.

CHAPTER 21

Carlos ate freshly baked cookies, and the rich smell of his coffee sifted through the air as he flirted with Violet in the kitchen.

"Carlos? May I have a word with you?"

He looked at Violet and said, "You told me we could speak freely in front of Violet."

"I need to see you in the library," I said, my voice as dark as my spirits. Carlos caught my meaning and gave Violet a quick glimpse before following me.

"What's so urgent?" he asked.

I didn't utter a word until the double doors of the library closed behind us. "I know where the amulet is. Santa Anna has it. He took it with him."

"What! Why didn't you tell me?"

"I didn't know until a moment ago, and he'd have shot anyone who tried to take it away. When he left just now, only Jesse was there, unarmed."

"I can't believe you didn't take his gun away sooner!"

I sat down. "I meant to remind Angela to bring it inside the house, but I forgot."

"She should have known to hide it."

"Angela's been in too much of an emotional state for her to remember details," I said. Hunched over on the divan, I shoved my fingers into the hair at my temples.

Carlos sat down and put an arm across my shoulder. "Do you have any idea where he's gone?"

"No, but I know where he'll be tomorrow night."

"Then we'll get it back."

"He's demanding the rest of Herrera's shipment."

Carlos jumped up. "How did he know about it?"

"He didn't say." He rubbed his day-old beard.

"We don't even know where the cavalry is keeping their supplies. There's not enough time for a thorough search to find where more guns and ammunition are stored." On top of losing my necklace, Carlos just confirmed that the military was the source of the guns we resold for profit.

"Santa Anna said the guns are at Castro's old ranch."

"How does he know that?"

"I don't know, nor do I care. He said he'll give me the amulet when we give him the weapons."

"Why the hell doesn't he get them for himself?"

"I only saw about three men at the front gate. There's probably a small army guarding the weapons."

"You have no choice, Carmena."

"Will you help me?"

"You don't have to ask."

"Yes, I do. I didn't want to place any one of us in danger ever again. That's why I bought all those stocks, so we could bring in money to the ranch without putting ourselves in danger." I stood up and paced. "Why this? Why now, when I was feeling so close to leaving?"

"Perhaps you were not meant to leave."

I wiped the chill off my arms. "I need to return."

"We need to see how many guards are on duty," Carlos said. "Maybe there's not much security since it's such an unlikely place for storage, and it'll be easier to take them since we only need half the shipment."

I took my seat again, threw my head back, and closed my eyes. "Who did we lose in the last raid?"

"A drifter. Temporary help. We barely knew his first name. Javier said he could still smell the whiskey on his breath when he buried him. That was why everything went wrong, but there will be no problem with the proper planning."

"And God willing, no casualties," I said.

"I want Javier and Jesse well rested before they scout the ranch tonight. I'm going to pull them off their chores right now."

"Good luck with that. Should we invite the new men to the raid?"

"Let's get Jesse's opinion on that. He knows them better than we do." Carlos put a hand on my shoulder. "Everything will work out fine, Mandy. We won't be caught, and we'll get your necklace back." He chucked me under the chin, and I smiled half-heartedly.

"I need some time alone. Why don't you go back to the kitchen?" I lifted my eyebrows up and down in rapid succession.

For the first time, I saw Carlos blush.

"*Ay, Diós,*" he said and left the room.

ↄ∕ↄↄ∕ↄ

The talk of the table over breakfast the next morning was Dusty's return to the ranch about twenty minutes after she left with Santa Anna, and everyone had a lighthearted chuckle. If horses could talk.

I asked Violet to make another batch of her delicious coffee.

"I'll be with the field hands," I said and took the entire pot to the bunkhouse, filling every cup. The mood was somber. Javier and Jesse cleaned and polished their guns. Joe drew a map and Roy stood over him.

I joined them at the table. "What's this?"

Joe was the verbal one of the two. "A map of Castro's place. Me an' Roy worked it a time back."

"Get out!" I said.

Joe and Roy exchanged glances and the men stood to leave. Javier's lower lip dropped.

"Wait! That's not what I meant." I pulled on Joe's arm. "So, you really worked there?"

"Yes, ma'am," he said and sat back down.

"You know, none of you have to do this. I mean, you won't lose your jobs or anything."

Carlos walked in. "That's what I said."

"He did at that," agreed Joe. Roy bobbed his head. "All them no account soldiers do is kill off them injuns," Joe said. "Don't rattle me none ta take guns from 'em." Roy bobbed his head again.

"Thanks, guys. Now, give me the dour-one-one on this map."

"Beg yer pardon, ma'am?" Joe mimicked the puzzled expressions of the other men. Carlos smiled and shook his head.

I sighed. "Tell me about the map." For fifteen minutes, Joe gave us a number of details, and when he finished, we all thought we could walk the property blindfolded.

Carlos turned to Jesse and Javier. "If you leave at ten tonight at a decent trot, you'll get there about eleven. Jess, take count of the soldiers. Find out how often they change shifts. Javier, you need to find out where they're holding the weapons and make sure there are enough. I want you back by sunrise tomorrow."

I stood, and the men followed suit. I picked up the empty coffee pot. "I want to know the second Jesse and Javier are back."

In the kitchen, the metal pot clanked when I set it down too hard on the counter. Angela set the last of the dishes inside the drainer and told me to sit down. She rubbed out every stiff muscle above my shoulders, and Violet set a mug of herbal tea in front of me, a recipe prescribed by Sadie for nerves.

୧๑୧

Late at night, we wished our reconnaissance team a safe journey. Several tense hours passed with little or no sleep for the adults. The men returned to the ranch before the sun rose. We gathered in the bunkhouse and, as it turned out, the surveillance passed without incident.

"Ain't no more than eight men guardin' the entire ranch," Jesse said. "Only two of 'em was outside fer a three-hour shift bafore two others come out an' replaced 'em at the back door."

"Did they inspect the barn right away?" Carlos asked.

"They never did," Javier answered. "They just took a walk about the place before they sat down for a smoke."

"They done left the barn windy wide open, too," Jesse added.

"What's inside the barn?" I asked.

Javier answered. "Lots of crates filled with pistols, rifles, and bullets. The barn is on the opposite side of the house, and the window faces the fence line, only about twenty feet away. We can hide the wagon behind a mess of mesquite trees."

"Thar's an old gate without a lock right next ta them trees. We kin grease up them hinges, an' they'll be quieter than a pig after slaughter. It'll be a walk straight from the wagon ta the windy without bein' seen," Jesse said.

"Javier and Joe are the biggest men here," Carlos said. "You men knock out the two soldiers on duty, if they're not inclined to stop for a smoke, and move them out of the way. You'll climb through the window and pass the guns and ammo to Roy and Jesse while Carmena and I keep watch from the front and rear of the ranch."

"How long you figger it'll take ta load the wagon?" Joe asked.

"If we move quickly, no more than ten minutes or so to get what we need," Carlos answered. "Jesse, you'll take the guns to the delivery site, and I'll ride behind you, covering the rear. Joe and Roy, you'll ride in the brush alongside the road in case we're ambushed by soldiers or highwaymen. Javier, you ride back to the ranch with Carmena."

"Me?" I said. "What do I need an escort for? I'm coming with you."

"It's too dangerous since you were last injured." Carlos stared me down. I think he was trying to remind me that I might have no idea what to do in a raid. "Besides—" He leaned over and added in a near whisper, "—if your memory fails, how will you be able to get back to the ranch in the dark alone?"

It was a good argument by itself. There was a chance I could get lost even if it wasn't dark. I couldn't depend on Carmena's memories always coming through for me.

"But why should I miss out on any of the fun?" Javier protested. "Besides, we need you to run the ranch if we're caught."

"Javier, you have a wife and children," Carlos said.

"And so will you one day," Javier said, "if Violet's desperate enough to hitch up."

We all laughed, except Carlos who ignored the ridicule. "Regardless, I'm a single man now. Without children."

Javier stood up to his supervisor. "I'm riding with Jesse. We've always worked as a team, and you're not gonna break us up now."

"He got hisself a point there, Carlos," Jesse said. "Tain't like we ain't done this bafore."

Carlos sighed, deferring to Javier's wishes. "Be careful. My gut says this one sounds too easy."

"Why don't we wear them disguises that Angela made fer us the last time?" Jesse suggested.

The new men looked hopeful. "Ya mean a mask jest like them stage coach robbers wear?" Joe asked. Roy showed his enthusiasm with a quirky smile.

"That's not a bad idea," Carlos said. "Even though the almanac said the overcast we've had all week will give us good cover, I'm all for taking extra precautions. Carmena, if you see anything go wrong, give a warning whistle, and I'll fire off a shot or two to raise a ruckus. That should get the soldiers going in my direction at the front of the ranch."

"Javier, don't forget to give the all clear signal when you're finished in the barn," I said.

Javier sang out a slow owl call. "Hoooo-hoooo!" The eerie sound floated to the rafters and descended like an ethereal portent, not exactly comforting.

Jesse shouldered him. "That was jest outright scary, Javi. Y'all tryin' ta curse us or somethin'?"

"Whatever," Javier said.

Carlos deflected their bantering. "We'll go over it again before we leave tonight. We all need to save our strength and keep our chores to a minimum throughout the day."

Joe and Roy cooled off the horses while the rest of us headed to the house for a few hours of sleep. A gradient strip of lavender hemmed the top of the horizon, and the jagged hills looked like monstrous shadows coming to life.

When we reached the front steps, I asked Carlos, "How bad is that gut feeling of yours?"

"Let's just be extra careful," he said. "I'm thinking the sooner we have done with this, the better."

We ambled up the stairs. "We only need a small amount of ammo, and we'll be wearing masks," I rationalized.

"Good morning, Carmena." At the top of the stairs, he veered left down the hallway, although his room was in the opposite direction.

Violet was more than likely waiting for him.

୧⁓ଦ⁓ଦ

Later, after a few hours' sleep, everyone acted normally, as if we weren't conducting a raid against the military that night. The captain's pending visit for lunch gave us something else to think about.

Violet and Angela acted like the Pope awarded me a private audience. The house had been meticulously cleaned and dusted. Violet sent the kids out to collect any type of flower in bloom and, thanks to her artistic talents, stunning floral arrangements colored the rooms downstairs.

My ranch foreman reacted quite the opposite about the captain's lunch visit. Carlos knew that Captain Sanders was sweet on Carmena, and that I had developed a sweet tooth of my own.

Carlos prepared a duplicate inventory sheet, recording stores depleted by Franz, and the list included an unnecessary but thorough account of Franz's assault. If anyone had picked their nose that day, I was sure Carlos included it in his report.

He held out the papers to me. "Remember when you said you had no idea how Santa Anna's premature death could affect history?"

"Yes, but what does that have to do with your report?"

"You don't know what will happen if you interfere in the relationship between Carmena and Captain Sanders. I suggest you keep your feelings out of this."

I yanked the papers out of his hand. "Thank you for the reminder, Carlos, as unnecessary as it was."

℘℩℘℩

Javier and Jesse selected the most pitiful specimen of horses, a few nags we rescued from neighboring ranches, and runty yearlings, and placed them in the lower corrals. Roy and Joe helped herd the prime stock, cattle and horses alike, to graze in the high meadow.

Martino swept the patios and covered a table in the large gazebo. Violet set out place settings of imported bone china and cut Irish stemware from the cabinet in the ballroom. Martha Stewart would have tweeted over the table arrangements.

Carlos, on Angela's orders, burned a variety of herbs that were known to keep insects at bay. Violet informed me that the menu was nothing special. She and Angela decided to prepare part of our dinner early and use a fraction of it for the captain's visit.

My first choice of standard gauchos and cotton blouse had been vetoed by my female staff. Violet handed me a pale pink cotton dress, most likely chosen for the low-cut bodice.

My two housekeepers, turned stylists, pinned up my hair with long tendrils curling down my back and sides. Tiny white and pink flowers were planted in the strands. Angela instructed Gracie to dab a bit of French perfume on either side of my neck. Carlos wanted to play on the captain's guilt, but the women were having a shot at feminine stratagems.

None of the ruses was necessary. I knew Captain Sanders would do anything for Carmena, and I shoved Carlos's warning to the back of the bus.

There was an urgent knock on my bedroom door, and Angela huffed, annoyed by the interruption of the vital makeover.

"Come in," I said as I clipped on dainty pearl earrings. Violet closed the clasp on a matching strand at my neck.

"He's here!" Martino announced. He spied my attire and coiffed hair, and his eyes lit up. He walked slowly to the vanity and took my hand. "Gee, you're pretty, Carmena."

He kissed the back of my hand, and I caught Violet out of the corner of my eye holding back Angela's reprimand.

"Thank you, Martino. I'm pleased that you noticed."

He looked down at his hand holding mine and blushed. Then he dropped it and darted out of the room. Violet and I laughed. Angela smiled.

"¡*Ay, Diós*!" Angela said. "He is too young to act like the captain."

At the mention of the man, my corset felt too tight, and I felt my face grow hot.

Violet fanned me. "Breathe!" she ordered.

"It's not like you haven't seen the captain before," Angela reminded me.

I stared at my heaving chest in the mirror. "Yeah, but I truly doubt he'll have seen this much of me before."

"You look beautiful, *mijita.*"

I stood and posed before the floor length mirror. "I look like a prom queen." The Georgian style gown surrounded my body three feet in every direction. "Don't you think I'm a bit overdressed for the occasion?"

"Not for this one," Violet answered.

The women ushered me out the door and accompanied me down the hall. They took the staircase on the opposite wing to the kitchen. Following their instructions, I waited five minutes before I stepped gracefully down the stairwell as if I were attending a debutante ball.

Sanders's deep voice carried as he conversed with Carlos in the parlor. Angela poured him a glass of her lemonade. He tasted the tangy drink, and at that precise moment, gazed up at me and said, "Delicious."

Carlos came into view, and for an instant he wore the same wide-eyed look of wonder. He studied the captain, and his eyes turned to red laser beams, targeting the officer for destruction. Carlos turned his burning orbs onto me as Charles absent-mindedly handed his glass to him and met me at the bottom of the stairs. He held his hand out, and I took it. It felt like the first time we had ever seen each other.

"For heaven's sakes!" Carlos said.

Angela scurried into the foyer and told Carlos she needed him to check the stove to see why it wasn't heating up properly.

As she dragged him past the stairs, Carlos pointed a finger at us. "I'll be right back. Don't you two do anything until I return!"

Angela smacked him on the back of the head, and he asked, "What did I do?"

CHAPTER 22

Charles took a few more moments to ogle, and I welcomed his attention.

"You are absolutely beautiful," he finally said. Warm lips pressed against the back of my hand.

He smiled, and I gushed. "If I am beautiful, then you, Captain, are radiant."

He laughed, and his cheeks turned a little crimson. "Please, call me Charles, Carmena." He held out his arm, and I rested my hand on it as he escorted me inside the parlor.

We heard Carlos throwing a hissy fit across the house. "Would you mind closing the doors behind you, Charles? It may not be appropriate but neither is the behavior of my foreman."

"I shall be only too happy to accommodate you," he replied and closed both doors to the parlor. They squeaked a bit, and I gathered from Carmena's memories that it was the first time they had been closed in quite a while.

"Did I see you with a drink?"

He looked around the tables. "It seems to have disappeared."

"Let me pour you another. Would you care for lemonade, tea, brandy?"

"The lemonade was rather—" Charles scanned me up and down. "—tasty."

Even if I wasn't the only woman in the room, the captain would've made me feel like it. The longer I stared at his handsome features, the more I wanted to grab the sides of this face and plant a lip lock on him with more suction than my Dyson vacuum.

He grinned. "Are you all right, Carmena?"

"Yes, why do you ask?"

"You appear to have trouble…breathing." He glanced at my chest, and I heaved in a breath of air that nearly made my bodice rip and his eyes pop out. My hand below my throat reminded me to exhale.

"I'm fine."

He gave me another one of those great blinding smiles then leaned forward. Up close, his blue eyes brightened and intensified. His lips were just a fingertip apart from mine when the parlor doors flew open.

"Lunch is served."

Carlos sounded winded, as if he'd run from the kitchen.

∽∼∽∼∽

Charles took in the decorated gazebo, pleased we went through so much to impress him.

Carlos stood by the table like a private maître d'. Maybe more like a hitman. He helped me with my seat and pointed at a chair across the table. Charles smiled, picked up his chair and moved it right next to mine.

Carlos stormed off to the kitchen. Violet appeared and moved the place setting for the captain.

"Thank you," he said and stood. "We haven't been properly introduced, ma'am."

Violet had already started blushing, a common effect his handsome face and gorgeous body had on the opposite sex, regardless of age or marital status.

"I'm Violet, Captain."

He bowed. "I'm charmed, Violet. Captain Sanders at your service."

She smiled and rushed back into the house, fussing with her hair and straightening her apron.

Charles and I engaged in small talk. It didn't matter what we said. We knew what the other was thinking.

Angela came out with Gracie and each carried a small covered dish. Violet marched behind them, a large water pitcher in hand. She poured cold spring water into our crystal goblets, strained more than once to remove the sediment.

Violet scooped a fried corn tortilla topped with what looked like refried beans, shredded lettuce, and melted cheese onto each of our bread plates. "Legumes on flatbread," she said. She spooned the contents of another small dish onto the cheese. "With tomato coriander chutney."

I could have sworn it was Angela's salsa on mini tostadas.

"It looks wonderful," Charles said. His smile had the same effect on her as it did me. The silly grin never left Violet's face. He took one bite and would probably have married the cook if he weren't so in love with me, or rather, Carmena. "Delightful, Violet."

She blushed. "It's Angela's recipe. I'll be back with your main course in a short while."

For a split second, I saw Carlos at the back door. Someone's hand clamped down on his shoulder and dragged him back inside.

To the captain, I said, "I'm lucky to employ two wonderful cooks on my ranch."

"I can't believe you can eat like this and still look like that." He held up his water glass. I wasn't certain what we toasted to, but I clinked my glass against his.

"I'm so glad you were able to join me for lunch today, Charles." My eyelashes batted on their own.

He held my hand. "Carlos might be upset if he sees me holding your hand."

I glanced covertly at the back door.

"Second level, far right window," Charles said.

"That would be Angela and Javier's room."

"Maybe he had to speak to them."

"Javier's shoeing horses, and Angela's in the kitchen. Maybe he's spying on us."

Charles wasn't fazed by the idea. "What would you have me do?"

"I would ask you to act as if you didn't see him."

He grinned, brought my hand up to his lips, and kissed it.

"Now what is he doing?" I asked.

Charles barely glanced at the window. "I believe he has smashed his nose into the glass."

I laughed. "I wonder what he would've done if it wasn't my hand that you kissed." I blurted the innuendo, forgetting that a flirtatious remark from my time was taken a lot more seriously in this era.

Red crossed the captain's cheeks, but after the shock of my bold remark wore off, he tilted my chin with his free hand and kissed me. Soft and warm, but with a jarring consequence. My body shuddered from the inside out. My corset selfishly guarded the air I should have been breathing.

As soon as oxygen managed to reenter my lungs, I whispered through closed eyes, "What is Carlos doing now?"

The captain chuckled. "I don't see him anymore."

I lifted my lids, and his staggering blue eyes pierced me like an ice pick in a soft stick of butter.

"I have a feeling we'll see him at any moment," I said.

Sure enough, Carlos barreled through the back door, Angela running after him. Carlos, clearly incensed, charged the table, shaking off Angela's hand. "Captain! I'm afraid I must call you out on your impertinent behavior!"

Charles was about to stand, but I held onto his arm

Angela stepped between the chairs and whispered, "I sent Gracie to get Jesse."

On cue, Jesse jogged through the iron gate and said, "Wha, Cap'n Sanders, it's shorely nice ta see ya agin."

Charles stood and shook hands with Jesse across the table. "Mr. Calhoun."

"I'll have none a that mister business. Y'all jest call me Jesse." He turned immediately to Carlos and put his arm around the tense shoulders. "Say, Carlos, I kin sure use some help with that door on the side of the barn."

"Why isn't Javier fixing it?" he snapped.

"He's shoeing taday. Mind helpin' me a spell?" He pulled Carlos by the arm. Carlos shot me with a squinty-eyed threat, then the captain, as he was swept away by the smooth-talking wrangler.

"Captain, please sit down," Angela said. "I'll bring out your lunch in a moment."

"Thank you, Angela."

She smiled like a doting mother hen and left us alone.

"Perhaps Carlos feels I'm stepping into his territory," Charles said.

"He wants to take care of the ranch and everything on it."

He brushed a strand of hair from my face. "And what do you want?"

"At this point?" I heard footsteps coming across the patio. "A little more privacy."

He kissed my hand again, right in front of Angela and Violet. They giggled at each other.

Violet announced the main course, pork roast on a bed of wild rice with a side of vegetables. At any other time, we would have called it carnitas and grilled corn. Charles and I dined while he kept my attention with enjoyable stories of his travels and the happier moments of his military assignments. He listened as I borrowed from Carmena's memories and shared tales about our fun adventures on Holiday Ranch. We never took our eyes off of each other.

I didn't want to discuss my problems with Franz or our proposed contract with the military. What I really wanted was complete honesty, to tell him about the upcoming raid and how desperately I needed my amulet back.

"How long have we known each other, Charles?"

He leaned back into his chair, his hands intertwined behind his head. His biceps stretched the seams of his jacket. "I think it's been almost a year now."

"Only one?" I asked. He nodded. "In some ways, it feels that I've known you so much longer."

"True, but I fear that I don't get to see you as often as I'd like. In fact, that brings to mind something I've been wanting to ask you about, Carmena." He leaned forward and covered my hand on the table. "I want to talk to you about something to ensure that we will see each other much more in the future."

"Dessert!" Gracie thankfully announced.

I didn't know for sure what the captain was going to say, but no doubt, it wasn't mine to hear.

Gracie set down two slices of a triple-layer chocolate cake with ganache filling and fudge frosting. My mouth instantly watered. Gracie's little hands were clasped behind her back as she twisted side to side. "I helped make the cake, Captain."

"I can't wait to taste it!" Charles said. She grinned, and he asked, "Would you like to join us for dessert, Gracie?"

"Yes, but Mama said we have to stay inside so you can kiss Carmena again." She immediately covered her mouth. Charles and I laughed.

"You go grab some cake and a fork, then come back out here. Tell your mother I said that was an order." He winked at Gracie who answered with a huge smile and happily ran back to the kitchen.

"Why, Charles, I do believe you have a soft spot for the little ones."

"Actually, I despise children, but I'm hoping Gracie won't finish her cake, and I can eat the rest of hers."

"Go ahead and deny it, but I know otherwise."

"The truth is—" His brilliant blue eyes lit up as he took both my hands into his and did that wonderful soul-penetrating stare. "Someday soon, I hope to have a few of my own, with the only woman who has ever captured my heart." We heard Gracie giggle as she took her seat, saving me from stammering through a response.

My taste buds exploded as I bit into the chocolate dessert. Gracie ate all of hers, but I gave most of mine to the captain.

Charles was the only dessert I wanted.

჻჻჻

"Thank you for your invitation to lunch, Carmena."

Angela, Violet, Martino, and Gracie followed us to the front door. "It was my pleasure, Charles. Perhaps next week you can join us for dinner?"

"I'd like that." Someone sighed and he said, "Angela, Violet, thank you for a superb meal."

"*Gracias*, Captain."

"Glad you enjoyed it, sir."

He bent over Gracie and lightly tapped the tip of her nose. "And that was the best chocolate cake ever." She giggled and hid behind her mother, suddenly shy with so much of his masculine attention.

"Martino." He shook hands with the boy. "You did a great job, too. Carmena tells me it's like having another man around the ranch with you working so hard around here."

The boy puffed out his chest and hitched up his pants. "Carlos said he'll teach me how to take inventory real soon."

"Did he?" Violet asked.

"After my homework," Martino explained.

Charles opened the front door, and I pulled it shut behind us before we were followed. We stepped down to the hitching post.

"Charles, I have to tell you something."

"What is it?" He gently placed his hands on my shoulders, and he reignited that feeling in me of a love-struck freshman in a teen movie.

"I was supposed to present you with a contract, asking the military to allow us to produce livestock for the fort instead of having our best breeding stock confiscated. We've been losing money on the ranch. I guess I got so carried away with your visit that I forgot to bring it up."

"You didn't have to go through all this trouble. I'd speak to President Polk himself if you asked me to."

"It was no trouble and speaking to your commanding officer will do."

"I can wait here if you want to get the contract."

I thought about it. "No. I'd rather you come back next week and get it."

Charles pulled me into his arms. He gave me a possessive ten-point-oh cave-man kiss, the kind most women dream about. My legs wobbled like Jell-O.

We must've spun in a circle because, when I pulled back, I saw Carlos standing at the overhead veranda. He shook his head, slowly, like I'd failed him. Like I'd betrayed Carmena, and suddenly it felt like I had. Carlos stepped away from the rail, and I heard a door close.

My foreman may have been acting out of jealousy, but he could've also been reminding me that I wasn't the Carmena Charles fell in love with. Even if I couldn't find a way back to my own time, I had to keep reminding myself that I had no right to infringe on a love that belonged to someone else.

"What's this sad face?"

"Honestly? I miss you when we're apart."

Charles stroked my cheek and said, "I don't know why things have changed the past couple of weeks, but my heart can no longer contain all the love I feel for you. It feels like it's going to burst."

Then he planted another fantasy kiss on me. Lucky thing Carlos hadn't hung around. What I would've given to live forever in that moment, with one of his hands at the nape of my neck, pulling my mouth deeper into his, and his other hand at the small of my back, drawing my body closer.

The captain pulled away and rested his forehead against mine. "Carmena." He gulped air.

"Charles."

"We have to talk soon, sweetheart. About our future."

Why did he have to ruin it for me and talk about the future? I couldn't have him, and I didn't know for certain how the real Carmena felt about him. I'd have to let him down very gently, leaving the possibility open of his getting back together with my ethereal counterpart.

"I'm on a special assignment this weekend, but I'll come calling next week, if I may, for that dinner."

Instead of ending it right then, I said, "I'll be glad for another visit."

He embraced me. "I don't want to let you go. It's too hard saying good-bye to you, Carmena."

"Then just say 'See you later, alligator.'"

The captain stared as if I'd lost all sanity. Then he laughed. "All right." This time he gave me a quick kiss and climbed onto his horse, a former thoroughbred tenant of my ranch. "See you later, alligator." He winked.

"After a while, crocodile." Charles laughed again. I stepped back and blew him a kiss. His stallion cantered down the gravel lined drive, and then Charles motioned his horse about and waved. I blew him another kiss.

I turned to the front door. It was wide open, filled with my housekeepers, the children, Jesse, and Javier. They were all smiling.

Carlos wasn't there.

ϵ↷ϵ↷

It was my turn to say grace at dinner. I prayed, "Dear Lord, thank you for all of my amazing employees on the ranch. They are loyal and discreet in every way. I'm so glad they respect my privacy and don't make snide comments about my personal life, especially at the dinner table. We give thanks for this meal. Amen."

"Amen," came the disappointed replies.

Violet set two platters of carnitas tostadas on either end of the table next to the salsa and refried beans. Angela brought out rice and Mexican style corn with peas and peppers.

The meal was delicious and as I started in on seconds, I called across the table to Violet, "Would you please pass the tender seasoned pork and the tomato coriander chutney?"

She grinned.

"I don't believe we got nothin' like that on this here table," Joe said.

Violet passed the carnitas and salsa.

For dessert, we enjoyed the best chocolate three-layer cake on the planet.

CHAPTER 23

Carlos stood next to the library doors after dinner. He leaned against the jamb and toyed with his cigar. "Well?"

"Well, what?" I rummaged through my notes, recording the amounts of the drafts prepared for Beauford.

"How did it go?"

"You saw for yourself, Carlos. You stared out every single window during the entire visit."

"I did not," he denied. "Only from Javier and Angela's. And Gracie's room. Mine didn't count."

"What about from the veranda?"

"There, too."

"Don't worry. I'm not going to make any romantic decisions for Carmena."

"I know she'd appreciate the gesture." He strolled to the fireplace and toyed with a candleholder on the mantel. "It seems I have to apologize for my behavior more and more around you."

"You probably wouldn't have to if I didn't forget my place so often."

"Perhaps this is your place."

"I'd agree, but I'm too easily filled with guilt when I think about Carmena," I said. "Is she happy wherever she is? And then I think of my home, my family. I have so much yet to do."

"Maybe you and Carmena are both happier in your new homes," Carlos said.

"Yeah, and maybe we both feel too guilty to enjoy it." A moment passed.

"What did the captain think about your contract?" He chuckled. "I'm sure he didn't know you could write like a solicitor."

"Uh, yeah. About that contract…"

"He did agree to deliver it to his commanding officer, didn't he?" He sat down at the edge of the leather chair. "After all the animals they've stolen, he didn't have the nerve to refuse us?"

I didn't know what to say.

"Mandy?"

"I didn't actually give it to him."

"What?" His voice boomed.

"Sshhh! You're ranting like Beauford Jones."

"Do you know how much trouble we went through to make this the perfect opportunity for you to present the idea to him?"

"Yeah. You wanted me to act like a saloon girl so we could have our way with him, and when I did you went off the deep end." He crossed his arms. "I told him about the agreement, and he's coming for dinner next week so we can discuss it in more detail," I continued.

"For gawdsakes." He stood and paced the room. "Not only do we have to worry about the raid, but now we have to put on another performance for that heartsick puppy!"

"You shouldn't throw stones, Mr. Take-Measurements-for-the-Stove-a-Million-Times."

He humphed and left the library.

芝芝芝

I woke up in the dark from a power nap just before eleven. I dressed, finding comfort in wearing my Brazilian jeans. I planned on winding the amulet as soon as the raid was over, and gauchos weren't the current height of fashion in the future. Besides, if there was a chance I was going to die, I wanted to do so in style. I decided to keep my screwdriver with me, too. I had a feeling we might need it, maybe to pry open the barn window if it was locked. The pink plastic handle formed a bulky lump inside my back pocket, but better to keep the unusual color under wraps.

We gathered inside the bunkhouse, and the men stared at my jeans, but no one dared comment on the tight pants. It was my rubber-soled running shoes that really commanded their attention.

"What in tarnation are y'all wearin' on yer feet?" Joe asked.

"You only see her boots." Carlos spoke in a deep voice, his dark eyes filled with warning.

I hadn't heard him speak like that before, and it scared me as much as it did Joe. The subject was instantly forgotten.

Thick cloud cover darkened the night, yet our surefooted horses easily negotiated dips in the trail. Just after midnight we were within a quarter mile of the Castro Ranch at the corner of the immense property. A clink of metal startled us, and Jesse slowed the team.

Javier, a dark shadow atop his mount, said, "I think it's a chain that came loose from the wagon. Happened to us on the way inta town the other day, but I thought I fixed it."

"We prob'ly jest need ta tuck it inta place agin," Joe said. He dismounted and softly cried out as he lost his footing and fell to the ground. Roy and Carlos flew off their horses.

"What happened?" Carlos demanded.

"Got maself stuck in a pothole. 'T'ain't nothin' but a little ol' sprain is all."

"Little or not," Carlos said. "It's enough to keep you from climbing into the barn. Jesse, you're going to have to take Joe's place and help Javier. Hand the ammo out the window to Roy and me. Roy and I will load up the boxes. Joe, you drive the team. Javier, ride on up and find out where those guards are."

Javier took off, and Joe said, "Reckon I kin handle the wagon. I'm a might sorry fer undoin' yer plans, Carlos."

Jesse set the brake, stepped off the buckboard, and took Joe's horse. Roy put an arm under Joe's shoulders and helped him hobble into the wagon. Carlos tucked the loose chain into place and secured it with twine. Before long, Javier returned with his report.

"Two guards are on duty. They're smokin' on the far side of the ranch."

"We'll wait until a few minutes after the guards change shifts. Everyone put on your masks, and let's get a move on," Carlos ordered.

By the time I reached my position at the top of the rise behind the main house and hid with Dusty inside a copse of trees, the cloud cover disintegrated, and a full moon lit up the ranch below. Apparently, Carlos read the wrong night in the Farmer's Almanac. The only thing missing was a neon sign flashing "Robbery in Progress."

Joe steered the wagon down the fence line. My anxiety level caught up to my heart's quickened pace. Critters everywhere tapped into the strange undercurrent surrounding the makeshift storage facility. Quiet settled like a thick blanket. Even cicadas and crickets gave us the silent treatment. The night made no sound, but it breathed faster in the brightest moonlight possible.

Two soldiers stood at the back porch, smoking and shooting the breeze. We waited about twenty exasperating minutes, and I had a sudden urge to call off the foray. As I started to give the signal to abandon ship, a couple more soldiers stepped out of the back door and assumed guard duty. The two smokers went inside, and the two replacements gamboled along the perimeter of the house, then over to the barn. They hand rolled cigarettes and lit up, and I prayed they didn't hear our horses hidden in the tangle of mesquite trees.

The guards turned the corner of the barn and were out of sight. Javier cut the barbed wire and ran to the side of the building, Jesse staying close behind. From my vantage point, I saw their black silhouettes sink low against the building. They didn't climb into the window right away. Javier peeked around the corner, in case the two soldiers veered full cycle, and lucky thing they decided to wait.

In a few minutes, the guards came back around the far corner. Preoccupied with conversation and lighting up another cigarette, neither one saw the crouched men and were easily gun butted, collapsing like silent accordions to the ground.

Javier and Jesse quickly hog tied the unconscious guards and heaved the bodies next to the barn wall. Jesse pulled the window open and climbed over the sash. Javier dived in after him. The shadowed figures of Carlos and Roy stood outside the window and waited for the first hand-off.

Jesse and Javier pushed a large crate over the sill and the recipients struggled with the clumsy box between them. The moment it was placed on the wagon, Carlos and Roy jogged back to the barn window for another. Twelve minutes later, they held the last crate of weapons between them. Javier gave the owl signal. They were finished.

I barely took in my first relaxing breath when someone opened the back door.

A soldier in socks and an unbuttoned shirt stuck his head out the door. "Hey Frank! Henry! Y'all want some coffee an' hot apple pie?"

Carlos and Roy were midway to the wagon with the last crate and froze. Javier's torso and one of his legs hung out the barn window. My muscles tightened, and Dusty stood perfectly still.

"Frank! Henry! You guys up fer some pie?" the man blared again.

Roy, probably figuring that if there was no answer they'd come looking, bellowed, "Nah!"

"Suit yerselves," the man hollered and went back inside but not before one of the hitched horses whinnied nervously. The soldier at the back door did an about face on the stoop. "What the hell you fellers up to back there?"

Dusty took an anxious step back, and a twig snapped under her hoof. The man scanned the hill in my direction and took off at a sprint inside the house. I pursed my lips and whistled. Nothing came out. I puckered again and again with only fruitless results. As I mastered a decent swish of my tongue about my mouth and a thorough wetting of my lips, the back door flung open and six armed men ran outside. A shrill whistle shot out between my fingers, a call for "Drop everything and get the hell out of there!"

Carlos and Roy let the last box fall and made for their horses as Joe tried to get the team out of a rut. Jesse pushed Javier out of the barn window and started to climb over the sash. Three uniformed men ran between the house and barn to circle round the front side and the other three ran alongside the barn, straight toward the fence.

Javier jogged the short span to the fence but didn't jump high enough over the box of guns. His body flew over the crate and he landed nose to the ground as Jesse tumbled over the window sash.

The soldiers appeared from either side of the barn pointing their rifles directly at Jesse, and one yelled, "Halt or I'll shoot!"

Jesse threw his arms up. The soldiers crept out from their cover and set him in their sites. Tension charged the air. No one spoke, moved, or uttered a sound for three of the longest seconds before gunfire sparked from the trees, unleashing hell in all directions. Soldiers shot at the sparks, and I saw men falling.

At my command, Dusty broke into a full gallop and headed straight into the melee. In a matter of seconds, bodies littered the ground and groans of pain echoed around the barn. I reached the side of the building and saw Jesse running toward the wagon as a soldier raised his rifle. I kicked Dusty in the sides to put her between my man and the soldier. As Dusty swung around, I realized I was a few feet off the mark, and Jesse was a good target. The officer was taking aim.

On pure instinct, I grabbed the flathead screwdriver from my back pocket, the only weapon in my possession, and screamed. The uniform man jerked his rifle around and trained the barrel on me. I flung the screwdriver as hard as I could at the soldier.

A burst of light exploded as the tip of his barrel rocked upward. Several answering shots exploded in my ears from the bushes, soldiers, and from one of the fallen men. The soldier who shot at me fell forward with a pink plastic handle sticking out of his eye socket. At the same time, Jesse folded to the ground as if he didn't have a single bone in his body.

I jumped off my horse and raced to him. His blood-soaked shirt was riddled with holes. Carlos and Roy sprang from the trees, but Javier reached me first.

"It's Jesse!" I cried.

"Jess!" Javier pulled the man into his arms. "Are you okay?"

I couldn't see Jesse's eyes beneath Javier's shadow, but I knew they weren't open. Javier's voice choked up as he rocked back and forth.

"You're gonna be all right, Jess!" Jesse mumbled incoherently. "That's it, *amigo*. You're gonna be fine." Javier wiped his own eyes with his sleeve.

Carlos kept his cool and said, "Roy, take Jesse back to the ranch. Carmena, you keep watch behind Roy." Carlos whistled for Hammerhead, and his horse bolted from the trees, skidding to a stop beside his master. Roy mounted the nervous stallion. Jesse groaned as we lifted his body and propped him up against Roy's back.

"Hold on, Jesse," Javier encouraged. Carlos and Javier caught Jesse as he slipped off the horse.

"He's done got a weak grip at best," Roy told Carlos.

Carlos pulled the lariat off his saddle and helped Javier bind both men together. Jesse moaned when the rope was pulled tight to secure the knot. Hammerhead lurched at the smell of blood.

"I'll deliver the weapons with Joe," Carlos said. "Javier, you ride cover behind us."

"I think I should follow Roy and Carmena to the ranch," Javier said. "Make sure they arrive safely." He didn't want to leave Jesse's side.

"Fergive me fer inneruptin' but y'all should quit yer yammerin'," Joe said as he drove the wagon closer to the action. "I'm afeared Jesse's hurt mighty bad an' needs some tendin' to right away."

"Joe's right. Javier, ride ahead and have Angela ready to take the bullets out," Carlos said. "Carmena, cover them from the rear. Joe and I will deliver the guns."

"Let's go then," I said before we fretted any more.

Javier headed like lightning for the ranch, and Roy took off as fast as he dared with the injured man tied to his back.

I raced to the dead soldier with my screwdriver protruding from his eye socket, and it slurped out. A quick swipe on his jacket removed the gray gelatinous residue. Joe hee-yawed at the team and rode in the opposite direction as Carlos followed the wagon. I mounted Dusty faster than ever and took off after Roy.

❧❧❧

In the moonlight, Jesse's blood looked like a patch of black on the back of his jacket. I heard Roy say, "Hang in thar, Jess. It's only 'bout thirty-five minutes ta the ranch." Every few minutes he'd shell out more hope. "Jest a bit more, Jess."

Twenty minutes from the ranch, Roy unexpectedly reined in his mount and Dusty caught up to Hammerhead. The field hand pointed to the trail on the right.

"Ma'am, there's a pack a soldiers coming up the trail."

The braids decorating the shoulders of the lead rider glittered in the moonlight. Captain Sanders, with four men behind him. "Roy, take Jesse back to the ranch."

"But ma'am, Carlos will pitch a doozy if I—"

"Don't argue, dammit! Get back to the ranch now or you won't have a job in the morning!"

"Yes, ma'am," he said and held an arm behind poor Jesse who arched and grunted like an injured animal. Roy kicked Hammerhead in the sides and in no time was in a full gallop, disappearing behind a thick line of trees.

I rode straight ahead to intersect the captain and his men before they had a chance to spot Roy. An outcrop of rocks and saplings prevented any easy escape. In the clearing, the soldiers held up their guns, perfectly level with my chest.

Sanders knew I was cornered and calmly said, "Keep your hands on your reins, or I'll order my men to shoot." The taller trees darkened the corner and if not, Charles would have easily recognized Dusty's perfect palomino tan.

"Take off your mask," the captain ordered. I hesitated. "We have confiscated your wagon of stolen goods and your associates are in custody. Now, who are you?"

Apparently, Sanders didn't yet know that Carlos and Joe were my partners in crime. He probably left the wagon before their masks were removed. I sat still in the saddle. The captain's horse clopped next to mine and before I blinked, his hand swept the mask over my head.

Charles plastered his eyes on me as if he'd just found out that I traveled from the future.

CHAPTER 24

The captain formed a barrier between me and his men. No doubt they would've reacted with equal shock had they known the owner of Holiday Ranch was beneath the mask.

"Sergeant Adams!"

"Yes, sir?" The soldier cantered forward, and I heard his quick intake of breath.

"Assign two of your men to join the rest of the squad at the outlaw wagon and bring it back to Castro's Ranch. You will ride ahead with another soldier and approach the Castro property with extreme caution. Assess the casualties and any further losses. We'll hold the prisoners in custody inside the house until we take them to town tomorrow morning."

"But, sir," he protested, keeping his eyes fixed on me.

"You have your orders. You will use all discretion and hold your tongue. Is that understood, Sergeant?"

"Yes, sir!"

The young man obeyed. The sergeant gave the order to Boyce and a boy I knew to be named McFaddin, one of the bystanders when Carmena was attacked, to bring my men and the wagon back to Castro's Ranch. Each boy stretched their neck, trying to get a peek at the highwayman, as they tore off to their destination. Sergeant Adams left with Corporal Scott to count the dead.

After the sound of hooves faded into the night, Charles asked, "What do you have to say for yourself, Carmena?" His disappointment cut through me but not deeply enough. Like a trapped animal, I immediately sought a way out while distracting the captain.

"I thought you were on a special assignment, Charles. I didn't expect to see you tonight."

"This is my special assignment." He pulled his horse closer to Dusty. "I find myself in a precarious situation."

"Do you?" I asked coyly.

He rode to the other side and examined the dark stain on my jacket. "Carmena! Are you injured?"

There was a sudden change in his demeanor. His soft spot was exposed, and I had to step on it while I had the chance.

"Neither of your other men were hurt. Whose blood is this?" he persisted.

There was no way I'd give away the fact that any more of my men participated in the raid. I let my voice crack with a contrived story. "I was involved in a skirmish with one of your soldiers. He was trying to attack me in the most brutal way, and someone shot him before he could do anything to me," I sobbed for good measure.

"My God," he said, looking over his shoulder to make certain his men were gone. "Did you shoot anyone, Carmena? Are you armed?"

"No. I don't have a gun," I answered honestly. It was easier to stick to household tools.

The captain's hand shot out, and he seized Dusty's reins. In a matter of seconds, he swung himself off his stallion and swiftly plucked me from my horse with his free arm.

Santa Anna taught me to play cards to my advantage, and this was one move I was going to overly exploit. I slid downward, similar to the first time I rode with Carlos, only now it was quite deliberate when my breasts rubbed the captain's profile as I slithered down against his body.

"I'm so sorry, Charles. You must hate me!"

"All this time, I thought it was Mexican *bandidos* or common outlaws robbing us." The captain swiped a hand down his face then shook me by my shoulders. "Why did you do it?"

"Your men were depleting my stock," I whined. "What other recourse did I have? The ranch was suffering such big losses!"

"But Franz was ordered not to take more than the surplus of any ranch."

"It seems he wasn't complying with your orders."

"I wished you'd told me. But what of the agreement you were arranging?"

His tone was gentler, more compassionate. I had to take advantage of his kind nature so I could get back to the ranch. I had to see if Jesse survived and find out if anyone came across the amulet. I had nothing new to add to my story, but I'd repeat myself until I found a way out. As long as Charles didn't touch my face, he might believe I was really crying.

"Even with approval of the contract, we had to make up the loss," I sobbed. "I didn't know what else to do! It was impossible to breed more animals at the rate Franz was taking them!" I folded into the captain's firm chest and wished I had more time to cuddle. "Oh, Charles!"

"I'm so sorry, Carmena." His hand smoothed down my hair and gently kneaded the back of my neck. "Maybe I can say that I conducted an interrogation and determined that you had no knowledge of what was happening. That it was one of your men who planned everything."

"But your men—Sergeant Adams saw me! Surely he'd inform someone else if you didn't report my involvement. I couldn't let you do that for me, Charles." I gazed up at him, desperate and pleading, willing my eyes to go big and round like a puppy. It worked as a child and it worked now, only far better than I had hoped.

The captain leaned down and kissed me. I indulged in the incredible sensation, like tasting cheesecake for the first time. My heart sang, and I was sorry this wasn't the appropriate time to make-out with the gorgeous soldier. After the satisfying sampling, I returned my thoughts to a course of action.

In my sexiest whisper, I said, "Charles!" I grasped his neck and jumped, hitching my legs around his slim waist, forcing him to hold onto me while my weight made our bodies

wobble downward. "Oh, Charles," I repeated in the same se-
ductive tone. Passion flowed like a steady stream of lava, hot
and burning my insides.

He knelt on the ground, and I plastered my body to every
square inch of him. He was tired and plopped his bottom on
top of his legs which folded beneath him. Good. He'd be off
balance. I sat on top of his beefy thighs and kissed him. In case
my escape didn't work, at least I had the chance to savor this
last exchange.

I kept my mouth on his and hastily searched about. With
one leg wrapped around the captain's waist, I hooked my right
foot on a smooth rock, three times the size of my fist and
scooted the stone to within my reach.

"Carmena, I've wanted you for so long." His hands
rubbed up and down my back, and he pulled me more firmly
against him.

"I've wanted you, too, Charles," I confided. "Only, I never meant you any harm."

"What?" he asked, confused by my comment. I pelted
him with the rock on the side of the head and he slumped
against me.

"You're a little too old for me," I said. "Over a hundred
and seventy years my senior."

It proved hard to willingly disentangle from the captain's
enticing flesh. I felt for a pulse, kissed him on the cheek, and
laid him gently on the ground before riding as fast as Dusty
could carry me to Holiday Ranch.

૯୬૯୬

Angela nursed Jesse's body splayed out on the bed in the
secret bunkhouse room. The sight of the injured man devastat-
ed me, but my heart filled with gratitude seeing that my other
men had survived. Carlos finally looked his age, worn and
tired. We embraced, the fear of arrest lifted for the time being.

"I'm so glad you're safe!" I whispered.

We kept our voices low. He pushed my hair behind my ears, "Carmena." He hugged me again. "I'm glad you're safe, too."

"What happened? I thought we were supposed to have cloud cover, not stadium lighting!"

"Shhh!" Carlos admonished and peeked back at Jesse. "If you had known the truth you would've called it off and lost all hope of getting your amulet back."

"You're right." I looked at Jesse and my heart wretched. "How did you escape?"

"Sanders caught us delivering the guns," he whispered. "He left a few men behind to guard me and Javier, but he didn't have time to unmask us. Shortly after he left, a few of Santa Anna's men came out of hiding."

Thank goodness the captain left before the ambush. Relief doubled knowing my men weren't IDd. A chance still existed to keep them from being linked to the robbery or the shooting of the soldiers at Castro Ranch.

"Santa Anna didn't come out of hiding until all of the soldiers were killed. He had his men load the guns into an old carriage and let me and Joe leave, unharmed," Carlos said.

"Where's the wagon?"

"We left it so we could get back here faster."

"The wagon is all the evidence they need to link the ranch to the robbery."

"We have to go back for it." Carlos eyed everyone evenly in the group and kept his voice as quiet as possible. "Our former guest asked that I give this to you." He pulled my necklace from his pocket, and I stared at the amulet, the cause of so much havoc.

"Santa Anna wasn't known in history books for being true to his word," I whispered. "I'm lucky I got it back." The chain fell over my head and I tucked the charm into my shirt. We were both aware of what it cost to get it back.

"I'm not sure what he was referring to, but Santa Anna said his offer still stands."

"Humph."

"What of the captain?" Javier asked quietly from Jesse's side. "Roy said he was about to capture you."

"He did but he sent his men away. I knocked him out with a rock then rode here."

"You knocked him out? You didn't kill him after he saw you?" Carlos asked. He tried to keep his voice down. "His men were responsible for shooting Jesse!"

"He didn't pull the trigger!"

Jesse groaned, and we turned toward him.

I stepped to the bedside. "Jesse?"

Blood saturated the bedding and multiple bullet holes riddled Jesse's chest. His lids fluttered, and his empty eyes pointed toward the footboard. "Ma'am? Did we git them boxes delivered?"

A tear trickled down my cheek. I glanced at Angela, hopeful, but she responded with the smallest shake of her head. Jesse wasn't going to make it.

"We sure did, Jess. You fought bravely."

He grimaced under a wave of pain. "I'm glad to have done ma part."

"What can I do to make you more comfortable?"

He coughed, and spittle mixed with blood oozed between his lips. I grabbed a dry cloth from the end table and gently dabbed at his mouth.

"I'd shorely appurshiate a bit mora that thar pain tonic." Angela held up a bottle and pointed at it. He'd gone through nearly a third of the vial of laudanum. He'd die if we gave him anymore. The housekeeper shook her head at me.

"Hand me the bottle, Angela."

She was horrified. "Carmena! That would—"

Carlos stepped between us and took the bottle from Angela, knowing it was the most humane thing we could do for Jesse. I took the proffered bottle and wrenched the cap off. Javier was closest to the bed.

"Help him sit up," I ordered.

Jesse groaned as Javier lifted him to a partial sitting position. "Drink this," I cried, my sight clouded. "It'll make you feel better."

Always the gentleman, he expressed his gratitude before taking a drink. "Ah, kindly thank ya, ma'am." Javier, drenched with tears, held onto his friend while I poured the laudanum into Jesse, enough medicine to put him out of pain in a matter of seconds.

I wanted to say something before he was gone forever, but nothing came to mind. No words of comfort, no promises of eternal life. I simply told him the truth. "You're a good man, Jess."

"I'm so glad ya done took me in, Carmena, all them years ago." he choked out. Blood dribbled out the side of his mouth, and Javier wiped it away with his hand. "Jest a little bitty girl, not afraid a' helpin' an ol' drunk."

"You were never that to me, Jesse. I'm so sorry. This is all my fault," I cried.

Each word in his reply was slow and painfully stated. "Now, don't git yerself all riled up. I done decided long ago that if I was gonna meet my maker, it was gonna be fer the folks at Holiday Ranch." Jesse forced out a smile. "Ain't no better family than the one I done had me here." He turned his head in the general direction of Javier. "I been only too blessed ta have ya fer my best friend, Javi."

"I shoulda done a better job protectin' you," Javier told him.

"Ya done good, *amigo*."

Then Jesse closed his eyes for the last time.

❧❦❧

We listened to Javier mewl like a wounded animal while Angela rocked in the chair and prayed a rosary for Jesse's soul. The rest of us congregated in the common room and wiped the salty traces of sorrow off our faces. Not one of us was spared puffy red rims or runny noses.

"Who shot him?" I asked Carlos as I swiped tears off my face with the back of my hands.

"I don't know. Angela pulled too many different sized slugs from his chest," Carlos answered. "He was shot at least seven times before he fell, Carmena. He's lost too much blood."

"I have no idea what's going to happen in the next few hours," I said to the three men circling me. "I'd like to act as if nothing has happened, as if Captain Sanders never knew that we were conducting the raids. We need to clean everything up and act like we've been on the ranch all day and night."

"But what about the wagon and them men who was ridin' with the captain?" Joe asked. "Did any a' them sees ya?"

"Yes."

"How many were there?" Carlos asked.

"Two were going back to the ranch to assess damages," I answered as Javier entered the main room and struck at his tears like they were an inconvenience. "The other two soldiers were sent to the wagon and were told to take it back to Castro's ranch with any prisoners."

"Carmena," Carlos said. "Have Angela and Violet gather all the blood-stained clothes and shoes and burn them in the pit behind the kitchen. Javier, unsaddle the horses, except Hammerhead and Dusty, and put the remaining tack away."

We walked out the door behind Carlos as he doled out orders.

"Roy, we're going to have to take care of the remaining soldiers that Sanders sent back to Castro's ranch and bring the wagon back."

"That's too dangerous," I protested.

"If they're the only witnesses left, it must be done," Carlos explained.

"But Sanders saw me. Are you going to take him out, too?"

"Take 'im out where?" Joe asked.

"I don't think he'd turn you in," Carlos said. "Me, and everyone else here, yes, but not you." It wasn't a direct answer, but I was afraid to ask for clarification.

"I'm coming to Castro's place with you," Javier said to Carlos.

"No," Carlos argued. "You're too emotional and may make a mistake."

"I want to go with you. Martino can keep watch so Joe and Roy can ride up Turtle Hill in the wagon and bury Jesse." Carlos rubbed his chin and considered Javier's suggestion.

"That's a good idea," I said. "We can't have any evidence left over from the raid, especially a body." I hated referring to Jesse as if he was a dead animal, but I'd do anything to ensure the safety of everyone else.

"'T'aint right ta have no funeral," Joe commented.

"We'll have to postpone the service until we're sure no one is watching the ranch," Carlos said.

"We'll have a funeral tomorrow, that is if we're not arrested," I said. "We have to get all the cleanup done tonight. Tomorrow, no one riding in will be able to see us up on the hill."

"Maybe someone kin make some kinda headstone for Jesse," Joe said, and Roy bobbed his head. Joe voiced our fears out loud. "An' if we is on the hill an' gotta git along bafore them soldiers, we kin cross Sealsfield's property an' head fer the United States."

"I hope there's no need for that," I said.

℘℘℘

Carlos and Javier changed and brought Violet their shirts, the first of the bloody clothes to be collected for incineration. Before they remounted and rode out to the Castro property, Carlos said, "Tell me as best you can remember where you knocked out Captain Sanders."

"What are you going to do?" I felt the hair on my back rise like a dog about to attack.

Carlos held me by the shoulders. "We have to know what his intentions are. If he tells us he's sending a regiment, we'll all have to leave Holiday Ranch tonight."

"You're not going to kill him?"

"Not unless I have to. Where is he?" Carlos demanded and gave me a furious shake.

I reluctantly described the location where I knocked out Charles and the two men rode off.

Violet built a fire behind the kitchen in the deep barbeque pit. We collected clothes from Joe and Roy. I added mine, including my beautiful designer jeans and Adidas shoes. Martino brought Jesse's bloodstained clothes from the bunkhouse. In no time, the fabric was up in flames. I had Violet scrub the dirt and mud from everyone's boots as they finished their jobs.

Angela washed Jesse's body and dressed him in his finest clothes, an old suit, clean but twice his size. It was the first time he'd been seen in it. Thirty minutes later, I joined Joe and Roy at the top of Turtle Hill to dig the grave. They dug out three feet of soil when we heard the faraway ringing of the alarm.

"Someone's a comin'!" Roy said.

"Can't ride all that way an' take out five men an' ride back home agin in that shorta time," Joe said.

"You're right. Joe, can you finish digging with that sprain?"

"'T'aint a problem, ma'am."

"Good. Roy, come with me. I'm going to see who it is, and I may need some cover." I left Joe to shovel more dirt out of the grave and, by the light of the moon, Roy and I stumbled downhill. When Roy found out it was the men, he climbed back up the hill to help Joe, and I raced to the stable.

"Where's Javier?" I asked Carlos.

"He's coming back with the wagon."

"How did you manage to get back so soon?"

Carlos hesitated. "They were already dead, Carmena."

"Sander's men were dead? The ones he sent to the ranch?"

"Yes. Three of them. They were killed just about the same place Jesse was shot." He licked his lips. "Like they were executed."

"But who did it?"

"It was hard to tell. We guessed Santa Anna's men probably went back for the rest of the ammunition."

"How do you figure? Were more weapons missing?"

"No, but one of the dead men at the ranch was a Mexican," Carlos explained.

"There were four young soldiers that the captain had with him, but you only saw three of them?"

Carlos nodded and knew full well what that meant. There was a witness to the raid.

"What happened to the captain?" I asked.

"We never saw him," Javier said. "We checked the barn and the house. We looked over all the dead bodies. The captain wasn't there."

The fact that they searched for Charles told me they planned to kill him. It felt like I had been holding my breath the entire time they were gone. My shoulders relaxed, glad that chances were Charles was still alive.

"He murdered them, Carmena." Carlos's words were layered in rage. "Santa Anna didn't even go back for the rest of the guns. They were still in the barn. He just wanted to kill the rest of the soldiers."

"I suppose I should be grateful," I said in a stupor. "Santa Anna didn't do this for me, but I don't know what his motive was."

"The man is crazy," Carlos said.

"The fate of our ranch and those who live on it depend on whatever action Captain Sanders takes tonight and what the last soldier standing has to say."

"The captain is an honorable man. He'll do the right thing."

"That's what I'm afraid of," I said.

CHAPTER 25

The wagon clambered up the gravel driveway, and Javier sidled it up to the side of the house.

"If nothing happens in the next couple of days, some of us can ride into town," Carlos said. "If we're not waylaid when we get there, we can ask around if we're wanted by the law."

"The sooner we start breeding horses and cattle, the better," I said.

"Javier and I will unhitch the team and cool the horses." He walked to the wagon and grabbed the reins as Javier jumped down.

"We'll need to get a fresh change of clothes for Joe and Roy soon," I said. "They're covered in dirt and they didn't bring much when they arrived."

The women ran out the door. Violet hugged Carlos and Angela latched onto Javier's arm. "Everyone was here tonight," Carlos addressed us all. "No one went anywhere. If you're questioned, repeat details of last night after dinner. This way all our stories will sound the same. Javier, tell Joe and Roy the plan when they come down the hill."

"What if someone asks where Jesse is?" Violet asked.

"He left to visit relatives in Virginia," I said. "His cousins live in the city, and he just received word that they need him for family matters. We don't know when, or if, he's returning."

Angela whispered something in Spanish to Javier and their arms linked together as they walked toward the back of the villa. Violet, without caring who was watching, flung herself into Carlos's arms. He bumped into me. She slathered kisses on him and he, in turn, slathered back.

I did my best Jesse imitation. "Guess I'll mosey inside an' on up ta ma room."

They didn't hear me nor did they stop what they were doing, so I moseyed on up to my room.

 презен

The sun broke through the horizon in a violent shade of red, or perhaps it mirrored my apprehensive feelings about military retaliation. Carlos ended his watch at six a.m., and we all gathered solemnly in the dining room, keenly aware of Jesse's empty chair.

"Joe volunteered to take watch while the rest of us have our breakfast," I said. "In honor of our dear friend, Jesse, I'd like to pass this meal in silence. Then, we'll walk up Turtle Hill for his burial service. During the service, Roy, I'd like you to stand back a ways, enough to get a glimpse of the road, just in case any unwelcome visitors show up."

"I'm obliged an' ready ta do ma part." Now that Jesse wasn't with us, I found Roy and Joe's lazy twangs rather endearing and vowed never to complain about a person's accent again.

"Thank you, Roy." To everyone, I said, "If any of you are forced to talk about the raid, you're to say that I planned it, and Carlos was responsible for selling the guns. This will keep the damage minimal and the rest of you can continue to work the ranch. After the funeral, I think Jesse would want us all to get on with life, so if you find it hard to get through your work in the coming days, do it for him."

Begrudging nods and grunts rounded the table. "Javier, since you're Jesse's best friend, I was wondering if you might say grace."

He bowed his head a bit then said, "I have my words in my heart, but I don't think I can call them out."

"I understand. Carlos?"

"Of course. I'd be honored," he said. "Let us pray." We all bowed our heads. "Lord, we are grateful to have been blessed with the presence of our dear friend, Jesse. He was a good man and a dear friend. Jesse was an asset to the ranch." Someone sniffled. "Forgive those who had the opportunity to make amends for his death but didn't take it."

I looked up at him, but he dropped his head before we made eye contact. I suppose he wasn't alone in thinking I should have disposed of the captain while I had the chance.

Carlos continued. "Lord, we pray you keep us all safe and in your grace. Amen." Unenthusiastic "amens" went around the table, and without the familiar mealtime chatter a sullen atmosphere prevailed. I wondered what the others were think-ing as our forks scraped plates and a slurp of coffee sounded five times louder than usual.

I, for one, wondered if things could have gone differently had I taken a chance on asking Jesse to stop Santa Anna from stealing the amulet without a weapon in hand before the thief mounted my horse. If I had an ounce of control and hadn't en-couraged Charles to visit, Santa Anna would never have had the opportunity to steal my necklace in the first place. The downside of being in charge, being responsible, meant living with the consequences of every decision, big or small.

As soon as the last hotcake was swallowed, we made off for Turtle Hill. Javier carried a slab of wood, and we ended up marching behind him in single file, tracing his steps along the switchbacks. Joe had climbed down from the barn and held up the back of the line with only a tiny hint of a mild sprain after Angela had bandaged his ankle.

Javier dug a hole with his knife and worked several inch-es of the gravestone into the dirt. It read, *Jesse Calhoun, Born 19 Aug, 1783, Died 22 Feb, 1845. Jest restin' a spell.*

"Now, ain't that a purdy headstone if I ever done saw one?" Joe said.

The rest of us gave Javier tiny smiles of approval. Gracie laid a bunch of daisies on the grave. I couldn't recall exactly what Carlos said that day, but every word held meaning and admiration for the oldest member of our ranch family.

My mind lingered on the thought that Jesse was dead as a result of my carelessness. Now more than ever, it wouldn't be fair for me to wind the amulet. Not until I knew if and when Captain Sanders and his men were going to bear down on the ranch.

༄༅༄

Tension ground our collective nerves on the second day after the raid. The third day was far worse. No one had anything agreeable to say to anyone. Anticipation of criminal charges lent itself to short tempers and rude remarks. Joe and Roy weren't happy about wearing borrowed clothing.

None of us deserved any more grief than what we were already suffering at Jesse's loss, yet our frazzled nerves left everyone emotionally raw and exposed.

I ran into Carlos as he walked through the kitchen door, precisely as Angela rang the dinner bell. "I'm thinking of going into town tomorrow, Carmena."

"Come with me a moment," I said. I kept pace with his long stride and entered the library where I shut the door behind him. "Don't you think going into town may be asking for trouble?" The dinner bell rang again, but I had to finish expressing my concern.

"It can't be any worse than sitting like a lame bull in front of a pack of wild dogs. I can't help thinking that if the soldiers were planning to attack or put us under arrest, they would have done so by now. Besides, the men are going crazy, and that's driving me crazy."

"What do you mean?"

"They're getting on each other's nerves. Today, Joe helped Javier in the stables because he was mad at Roy."

"They're almost inseparable. What did Roy do to upset Joe?"

"He didn't say, but when one of the geldings didn't want to be shooed, it kicked Javier in the rump. Joe broke into hysterics, and Javier punched him in the stomach."

"Oh my! How's Joe?"

"He's fine. Roy came to his rescue and jumped on Javier, who stumbled out of the stables, and they both fell into the water trough."

I suppressed my amusement as the dinner bell rang yet again. "I guess we've all been on edge. Since you're willing to go, why don't you take Violet with you?"

"No!" Carlos snapped. "It wouldn't be safe and besides, that woman is insufferable! She complained that Angela tried to ruin her roast by adding too much wood to the fire and that the children acted up during their study time."

"You need a drink."

"Please. Not you, too. Don't start nagging me, Mandy."

"What did I say?"

"Exactly what Violet said when I told her not to tell me her petty grievances. She said, 'Why don't you have a drink?'" Carlos roared. "Do I look like I need a drink?" He swiped a cigar from the crystal container and slammed the lid into place. He bit off the end and stared at the tobacco stick before spitting out the piece he'd bitten off. "This damn thing is stale!" He tossed the cigar into the ashtray.

We heard the children scream. Carlos and I ran out of the library and into the foyer. Javier tugged each one down the stairs by the ear and admonished them both.

"It was your job to ring the dinner bell tonight, Martino, not to play your silly games with your sister! Mama had to ring the bell three times!"

"It was homework, Papa! Violet told us to play it to learn our numbers."

Gracie came to his defense. "We were having fun and didn't know it was time to ring the bell."

"Hah! Everyone knows homework isn't fun!" He ushered the bawling children toward the dining room.

"It looks like Javier needs a drink," Carlos said.

Carlos and I entered the dining room. Pouts and scowls went around the table. Carlos didn't look at Violet when he sat down, and they leaned apart from each other.

"Who's turn on watch?" Carlos asked, knowing it was mine.

"It's my turn, but I have something to say over dinner first," I said.

"It's been days," Angela said. "Do we still need someone to take the watch?"

"Yes!" everyone lashed out.

"Humph," she grunted and skulked into her seat.

"Whose turn ta pray?" Joe asked.

Gracie, her cheeks tear-stained from her recent ear pulling, said, "It's Jesse's turn."

"I'll say the prayers," Carlos said.

"Why you?" Javier asked. "He was my best friend, not yours," he accused. "And you prayed last time."

"Whatever," Carlos snarled. "Pray then."

We bowed our heads and waited. And waited. "Say something, *Viejo*," Angela encouraged.

"¡*Callete*!" he said. "I'm praying in silence."

"How in tarnation is we s'posta know what yer sayin'?" Joe asked.

"Now, you're gonna tell me how to pray?" Javier glared.

"Enough!" I banged my hand on the table. Silence caved in on the room. "Now, all of you, bow your heads, and I'll ask for God's blessing, dammit!"

They were startled but complied.

I said, "Lord, you know I can't pray very well, but I hope this is good enough to take Jesse's place." Someone snickered, and my beady irises searched the table for the culprit, but no one raised their head. I looked down again. "Bless this food, and may none of us choke on it."

"Amen," we said.

Between the two women, they prepared the worst meal ever. We chewed and chewed but the meat never gave. It was like chomping on rubber. I broke into a fit of giggles. Violet chuckled, too.

We held back until Gracie said, "Mama, I'm too scared to swallow!" We collectively spit out various sized pieces of overdone roast, and the table erupted into laughter.

"This is the toughest meat I ever tasted," Javier complained.

"These here potatas are so hard ah nearly lost more a' my teeth," Joe said. Roy grinned in agreement.

"Why don't we skip dinner and have dessert?" Carlos suggested.

"Yeah!" reverberated off the dining room walls.

"We can't," Angela said.

"Why not?" I asked.

Violet laughed. "I burned the cake!"

"No. That's not it," Angela chuckled. "When Violet wasn't looking, I put extra wood in the stove. On purpose!" she confessed, and the laughter continued.

After the entertaining remarks died down, I said, "Look. We've been under a terrible strain these past few days waiting for soldiers to retaliate. Carlos suggested he go into town tomorrow." Violet's mouth scrunched to an O and clutched his hand. "He can make discreet inquiries. Violet, you can go with him and get whatever food and supplies Angela says we need."

"Ain't that a might dangerous an' all?" Joe asked, and Roy nodded agreement. "If we ain't knowin' fer sure Cap'n Sanders gave our names to his superiors, we might all be wannid men."

"If the captain meant to make an arrest, he would've done so already," I pointed out. "And surely that last missing soldier would've spoken up by now."

"Still, it may be risky," Javier agreed. "Not to mention that Franz is still lookin' for Violet."

"It's no riskier than falling into a trough of water," Carlos mentioned.

Javier looked younger with his lopsided grin. "I dunno about that."

"No matter. I'm going," Carlos said. "None of us can live under this tension."

"Hows 'bout I join ya an' if somethin' happens, I'll ride back with Violet?" Roy asked.

"I'd appreciate it," Carlos said.

Angela stood. "It won't take long to make a fresh batch of tortillas."

Violet jumped to her feet. "I'll start some bacon and eggs. Who's hungry?"

"Me!" we all squealed.

We had breakfast for dinner, and a lighter mood settled on the ranch. I canceled guard duty permanently, deciding we'd take our chances. The conversation was light and full of bantering, rehashing the day's events. Life was too short to spend it bickering or whining or wasting time fretting.

Lightheartedness permeated the room as I considered how my priorities had shifted dramatically since becoming responsible for so many lives. I treasured the thought of the quiet wooded landscapes of Arkansas since living in the scrub brush wonderland of Texas. I wanted to go home and check out some of the hiking trails Judge Parker told me about the day I went to court.

After I discovered the location of the captain and knew that the future of Holiday Ranch was secure, it would be time to leave.

I knew that because for the first time in weeks, I missed my real home.

ⲉⲟⲉⲟ

The next morning everyone made visible attempts at civility and cheerfulness. Smiles went around the ranch, and well wishes bounced between one person and the next.

From the fountain, I watched as Carlos, Violet, and Roy fearlessly headed into town. Violet, who still kept Carmena's small gun in her pocket, sat next to Carlos on the buggy. Roy would ride ahead, scout the area, then trail back to give an all clear. God willing, everyone would return without bullet wounds and news of our full pardon.

ⲉⲟⲉⲟ

In the late afternoon, a series of rapid knocks against the bedroom door interrupted my long nap. Angela stuck her head in the room. "They're back!"

We ran downstairs, and I stood on the front porch. Roy rode aside the wagon. From a distance, the three carried on as if there wasn't any consequence of our raid gone sour.

"Everything's all right!" Violet hailed.

That was a relief, but I wanted a full explanation. I walked through the house and met them outside at the back gate. Carlos offered his hand to Violet, and she removed a few packages from the back of the wagon. Roy thanked me for his and Joe's new clothes.

I hugged Carlos. "You're back!" He smoothed my hair. "Tell me everything before I burst."

He cloaked my shoulder with his beefy arm and walked me to the kitchen. Violet placed a hot cup of tea in my hand and put on a pot of coffee for the men. Martino ran past us and out the backdoor to help unhitch the team and cool off the horses.

"The only thing anyone knows is that Santa Anna's men were responsible for the theft."

"And Charles?" Eyebrows raised around the room. "Captain Sanders. What did he have to say?"

"We didn't see him, but we heard that he's done been relieved a' his command," Roy said.

"What? I'm not hearing this!"

"I said—"

"I heard you, Roy!" I turned to Carlos. "How could he be relieved of his command? He's a well-respected officer, revered by his men, and esteemed by his superiors." Violet took the cup and saucer from my shaking hand and set it on the table.

"He's being court-martialed for dereliction of duty," Carlos explained.

"But why?" I asked.

"The soldier who initially survived the raid at Castro's ranch said the captain's men were killed when he wasn't there. He reported that the captain wasn't at the delivery site or the storage facility during the attacks," Carlos said.

"Scott." Roy gave the name of the witness. "He was a corporal."

"They asked the corporal who stole the guns, but he died before he could say another word," Carlos concluded.

"My God." I sat down, and Violet pushed the fresh cup of tea in front of me. I picked it up but didn't drink. "But where's the captain?" I asked again.

"He's staying at Ol' Sally's on his own recognizance until the court martial," Carlos said.

"The military wants a speedy hearing because of all the deaths involved," Violet said. "The captain said he wanted to make sure none of the thieves were still at Castro's Ranch before he brought the guns back, but his superior officers weren't in agreement with the captain's decision."

"When is the hearing?" No one spoke. "Give me an answer before I ride into town and find out on my own."

"Tomorrow," they answered in unison.

Carlos must've known what I was thinking. "Carmena, it wasn't your fault. You're not responsible for him."

"Don't ferget what we heard about Mr. Jones," Roy said to Carlos.

I looked at Carlos, and he said, "His assistant clerk said he's in New York meeting with another solicitor."

"I hope he comes back with good news. We can sure use some."

"Everyone out of the kitchen," Angela said. "We need to make dinner." She shooed us out, except for Violet.

I lumbered up to my room and reclined in the chaise lounge. Hours passed as I mulled over how I destroyed Sanders, Jesse, and a number of young soldiers. I pulled the amulet out of my shirt. If I wound it up, I'd be rid of this place but only a coward would run now. I had to see the captain's trial through. A light knock on the door shook me from my desperate considerations.

"Come in," I answered.

Carlos entered and closed the door behind him. "Don't do this."

"Do what?"

"You've been through enough," he said. "Don't punish yourself with a problem that isn't yours."

"The court-martial is another result of my losing the amulet."

Carlos noticed the necklace hanging outside my shirt. "Are you leaving us?"

"Even if I knew how, I couldn't leave until I know what happens to Charles."

He sighed. "Mandy."

"Save your argument."

Carlos bent down and kissed me tenderly on the cheek. "Dinner is ready. Come join us."

"I'd rather eat in my room."

"I'd rather you didn't," he said. "Everyone is celebrating downstairs."

"It's too early to be optimistic. Sanders may buckle during his court-martial."

"Are you going to be the one to tell them that? And aren't you the one who said Jesse would want us to carry on like before?"

I sighed. "I'll be down in a minute. First, I have to get dressed and find a cheerful face to put on."

"That's my girl." He smiled and left the room.

I rubbed one of the smooth hat charms that dangled on the bracelet the captain had given me. If Charles was jailed, I would lead the men on a rescue mission, futile at best, but I'd do what was necessary to keep him from paying the price for my mistakes. I had to do whatever I could to protect him.

It didn't matter whether the captain's heart belonged to Carmena or to me. What mattered was that my heart belonged to him.

CHAPTER 26

Festive place settings and a spring bouquet decorated the dining table. I wore a bright smile because Carlos asked it of me. He raised his shot glass of tequila and I raised a glass of merlot. Plates of hot food littered the table and the room quieted after everyone took their seats.

"Whose turn is it to pray?" Carlos asked.

"I believe we have to work a few more people into the prayer schedule," I said. "Violet, would you please say grace tonight?"

It was the first time she had been assigned prayer duty and she cast a nervous eye about the table. She reverently bowed her head, and the rest of us did the same.

"Lord, thank you for intervening with all that happened with the soldiers. Many lives ended, including our dear Jesse's, but many lives were spared. I didn't know Jesse well, but he and Javier rescued me from a terrible situation. I don't know why Jesse had to leave like he did, but I've learned that your ways, Lord, are not our own. I can only hope to leave such a mighty impression on this world when my time comes.

"I ask that I never take anyone here for granted and will try to celebrate the routine and special events in my life with the same joy. Thank you for allowing me to share this meal and this home with all these wonderful people. In your name we pray. Amen."

Violet put our lives into perspective, and I felt guilty for using prayer time as a sounding board. We remained silent. Violet snapped her napkin in her lap and smiled warmly.

"Thank you, Violet. That was a beautiful prayer," I told her.

"I don't think I deserve ta eat," Javier said.

"No one ever said a prayer that made me feel so bad," Angela said. The rest of us nodded agreement and gazed down at our plates. The room filled with regrets.

Finally, Martino spoke up. "I feel bad, but I'm hungry, too." He rolled up a tortilla and started chewing. One by one our appetites returned, and I had a feeling that prayer time would never be the same.

The meal was delicious, and I mimed a silent 'thank you' to Carlos for insisting I come down from my gloomy tower of self-pity.

☞☜☞☜

Carlos joined me in the library after the meal and picked up a fresh cigar from the crystal container. I took my place behind the desk.

"I'd like you to go into town tomorrow and find out the results of the court-martial."

He nodded and we both basked in the pleasure of the sweet-smelling cigar.

After a moment, I said, "I saw Sadie the day I found Santa Anna in the canyon. I know the real reason why you didn't want me to speak with her."

Carlos appraised me while he chugged his cigar like a steam locomotive. "And?"

"You knew all along that I was here to take Carmena's place."

Cherry tobacco smoke streamed through his pursed lips. "How could I have believed the ranting of an old crazy lady?"

"I don't know. You tell me, Carlos."

A sly smile crept up. "Your clothes. Franz had tossed your clothes aside in a pile—those inappropriate pants with that absurdly strange colored tool in your pocket. And those black Danish clogs on your feet."

"My running shoes."

"I don't know how you could run in those."

"So, you packed my clothes away and didn't tell me because Sadie told you that there was no chance of a future between you and Carmena, but you didn't want to believe it. The entire time you knew that she might know how I could get back to my own time."

The accusations burned, but he kept quiet. I should have been angrier than I felt with Carlos, but how could I be? Not after all the love and adventure I experienced on the ranch and meeting Charles, literally the man of my dreams.

Another long shaft of gray smoke flowed past his lips. "Does this mean that you know how to get back?"

"Sort of. It might be a little tricky since I didn't get a chance to ask Sadie any specific questions. Supposedly, I already have all the answers, even though my best field hand is dead, and the captain might be imprisoned in a military jail."

"You've done the best with what you know."

I shook my head. "I can't say I was the best history student. I don't know if I gave Beauford all the right names of the companies to invest in. There's still a chance that I could have destroyed the future of Holiday Ranch. I can't leave under these conditions, even if I wanted to."

"Would it be so bad to stay with people who care about you?"

"No," I admitted. "But people care about me there, too. Besides, Sadie made it sound like there'd be severe consequences if I stayed."

"I'll always look after the ranch. You know you can count on me."

I smiled weakly, too tired to give it my all. "Let's go over the books now. I'm sleepy, and I'd like to get to bed early."

He nodded, and we hit the books. With so little livestock to account for, it didn't take long to discuss the current inventory, but that also made it easier for Carlos to determine how many horses and cattle to purchase once the Sanders affair was settled.

We trudged out of the library. The bleak cloud surrounding me wouldn't lift until I had confirmation that the U.S.

Cavalry was none the wiser in the matter of our double lives as gunrunners.

And I wasn't going anywhere until I knew that Charles was safe.

⋰⋱

Everyone threw themselves into their work after breakfast the next morning. Carlos entered the library and said, "I'm going into town now." It was then we heard the clopping of horse hooves near the fountain.

Angela tore into the room and practically slid into Carlos. "It's him! It's that *bendejo* lieutenant. He's *muy borracho* and waves his gun!"

"Go upstairs with Violet and the children!" I snapped, and she scurried out of the library to find the others. Carlos grabbed a shotgun from the hidden cupboard near the front door.

"Where are the men?"

"Scattered about the ranch," I said.

He opened the front door and stepped onto the front porch as the inebriated lieutenant wobbled off his mount.

"Gawdammit, Violet, you two-timin' bitch!" Franz shouted like a mad dog. "Come outta there right now. I know yer in there!"

Carlos cocked his gun, and the swaying man looked up.

"I come fer my woman," Franz mumbled.

We stepped outside and kept an eye on the sot's trigger finger. I closed the door behind us.

"She divorced you months ago, Franz," Carlos said. "Get the hell off this property before we send for Captain Sanders." He wasn't frightened of the lieutenant, but I was sure Carlos wanted to avoid another shootout.

Franz flailed his gun to and fro. "You can't hide behind his fancy rank no more cuz he ain't got any!"

Carlos glanced back at me then told the man, "Leave now, Franz. None of us care to hear the blabbering of a drunkard."

He staggered forward, and Carlos raised his rifle. "Stay where you are!"

"I ain't afeared a you," Franz said, stopping in his tracks. "Yer nothin' but a dirty Mexican taking advantage of these poor women folk. 'Specially the white ones."

I touched Carlos on his tense shoulder and whispered, "He's drunk. He's not worth the bullet."

"Take your whittle-wabble someplace else or Captain Sanders will hear of this visit!" Carlos warned.

The man bent over and held his jiggling stomach. "Whoah! If that ain't a hoot! Your little puppet done pulled his last strings." His rage bellowed to the surface. "Filthy liar told the colonel lies! Told 'em I was stealin' personal property!" The man teetered and belched loudly. He fisted his chest. "Thar. Thas better. Now, where was I?" He scratched his grizzled beard with the barrel of his six-shooter.

"Oh, yeah. That bastard didn't wanna be court-martialed alone. He got kicked out for derelicshion a duty and I was disho'erably dissharged for conduct unbecoming," he slurred. "Now, he's drinkin' hisself ta death at Ol' Sally's like some poor drunk bastard!"

"Think there's any truth to his ramblings?" I whispered to Carlos.

He shook his head, unsure. "I'm done hearing your lies, Franz! Get the hell outta here!"

Franz pointed his gun our way, and Carlos pulled me behind his back.

"Not without my woman. Where the hell is that bitch? Gawdammit, Violet! Get yer butt outta here!" Franz broadcasted at the top of his lungs.

To our chagrin, the door opened, and Violet stepped out.

"Get back in the house!" Carlos ordered.

"I've seen him addle-headed before, Carlos. I can talk to him."

Franz pointed his gun at Violet. "You slut!" He fired a round and sent plaster spattering over our heads.

Carlos slammed Violet behind an arch then shoved me into her back. "Stay put!" he ordered and stepped onto the gravel drive. I held onto Violet when she made to run after Carlos and kept her behind the arch, a challenge as she was nearly a head taller than me.

"I'm going to tell you one last time, Franz. Get the hell off our land."

"Oh ho! First, you take my woman, and now you go after the other one's land." He pounded his fist in the air and yelled, "I hope ya got your money's worth, Mish Luebber!"

Carlos shoved the shotgun into his left hand and let it drop parallel to his leg. Gravel shot under his leather soles as he stormed right up to Franz and slugged him square in the nose. Franz flew backward and shot off another round into the sky. With the violent kickback, his pistol fell out of his hands.

Violet screamed at the sound of gunfire and her high-pitched wail startled the horse. Carlos stooped to pick up Franz's weapon at the same moment the horse spun and reared. It bumped Carlos with its large flank, enough force to spin him around and knock him into the gravel. The rifle fell out of his hands.

Franz rolled in a disjointed heap and reclaimed his pistol. He rose to his feet, off-balance, and pointed his gun at Carlos, swaying as he tried to target him. I charged the man like a linebacker and plowed into his side before he had a chance to fire.

My frame didn't have enough bulk or velocity to knock the drunken man down, and we struggled. I smelled his horrible breath and bodily odors. He whacked me hard on my cheek with the back of his hand, and I fell down, barely conscious. Lights spun in my head, and I shook them out.

Violet screamed.

Carlos placed his hand behind his head and came away with bloody fingers. Franz staggered back to where Carlos lay on the ground and stood directly over him.

Franz's words flowed out in a demonic whisper. "You're gonna die now."

He pointed his revolver right between Carlos's eyes, which were rounded and full of fear. Franz's head jerked forward then back. He swore and twirled around, rubbing the back of his head but was confused when he didn't see anyone behind him. Blood dripped down the back of his neck. I looked up at the veranda, and Martino smiled at me with his slingshot in hand.

"Get back inside!" I yelled at the boy, grateful for his lucky shot. Martino ducked behind the plaster railing and crawled toward the patio doors. Carlos was woozy and had a hard time scrambling off the ground. I staggered to my feet as Franz turned around and took aim at Carlos for the second time.

I tackled the lieutenant again, pummeling like a battering ram into his back, but he managed to get a shot off. Carlos grimaced and took the bullet in his thigh. He fell backward.

Franz elbowed me in the stomach. Air whooshed from my lungs, and I fell to my knees. He aimed his gun at Carlos and his hoarse voice held more poison than a black widow. "This is what happens ta men who can't keep away from women who don't balong ta them."

"No!" I screamed, but the air had yet to find its way back into my lungs, and my appeal went unheard.

A blast rang in my ears, and Franz's horse sprinted for the road, too alarmed to wait for its owner. Everything turned a dark shade of gray and blurred around the edges.

The lieutenant slowly pirouetted and stared at Violet. She stood her ground, her arms thrust forward, and elbows locked with the tiny gun riveted to her hands. Franz, eyes filled with shock, fell to his knees, aware that it was his last moment alive. Violet stepped aside, and he crumpled face first into the gravel.

Violet dropped the single-round gun and ran to Carlos. She ripped the hem of her slip. He cried out when she knotted it tightly above the wound.

"You lost a lot of blood, sweetheart. It might be an artery."

"I'm fine for now." He winced. "See to Carmena."

She ran over to me. I sat on my legs, wide-eyed, and knew my body was nearing collapse without oxygen. My vision faded, and I teetered onto my side.

Violet rolled me on my back. "She's turning blue!" she yelled back to Carlos.

"Pinch her nose and blow into her mouth!" he shouted.

Violet put a firm hold on my lower jaw. She pinched my nose and placed her lips full over mine. Her warm breath entered my body, and my lungs expanded. She blew again and again.

When I finally breathed on my own, I pushed up on one elbow, coughing. "I'm all right! I'm all right!"

"You sure, now?" she asked.

"Yes," I wheezed. "Please. Tend to Carlos."

Angela ran outside. "¡Ay, Diós!" she cried and joined Violet at Carlos' side.

I lay back down on the ground and gulped the sweet taste of fresh air. Footsteps thundered behind me, those of the field hands barreling across the yard.

"What in tarnation happened?" Joe yelled. With Roy's assistance, they lifted Carlos to his feet and carried him inside the house. Javier scooped me up and followed everyone else.

Angela barked orders to Violet who kept a cool head, although her boyfriend had just been shot in the leg with a good chance that his artery had been hit, and he may have been bleeding to death on the dining room table. Carlos bit down on a leather strap while Angela dug through his flesh for bullet fragments. After she plucked the last hint of metal from his thigh, she expertly sewed tiny stitches into his skin.

Joe and Roy found an old piece of canvas tarp and wrapped Franz's body in it, then unceremoniously tossed the corpse into the back of the wagon. I had them deliver Franz to the military headquarters in town and asked the men to make a discreet inquiry as to the latest update on Captain Sanders.

That evening, Carlos, Javier, and I greeted the wagon when Joe and Roy returned to the ranch.

"The US Cavalry wanted nothin' ta do with Franz's body," Joe said. "We hadda take it ta be buried in the church cemetery. Reverend Craig said he'll be contactin' the marshal an' tell 'im that Franz was shot in self-defense at Holiday Ranch."

"Thanks, you guys."

"That is good news," Carlos said. "I've got to finish some paperwork. Let me know if anything else arises."

It wasn't until Carlos left the group with the help of a cane and a healthy dose of laudanum that Joe finally spoke up. "Ma'am, there's somethin' you otta see," he said.

He strode to the back of the wagon. Roy and I followed.

Captain Sanders was laid out in the buckboard, with matted haired, beard and moustache scraggly and overgrown, and hygienically unfit to be in human company. He was far more wasted than Franz had been. It was the first time I'd seen him out of uniform.

"The captain was on Ol' Sally's porch an' she dint take kindly ta his bein' passed out in fronta the whole town an' all," Roy said. The field hand must have been possessed by Jesse. He didn't say much, but he had the same soft heart. The same endearing dialect.

"Would you two please put the captain in the second floor guest room nearest to mine? Angela or Violet can show you which one it is." Looks were exchanged, but I didn't care, and my lack of concern felt oddly liberating. "Just do it!"

I heard "Yes, ma'ams" behind me as I stormed away.

I called for Angela as I stomped up the stairs. She rushed into my room. "Please get a hot bath set up in the guest room next door. We'll need clean towels and clothes for the captain."

"Captain Sanders? He's here?"

"And send up some fresh coffee and a decent meal for both of us."

"Carmena." Angela's intonation told me of the potential disgrace in store.

"For gosh sakes, I'm going to get the man cleaned up and full of food. I'm not taking him to bed, at least not while he smells like the bottom of a hamper!"

She huffed at my brash retort and left the room. Carlos was right when he accused me of feeling responsible for the captain's deteriorated condition.

The heart had a mind of its own. We might have lost Jesse to a bullet, but I wouldn't lose Charles to a bottle.

CHAPTER 27

The men laid the captain on the featherbed, and he muttered as if he had a pound of peanut butter in his mouth. I asked them to leave the room and dragged a chair next to the edge of the bed. Charles reeked of sweat and cheap alcohol, and his handsome features were distorted by grime and frown lines. His haggard figure looked all the filthier on the white hand quilted comforter.

Someone tapped on the door.

"Come in," I said, not taking my sight off the man.

"Mama said to bring you this." Gracie approached with timid steps holding onto a water-filled bowl. A washcloth drifted in the liquid.

I mustered up a smile for her. "Thank you, honey. Please set it on the table."

"Is the captain going to die?"

"No. He's very sick, is all."

"Violet said he's drunk."

"I bet he is. Go on, now."

She left the room, and I proceeded to mop Charles's brow. His hand suddenly shot out and latched onto my wrist. Strong fingers pressed into my skin, and he breathed erratically. I waited as he mastered his bearings and lessened his grip.

His rough voice scratched like sandpaper. "Carmena? What are you doing here?"

"The question is what are *you* doing here?"

He cast a distrustful eye at the decor. Sheer curtains, square framed windows, and a four-post bed.

"How'd I get here?"

"My boys found you passed out at Ol' Sal's, and she asked them to remove you."

There was another knock on the door. "Come in." The captain attempted to get up, but I gently pushed him back onto the mattress.

Joe and Javier carried in a big washtub, partially filled with hot water. Roy, Violet, Angela, and Martino paraded behind with buckets of steaming water and emptied them into the tub.

Gracie scuffled in with half of another. She waved at the captain and gave him a darling smile. Charles looked like he'd seen his first alien and robotically waved back.

The bath entourage left the room, and the captain settled back into the frilly pillows. "I really don't want you to see me like this."

"Too late. Can you undress yourself, or do you need someone to do that for you?" I teased.

He mulled it over. "I need help."

"Fine. I'll call for one of my men."

I rose from the bed, but he clawed my arm again. "Carmena. Why are you doing this?"

"Why not?"

He huffed and looked the other way but kept my arm clamped in his hand.

"I owe you," I said.

He stared at the wall. "You owe me nothing."

"I care about you, Charles."

He eyed me as if he had emotional X-ray vision. "You smashed my skull with a rock."

I shrugged. "Only out of necessity."

Another knock on the door. I sighed and tried to pull my arm free, but the captain refused to yield.

"Yes?" I said impatiently to the intruder.

Angela entered with a tray of food and coffee. She set it on the nightstand. The man looked over at what she brought in.

"Good evening, Captain," Angela said. The housekeeper glanced at his tight grip on my arm but said nothing and left the room.

"Did you tell your staff to be nice to me?" Charles asked. His voice betrayed a hint of confusion at being treated with the same regard commanded by his former rank.

"No," I smiled.

"Well then, what's wrong with them?"

"You're a hero at Holiday Ranch. We're in your debt. Especially me."

A glimmer of hope sparked in his eyes but rapidly faded, and he looked back at the wall. I pulled out of his grasp and unlaced his shoes.

"What are you doing?"

"Getting you ready for a bath." I loosened a tongue and slipped off one boot. "Oh!" cannonballed out my mouth.

Charles said nothing, his eyes silently daring me not to grimace as I helped the afflicted wearing the smelliest socks on the planet. I tugged at the top of the odorous woolen garment, touching the fabric as little as possible, and let it drop. His other boot came off, and I pinched the second sock with the very tips of my thumb and pointer finger. It fell to the floor with the other.

"I'll have Violet wash your clothes."

"Don't bother," he said.

One by one, I unbuttoned the metal shanks on his shirt. At his belt, I yanked on the fabric and it draped open to reveal a rippled stomach. A thin line of hair pointed downward into his pants. I sucked in air, and his eyes took in my reaction.

My words were unintentionally husky. "I'll have one of the guys finish the rest."

He reached out for me, desperation stamped on every feature. "Carmena, don't go."

It was dismaying to see the strong, confident captain reduced to the emotional wreck lying in bed.

"Eat your dinner while the coffee is still hot. Finish your bath and rest a while, then I'll come back for a visit."

When I reached for the door, he grumbled, "I can undress myself. I don't need your men pawing on me like I'm an invalid."

"I know." I paused before saying, "Charles, you're welcome to stay with us."

He stared at the wall. "I'll be on my way soon."

"What I mean is, you're welcome to live here."

My comment surprised him. "Why would you invite me to stay here?"

"Why not?" I said. "There's plenty of room. You can earn your keep plus an allowance like the others. I'm sure you have some skills to offer." He remained quiet and narrowed his gaze on me. "For gosh sakes, don't look at me like I'm offering you charity. Soon we're going to be getting in quite a bit of cattle and horses for breeding and can use an extra hand."

He sneered, as close to a smile as I could hope for. "So you're changing careers?"

"Yes. Permanently. Now, if only we can keep the government from taking our best stock."

"That's been taken care of," he said.

"What do you mean?"

"I explained to a few people what Franz had been doing. I suggested that they work out an arrangement with you. Maybe take your lesser stock and only the surplus at that."

"Thank you, Charles. I really appreciate it. I'm sure with the trial you had to yank on some tight strings."

"Cashed in my last chip, but it was worth it. Franz won't be harassing you either. He was dishonorably discharged, too. Only thing is, I don't know where the bas—where he went off to."

"Franz is dead."

"What?" The captain bolted upright. He clamped his mouth shut and furrowed his brows then reclined slowly back into the pillow. "What happened?" he mumbled through his hangover.

"Violet shot him after Franz shot Carlos."

"How is Carlos?"

"He's fine. Took one in the thigh, but it will mend well. Missed his main artery. Violet's taking care of him. They'll probably get married soon."

"Carlos and Violet? So you and he aren't..." He pointed his finger back and forth.

"No, we're not." Sanders visibly relaxed. "But don't get your hopes up. I'm not an available woman right now."

"Is there someone else in your life?"

"It's my ranch. I'm married to it. She comes first, before anyone. And then it's the people who work for me. I can't ever let my employees down."

"So if I worked for you I'd stand a better chance?"

I laughed. "You mean a great deal to me. Surely you know that." It was a bit intimidating to candidly express my heartfelt feelings about the man, yet I felt satisfied doing so.

He grimaced, wrestling for a more comfortable position. Unexpected tears trickled down the sides of his temples. "Gawdamn whiskey."

I closed the door and sat back down on the chair. "Charles? What is it?"

"I told you," he said gruffly. "It's the whiskey."

"Liquor only makes a man cry when he can't get it."

He smiled bitterly. "Gawdamn you, Carmena."

"Guess I hit a nerve." I kept silent and hoped he'd tell me the true reason for his distress.

Salty liquid dripped a crooked line on his unshaven face and puddled on the pillow. He laid his thick arm across his eyes, shielding himself from something.

I took the washcloth and wrung it out.

"Don't," he warned.

I wiped his neck. "This isn't what I expected to happen. I thought the government was coming after me. I didn't think you'd keep quiet and allow yourself the public disgrace of a court-martial."

"You think I care what anyone, especially the blasted army, thinks of me? They're no better than Santa Anna's cutthroats." He pushed my hand away and draped his arm back across his face.

"What is it, then? What would make you drink yourself into oblivion?" I only heard his ragged breathing and sniffled mucous. I persisted, "Charles, please trust me enough to share what's bothering you."

"It wasn't Santa Anna."

I almost missed his soft-spoken words. I gave him my hankie, and he swabbed his nostrils and cheeks.

"You mean he wasn't the one who attacked your men at the wagon?"

He shook his head. I barely heard his reply. "At Castro's ranch."

"I don't understand."

Bitterness infiltrated every word. "Santa Anna attacked my men at the wagon." He shivered. "But not at the storage site."

I tucked the blankets in around him. "Then who killed your men at Castro's ranch?"

He cried, and his grief broke my heart. It would've sounded like a shout, had his voice not been fettered from the phlegm buildup. "It was me, Carmena. I killed them. I shot my own men!" His shoulders heaved as he agonized over his terrible confession.

I heard him. He told me. I couldn't believe it. The idea of Charles bringing harm to his own men had never entered my mind. It took a few moments for both of us to recover.

"Why, Charles?"

He sighed. "He saw you. Corporal Boyce. Then he told the other soldiers." His arm remained over his eyes, hiding from his remorse. "They'd tell the commanding officer if I didn't. My men are—were loyal to me, but I trained them to do the right thing, to follow orders. They'd report the incident if I didn't. I had to do it, Carmena."

"But they said in town that there was a dead Mexican at the ranch. It had to have been Santa Anna!"

He let me pull his arm from across his face and hold his hand, but he didn't look at me. "After I came to, I rode to Castro's Ranch where my men were waiting for me. Once they learned about the ambush at the wagon, my men waited for me to lead them here to make arrests."

"Oh, dear," I said, my voice as tiny as I felt.

"When I gave the order to leave you be, they argued. They accused me of protecting gunrunners and wanted to do what was right. They just stood there, Carmena, and watched as I shot one and then the other." His tears gleamed and cut like a knife to my heart. "No one raised his gun to me. They were too shocked to see that I had become the enemy. They were young, loyal men, and I shot them dead," he cried, his throat as raw as his emotions.

"So...you killed them because of me?"

"Carmena." The name sounded like a curse. "Theft of military property is punishable by death. Surely you know that." He swallowed hard.

"No, I didn't know."

"You, and everyone on your ranch, even the women and maybe the children, would have been charged." Sorrow and shame emanated from his every word. "After I killed my men, I rode back to the wagon, where I assumed it was Mexican *bandidos* who outnumbered and killed the rest of my squadron. I checked all the bodies on the ground. Your masked men were gone. No one else was alive.

"I put the body of a Mexican on my horse and took it to Castro's ranch so it would look like bandits killed my men while stealing the ammunition. That's when I realized that Corporal Scott was gone. I rode into town to stop him from telling what happened, but he had already died."

"I don't know what to say to all this."

"You must think I'm a monster."

I lifted his hand to my chest and held it tight. "I never dreamed anyone would commit murder in order to protect me, to save my ranch. All I can say is thank you. I'm so grateful." I kissed his soiled hand. "I can't imagine how you feel. What a terrible decision you were faced with."

"I would do it again if it meant protecting you, Carmena."

We shared the agony of his choice, locking eyes and hearts.

"You need to find a way to make it up to them—their families," I said.

"How can I make it up to them, Carmena? How can I make their murders right? I turned my heart against every principle I held dear."

It didn't cost Santa Anna any integrity to kill most of the soldiers. The price of honor for men like Captain Sanders, however, was much too high in these times.

I took the washcloth from the basin and blotted the salty rivulets running down his cheeks. He pushed me away again, but I kept at it—tenderly stroking, rinsing out the cloth, and wiping over and over. I dabbed under his dark blue eyes made shiny by his tears.

"It's a horrible sacrifice you made for me," I said. "I'm so sorry."

"I despise myself right now, but you must hate me for being no better than those Mexican cutthroats." He curled toward the wall again. He hugged his arms to his chest and tried to lock me out.

"No. I don't hate you, Charles. I'm in your debt. Your sacrifice saved all of us."

He looked over his shoulder at me, puzzled.

"I don't like the idea of men being murdered, but sometimes we make the best choices we can, even if they're not right. You don't have to bear this burden alone. I'm here for you, Charles."

He tore upright and hugged me. "I thought you'd hate me."

"I feel only gratitude having you in my life," I whispered into his smelly neck. Streams flowed from my eyes, too, and forgiveness encompassed both our hearts. Mine for him and, I hoped, a bit for himself.

I pulled back and waited until we locked eyes. "I don't want you to ever kill another person who doesn't deserve it. If someone threatens you or me, we walk away. But if there's a danger to our immediate physical safety, we do what is necessary to protect ourselves and each other. Agreed?"

Charles stared at me, and I swear I saw appreciation swimming in those blue pools. He nodded.

"We don't need to mention this again. To anyone. I'm sure you'll punish yourself enough with your private memories of that night, but if you'll let me, I'll ease your torment. After all, I was the cause and deserve to take responsibility for their deaths as much as you."

"You didn't pull the trigger." He flinched at the alcohol-induced pain in his head and lay back down.

"No, Charles, but I did send my men to Castro Ranch to do what you had already done. My intention was the same. I gave orders to kill everyone. Everyone except you."

He was as stunned at my confession as I was by his.

"My men didn't get the chance to pull the trigger, although they were ordered to and would have if your men weren't already dead." It was my turn to wait for judgment.

"I'd never let anyone hurt you," Charles said.

"I know that." I cupped his cheek and kissed the other. "I'd never let anyone hurt you, and aside from my bashing your head with a rock, I would never hurt you, either."

"That was small compared to what I truly deserve."

"Charles, in my eyes, you deserve to be loved so let's do our best to make amends, maybe help the families of the men who paid the price for our affections."

"I already depleted my savings and sent each of their families a draft because I destroyed their means of support. But Carmena, you can't buy salvation. You can't redeem guilt or murder with money."

"No, but you can forgive yourself. We can forgive each other for not thinking clearly because we had both been consumed by passion for people we love."

He embraced me again and held me for several minutes. It was wonderful being the object of his affection.

"We can continue our discussion later, if you'd like, but right now I'd like you to take a bath. You smell horrible!"

He smiled, a small one, through lashes webbed with the last of his tears.

"But eat first. I'll come back and see you in a while."

"Thank you, Carmena."

I stood up and made for the door. "Believe me. It's the least I can do."

"I don't want you to do anything for me out of pity," he said.

As I started to pull the door closed, I smiled. "I'm not. I'm just being selfish."

I left Charles more at peace, and perhaps, with a little too much hope.

CHAPTER 28

We held off on hiring another housekeeper because Angela and Violet felt they had the chores, cooking, and children's schooling under control.

Wranglers weren't an option. When I put the word out to Roy that we wanted to hire new men, it took him only a day to find Roland, Pablo, and Snitch, whom we nicknamed the three musketeers because they took an instant liking to each other.

Violet couldn't stand the thought of anyone not feeling like part of our family and begged me to have all the hands share our meals. We still had four leaves left to expand the table so technically, I could hire eight more employees before I had to consider feeding the field hands separately.

I had the captain sit next to me. Shy and awkward, he had a difficult time jumping into the routine of ranch life. The spark went out of him after shooting his own men. It was a nightmare that would plague him the rest of his life, and I needed to see the return of at least a semblance of the man I fell in love with.

This Charles Sanders wasn't the confident captain who led his men into border battles along the Rio Grande. Before I returned home, I had to pull Charles out of his emotional prison. It took me days to convince him to leave his room, and he did so because I stopped bringing his meals upstairs.

Carlos was the only one I told of the captain's terrible choice to kill his men and made him promise not to tell a soul, not even Violet. I didn't want anyone to think less of Charles for sacrificing so much for me, for Carmena.

In the darkest hours of the night, I heard Charles sob in his sleep as he warred with his conscience and relived his painful decision. One such night I snuck into his room and quietly shut the door behind me. "Charles?"

He groaned and tossed in the blankets.

I sat on the edge of the bed and tapped his shoulder. "Charles?"

He rolled onto his side. The moonlight cast a heavy shadow, and his eyes were blackened sockets until my sight adjusted to the scant light.

"Carmena?"

"I'm here, sweetheart."

He bolted upright and held me tight enough to bruise my ribs. I gritted my teeth, and he lessened his grip.

He held my arms and looked me up and down. "What's wrong, Carmena?"

"I thought I heard you having a nightmare."

"Everything's fine now that you're here."

I brushed strands of silky stray hair out of his eyes, and he hugged me more gently, burying his face into my curls.

"Carmena." It sounded like a Shakespearian sonnet each time he said my name. "I don't know what I'd do without you."

"I feel the same way about you, Charles." It felt like emotional suicide each time I imagined returning to the future without him.

He kissed me, and Fourth of July fireworks couldn't compare to the light show that dazzled the inside of my mind. My heart burst with a mad release of feelings I had for the man. It might have been a point of no return if not for the light rapping on his door.

It had to be Carlos. Who the hell else would interrupt such a magical moment?

Charles kept his arms firmly around me when I tried to jerk free from his hold.

"Who is it?" Charles said.

"Javier. I thought I heard some trouble in here."

"No, it's fine. I'm okay. Thank you, Javier."

Javier mumbled something, and we heard solid footfalls padding down the hallway.

"Stay with me, Carmena."

"Despite all the things that have happened, I still consider you a man of honor, Captain."

"This doesn't have to do with honor, Carmena, but our feelings for one another."

I slid off the bed. "We already woke Javier. Who knows who else is awake?"

"I wish you would stay." Charles grabbed my hand and kissed it.

"Me, too."

"Thank you for visiting."

"I only wanted to make sure you were all right."

"Now, I am."

He pulled on my arm and grabbed a fistful of hair at the back of my neck. He kissed me enough to leave me wanting more, and I didn't think he could ever kiss me that well again. I stood on shaky legs and sensed his smile.

It took all my will power to leave him when I wanted to stay. In his room. In his bed.

"Good night, Charles," I said and closed the door, leaving my heart behind.

∾∾∾

Time had no meaning, and peace blanketed me when I held Charles's hand during our many strolls about the grounds. He stole some kisses, most I willingly gave, under the shaded gazebos, or we rode to secluded areas on the ranch property. When we were together, nothing else in the world mattered.

The captain's baritone voice never failed to hold me captive, and I melted into a sappy puddle every time his startling blue eyes looked at me longer than a split second. We learned we had lots in common. His feelings blossomed from infatuation into true love, and I did my best to hold my feelings at bay.

Charles was usually good about meeting me after lunch in the parlor for our afternoon constitutional. When he was late coming downstairs one afternoon, I went up to his room. I tapped on his door, and it unexpectedly swung open. Without concern for proper decorum, I entered as he was about to don a freshly washed shirt.

Curvy biceps bulged, and his torso resembled a bronze bust of a fierce warrior. I wanted more than his luscious body, and that was when I became aware of dangerous territory.

Now more than ever I didn't think I could leave the captain. Up until that moment I thought I was emotionally capable of easily slipping away to the future when the time came.

"Close the door, Carmena," Charles said in a husky whisper. "Stay with me."

I sprinted out of the room like a spooked rabbit and cursed my feet for not listening to my heart.

The more attention I paid to Charles, the less the amulet whirred against my sternum. If it hadn't already been stolen once, I would've been tempted to leave it on my dresser each morning. My gut instinct knew there was a definite correlation between the amulet's inert activity and the amount of time I spent with the captain. Carlos warned me not to let it happen, but it was too late.

I had fallen in love.

༒༺༒

Carlos, Javier, and Roy, the three musketeers, and a hired team of over a dozen wranglers took part in a roundup for our new acquisition of over two hundred and fifty head of Black Angus from a cattle dealer in Oklahoma. Joe stayed behind with a temporary field hand to take care of the routine activities on the ranch.

During the six-week run, Charles took an active part in managing the ranch for Carlos and helping with basic chores. He seemed to enjoy the paperwork side of the business, a good diversion from his tormented thoughts. He dispatched a letter to Beauford Jones requesting an update, but Jones had already left for New York the week prior to contact Sealsfield's solicitor.

Every time I entered the library while Charles recorded ranch activities and inventory, he took the time to enjoy a glass of coffee or lemonade and a brief conversation, the pretense to a high stakes game of sexual tension. Each time I drew near to him, his energy reeled me in, and I happily took the bait, knowing full well that there was no way for either of us to win.

Upon the men's return, on a scalding mid-June afternoon amidst a thunder of hooves, Charles withdrew again. It was like someone pressed the button on a vacuum cleaner, and he was the cord that whipped itself back into hiding, into a safe container.

A week passed after the cattle run, and Carlos and I were the first to sit down in the dining room. "Have any suggestions on how I can get Charles to feel like one of the family?" I asked him.

"For starters, you can stop acting like an indulgent mother hen."

Mildly outraged, I asked, "How can you say that?"

Carlos counted on his fingers. "You make sure he always has a favorite food at every meal. You have Angela or Violet wash out his laundry, daily, and every time he gets a sliver bringing in firewood you act as if the man requires surgery."

I opened my mouth to protest, but Carlos was right. He smirked when my shoulders fell.

I exhaled. "What should I do?"

"Only two things," he said. "First off, treat the man like you would any other person who works for you."

I nodded. "I can do that. What's the second thing?"

"Trust me," he said.

Before I could argue, the others sat in their chairs with washed hands and huge appetites. Platters of barbequed steaks, thick fried potatoes, heavily buttered corn, green beans— Charles's favorite vegetable—and freshly baked bread were set on the table.

The racket quieted down, and I said, "Charles, would you please say grace today?" All eyes flew to the former officer, whom the others continued to refer to as "the captain."

"Well, Carmena, I—I'm not much of a p—praying man," he stammered.

"Nonsense. You've heard the rest of us lead prayers for weeks. First, you give the order to bow our heads, and then allow yourself to be inspired."

"I don't think that it's, uh, fitting," he protested.

I looked about the table. "All those in favor of the captain saying grace, raise their hand." He was the only one without his hand above his head. "It's settled."

I folded my hands, and Charles peered at the expectant onlookers. Angela and Violet nodded encouragement. He glared at Carlos the moment Carlos winked at me.

"Well then, seeing how I have no choice, let us bow our heads." He waited a beat. "Lord, I thank you for letting me be a part of this squadron of good men. Er, and women. Uh, and the children, too. May we always be prepared to go into battle for you and, uh, well, you know, bless this food. Amen."

"Amen," we said in unison, except Javier who said, "Yes, sir!"

The lunch topic centered on livestock and the experiences the men had on the cattle run. Various pranks were played on the new wranglers. Pablo bit into his sandwich and pulled out a chunk of a cooked skunk, Roland found a dead snake in his boot, and someone slipped a non-poisonous scorpion in Snitch's bedroll.

In addition to the Black Angus, we also purchased several thoroughbred stallions and mares and at least thirty colts and fillies, which included saddlebreds and mustangs.

Roy turned out to be our resident horse whisperer. He could break the horses faster than Javier could shoe them. After we gave the military what they needed, we'd sell a portion for hefty profits at auction, and the prime stock would be saved for breeding.

At Carlos's request, Charles joined us in the library after lunch. Once there, they lit up from the stash on my desk. I took my customary seat. It felt good to be in the boss's chair.

"Roy found six more wranglers," Carlos said. "They heard we were the best place for an honest man to work for honest pay."

"Let me guess," I said. "He already promised them work."

Carlos smiled. "Yes, but I told him if they don't work out or we can't afford to keep them, he's the one who gives them the boot. And I told him the next person he brings to the ranch will have to live off his salary."

"That'll help keep him from bringing every stray wrangler home."

"You're just going to let one of your men call the shots on who and when to hire?" Charles asked.

"He has a gift," I said.

Carlos told us what tasks were assigned to whom, taking into consideration the talents each wrangler brought to the table. "One is a farrier, and another knows something about plumbing."

"Plumbing? To work on a ranch?" Charles asked.

"Indoor plumbing is every woman's dream," I said.

Carlos rolled his eyes, but Charles rubbed his chin and said, "It would be considered an improvement on the property."

"It means no more hauling water to bathe or flush the toilet. And I'm done putting up with smelly bodies over dinner. Let's add on a room behind the bunkhouse and rig a makeshift shower inside with a fireplace to heat up the water in the winter. See that the new guy gets started on some plans right away."

"I don't want to get up to full capacity in the bunkhouse," Carlos said. "The men need some breathing room, so let's not hire any more than that."

"I agree, but I'd like to add on a large living area to the bunkhouse with a game room," I said.

"A game room?" nearly everyone asked.

"You know, like checkers or a card table?"

"Like a saloon?" Charles asked. I nodded. "Why would you encourage such a leisurely pace with the field hands?"

Carlos seemed as perplexed as the captain.

"What I'm encouraging is their happiness and desire to remain here. Good food and the comforts of a cozy home environment will encourage a more dedicated team."

"It's like she can see into the future," Carlos said to Charles.

"And I guess it goes without saying that all the new men will sleep in the bunkhouse with the three musketeers," I said.

Carlos and Charles agreed.

"How do you propose to pay for the added salaries, plumbing, and a new room in the bunkhouse?" the captain asked. "And I'd also like to know why you asked me here."

Carlos smiled. I had a feeling he had been waiting for Charles to ask. Carlos blew out a slow stream of smoke, surrounding us with the calming aroma of the sweetened tobacco.

"It's time you carried your weight around here, Captain."

"Let's not be so formal, Carlos," Charles suggested. He made himself more comfortable in the wingback chair.

"You are profoundly admired and will always be the captain," I said.

He gave a slight nod. "How is it that I'm to carry my weight?"

"You weren't born into a farming or ranching community, am I right?" Carlos asked.

"You're right. My family was well to do Bostonians who never lifted a finger," he said with more disgust than pride.

"I find having to do any paperwork after a long day's work rather tedious. What we're proposing is—" He looked at me as if I were in on his plan. "I'll give you the figures, you make sense out of them and record your findings."

"You mean manage the books? Doesn't sound like much of a challenge. I did that while you were on the cattle run."

"Carlos will maintain the title of Ranch Foreman," I said. "You, Charles, are now the official Ranch Manager. We'd like you to oversee the financial records including the ranch portfolio, any legal proceedings, and household expenses. You'll place orders for supplies and equipment when Angela or Carlos requests them. You'll also make sure that all the employees on the ranch are paid, well fed, and happy. Plus, pick up any slack if the need ever arises when someone is laid up. Congratulations."

"Pay scale?" he asked.

"Same as me," Carlos told the captain. "It's a meager salary, but none of us are left wanting. Carmena is very generous. For me, the salary is a minor consideration."

"Free room, meals, clothing, camaraderie, and all the Virginian cigars you can ask for," I explained further.

Carlos stood. "Carmena can explain your duties in detail as I bid you both good night."

The moment Carlos left the room, Charles asked, "What's with him appointing me into my new position like he was the president?"

"Establishing territory, I think. You may be in charge of the books, but he's still in charge of the entire ranch."

"Great. My first pissing contest, and I didn't get off a shot." Charles was a teaser, too, and ought to have fit in well by now.

"Let me show you the books."

Charles pulled a chair next to mine. His close proximity had an immediate effect but giving into my carnal desires felt like an act of disloyalty to the real Carmena, who was more than an alter ego. By now, she was like an invisible best friend. I really liked being in her life, feeling what she felt, knowing what she knew. Through her memories, I grew up and learned to use my inner guidance to make wise decisions, not just in my best interest, but for everyone on the ranch.

Although I couldn't stay in this time and experience a full and satisfying relationship with Charles, the least I could do was keep away from her man while I was here. I knew that taking away Carmena's right to choose what she wanted wasn't fair to her. And staying would be the same as taking her life. Besides, I hadn't forgotten Sadie's warning if I chose to remain in the past.

None of this could be shared with the wondrous man beside me. All I could do was keep him at bay until I felt one hundred percent certain about leaving.

In the middle of my reverie, Charles unexpectedly leaned in and kissed me. His meaty fingers tangled in my hair and pulled my head back until I felt his lips press deep into mine.

Sparks didn't just ignite—they imploded. My reasoning melted into pure need. The occasional kissing and hand holding suddenly wasn't enough. I wanted his strong arms embracing me so tightly that he'd absorb me into his skin. I wanted to feel his tongue tantalizing me with pleasure. In a heartbeat, I forgot all about Carmena, my invisible best friend.

I pulled back to quell the overwhelming sensation that my heart was going to burst, as full as it was of raw desire for the man. Damn the captain for looking so self-satisfied, for knowing exactly how he made me feel.

I gasped for air and feigned composure. "Perhaps we'd better—"

He delved into my mouth again and this time, damn me, for letting him. My control was nearly undone. It took a lot of effort to force myself to push him back.

"Charles, let's get this job finished before we do anything else," I wheezed.

"Whatever you say," he said, self-assured, confident. The old captain was back.

For the next two hours, I showed him all the ledgers that included the inventory records for the main house and the outbuildings, banking transactions, provision lists, and legal documents. The first statement for our stock portfolio arrived a month prior. Beauford said it would take up to ten weeks, and only then did I realize how much time had passed since the captain's arrival at Holiday Ranch.

"Hmm. I'm impressed by your investments," he said. "No wonder you can afford to hire new hands." He thumbed through the papers. "Of course, I can't agree with all of your choices. This Morse fellow's a big risk, don't you think?"

"The returns will be great once he gets the patents straightened out on his equipment." It would happen around

1854, when the US Supreme Court upheld Samuel Morse's patent. "We'll make a fortune once electronic voice telegraphs get off the ground, too."

"So that's what this American Telegraph is all about. What makes you think it's going to happen?" he said.

"I have inside information."

"And who, may I ask, supplied you with it?"

"My gut instinct."

"Thank God I'm in charge of the books now."

I nudged him with my shoulder and got a whiff of his aftershave. Our eyes connected, and it was hard to speak. I saw his Adam's apple bob up and down.

"Here are the payroll ledgers," I eked out. "I recently upped the salaries."

"Hazard pay?" he teased.

I smiled. "That's in the past. Let's leave it there."

He nodded.

"In this envelope, you'll find a last will and testament. It will be revised soon to include your name as a beneficiary, share-and-share-alike, as long as you live here."

"That's very generous, but I hope you're not planning on leaving us any time soon." He kissed the back of my hand.

"I take care of my people. Of my home." I wanted to add "of my man" and wondered if I had the strength to leave him. Words clogged my throat, and I coughed to clear them out. I barely noticed that the grandfather clock had already blasted the entryway with eleven strikes to the chimes. As thrilled as I was to be with Charles, a big yawn escaped me. "It's time for bed."

"Please tell me that's an invitation."

I shook my head, smiling.

"Do you mind if I go over these records a bit longer?"

"Suit yourself." I leaned down and kissed him. His hands roamed, and I let them. "I'll see you in the morning," I said, and it took another ten minutes to say goodnight.

Finally, in a voice belying my ravenous yearning for the man, I whispered, "I need to get upstairs before I lose my last single ounce of decorum."

I turned away, but Charles held my arm. "You know, since that incident with Franz you've changed. You used to be too busy to bother with me, like there was just too much work for you to handle anything outside of your ranch. But now, there's something more to you, Carmena, that I never saw before." Without warning, he pulled me onto his lap. "I like it. Whatever it is that has made you want me."

"I imagine I always felt this way about you but didn't allow myself to show it. A life-changing event can make all the difference."

"I'm glad you decided to let me know how you really feel," Charles said. He pulled me in for a kiss, tender and heartfelt, pure and without expectations.

"Good night, Charles."

"Good night, sweetheart."

I smiled and floated all the way up to my room.

CHAPTER 29

Roland rode into town after breakfast to see if there was any word from Beauford Jones. We were lucky. He had returned from his trip to New York the day before. Roland let him know I had a will revision, and that Carlos and I were anxious to hear how his visit went with Sealsfield's solicitor. Beauford was kind enough to accompany our wrangler back to the ranch.

Charles joined us in the parlor. Beauford had barely stepped foot inside the room and greeted the captain when Carlos asked, "What news of Sealsfield, Mr. Jones?"

"Are you going to let him catch his breath?" I asked Carlos.

He nodded. "My apologies, Mr. Jones. May we offer you a refreshment?"

"No, thank you, Mr. Solis."

"Good. What news of Sealsfield?"

I shook my head, and Charles coughed into his hand.

Beauford was as anxious as Carlos to share the story. "Apparently, Mr. Sealsfield had been living under an assumed name all these years, in the United States and then England. Now, he doesn't even live in the United Kingdom anymore."

Violet brought in a tray of iced tea, despite Beauford's earlier refusal, and he quickly slugged down a glass.

"Where is he now?" I asked after his last swallow.

"In Switzerland, but Mr. Thompson still represents him as his attorney. Apparently, Sealsfield isn't even his real name."

"What is it?" Carlos asked.

"Carl Postl. Apparently, he wanted to live his dream of being a writer but succumbed to his mother's wishes to lead a religious life instead."

"So this Postl is the same man who owns the Sealsfield property?" Charles asked.

"Yes," I said. "Please continue, Mr. Jones."

"Mr. Postl regretted his decision in taking the vows. Once his mother died, he fled the priesthood. He heard that Germans were migrating to Texas and Postl moved to the United States under the assumed name of Charles Sealsfield, presumably so his mother couldn't locate him. Some years back, he received a generous offer from a newspaper in England for a journalist position. He wrote a few years before retiring and moving to Switzerland."

"What was Mr. Thompson doing in the United States?" Carlos asked.

"He was dispatched by Mr. Sealsfield, er, Postl, to handle all manner of business. But that's not the good news," Jones told us. "Why, I registered in the same hotel as Mr. Thompson and was able to contact him personally only a few days after I arrived."

"Outstanding," Carlos approved and Beauford beamed.

"I made a rather low offer to Mr. Thompson for the land, and told him there'd be an incentive on the condition that Postl sells."

"You bribed him?" Beauford looked worried until I said, "Excellent!"

Beauford straightened up and bragged further. "Mr. Thompson didn't seem to care how much I offered for the land, once he saw the amount of his bonus." Beauford pulled a parchment envelope from his pocket and handed it to me. "Here is the signed deed for your new property and your receipts."

Carlos, Charles, and I were equally astounded. Beauford saved us thousands and thousands of dollars and accomplished a task that I was certain would take up to at least a year.

"You are amazing, Beauford!" I said. He grinned.

"Well done," the captain said and clapped the attorney on the shoulder.

"Cigar?" Carlos offered him one of his finest hand-rolled tobacco sticks.

Beauford flushed. "No, thank you."

I pulled a small envelope from my desk drawer. Something we kept on hand in case it was ever needed for a quick service or a well-earned reward. "This is for you, Beauford, along with my thanks for doing such a brilliant job."

To his credit, Beauford didn't peek inside the envelope. "Thank you, Miss Luebber. It is always…" He thought a moment until he said, "…iteresting doing business for you."

Carlos saw Beauford to the door. A short while later we joined everyone else in the dining room for lunch. I let Carlos tell the others about our new land acquisition, the most coveted parcel north of San Antonio. It was cause for celebration and the women planned a special dinner for that evening.

Charles raised his drink to me, and his approving smile struck a nerve. Damn the captain's cheerful demeanor. He was truly a part of the ranch family now, a fully-fledged team member who celebrated the victory along with everyone else.

Carlos looked at me from the other end of table. He knew. It was near time for me to leave.

Whether I wanted to or not.

ల్యాల్య

After lunch, I gave Charles the all-my-workers-represent-the-ranch speech and explained how we expected him to dress the part and put on a good show. He was thrilled at the idea of us riding into town together, even though we were just going to visit the tailor's where he'd be fitted for new suits and casual wear.

It was my first time off the property, and the views were breathtaking. It was hard to believe that Texas would suffer any future droughts.

Once we were out of view of Holiday Ranch, Charles slipped his arm about my shoulders. He kept it lying comfortably around me until we saw people walking or riders in the distance. Then he'd discreetly put his hand back on his leg, next to his gun belt.

Everyone knew Carmena and the captain. I would've thought it was just country folk being friendly to us, but nearly every person we met knew us by name. It was a pleasant surprise to see that Charles addressed many people by their names, too.

"Good afternoon, Mr. Lewis. Did you get that fence finished yet?"

Three little girls waved to me. "Good afternoon, Miss Luebber!" And they just giggled at the sight of the captain.

The main street of the soon-to-be incorporated Fredericksburg was a one-block long ghost town—only, the people were still alive. The buildings were constructed of wood and most had a hitching post installed out front. Dozens of townsfolk greeted us with a friendly wave or warm sentiment, and a group outside the saloon applauded the captain as the wagon rolled by. Charles smiled proudly and gave quick nods and tips of his hat to the onlookers.

Carmena's memories were quick to rise to the surface, and I remembered all the people, their stories, and how they felt about her. She was well regarded. A few raised brows and envious stares told me that the captain and I instantly became an item.

Charles was fitted for new clothes while I ran a few errands at local businesses, which included the purchase of a new enclosed carriage with a black canvas cover, the Luebber crest handsomely displayed in brass and black leather on both doors. Carlos would probably pitch a fit, so I decided to let him find out about it when the carriage was delivered, and I was gone.

Charles met me at the general store, then we dropped in on Old Sally.

"My Lord, Cappin', I ain't ever seen ya look so happy." She gave me the once over and embraced me like a long, lost daughter. "An' I reckon I know why."

His goofy smile looked all the more endearing when he blushed.

"Sally, I don't believe I've ever seen the captain that shade of red," I teased.

She winked at him. "Now, don't fret none. Everybody likes a juicy tomato."

I think he wanted to rush out the door. Sally gave Charles a bigger bear hug than me.

"I can't help it, Sal," he said. "That's what happens when I'm around you."

"Well, if that ain't the biggest fib this side of the Mississippi, but I'm glad ta hear it!" Ol' Sal blushed as easily as all the other females in town and on my ranch—every place that Charles left a smile or a compliment. We left her in good spirits and with a box of her favorite hard candy from the general store.

A trail of people, adults and children alike, followed the wagon down the main street to the edge of town. Soon we were back on the road to home.

My left arm rested gently under the captain's and my right hand relaxed on the bench next to my side. "My arm hurts from waving to your fans."

"My what?"

"Your admirers."

"I heard 'Carmena' as many times as I heard 'Captain,'" he said.

"Yeah, but none of the girls or women giggled when they shouted my name."

"Maybe they think I look funny."

I leaned into his shoulder. "I doubt that."

Charles kissed the top of my head, easy to do as he was so much taller than me. The bumpy ride was hardly noticeable during the entire trip to and from Holiday Ranch. Eventually, the rocky west end of the property came into view, and in a minute, we'd be visible to anyone watching from atop Turtle Hill or the lookout perch on the barn. I imagined Carlos and his glowering disapproval.

"Charles, will you stop the wagon a moment?" He knit his worried brows as the team slowed to a stop. He turned my body toward him and examined my face.

"Carmena, what is it? Are you unwell?"

"I'm fine. I just wanted to tell you—what I mean is—that is, I'd like you to know—" It wasn't like me to be at a loss for words, but in his presence, staring into those sapphire eyes, each word tumbled over the other. Frustrated at my lack of verbal expression, I grabbed the captain by the cheeks and let my physical passion do the talking.

Charles responded appropriately to my kiss. He held me by the shoulders but then his hands wandered up and down my arms, across my back, and to my waist. I had to come up for air and gulped in oxygen.

His smile sparkled as much as his eyes. "I guess my new lucky stone is working."

"Your lucky stone?" I asked, still dazed.

He pulled a small ceramic disk out of his pocket. It was almost round, a muddy red with an embossed fleur de lis on one side, a lion on the other. Yep, the same lion.

"Where did you find that?"

"I didn't. Some old lady stopped me when I left the tailor's to find you in the general store. She gave it to me and among other things, she said it would bring me more luck than I ever imagined."

Sadie immediately came to mind. I was going to ask him about the things she told him but there was something else, and it took my attention away from the charm. And it wasn't just the buzzing of my amulet.

"Why are you looking at me that way, Charles?"

"Because I want to remember when you were so tongue-tied that you could only tell me how much you loved me in a kiss."

I made to protest his observation, however accurate, but my words jumbled up again, and I stuttered. The captain laughed at my impotent objection.

His smile faded into a serious line and he said, "Darling, marry me."

If I was at a loss for words before, I had forgotten how to speak after his proposal. It was more than a request—it was something desperate, as if his life depended on my answer, an answer I had hoped to avoid.

"There's nothing I want more, Charles, than to marry you, but your proposal is a bit too early. I have to see how the ranch is going to survive financially on our stock portfolio. I may lose everything, and we wouldn't have a leg to stand on."

"You can't possibly think I want you only for your property."

"Of course not, but other people depend on me for their livelihood, for their day-to-day survival."

"I can always fall back on my family. They may not speak to me now, but my mother made it clear that I stand to inherit quite a bit, Car—sweetheart. I will have enough to sustain the ranch for decades to come."

A potential financial loss was the only argument I had considered to stave off a proposal. I had no idea that Charles had the means to rescue Carmena from any economic plight. He knew I loved him, that I wanted him, but I couldn't stay to accommodate his desires, or my own.

And I couldn't put off leaving another moment longer.

"The ranch isn't your responsibility, Charles."

"It would be if we were married." He had kept me firmly in his arms as we sat in the shadow of a giant rock formation, and I felt as trapped as I did the night he had caught me riding from Castro's ranch.

"I don't want to depend on something we're unsure of, like your family's inheritance. We don't know that your parents are doing well—"

"My great-uncle James on my mother's side needs someone in the family to take care of the books for his company," he said, cutting me off. "Ames Manufacturing. My father used to manage the books for them and invested most of his salary back into shares in the business until he died a few years back. My great-uncle Nathan took over, but he has recently taken ill, and they want someone reliable in the family to do the accounting."

"Just how well is Ames doing?"

"They make all the swords for the US Cavalry." I raised my brows and he sneered. "There's a lot of money to be made in military contracts if you can supply the weapons." I knew more than anyone how much could be made in military weapons, and how much could be lost because of them. "They wrote to me last month, asking if I'd reconsider taking my great-uncle Nathan's place."

His bad news was the out I needed. "Why didn't you tell me? You shouldn't be here! You should be with your family, helping them take care of the business!"

"My family disowned me a long time ago, Car—my love." That was the second time he almost called me by name but stopped himself. "I haven't seen them for about fifteen years, since I enlisted. Both my parents were disappointed when I joined the cavalry." Charles spoke calmly, as if he had already dealt with the emotional repercussions. "I turned down many promotions to remain in Texas, so I could stay away from Massachusetts, but I'm willing to return if that's what it takes to help you keep the ranch going."

"I'd never ask you to do anything that made you miserable. I want you to stay here with Car—Carlos and the rest of us who take care of the ranch." I had almost said her name.

Charles embraced me in his firm arms. "I want nothing more than to be here, as long as I'm with you." He looked into my eyes and said, "Let's get married, sweetheart. Tell me you'll have me."

"Will you give me time to work out some of the finances first?"

He frowned.

"It should only take a month or two to get on our feet. Then we'll know if we have to rely on your future inheritance."

"What difference will that make?"

"I just want peace of mind. I want to make sure that I marry under ideal circumstances. Please, Charles. Just a month or two." I deliberately batted my lashes and pouted.

He laughed and gave me a short, rough kiss. "Six weeks."

"Fine. Just—I don't want to tell anyone until then. Agreed?"

He almost argued the point but then said, "Agreed." He snapped the reigns, "Yaw!" and the team strode forward. It took only moments to round the bend, and I looked up at Turtle Hill. The familiar outline of my ranch foreman, shielding his eyes from the sun, looked down at the wagon.

ᴄʌᴄʌ

That evening Carlos lit up a pre-dinner cigar and we sat at the library bay window together, watching Martino and Gracie play a game of chase around water troughs and hitching posts.

"We can move the cattle to Sealsfield's—" Carlos corrected himself. "—to your new pastureland tomorrow. The men have already started calling it the back meadow. While you were in town, I sent Joe to tell your friend, Sadie, that she could stay in the cottage."

"That's a surprise," I said and kept my eyes on the kids. "What did she say?"

"Nothing. She was gone."

I glanced at him.

"The place was deserted," he said.

"I sort of expected that."

We watched Gracie search for Martino, who crouched behind her. Through the glass, we heard him yell "Boo!" and she jumped higher than she was tall. Carlos and I laughed. It was a good memory to take with me.

"I'll be leaving soon."

"I know," he said.

"I'll miss you terribly."

"And I, you."

My tears dripped in a silent stream. "I'll wind the amulet sometime tomorrow and tonight at dinner, I'll say my goodbyes."

"How will you do that?" he asked.

"I'll tell each person what they mean to me. What I grew to like about them." Sharing sentiments with Carlos, and especially Charles, would be a greater challenge. "They might notice a change in the real Carmena when she comes back. I don't know what you should expect. You may have to fill her in on all the changes she's made."

"Do you have to leave?"

"Sadie warned me of severe consequences if I didn't return to my own time. Besides, there's no reason for me to stay. I believe I know how to get back, and I know the purpose of the amulet. It was about being willing to grow up on my part." I put my hand to my chest as the charm hummed and grew warm for the first time in months.

"Please help Charles through any rough times he may have as he deals with memories about the raid. He's had a fitful sleep nearly every night since he's been here."

"I will," he promised.

"You never asked me any more questions. About the future."

"Once I learned of the war to come, I decided it's probably better to live in ignorance than fear."

"Carlos, nothing eventful will occur here. I mean, other than typical cowboy and Indian stuff. The most important thing is that the stocks are all sold by September of 1929 because a month later the stock market will crash, and there will be a severe drought in the 1930s. I left you a note in the bunk safe telling you about the drought, the crash, and other things that may ensure the ranch remains successful during hard times. There's plenty of gold in the barn cellar and US dollars in the safe now."

He nodded.

The kids threw rocks at an old tin can. Gracie was very accurate.

"I made arrangements for you and Javier to each build your own homes on prime land, if you so choose. Beauford is having the land surveyed so Javier and Angela will each receive two hundred and fifty acres and you will receive five hundred, plus you'll be the President of Holiday Ranch Incorporated.

Carlos inhaled and scrunched his eyes closed for a moment. "Thank you."

"For the other employees, after their tenth year of service, each of the wranglers serving up to now will receive one hundred acres, and subsequent wranglers ten acres for every ten years served until up to one hundred acres have been given to them. Beauford will handle the paperwork. And the captain—if he stays on for more than a year, will receive two hundred and fifty acres. He might want to live separately with Carmena." My heart ached at the mention of it.

"That's quite a soft spot you have for him."

"Very soft," I conceded. "There are also provisions for Martino and Gracie. All their college expenses will be paid for by the ranch. Whether they choose to stay here or move away, they'll also receive land. I want them to always have a home here. The captain will see that the bulk of our profits are reinvested."

"I wish you could stay," he admitted.

"Even without the warning from Sadie, would you want to be the one responsible for destroying Carmena's life?"

He shook his head and gazed out the window. "It takes a remarkably strong woman to rise above her own desires. It must be hard for you to let go of everything here. To let go of him."

My eyes clouded over. "I should've left weeks ago." I sniffed and felt my throat close. "Carlos."

I heard him gulp down his emotions. We faced each other. He folded me into his strong and reassuring arms. I smelled that musky soap and the sweet tang of sugar cubes in his pocket.

"I still wish things had been different between us," he said.

"I don't. Things worked out perfectly—you with Violet, me, or Carmena rather, with Charles."

"I have to admit, it did."

"You're my best friend, Carlos, and you will be when I'm gone."

He kissed me on the forehead. We hugged a moment longer.

"I'm going to get dressed for dinner now," I said. I left him at the window watching the children play.

❦❦❦

Torturous thoughts of leaving my Texas family lumbered with me up the stairs. I wasn't a coward when I was fighting Franz, facing Santa Anna, or gunrunning, but the pain of leaving was unbearable. I didn't know if I could say goodbye to anyone else, especially Charles.

According to Sadie, once I was gone, the real Carmena would take my place, and although Carlos would be the first to notice, the captain would soon catch on. I wondered if he loved Carmena before I came through the mist or if he fell in love with the real me. He did say I was different since the attack. I wondered if Charles would continue to love Carmena after I left.

The necklace hummed. I looked up and down the hall before I pulled it out of my bodice. It glowed an incandescent blue. I tugged at either end and pulled the little cogs away from the amulet. I twisted them only once and quickly set them back into place, not certain if I was ready to commit to officially winding it.

Light shone under Charles's door. I tucked the charm under my clothes before I rapped lightly.

"Come in."

"Hello, there," I said as the door swung open.

His bright smile undid me. That and his unbuttoned shirt and unfastened pants. I saw the ledgers on his bed, and he glanced back at them.

"Thought I'd go over these records," he explained.

"From here on out, those books remain in the library."

"Done."

"You're welcome to work at my desk. You'll find that we have no secrets here at the ranch."

"Is that why you wanted to see me?"

I took a deep breath. "I wanted to say that I might seem...different in the next few days. The ranch is going through a lot of changes, and I'm starting to feel a bit nervous."

"Does change upset you?"

"No. But right now, it's happening all at once, and I don't think I'm handling it well, so I'm asking for your patience ahead of time."

"You'll have it. That, and anything else that is mine to give you."

"I can only think of one thing I want right now."

Charles read my thoughts. He moved faster than floodwaters in a creek bed. Either he pulled me into his arms, or I deliberately flew into them. An eager arm wrapped about my waist, and he grabbed a handful of my hair. He gave me the most incredible kiss, and I swooned, inundated with goose bumps and shivers at the same time.

We came up for air and Charles said, "Are you all right?"

"I will be when I get my breath back."

He grinned, the happiest I'd seen him in months. "Darling, tell me you love me. Or tell me it isn't so. I need to know how you truly feel."

Nothing could convince me to take Carmena's place, yet I wanted him to know how much I cared. I mustered the strength to look into his eyes and not melt into them like I usually did.

"I feel that there will never be enough words, and especially, enough time, Charles, to tell you how much I love you."

He grinned. "It worked again." He held up the ceramic disc, his lucky stone. Charles put it in his pocket and pulled me as close as possible and said, "With all my heart, I love you, Car—I love you, sweetheart."

"That's not the first time you started to say my name and stopped. What aren't you telling me, Charles?"

"That I'll never want more than to love only you."

He held my chin, kissed me better, and longer than ever. I swooned yet again, and he smiled, pleased at my dazed reaction.

It took a second to swallow and breathe in deeply, then I said, "Regardless of time, or if we ever find ourselves physically apart, I'll always feel this way about you, Charles."

His embrace was like a glove's perfect fit. He whispered, "It will only take a minute to clear off the bed—"

I sighed and had barely enough resolve to shake my head the tiniest bit. "I want to, but right now, I just can't."

"Then I'll see you at dinner."

His eyes sparkled before he closed them to kiss me, a closed mouth peck, soft and sweet. Charles playfully pushed me out of his room, knowing I wanted much more. He grinned at me and shut the door.

I heard him laughing and couldn't keep myself from smiling, too.

CHAPTER 30

A knock on the door interrupted my nap before dinner. I rubbed my eyes, and someone knocked again. "Come in."

"Oh, you're up. Marco and I have been debating on waking you."

I blinked a few times and stared at my cousin. "Nicole!"

"I'm sorry. I didn't mean to startle you—"

"It's great to see you!"

"Uh, thanks."

I looked about the room. "Where did everybody go?"

"You okay, Mandy?"

I smiled and snapped out of the daze. "Never better. Where did you get that skirt?" Nicole wore a red-leather skirt with curly black embellishments. The design was familiar.

"This?" She twirled. "Barbara ordered it from the neatest little wholesale boutique in Texas."

"Huh. What happened after I disappeared into the mist?"

Nicole tilted her head. "What do you mean? What mist?" She squinted at me. "Mandy?"

"Never mind. Do you recall when I left the kitchen?"

"When I got home from work last night?" I nodded. "Yeah. You looked pretty tired when you went to bed. Actually, kind of dazed, like you look now."

"Huh. That's just…interesting." My gauchos felt tighter than usual as I sat up. I looked down at my Brazilian jeans hugging every curve, the same jeans I saw burned in a barbeque pit. I wore my running shoes, and an uncomfortable bulge poked out my back pocket. My screwdriver. No point trying to figure out how that happened.

Something else had been tucked into my pocket. My gold bracelet from the captain. My heart swelled, and my eyes flooded as I clasped the memento onto my wrist.

"I'm glad you missed our argument," Nicole said. "Marco was ticked off because I came in late. I told him I had to close the store, but he brought up the subject of my working again."

"I'm sorry to hear that. Hey, you know the note from Maizy and the amulet?"

"Are you kidding? I've been waiting for you to wake up so we could talk about it." She sat on the bed and said, "Where are they? You found something out, didn't you?"

"Yes. No. I mean, I think so. I'd like to shower first, if you don't mind."

"I can hold out a while longer. I'll be downstairs." She headed for the door.

"Nicole?"

"What is it?"

"Thanks for letting me stay here. I'm really glad for everything that's happened."

"We're glad to have you." She smiled and closed the door behind her. Her steps were light and swift on the stairwell.

The amulet and note would be passed to Nicole, but it wasn't my gut instinct that told me. It was her red-leather skirt, made of the same leather-like fabric and curly black designs as the outside of a bowl I saw sitting on a weather-beaten table in a cozy adobe cottage.

I didn't get the meaning of "He wears a pink hat and rides a purple hippo" but my intuition said the message would reveal itself. Not knowing the next step wouldn't be a problem either, because my future no longer intimidated me. Not another second of my life would be wasted, and I'd embrace the unknown with arms and eyes wide open.

I took the parchment note out of my back pocket. The four-line poem was still there but the hippo line had disappeared.

I packed a small valise of clothes and my make-up bag then phoned for a taxi. With paper and pen in hand, I sat at the table and wrote a note to Nicole.

Dearest Nicole,

Thank you so much for your hospitality. I'll contact a mover, and I'd appreciate it if you'd have them pack and ship the rest of my things.

I know this is more sudden than my move to California, but something is calling me back to Arkansas. I can't say I know why I have to go back. Maybe it's to find my purpose in life or to figure out what kind of work I should be doing. Maybe they're the same. At least I know the answer is there.

Love, ~~Car~~ Mandy

P.S. Don't forget to wind it and tell me everything when you get back!

As Sadie instructed, I scribbled the memorized line on the parchment paper under the once cryptic poem. *Kick up your heels and take charge!* I set my note for Nicole, the amulet, and Maizy's poem on the table.

A lot happened to me in the two days of my own time that I was gone. It wasn't so much that I changed on Holiday Ranch. I think I was always responsible, brave, and smart, but I didn't know how to uncover it all. Those traits were tucked deep inside, like seedlings that had to be watered and nurtured. Holiday Ranch was the perfect garden for that to happen.

On the ranch, I learned that life is less about having lots of choices and more about using my inner voice to do what felt right with the fewer choices I had.

The shuttle pulled along the curb and didn't honk, as I requested. With luggage and purse in hand, I quietly left my temporary shelter to resume my life in Arkansas.

❦❦❦

I landed at Fayetteville XNA in the late evening and a taxi took me home. The farms, silos, fields of barley, and wooded acres were barely visible at night, but I knew they were behind the twilight mist.

I called the realtor and let them know I wasn't going to be renting out my home after all. The voice mail notice popped up on my answering machine, and I checked to see who had called.

"Hey there, Miss Ruhe! How about a ride in my jeep? We kin have a picnic right next to the purdiest little lake on my property. Gimme a call if you think you'd like that."

I swore I'd erased that message before leaving to California. The judge's voice was as deep and as smooth as the captain's. His southwest patois was music to my ears. I jotted his number down. It was Thursday. Nine in the evening. I hoped it wasn't too late to call. His phone rang once, twice. He picked up.

"Mandy Ruhe. It's nice to see your name pop up on my caller ID."

"I'm glad I didn't chicken out and hang up."

"I mighta issued an arrest warrant if you had."

"Do you, by any chance, know how I could find out who gave me an inheritance a little over two years ago?"

"Maybe. Did they live in Arkansas?"

"No. The legal papers came from a court in Texas."

"That'll help."

"Can I ask you something else?"

"Shoot," he answered.

"Are you still available for a picnic and a ride in that Jeep of yours?"

"I am an' I can pick you up Saturday mornin' if it's too long a drive for you. I'm about an hour south of you near Lake Sequoyah."

"On horseback it'd be too long, but not in my car," I said.

"Grab a pen an' I'll give you directions."

We spoke for about two hours, easy and enjoyable conversation. After hanging up, I only unpacked pajamas. Maybe I'd go shopping the next day to buy a new outfit. Gauchos, if I could find them.

In the morning, I phoned Nicole to apologize for my hasty departure, but Marco said she locked herself in the bedroom. She was acting funny and yelled at him in an English accent.

Out of curiosity, I started a search on my cell phone to see how many Sanders they had listed in the Fredericksburg area. A prompt asked me to say the name of the party I wanted. I clicked off the phone.

Some things were best left alone.

e/୬e/୬

The drive to Judge Parker's took just over an hour. He lived in a rural area of Fayetteville.

I pulled onto the private road of the judge's property. Wrought iron letters arched above the lengthy driveway leading to the house and read, *Jest Restin' A Spell Ranch*, the same epitaph Javier had carved on Jesse's tombstone. It might have creeped someone else out, but the name put me at ease. I thought it no hokier than "Holiday Ranch."

I pulled up near the front doors of the white columned mansion, similar to the construction of the eastern colonials in the mid-1800s. The property was smaller than Carmena's villa, but no less impressive. It had an amazing panoramic view of the lake and surrounding hillsides.

A dark colored Jeep was parked under a well-shaded area outside of a three-car garage. In the center of the circular drive sat a beautiful garden with a rock fountain. His Honor stepped off the porch, wearing a huge smile and his cowboy hat. He was more handsome than I remembered with an older man maturity but a Peter Pan grin.

I got out of the car and my feet crunched on the gravel, a sound I enjoyed hearing.

"You sure are a sight for sore eyes," the judge drawled.

"Have you shackled any kids lately?"

"Only on holidays. C'mon inside."

He sprawled his muscular arm across my shoulders and left it there as we walked up the steps to two double doors of white ash.

"So far, I've only found out that your inheritance came from someone by the name of Sanders." I tripped over the last step, but his strong arm kept me upright. "You okay there?"

"Yeah. Thanks. You don't need to dig anymore."

"Lost relative?"

"Sort of. A family friend from long ago."

We entered a sitting room past the foyer, impeccably furnished with warm autumn tones and masculine built-in cabinets.

"This way to the kitchen. I'll get my keys an' we'll be off." A phone rang in the opposite room. He sighed. "I have to answer that. Never know when someone needs a warrant for a speedin' ticket." He winked.

"Very funny," I said.

He tossed his hat in the air toward a hat rack near the portico, but it missed the large wooden hook. The phone rang a second time, but he went for the hat.

"I'll get it," I said.

"I'm much obliged." He jogged to the phone in the next room and called over his shoulder, "That's the first time I missed that rack."

"Yeah, right!"

I picked up the Stetson and nearly fainted at the sight of the pink satin lining. I didn't know why I was surprised after everything else I'd been through and my eyes wandered with my thoughts.

Looking outside, I had a clear view of a dragonfly skirting one daisy to the next in the circular garden, past the bubbling fountain. I also had a view of the back of Judge Parker's Jeep. It was painted deep purple. The vanity license plate read, "HIPPO."

The meaning of the pink hat and purple hippo at last.

"What's that beautiful smile for?" The judge walked over to me and took the hat out of my hand. He set it on his head, tapped the rim, and cuddled me in his secure embrace, a gesture feeling as natural as my instant attraction to Charles.

"Actually, I've been admiring the plate on your jeep."

He looked out the window. "That's my purple hippo. Sound too sissy?"

"Not at all." I couldn't help grinning. "It's enchanting."

"Apparently, you didn't have a chance to move." He started to lean my way. He topped me by at least a foot and had a lot of leaning to do.

"I decided against it," I said. "A lot has happened in two days."

He kissed me. A gentle little peck, a promise of more to come. "How would you like to take the ride of your life?"

"I already have, Judge Parker."

"Call me Vince," he said. "And not like this, you haven't."

A newly inspired sense of feminine power enveloped me. I clutched his shirt collar and pulled him back down. I planted a kiss on the man with more shivers than I ever felt with Carlos, more warmth than the air that Violet blew into me, and with as much passion as Charles Sanders poured into my body.

Unlike with Charles, I didn't have to hold back with Vince. He ran his hands slowly across my back and shoulders.

"Show me that ride, Vinny."

He smiled. "Great-grandma Esther used to call me that. She was an antique when I was just a little feller."

"I'm an old soul. Been around more years than you can imagine."

"I have a feelin' the hippo's gonna be very good for you."

I smiled, at a loss for words. We walked out the door. Vince's arm rested comfortably, protectively, on my shoulders.

My gut instinct spoke softly. It said, "Welcome home."

CHAPTER 31

Nicole's frustration grew, not because Mandy snuck away an hour or so before, nor because Nicole didn't understand the latest scribbled message, "Kick up your heels and take charge!"

What bothered Nicole was not knowing how to wind the amulet.

The pictures on the hexagonal charm should've readily lined up when one was set into place. No matter how she twisted and turned the sections, the only unbroken picture under the magnifying glass was the one depicting famous landmarks in England.

Marco interrupted her for the umpteenth time and tried the knob on the bedroom door. "Hey, babe?"

Nicole almost shouted something nasty, but the humming of the necklace distracted her.

"There's a friend of yours on the phone," Marco said. "Alanna. She's leaving a message. She wants to talk to you."

She doubted Marco could've made up the story to lure her out of the room. He hadn't even met Alanna, the girl who was enrolled in Nicole's first karate class in junior high. The petite eighth grader couldn't cut the physical demands of the sport and dropped out after three sessions. Somehow the girls remained friends through high school and college, meeting maybe once a year for lunch, and texting or e-mailing a few times. Their last visit was six months ago. Why was Alanna calling now?

"Did you hear, Nicole?" Marco shouted through the door. "Alanna's on the phone! She said she's in town attending some kind of agricultural convention." He hushed a moment. "Never mind. Your phone just shut off." After a pause, he asked, "Nicole? Aren't you going to fix me dinner, baby?"

She didn't answer.

Marco pounded on the door, his voice unsettled. "Are you going to talk to me or what?"

Before she could shout at him to leave her alone, a swirling mist seeped from the walls and floorboards and clouded her vision. Nicole looked all around her, and in no time, she couldn't see beyond her shoulders. The mist mushroomed like the delicate spray from a waterfall but felt laden with real substance.

Marco's demands and his incessant rapping on the door gradually muted. Her body sank into a long, dark tunnel. She floated at the opposite end and watched the door fly open. Marco kicked in the door, using his crutch as leverage and slamming his good foot against the wooden barrier. But it was too late. Nicole had been pulled deeper into the darkening void.

He screamed her name, but she couldn't hear him.

Everything grew quiet, and all that she knew of the world faded to black.

About the Author

Carole Avila is an award winning writer and poet, as well as a playwright. Her published works include *Death House*, a young adult horror story, several short stories, and brief memoirs. She is currently working on the Eve's Amulet series, other stand-alone novels in women's fiction, and her non-fiction work, *The Long- Term Effects of Sexual Abuse*. Her non-fiction work comes from her experiences as an intuitive life coach and a survivor of abuse. Carole currently resides in Arkansas, and when she isn't writing, reading, or visiting with friends, she enjoys the company of her husband, children, grandchildren, and Cleo, the family shepherd-mix.